James Anthony Froude, Thomas Carlyle, Jane Welsh Carlyle

Letters and Memorials of Jane Welsh Carlyle

In three Volumes. Vol. III

James Anthony Froude, Thomas Carlyle, Jane Welsh Carlyle

Letters and Memorials of Jane Welsh Carlyle
In three Volumes. Vol. III

ISBN/EAN: 9783744688499

Printed in Europe, USA, Canada, Australia, Japan

Cover: Foto ©Raphael Reischuk / pixelio.de

More available books at **www.hansebooks.com**

LETTERS AND MEMORIALS

OF

JANE WELSH CARLYLE

PREPARED FOR PUBLICATION BY

THOMAS CARLYLE

EDITED BY

JAMES ANTHONY FROUDE

IN THREE VOLUMES

VOL. III.

LONDON

LONGMANS, GREEN, AND CO.

1883

LETTERS AND MEMORIALS

OF

JANE WELSH CARLYLE.

LETTER 207.

Miss Barnes, King's Road, Chelsea.

Auchtertool House, Kirkcaldy: Aug. 24, 1859.

My dear Miss Barnes,—How nice of you to have
written me a letter, ' all out of your own head' (as the
children say), and, how very nice of you to have
remarked the forget-me-not, and read a meaning in
it! It was certainly with intention I tied up some
forget-me-nots along with my farewell roses ; but I
was far from sure of your recognising the intention,
and at the same time not young enough to make it
plainer. Sentiment, you see, is not well looked on by
the present generation of women ; there is a growing
taste for fastness, or, still worse, for strong-mindedness! so a discreet woman (like me) will beware
always of putting her sentiment (when she has any)
in evidence—will rather leave it—as in the forget-

me-not case—to be divined through sympathy; and failing the sympathy, to escape notice.

And you are actually going to get married! you! already! And you expect me to congratulate you! or 'perhaps not.' I admire the judiciousness of that 'perhaps not.' Frankly, my dear, I wish you all happiness in the new life that is opening to you; and you are marrying under good auspices, since your father approves of the marriage. But congratulation on such occasions seems to me a tempting of Providence. The triumphal-procession-air which, in our manners and customs, is given to marriage at the outset—that singing of *Te Deum* before the battle has begun—has, ever since I could reflect, struck me as somewhat senseless and somewhat impious. If ever one is to pray—if ever one is to feel grave and anxious—if ever one is to shrink from vain show and vain babble—surely it is just on the occasion of two human beings binding themselves to one another, for better and for worse, till death part them; just on that occasion which it is customary to celebrate only with rejoicings, and congratulations, and *trousseaux*, and white ribbon! Good God!

Will you think me mad if I tell you that when I read your words, 'I am going to be married,' I all but screamed? Positively, it took away my breath, as if I saw you in the act of taking a flying leap into infinite space. You had looked to me such a happy,—

happy little girl! your father's only daughter ; and he so fond of you, as he evidently was. After you had walked out of our house together that night, and I had gone up to my own room, I sat down there in the dark, and took ' a good cry.' You had reminded me so vividly of my own youth, when I, also an only daughter—an only child—had a father as fond of me, as proud of me. I wondered if you knew your own happiness. Well! knowing it or not, it has not been enough for you, it would seem. Naturally, youth is so insatiable of happiness, and has such sublimely insane faith in its own power to make happy and be happy.

But of your father? Who is to cheer his toil-some life, and make home bright for him? His companion through half a lifetime gone ! his dear ' bit of rubbish' gone too, though in a different sense. Oh, little girl! little girl! do you know the blank you will make to him?

Now, upon my honour, I seem to be writing just such a letter as a raven might write if it had been taught. Perhaps the henbane I took in despair last night has something to do with my mood to-day. Anyhow, when one can only ray out darkness, one had best clap an extinguisher on oneself. And so God bless you !

Sincerely yours,
JANE W. CARLYLE.

LETTER 208.

To George Cooke, Esq.

Auchtertool House, Kirkcaldy: Friday.

I am not at the manse, but within a quarter of an
hour's walk of it, in a large comfortable house lent us
by a Mr. Liddell; and we should have done well here
had not Mr. C. walked and rode and bathed himself
into a bilious crisis just before leaving Humbie; so
that he began life under the most untoward auspices.
For the first fortnight, indeed, it was, so far as myself
was concerned, more like being keeper in a madhouse
than being ' in the country' for ' quiet and change.'
Things are a little subsided now, however, and in spite
of the wear and tear on my nerves, I am certainly less
languid and weak than during all my stay in the
farmhouse. Whether it be that the air of Auchtertool suits me better than that of Aberdour, or that
having my kind little cousins within cry is a wholesome diversion, or that it required a continuance
of country air to act upon my feebleness, I am not
competent to say, nor is it of the slightest earthly
consequence what the cause is, so that the effect
has been as I tell you.

LETTER 209.

T. Carlyle, The Gill, Annan.

York, Scawin's Hotel: Thursday, Sept. 22, 1859.

There! I have done it! You prophesied my heart would fail me when it came to the point, and I would 'just rush straight on again to the end.' But my heart didn't fail me, 'or rather' (to speak like Dr. Carlyle) it did fail me horribly! but my memory held true, and kept me up to the mark. With the recollection of the agonies of tiredness I suffered on the journey down, and for many days after, still tingling through my nerves, I took no counsel with my heart, but kept determined to not expose myself to that again, whatever else (bugs inclusive). And, so far, I have reason to congratulate myself; for I was getting 'quite' done up by the time we reached York, and I am now very comfortable in my inn, with prospects for the night not bad! If only there be no 'small beings' (as Mazzini prettily styles them) in the elegant green-curtained bed of number 44, Scawin's.

I am sitting writing in that number, by the side of a bright little fire; which I ordered to be lighted, the first thing, on my arrival. While it was burning up, I went down and had tea in the 'ladies' coffee-room,' where was no fire, but also no ladies! They

brought me very nice tea and muffins, and I 'asked
for' cream!! and for an egg!!! 'And it was all
very coonfortable!' I think I shall order some supper
when the time comes; but I haven't been able to
decide what yet. There isn't a sound in the house,
nor in the back court that my windows look out on.
It is hardly to be hoped such quiet can last. Trains
will come in during the night, and I shall hear them,
anyhow; for this hotel, though not the Railway
Station Hotel, is just outside the station gate. It was
Eliza Liddell who recommended it to me. I never
was in an inn, all by myself, before; except one night
years ago, in the 'George' at Haddington, which was
not exactly an inn to me; and I like the feeling of
it unexpectedly well! The freedom at once from
'living's cares, that is cares of bread,' the pride of
being one's own mistress and own protector, all that
lifts me into a certain exaltation, 'regardless of
expense.' And now I am going to ring my bell, and
order a pair of candles!

Candles come! a pair of composite—not wax,
'thanks God!' I shall breakfast here in peace, and
quietness to morrow morning; and leave by a train
that starts at ten, and reaches London at four; and
shall so avoid night air, which would not suit me at
present. It has grown very cold, within the last
two weeks; and I was as near catching a regular
bad cold as ever I was in my life without doing it!

The habit I took of waking at four at Auchtertool continued at Morningside, where there was much disturbance from carts 'going to the lime.' The morning I left was chill and damp ; and I rose at six, tired of lying still, and dawdled about my room, packing, till I took what Anne used to call 'the cold shivers.' Mrs. Binnie's warm welcome and warm dinner failed to warm me; which was a pity; for Mrs. Godby had arrived and the short visit would have been extremely pleasant, but for my chill. My tongue and throat became very sore towards night. Next day I felt quite desperate ; but Mrs. Godby gave me a stiff tumbler of brandy toddy, in the forenoon, before I started ; and her brother sent me, in his carriage, straight to Sunny Bank, so as to avoid the cold waiting at Long Niddry, and the other risks of the train ; and on arriving at Sunny Bank, I swallowed two glasses of wine, and then, at bedtime, a stiff tumbler of whisky toddy !!! and so on, for the next two days fairly battling down the cold with 'stimulants.' I think I shall escape now, if I take reasonable care. Pity there should be 'always a something'! But for this apprehension of an over-hanging illness, and these horrid 'cold shivers,' I should have enjoyed my last visit to Sunny Bank so much. They were so much better—the house so much cheerfuller with Eliza there, and so many people came to see me that I liked to see. Even when I left, this morning, I did not despair of seeing them again ! [1]

Surely you will never be so rude to that good-humoured Lady Stanley as to fling her over after all. Besides, Alderley would make so good a resting-place for you on the long journey. I hope to get things into their natural condition before you arrive.

Ever yours,

J. W. C.

Love to Mary. I hope she liked her picture. You never saw such a pen as I am writing with !

LETTER 210.

T. Carlyle, Scotsbrig.

5 Cheyne Row, Chelsea: Monday, Sept. 26, 1859.

Two letters to be forwarded, or catch me having put pen to paper this day, I am so tired, Oh my ! I never ! A good sleep would have put me to rights, but that hasn't come yet. In spite of the stillness, and the good bed, and the all-my-own-way, I do nothing but fall asleep, and start up, and light matches, till four o'clock strikes, and after that I lie awake, wishing it were breakfast-time. What a wise woman I was to come home by myself, and get my fatigues done out before you arrived. I am not going out to-day, nor was I out yesterday, but on Saturday afternoon I trailed myself to Silvester's, and saw the

[1] Never did, alas !

horse—'just come in from being exercised,' 'in capital condition,' 'so fat!' Silvester said, clapping its buttock, 'and so spirity that he never——!' The stable seemed good and very clean. I think them most respectable people. And the distance is less than to ——'s.[1]

.If you could conveniently bring a small bag of meal with you from Scotsbrig, it would be welcome; we have none but some Fife meal, which is very inferior to the Annandale. At all events, you could ask Jamie to send us a few stone, say four, and if Mary would give us a little jar of butter, like what she sent with me last year, it 'wud be a great advantage.'[2]

I find everything in the house perfectly safe—no bugs, no moths, grates unrusted, much more care having been taken than when Anne was left in it, with wages, and board wages, at least in the last years of Anne's incumbency. Mrs. Southern is an excellent woman, I do believe, and Charlotte is already the better for being back beside her—away from Thomson's and Muat's.[3]

Ever yours,
J. W. C.

---

[1] The *arsenic* place! My poor 'Fritz' had been suddenly taken to Salter's, Eatou Square, and for a year or more had been quite coming round then.

[2] Good East Lothian woman's speech to me, on the return from Dunbar and the plagues of Irishry, &c., &c. (? seventeen years ago): 'If the wund would fa', it wud be,' &c.

[3] Names merely—unknown.

LETTER 211.

T. Carlyle, Esq., at Alderley Park, Congleton.

5 Cheyne Row, Chelsea: Thursday, Sept. 29, 1859.

Thanks! Just one line, that you may not be fancying me past writing. But there is no time for a
letter. I am shocked to find how late it is. I fell to
putting down the clean drugget, in the drawing-room,
'with my own hands,'[1] that you might not on your
first arrival receive the same impression of profound
gloom from the dark green carpet, that drove myself
towards thoughts of suicide! And, behold, the seams
had given way in many places at the washing; and I
have had to sit on the floor like a tailor, stitching,
stitching, and so the time passed away unremarked,
and it now is long past my dinner-time, and no dinner
so much as thought of, in spite of Charlotte's repeated
questions.

I will put myself in an omnibus, and go up to
Michel's in Sloane Street, and dine on a plate of soup.
Woman wants but little here below—after a railway
journey from Scotland especially.

I am glad you have gone to Alderley. I have
slept a degree better the last two nights; but have
still much to make up in that way. Don't hurry on,

---

[1] 'Signed it, with my own hand' (Edward Irving, forty years ago).

if you do well at the Stanleys'. Kind regards to the lady.

Yours ever,

J. W. C.

LETTER 212.

'Butcher's cart passed over Nero's throat.' Poor little foolish faithful dog! it killed him after all; was never well again. He died in some four months (Feb. 1, 1860, as the little tablet said, while visible) with a degree of pitying sorrow even from me, which I am still surprised at.

The wreck of poor Nero, who had to be strychnined by the doctor, was, and is still, memorable, sad and miserable to me, the last nocturnal walk he took with me, his dim white little figure in the universe of dreary black, and my then mood about ' Frederick ' and other things.

Holmhill is half a mile from the village of Thornhill. Dr. Russell withdrawing from regular business there.—T. C.

Mrs. Russell, Thornhill.

5 Cheyne Row, Chelsea : Wednesday, October 30, 1859.

Dearest Mary,—' If you but know how I have been situated ! ' (my husband's favourite phrase). First, I arrived so tired ! oh so dead tired ! Notwithstanding that, I actually summoned nerve to put in effect my often cherished idea of sleeping at York (half-way) alone in an inn. Odd that I should never, at this age, have done that thing before, in my life, except once, when, after an absence of eighteen years, I spent a night *incognita* in the George Inn of Haddington, where I could not feel myself a mere traveller. It was a proof that my nerves were stronger, if not my limbs, that I really carried out the York speculation, when it came to the point. It would certainly have been again a failure, however, but for a lady in Fife telling me of a comfortable inn to stop at. I was to ask, on getting out of the carriage, 'was any porter from Mrs. Scawin's here?' which I had no sooner done, than the name Scawin was shouted out in the sound of 'Sowens!' to my great shame! I feeling as if everybody knew where I was going, and that it was my first adventure of the sort!! But I was comfortably and quietly lodged; no bugs, no anything to molest me, only that the tumult in my own blood kept me awake all night; so that I arrived here as tired, next evening, as if I had come the whole road at one horrid rush. And I hadn't much time allowed me to rest; for, though Charlotte had got down all the carpets, there were still quantities of details for me to do, before Mr. C. came. And he stayed only a week behind me.

When the house was all in order for him, my cares were destined to take another turn, even more engrossing. Just the night before his arrival, Charlotte went to some shops, taking the dog with her, and brought him home in her arms, all crumpled together like a crushed spider, and his poor little eyes protruding, and fixedly staring in his head! A butcher's cart, driving furiously round a sharp corner, had passed over poor little Nero's throat! and not killed him on the spot! But he looked killed enough at the first. When I tried to 'stand him on the ground' (as the servants here say), he flopped over on his side, quite stiff and unconscious! You may figure my sensations! and I durst not show all my grief; Charlotte was so distressed, and really could not have helped it! I put him in a warm bath, and afterwards wrapped him warmly, and laid him on a pillow, and left him, without much hope of finding him alive in the morning. But in the morning he still breathed, though incapable of any movement; but he swallowed some warm milk that I put into his mouth. About midday I was saying aloud, 'Poor dog! poor little Nero!' when I saw the bit tail trying to wag itself! and after that, I had good hopes. In another day he could raise his head to lap the milk himself. And so, by little and little, he recovered the use of himself; but it was ten days before he was able to raise a bark, his first attempt was like the scream of an infant! It has been a revelation to me, this, of the strength of the throat of a dog!! Mr. C. says, if the wheel had gone over anywhere else, it would have killed him. A gentleman told me the other night that he once saw a fine large dog run over; the great wheel of one of Pickford's heavy-laden vans went over its throat!! And the dog just rose up and shook itself!! It next staggered a little to one side, and then a little to the other, as if drunk, then it steadied itself, and walked composedly home!

When I was out of trouble with my dog, I had time to feel how very relaxing and depressing the air of Chelsea was for me, as usual, after the bracing climate of Scotland. I was perfectly done, till Mr. C. insisted on setting up the carriage again, and Providence put me on drinking water out of a 'bitter cup;' that is a new invention, very popular here this year!—a cup made of the wood of quassia, which makes the water quite bitter in a minute; of course, a chip of quassia put into water would have the same effect; but nobody ever bid me take that! I thought, for three or four days, that I had discovered the grand panacea of life! I felt so hungry! and so cheerful!! and so active! But one night I was seized with the horridest cramps! which quite took the shine out of quassia for me, though I daresay it was merely that I had quite neglected my bowels. I haven't had courage to re-commence with the 'bitter cup;' but it will come! Meanwhile I am pretty well over the bilious crisis that has befallen, to 'remind me that I am but a woman!' and a very frail one (I mean in a physical sense)!

How pleasant it will be to think of you at that pretty Holmhill! though one will always have a tender feeling towards the 'old rambling house,' where we have had such good days together. But the other place will be for the good of your health, as well as more agreeable, when you have once got over the pain of change, which is painful to good hearts, though it may be joyful enough to light ones. It will also be a comfort to my mind to think of that drawing-room getting papered all with one sort of paper !

God bless you. Love to your husband.

J. W. CARLYLE.

LETTER 213.

To Mrs. Stirling, Hill Street, Edinburgh.

5 Cheyne Row, Chelsea : October 21, 1859.

You dear nice woman ! there you are ! a bright cheering apparition to surprise one on a foggy October morning, over one's breakfast—that most trying institution for people who are ' nervous ' and ' don't sleep ! '

It (the photograph) made our breakfast this morning ' pass off,' like the better sort of breakfasts in Deerbrook,[1] in which people seemed to have come into the world chiefly to eat breakfast in every possible variety of temper !

Blessed be the inventor of photography ! I set — him above even the inventor of chloroform ! It has given more positive pleasure to poor suffering

[1] The Deerbrook breakfasts refer to Miss Martineau's poor novel.

humanity than anything that has 'cast[1] up' in my time or is like to—this art by which even the 'poor' can possess themselves of tolerable likenesses of their absent dear ones. And mustn't it be acting favourably on the morality of the country? I assure you I have often gone into my own room, in the devil's own humour—ready to swear at 'things in general,' and some things in particular—and, my eyes resting by chance on one of my photographs of long-ago places or people, a crowd of sad, gentle thoughts has rushed into my heart, and driven the devil out, as clean as ever so much holy water and priestly exorcisms could have done! I have a photograph of Haddington church tower, and my father's tombstone in it—of every place I ever lived at as a home —photographs of old lovers! old friends, old servants, old dogs! In a day or two, you, dear, will be framed and hung up among the 'friends.' And that bright, kind, indomitable face of yours will not be the least efficacious face there for exorcising my devil, when I have him! Thank you a thousand times for keeping your word! Of course you would—that is just the beauty of you, that you never deceive nor disappoint.

Oh my dear! my dear! how awfully tired I was with the journey home, and yet I had taken two days to it, sleeping—that is, attempting to sleep—at York. What a pity it is that Scotland is so far off! all the

---

[1] Turned.

good one has gained there gets shaken off one in the terrific journey home again, and then the different atmosphere is so trying to one fresh from the pure air of Fife—so exhausting and depressing. If it hadn't been that I had a deal of housemaiding to execute during the week I was here before Mr. C. returned, I must have given occasion for newspaper paragraphs under the head of ' Melancholy Suicide.' But dusting books, making chair-covers, and ' all that sort of thing,' leads one on insensibly to live—till the crisis gets safely passed.

My dear! I haven't time nor inclination for much letter-writing—nor have you, I should suppose, but do let us exchange letters now and then. A friend-ship which has lived on air for so many years together is worth the trouble of giving it a little human sustenance.

Give my kind regards to your husband—I like him.—And believe me,

Your ever affectionate

JANE WELSH CARLYLE.

LETTER 214.

In October, after getting home, there was a determined onslaught made on ' Frederick,' an attempt (still in the way of youth—16 rather than 60 !) to vanquish by sheer force the immense masses of incondite or semi-condite rubbish which had accumulated on ' Frederick,' that is, to let the printer straightway drive me through it !—a most fond and foolish notion, which indeed I myself partly knew, durst I have confessed it, to be foolish and even inpossible! But this was the case all along; I never once said to myself, ' All those chaotic mountains, wide as the world, high as the stars, dismal as Lethe, Styx, and Phlegethon, did mortal ever see the like of it for size and for quality in the rubbish way? All this thou wilt have to take into thee, to roast and smelt in the furnace of thy own poor soul till thou fairly do-smelt the grains of gold out of it!' No, though dimly knowing all this, I durst not openly know it (indeed, how could I otherwise ever have undertaken such a subject?) ; and I had got far on with the unutterable enterprise, before I did clearly admit that such was verily proving, and would, on to the finis, prove to have been the terrible part of this affair, affair which I must now conquer *tale quale,* or else perish! This first attempt of October–February, 1859— 1860 (after dreadful tugging at the straps), was given up by her serious advices, which I could not but admit to be true as well as painful and humiliating! November 1860 had arrived before there was any further printing : nothing thenceforth but silent pulling at a dead lift, which lasted four or five years more.

My darling must have suffered much in all this; how much! I sometimes thought how cruel it was on her, to whom ' Frederick ' was literally nothing except through me, so cruel, alas, alas, and yet inevitable! Never once in her deepest misery did she hint, by word or sign, what she too was suffering under that score; me only did she ever seem to pity in it, the heroic, the thrice noble, and wholly loving soul!

She seemed generally a little stronger this year, and only a little ; her strength, though blind *I* never saw it, and kept hoping, hoping, was never to come back, but the reverse, the reverse more and more! Except a week or two at the Grange (January 1860), which did not hurt either of us, I think we had intended to make no visits this year, or as good as none. We did, however, and for good reasons, make two—hers, a most unlucky or provoking one, provokingly curtailed and frustrated, as will be seen. This was in August, to Alderley, and she could have gone further but for blind ill luck. Beginning of July she had tried a week or thereby of lodging at Brighton, and invited me, who tried for three days but could get no sleep for noises, and had to hurry home by myself; where also I could not sleep nor stay to any purpose, and was chiefly by brother John, who accompanied, led by sea to Thurso, for a 'long sail' first of all.

To Mrs. Russell, Thornhill.

5 Cheyne Row, Chelsea: Friday, Jan. 28, 1860.

Dearest Mary,—A letter from me would have crossed yours (with the book) on the road, if it hadn't been for a jacket! Things are so oddly hooked together in this world. The connection in this case is simple enough. I needed a little jacket for home wear, and, possessing a superfluous black silk scarf, I resolved, in a moment of economical enthusiasm, to make with my own hands a jacket out of it. For, in spite of the ' thirty thousand distressed needlewomen ' one hears so much of, the fact remains that nobody can get a decent article of dress made here, unless at enormous cost. And besides, the dressmakers who can fit one won't condescend to make anything but with their own materials. So I fell to cutting out that jacket last Monday, and only finished it to-day (Friday)! and was so much excited over the unusual nature of the enterprise (for I detest sewing, and don't sew for weeks together) that I could not leave off, for anything that could be postponed, till the jacket was out of hands. But Lord preserve me, what a bother; better to have bought one ready-made at the dearest rate. I won't take a needle in my hands, except to sew on Mr. C.'s buttons, for the next six months. By the way, would you like the shape of my jacket, which is of the newest? I have it on paper, and could send it to you quite handy.

Oh my dear, I am very much afraid, the reading of that book will be an even more uncongenial job of work for me than the jacket, and won't have as much to show for itself when done. If there be one thing I dislike more than theology it is geology. And here we have both, beaten up in the same mortar, and incapable, by any amount of beating, to coalesce. What could induce any live woman to fall a-writing that sort of book? And a decidedly clever woman— I can see that much from the little I have already read of it here and there. She expresses her meaning very clearly and elegantly too. If it were only on any subject I could get up an interest in, I should read her writing with pleasure. But even when Darwin, in a book that all the scientific world is in ecstasy over, proved the other day that we are all come from shell-fish, it didn't move me to the slightest curiosity whether we are or not. I did not feel that the slightest light would be thrown on my practical life for me, by having it ever so logically made out that my first ancestor, millions of millions of ages back, had been, or even had not been, an oyster. It remained a plain fact that I was no oyster, nor had any grandfather an oyster within my knowledge ; and for the rest, there was nothing to be gained, for this world, or the next, by going into the oyster-question, till all more pressing questions were exhausted! So— if I can't read Darwin, it may be feared I shall break down in Mrs. Duncan. Thanks to you, however, for the book, which will be welcome to several of my acquaintances. There is quite a mania for geology at present, in the female mind. My next-door neighbour would prefer a book like Mrs. Duncan's to Homer's ' Iliad ' or Milton's ' Paradise Lost.' ' There is no accounting for tastes.'

I have done my visit to the Grange,[1] and got no hurt by it ; and it was quite pleasant while it lasted. The weather was mild, and besides, the house is so completely warmed, with warm-water pipes, that it is like summer there in the coldest weather. The house was choke-full of visitors—four-and-twenty of us, most of the time. And the toilettes! Nothing could exceed their magnificence ; for there were four young new-married ladies, among the rest, all vieing with each other who to be finest. The blaze of diamonds

---

[1] Finished January 13.

every day at dinner, quite took the shine out of the chandeliers. As for myself, I got through the dressing-part of the business by a sort of continuous miracle, and, after the first day, had no bother with myself of any sort. The new Lady[1] was kindness' self and gave general satisfaction.

Affectionately yours,
JANE CARLYLE.

LETTER 215.

To Miss Barnes, King's Road, Chelsea.

5 Cheyne Row: Saturday, Jan. 14, 1860.

My dear Miss Barnes,—I send you a pheasant, which is a trophy as well as a dead bird! For I brought it home with me last night from one of the most stupendous massacres of feathered innocents that ever took place 'here down' (as Mazzini expresses himself)—from seven hundred to a thousand pheasants shot in one day! The firing made me perfectly sick. Think of the bodily and mental state of the surviving birds when the day's sport was ended! Decidedly, men can be very great brutes when they like!

We have been away for ten days at the Grange (Lord Ashburton's place in Hampshire), where I always thrive better than anywhere else ; and where, as you see, there are many pheasants.

[1] Lord Ashburton married secondly, November 17, 1858, Louisa Caroline, youngest daughter of the Right Hon. James Stewart Mackenzie.

I went to take leave of you before we went ; but saw all the blinds down, and grew sick with fright ! I went into Mr. Gigner's shop and inquired was anything the matter ; and he told me of your new loss. At least, it was an immense relief to me to hear that your father and yourself were not ill or worse. After that I thought a note about my insignificant movements would only bother your father ; so I left him to learn my whereabouts from the ' Morning Post,' certain he would be too much preoccupied for looking after me at all. Do come soon, if I don't go to you. Do you care to have this card ? It will do for an autograph if you don't want to use it.

Affectionately yours,

J. CARLYLE.

LETTER 216.

To Mr. Barnes, King's Road, Chelsea.

5 Cheyne Row : Thursday night, Feb. 1 [Nero died].

My dear good Mr. Barnes,—I cannot put into words how much I feel your kindness. It was such a kind thing for you to do ! and so kindly done ! My gratitude to you will be as long as my life, for shall I not, as long as I live, remember that poor little dog ? Oh don't think me absurd, you, for caring so much about a dog ? Nobody but myself can have any idea what that little creature has been in my life. My inseparable companion during eleven years, ever doing his little best to keep me from feeling sad and lonely.

Docile, affectionate, loyal up to his last hour. When
weak and full of pain, he offered himself to go out
with me, seeing my bonnet on ; and came panting to
welcome me on my return, and the reward I gave
him—the only reward I could or ought to give him,
to such a pass had things come—was, ten minutes
after, to give him up to be poisoned.

I thought it not unlikely you would call to-day ;
because your coming to-day would be of a piece
with the rest of your goodness to me. Nevertheless,
I went out for a long drive ; I could not bear myself
in the house where everything I looked at reminded
me of yesterday. And I wouldn't be at home for
visitors to criticise my swollen eyes, and smile at
grief 'about a dog,' and besides, suppose you came,
I wished to not treat you to more tears ; of which
you had had too much ; and to-day I couldn't for
my life have seen you without crying dreadfully.

Tell your little jewel of a daughter I have not
forgotten her wish, for which I thank her. I wish
all her wishes were as easy to fulfil.

Yours affectionately,

JANE WELSH CARLYLE.

LETTER 217.

To John Forster, Esq., Montagu Square.

5 Cheyne Row : Thursday, Jan. 1800 ? or March ?

All right, dear Mr. Forster—nothing but ' yeses
out of that man's mouth, when your proposal was

stated to him. Willing, pleased yeses. I am afraid
something must be going to happen to him. 'Yes,'
he would go on Sunday; 'yes,' he would be there a
quarter before six; yes, he would walk there, and let
you send him home. Exactly as you predicted, he
did not come in till half-past six by the clock. It is
a pity for poor me; I daren't do anything pleasant
ever. Though, like the pigs, I get used to it, and
am thankful if I can but keep on foot in-doors.

I am bent on seeing her and Katie, however,
before we go to the Grange.

Yours affectionately.

JANE CARLYLE.

[*In T. C.'s hand*:—]
Yes, Saturday;—for the brougham to fetch me, no, with
thanks.—T. C.
(Written then!—T. C.)

LETTER 213.

Autumn 1860, I made a visit of four or five weeks to
Sir George Sinclair at Thurso. Early in the summer of
that year, I was visited by sleeplessness; and first began to
have an apprehension that I should never get my sad book
on Friedrich finished, that it would finish me instead. I
still remember well enough the dark, cold, vague, yet
authentic-looking feeling of terror that shot athwart me as
I sat smoking 'up the chimney,' huddled in rugs, dressing-
gown and cape, with candle on the hob, my one remedy in
sleepless cases; the first real assault of fear, pointing, as it
were, to undeniable fact; and how it saddened me the
whole of next day. The second day, I compared it to

Luther's temptings by the devil; and thought to myself in
Luther's dialect, ' Well, well, Herr Teufel, we will just go on
as long as we are alive; and keep working, all the same,
till thou do get us killed ! ' This put away the terror, but
would by no means bring the sleep back. I recollect lying
whole nights awake, still as a stone; getting up at six, and
riding to Clapham Common, to Hammersmith region, by
way of surrogate for sleep. My head had an unpleasant
cloudy feeling; I was certainly far from well, far below my
average of illness even. Brother John, who lived in his
Brompton lodgings then, recommended strongly a sea-
voyage; voyage to Thurso, for example, whither the hospitable Sir George Sinclair had been again, perhaps for the
third or fourth time, eagerly inviting me. Nothing else
being so feasible, and something being clearly indispensable,
we both set off, John volunteering to escort me to Wick;
and generously and effectively performing that fraternal
service. The very first night, in spite of the tumults of the
crowded Aberdeen steamer, and such a huddle of a sleeping-
place as is only seen at sea, I slept deep for six or seven
hours; and had not again, during this visit, nor for years,
any real misery about sleep.

On the part of my generous host and household, nothing
was left wanting; I was allowed to work daily some hours,
invisible till three P.M. I bathed daily in the Pentland
Firth in sight of the ' Old Man,' roamed about, saw
' John o' Groat's House' (evidently an old lime-kiln!) &c.
&c., a country ancient, wild, and lonely, more than enough
impressive to me. I was very sad, ' soul exceeding solitary;'
nothing could help that. Sir George was abundantly con-
versible, anecdotic, far-read, far-experienced, indeed a quite
learned man (would read me lyrics &c., straight from the
Greek, any evening, nothing pleased him better), and full of
piety, veracity, and good-nature, but it availed little; I was

sad and weary, all things bored me! Here at Chelsea, with my clever Jeannie for hostess, and some clever Mrs. Twisleton for fellow-guest, Sir George was reported to be charming and amusing at their little dinner, while I sat aloft and wrote. But not here could he amuse; not here, though his constant perfect goodness, and the pleasure he always expressed over me, were really welcome, wholesome, and received with gratitude. I had many invitations from him afterwards, saw him here annually once or twice; but never went to Thurso again; never could get going, had I even wished it more.

Few letters went from me in that Thurso solitude, none that I could help. From my darling herself I seemed to receive still fewer than I wrote; the tediously slow posts, I remember, were unintelligible to her, provoking to her! Here is one, beyond what I could count on, come to me last week among four of my own, printed ' on approval,' in some memoirs of Sir George, which the relations have set a certain well-known Mr. James Grant upon writing! To Miss Sinclair's poor request, I said reluctantly yes—could not say no; corrected the five letters (not without difficulty); returned my own four originals; retained (resolutely) the original of this, and a printed copy as well as this. (December 13, 1869.)—T. C.

The letter from Mrs. Carlyle to Sir George Sinclair is not dated, so far as regards the year; but evidently follows close on the foregoing. It is felicitously playful in reference to her own husband. It is as follows :—

5 Cheyne Row, Chelsea: August 1, 1860.

My dear Sir,—Decidedly you are more thoughtful for me than the man who is bound by vow to ' love and cherish me;' not a line have I received from him to announce his safe arrival in your dominions. The more shameful on his part, that, as it appears by your note, he had such good accounts to give of himself, and was perfectly up to giving them.

Well! now that you have relieved me from all anxiety about the effects of the journey on him, he may write at his own ' reasonably good leisure.' Only I told him I should not write till I had heard of his arrival from himself; and *he knows* whether or no I am in the habit of keeping my word —to the letter.

A thousand thanks for the primrose roots ; which I shall plant, as soon as it fairs! To-day we have again a deluge ; adding a deeper shade of horror to certain household operations going on under my inspection (by way of ' improving the occasion ' of his absence !). One bedroom has got all the feathers of its bed and pillows airing themselves out on the floor! creating an atmosphere of down in the house, more choking than even ' cotton-fuzz.' In another, upholsterers and painters are plashing away for their life ; and a couple of bricklayers are tearing up flags in the kitchen to seek ' the solution ' of a non-acting drain ! All this on the one hand ; and on the other, visits from my doctor, resulting in ever new ' composing draughts,' and strict charges to ' keep my mind perfectly tranquil.' You will admit that one could easily conceive situations more ideal.

Pray do keep him as long as you like ! To hear of him ' in high spirits ' and ' looking remarkably well ' is more composing for me than any amount of ' composing draughts,' or of insistence on the benefits of ' keeping myself perfectly tranquil.' It is so very different a state of things with him from that in which I have seen him for a long time back !

Oh ! I must not forget to give you the ' kind remembrances ' of a very charming woman, whom any man may be pleased to be remembered by, as kindly as she evidently remembered you ! I speak of Lady William Russell. She knew you in Germany, ' a young student,' she told me, when she was Bessy Rawdon. She ' had a great affection for you, and had often thought of you since.' You were ' very romantic in those days ; oh, very romantic and sentimental,' she could assure me ! Pray send me back a pretty message for her ; she will like so much to know that she has not remembered you ' with the reciprocity all on one side.'

I don't even send my regards to Mr. C., but—

Affectionately yours,

JANE W. CARLYLE.

LETTER 219.

T. Carlyle, Esq., Thurso Castle.

5 Cheyne Row, Chelsea : Friday, Aug. 10, 1860.

Oh my dear ! If ' all about feelings ' be bad in a letter, all about scenery and no feelings is a deal worse! Such a letter as that I received from you, yesterday, after much half-anxious, half-angry waiting for, will read charmingly in your biography! and may be quoted in ' Murray's Guide Book ;' but for ' me, as one solitary individual,' I was not charmed with it at all! Nevertheless, I should have answered it by return of post, had I not been too ill for writing anything yesterday, except, on the strength of phrenzy, a passionate appeal to the ' retired cheesemonger,' about his dog, which, I am happy to say, like everything coming straight from the heart, went straight to the heart of the good little old cheesemonger. You will infer, from my going ahead against ' noises ' on my own account, that the ' extraordinary disturbance of the nervous system,' which Mr. Barnes found me suffering under when he came, has not yielded yet to an equally extraordinary amount of ' composing mixture !' My sleep had been getting ' small by degrees, and beautifully less,' till I ended in lying awake the whole nights through ! not what you call ' awake,' that is, dozing ; but broad wide awake, like a hawk with an empty stomach ! Still the mixture was to be persevered in, nay, increased, and I was assured that it was ' doing me a little good,' so little I myself couldn't perceive it, even through the powerful microscope of my faith in Mr. Barnes ! and, in spite of his assurance that ' home was the best place for me at present,' I had wild impulses to 'take the road' (like the 'Doctor,' and with the Doctor's purposelessness !). The night before last, however (Wednesday night), I fell into a deep natural sleep, which lasted two hours, and might have lasted till the masons began, but for cheesemonger's dog, which was out that night (bad luck to it !) on a spree ! and startled me awake at three of the morning with furious continuous barking—just as if my head was being laid open with repeated strokes of a hatchet ! Of course I 'slept no more ;' and yesterday was too ill for anything except, as I have said, writing a wild appeal to the cheesemonger. I will inclose his comforting answer which he handed in himself an hour after. It will be comforting to you also, in reference to your own future nights.

I have nothing to tell that you will take any interest in, except about the horse. He is still under the process of 'breaking,'[1] poor creature ! Is 'so nervous and resolute,' so 'dreadful resolute,' that the breaker 'can't tell how long it will take to get the better of him !' I must see Silvester to-day before writing to Frederick Chapman. I saw the poor horse three days ago, just coming in from the breaker's, like a horse just returning from the Thirty Years' War !' Poor beast ! I could have cried for him—

---

[1] To run in harness; but he wouldn't—couldn't—though the best-natured of horses, poor Fritz !

required to turn over a new leaf in his old age! I
know what that is!

'The nephew of Haggi Babda,' dropt in 'quite
promiscuously' last Sunday evening, when old Jane
was out at church, and I was alone, except for
Geraldine, who opened the door to him, and afterwards talked social metaphysics with him! He is
the fattest young large man I ever saw, out of a
caravan! but in other respects rather charming.
He wished me to impress on you how happy he
would be to transact any commissions for you at
Berlin, 'for which his connection with the embassy
might give him facilities &c. &c.' He seemed heartily
in earnest about this, and a hearty admirer of your
'Frederick.' He is the best-bred, pleasantest man I
have seen ' for seven years,' and the hour and half he
stayed would have been delightful, if I hadn't been
deadly sick all the while, and my nervous system ' in
an extraordinary state of disturbance.'

Tell Sir George I have planted the cowslips, ' with
my own hand,' and have not needed to water them,
' the heavenly watering-pan ' (which Mariotti spoke
of) having spared me the trouble. I gave them the
place of highest honour (round poor little Nero's
stone). I have had fires all day long for the last
week—such a summer! Lady Stanley sent me her
portrait. The only bit of real pleasantness, however,
that has come my way has been, last Wednesday, a

visit from William Dodds and his wife. They told me such things about the behaviour of the London Donaldsons, when they went down to Miss Jess's funeral!

Your situation sounds as favourable as a conditional world could have afforded you. I trust in Heaven that you will go on improving in it.

You remember, no pens got mended, so you won't wonder at this scrawling.

Yours ever,

J. WELSH CARLYLE.

LETTER 220.

T. Carlyle, Thurso Castle.

5 Cheyne Row, Chelsea: Friday, Aug. 17, 1860.

Thanks for the two letters, dear! I ' did intend ' to have answered them together, at full length, by to-day's post, but have been hindered sadly, and ignominiously, by—' what shall I say?'—an attack of British cholera! Don't be alarmed; it is over now! and it is still but two o'clock, and, though I was ill all night as well as all the forenoon, I don't feel disabled for writing. It is an appointment with Lady Sandwich, which I don't like to break, that takes away the remaining two and a half hours, in which I might have written a sufficient letter. She sent the coachman last night, with a note to say she had returned to Grosvenor Square, on account of a

slight attack of bronchitis, and would I tell the
coachman when to bring the carriage to fetch me ; I
appointed a quarter before three to-day, not fore-
seeing what the night had in reserve for me ! Indeed,
I had no reason to expect anything of the sort,
having been sleeping better, and feeling better in
every way for the last week. I rather ' happrehend '
it was my own imprudence, in taking a glass of
bitter ale at supper that caused this deadly sickness,
and—other things. Trust me for doing the best for
myself, in the circumstances. I am the last person to
let myself be humbugged by a doctor; Mr. Barnes
was perfectly right in ordering me, at the time you
left, to put all ideas of travelling out of my head, and
' go to bed for two hours every forenoon instead.'
And the mixture, which for many days failed in its
intended effect, on account (he said) of the excitement I was in, got to do me palpable, unmistakable
good at last, and is now discontinued by his own
order. At the time you. left I was hanging on the
verge of nervous fever, and have made a very near
miss of it ! He does not disapprove of my going
away now, provided I keep short of fatigue and
excitement, and I am taking steps towards forming a
programme. I will tell you in a day or two what
direction I have decided on. I should like very well
to spend a day or so at the Gill; but a stay of any
length there would not suit me at all. Milk is no

object, as it is not strong enough food for my present weak appetite; and solitude is positively hurtful to me. Human kindness is precious everywhere, and nobody appreciates it more than I do; but just the kinder they are, the more I should be tempted to exert myself in talking, and putting my contentment in evidence. In short, there would be a strain upon me, while I was supposed to be enjoying the height of freedom! I mean were my stay prolonged beyond the day or two during which the enthusiasm of meeting after so long absence, and having things to tell one another, holds out. I am so sorry to put you off with such a scrubby letter, but the carriage will be here before I am dressed; and here is my beef-tea— my first breakfast.

Kind love to Sir George.

Yours ever,
J. W. C.

LETTER 221.

Mrs. Russell, Thornhill.

5 Cheyne Row, Chelsea: Friday, Aug. 17, 1860.

Dearest Mary,—I haven't leisure to commence this letter with reproaches; for the reproaches would be very long, and my time for writing is very short. In an hour hence a carriage will come to take me to a sick old lady, I myself being quite as sick and

D 2

nearly as old, and there are directions to be given to divers workmen before I start. For Mr. Carlyle is absent at Thurso, and I have taken the opportunity of turning a carpenter, and a painter, and a paper-hanger into his private apartment.

Yes, after repeatedly assuring you that Mr. Carlyle would not go north this summer, but restrict his travels to some sea-side place near hand, I am almost ashamed to tell you that he has gone 'north' after all, and further north than he ever was in all his life before, being on a visit to Sir George Sinclair at Thurso Castle—the northernmost point of Scotland. A trial of Brighton had been made, and had ended abruptly and ignominiously in flight back to Chelsea, to get out of the sound of certain cocks. Of all places in the world, Brighton was the last one could have expected to be infested with poultry. But one week of Brighton had only increased Mr. C.'s desire for sea, and indeed he had got into such a sleepless, excited condition through prolonged over-work, that there could be no doubt about the need of what they call 'a complete change' for him. So he looked about for a sea-residence, where he might be safe from cocks and cockneys, and decided for Thurso Castle, which could moreover be reached by sailing, which he prefers infinitely to railwaying, and whence there had come a pressing invitation for us both to spend a couple of months. Accordingly, he streamed off there a fortnight ago, I remaining behind for several reasons; first, that sailing is as much as my life is worth, and seven hundred miles of railway would have been just about as fatal. Second, if I was going to undertake a long journey, I might take it in directions that would better repay the trouble and expense. And third, the long worry and anxiety I had had with Mr. C.'s nervousness had reduced myself to the brink of a nervous fever, and my doctor was peremptory as to the unfitness of my either going with Mr. C., or rejoining him at Thurso. Indeed I was not to leave home at all in the state I was in, but to take three composing draughts a day! and go to bed for two hours every forenoon. A fortnight of this and perfect quiet in the house has calmed me down amazingly, only I feel as tired as if I were just returned from the ' thirty years' war.' And now Mr. Barnes does not object to my going away, provided I don't go to Mr. C. ! and don't over-exert myself. Mr. C., who is already immensely improved by his residence at Thurso Castle, is all for everybody ' going into the country,' and has made up his mind that, like it or not, I must go ' instantly ' to—the Gill (Mary Austin's), which, as it suits his milk-loving habits, he thinks would equally suit me. And I myself would like very well to turn my two or three remaining weeks of liberty to some more agreeable use than superintending the house-cleaning here !

But decidedly mooning about, all by myself, at the Gill, lapping milk, which doesn't agree with me, and being stared at by the Gill children as their ' aunt ! ' is not the happy change for which I would go far, much as I like Mary Austin.

Now, I want to know how you are situated, whether the invitation held out to me, and which I, ' ignorant of the future,' declined for this year, be still open to me ; for if I had it in my power to go on to you for a week or so from the Gill, I might give myself the air of a charmingly obedient wife, and agree to go there, without my obedience costing me any personal sacrifice. I could break the long journey by staying a few days at Alderley Park (Lord Stanley's), where I have half engaged to go in any case. But I don't know if you are settled yet, or if you are not gone somewhere for change of air yourself, or if somebody else be not located, for the present, in my room, and unfortunately I am tied to time. I must be back in London—some weeks before Mr. C. ; for reasons I will explain later, for they require time to explain them.

In the meanwhile you will, in any case, answer me, as briefly as you like, by return of post ? for I shan't answer Mr. C. till I get your letter. And I do beseech you to be perfectly frank, to tell me if you are going anywhere, or if anybody else is coming to you, or if my room is not ready yet, or, worst of all, if you are poorly, and can't be troubled.

I understand that state so thoroughly well.

Your affectionate

JANE W. CARLYLE.

LETTER 222.

T. Carlyle, Thurso Castle.

Alderley Park, Congleton, Cheshire: Thursday, Aug. 23, 1860.

There! What do you think of this? If you knew all you would admit that I have as much ' courage ' as your horse, which ' goes whether he can or not.' But the present is not a moment for entering into details, of how ill I was after my last letter, and of how my illness was complicated with household griefs, and of how it was necessary to leave for here at hardly a day's notice, or give up altogether the idea of going anywhere. All that will keep till I am in better case for writing a long letter, or even till we meet ' on our return from the thirty years' war.' Enough to say, for the present, that I am here on a most kindly pressing invitation from Lady Stanley, to stay ' a week,' and ' be nursed ' (you may be sure it was pressing enough when *I* accepted it), and that my intention is, if I get as much better as I hope, to go on from here to the Gill, and from there, after a day or two's rest, to Holm Hill (Mrs. Russell's), where I can remain with advantage as long as I find expedient with relation to the time of your return home.

Mrs. Russell had been urging me to visit them for the last three months at intervals. And I am always much made of, and very comfortable there. And to have a doctor for one's host was a consideration of some weight with me, under the circumstances, in choosing that ultimate destination. I couldn't have travelled all the way to Dumfriesshire at one fell rush; but the invitation to Alderley broke the journey beautifully for me. It (the coming to Alderley) had been spoken of, or rather written of, by Lady S. before I last wrote to you, but I was afraid to say a word about it in case you had played me the same trick as in the case of Louisa Baring. No time had been specified then. So that when I received a letter on Monday (written in forgetfulness of the intervening Sunday), urging me to be at Chelford station on Tuesday by four o'clock, where Lady S. would send the carriage for me, it quite took away my breath. I could not possibly get myself and the house packed by Tuesday. Besides, Lady Ashburton had offered to come to tea with me on Tuesday, and been accepted, ' in my choicest mood;' so I answered that I would, D.V., be at Chelford station by four on Wednesday.

A more tired human being than myself, when I got into the train at Euston Square yesterday, you haven't seen ' this seven years.' Geraldine and

Mr. Larkin escorted me there, and paid me the last attentions. I was hardly out of sight of the station when I fell back in my seat and went to sleep, and slept off and on (me, in a railway carriage!) all the way to Crewe, where I was roused into the usual wide-awakeness by seeing the van containing my portmanteau go off as for good. It came back, however, after much running and remonstrating; and I was put down at Chelford 'all right' in a pouring rain, which indeed had poured without a moment's intermission all day. The carriage was waiting with drenched coachman and footman, who I had the discomfort of thinking must wish me at Jericho, at the least, and I was soon in the hall at Alderley, into which Lady S., with the girls at her back, came running to welcome me with kisses and good words, a much more human mode of receiving visitors than I had been used to in great houses. In fact, the whole thing is very human, and very humane as well. Lord S. is still in London, Postmaster-General you will have heard—nobody here but Lady S. and the girls, which suits my nervous system, and also my wardrobe (which I had no time or care to get up) much better than company would have done. Indeed, I had made the aloneness and dulness, which Lady S., had complained of, my conditions in accepting her invitation. Mr. Barnes had been saying all he could about 'the excited state of my brain' (I too have a brain it seems?) to frighten me into ' taking better care ' of myself, and ' avoiding every sort of worry, and fuss, and fatigue,' as if anybody could avoid worry, and fuss, and fatigue in this world. Worry, and fuss, and fatigue under the name of ' pleasure,' of ' amusement,' that however one certainly may avoid. So I should not have gone wilfully into a houseful of visitors.

I shall write to Mary to-day. I had the kindest little letter from her.

Love to Sir George. I have had no letter from you since—I cannot remember when.

Yours ever,

J. W. C.

F. Chapman will have written about the horse he undertook to break. Silvester says the horse is not broken, has a nasty trick that would break any brougham—turns sharp round, and stands stock still, in spite of all you can do, holding his head to one side as if he were listening. Poor dear Fritz. The breaker, who I suppose desires to be rid of it, says to Chapman it is broken, and Frederick means to try it himself.

LETTER 223.

Mrs. Russell, Holm Hill.

Alderley Park, Congleton : Saturday, Aug. 25, 1860.

My dearest Mary,—I could sit down and take a good hearty cry. I am not to get to you after all. This morning is come a letter from Mr. C., forwarded from Chelsea, giving me the astounding news that there is every likelihood of his coming home by next Wednesday's steamer. Always the way, whenever I go anywhere to please myself—plump he appears at Chelsea, and, just now, his appearance there in my absence would be (as Lord Ashburton would say) ' the devil ! '

I cannot enter into an account of my household affairs just now—being long, and most ridiculous. I was keeping it as an amusing story for you when we met. I will write the story from Chelsea at my first leisure (when will that be ?). But just now I am too vexed for making a good story, besides being too busy, having so many letters demanding to be written about this provoking change of plan. When I leave here, it must be straight for Chelsea, and I must go on Tuesday morning. What a pity! I was just beginning to recover my sleep in the fresh air and the absence of worries—have had actually two nights of good sleep ; and they are so kind to me, and they to whom I was going would have been so kind to me! But when one has married a man of genius, one must take the consequences. Only there was no need for him to have spoken of staying at Thurso till the beginning of October, and misled me so.

Your loving friend,

J. W. C.

LETTER 224.

T. Carlyle, Thurso Castle.

Alderley Park: Sunday, Aug. 26, 1860.

Oh, dear me! this length of days needed for a letter written to or from Thurso, to get an answer in the course of post, is very trying to impatient spirits! Not on account of the slowness only, but on account of the 'change come o'er the spirit of one's dream' in the interval between the post's going out and coming in. Not once, since you went to that accursedly out-of-the-way place, has a letter from you found me in the same mood and circumstances to which it was addressed, as being the mood and circumstances in which my own letter had left me, and of course it has been the same with my letters to you. For example, your announcement that you might be home immediately, crossing my announcement that I was on the road to Scotland. Now I write to say I am turning back, and shall be at Chelsea, D.V., on Tuesday afternoon, to prepare for you, in case you do come soon, which I shall regret for your sake; a few more weeks of sound sleep would be so good for you. What will be the contents of the letter that crosses this? Something quite irrelevant I have no doubt. Perhaps assurances that you can do perfectly well at Chelsea without me, and that I am to stay in Scotland as long as I like, when I shall be reading the letter at Cheyne Row, and as sure as ever woman was of anything that you could not have done at Chelsea without me for twelve hours.

The week before my departure, which should have been devoted to setting my house in order, was devoted to British cholera, which, coming on the back of low nervous fever, reduced me to a state of exhaustion, which even 'zeal for my house,' couldn't rouse to the requisite activity. Many things had been begun, but few of them finished—for instance, your bed had been all taken to pieces to look for bugs, and it had been ascertained that not one bug survived there, and the bed had been put together, but the curtains were away being cleaned.

Fancy your coming home to a curtainless bed, and 'Old Jane'[1] would have made no shift! for 'Old Jane,' my dear, I may as well tell you soon as syne, is a complete failure and humbug! Although you provokingly enough attributed the silence I systematically observe on the shortcomings of servants to want of 'care about it,' I still think that until I am arrived at parting with a servant, and have to show reason why, the more I hold my peace about them, and make the best of them, the more for your comfort and for my own credit.[2] 'Old Jane' then disappointed me from the first day. Before you left I had satisfied myself that she was a perfectly incompetent cook and servant,

---

[1] I have quite forgotten.
[2] Alas! can that need to be said?—insane that I was!

and soon after you left I satisfied myself that she—
told lies! and had no more sense of honour in her
work than Charlotte. There was no need to worry
you with the topic of her, which was to myself perfectly loathsome, until I had to account for replacing
her. I mention her now to reconcile you to the idea
of my having gone back home to wait for you. You
couldn't have done without me, you see. I have
engaged a woman of thirty-four, who is really promising (the woman Miss Evans wanted to have), and a
remarkably nice-looking girl of sixteen to be under
her.[1] She would not have taken a place of ' all work,'
and indeed it is very difficult to find even a respectable servant who will take it—naturally, when they
can find plenty of less confused places. She, the
elder woman, comes home on September 14, and
I wished the girl to wait till then. I think the house
will really be comfortable and orderly by-and-by—
at more cost; but that, you said repeatedly, you
didn't mind. At all rates, I have taken immense
trouble (two journeys to Richmond included), to find
respectable and competent servants. If I have failed,
it will just be another instance of my ill-luck, rather
than my want of zeal.

---

[1] Yes, I recollect these two. I had often latterly been urging ' two
servants,' but she never till now would comply. The *elder* of these ' two'
did not suit either. A conceited fool ; got the name ' Perfection,' and (to
the great joy of the younger, who continued worthily) had to go in a
few months.

Maud[1] has been sitting in my room waiting till I am done. Excuse haste and abrupt ending. I can't write on this principle, and I shan't get a chance again before post-time.

Yours,

J. W. C.

LETTER 225.

Surely this is one of the saddest of letters—the misery of it merely slowness of posts, and on both sides hardly bearable heaviness of load. Oh, my own much-suffering little woman !—T. C.

T. Carlyle, Thurso Castle.

5 Cheyne Row, Chelsea : Sunday, Sept. 2, 1860.

This is all—'what shall I say? strange, upon my honour!' On Friday morning comes a note from Sir George (that had gone round by Alderley) to the effect that his ' dear friend's pen being more devoted to the service of unborn generations than to mine' (truly! and if the ' unborn generations ' will do the answering, I shan't object !), and another expedition to John o' Groats being on foot, he writes to tell me the dear friend has been prevailed upon, &c. &c. Well! 'I am most particularly glad to hear it,' like Archivarius Lyndhorst. The more of Thurso Castle, the better for his sleep, and his head ; and, as concerns myself, the more time for putting things straight here, the better for my sleep, and my head! (if so insignificant an in-

[1] Stanley.

dividual can be said to have a head!) But certainly on the following morning (Saturday), there would be a few lines from the dear friend's self, snatched from his service to ' unborn generations,' to tell me, ' with his own hand,' of his change of plan! No! On Saturday morning the postman didn't so much as call! and when I ran out at the house door to see if he could really mean it, he merely shook his head from the steps of No. 8.   Late at night, however, I hear of a letter from you, received that morning by Neuberg.   There had been time found or made to write to him.   And he ' thought it his duty to,' not forward your letter to me, but interlard his own note with single words or whole lines of yours ' in ticks '[1]—' means to move *gradually* southward again, wishes *you* could be persuaded to start again, if able at all, and to rectify her huge error !' &c. Who was to ' persuade ' me to start again ?   Neuberg himself, perhaps?   Not you it would seem, who send not a single line to, as it were, welcome me home, though come home entirely for your sake ! No matter ! there is the less to be grateful for !

Meanwhile I am glad to know, even indirectly, that you are positively coming south by land, and ' gradually.' The two notes written after hearing I was at Alderley, and bound for Dumfriesshire, which were received together (on account of the mis-direction), within an hour of the time the carriage

---

[1] Her own Scotch name for double commas.

was ordered to take me to the station, threw no certain light for me on your plans. When you first fixed to go to Thurso, your grand inducement had seemed to be that you ' could sail there, and back, and avoid all that horror of railways.' You had never once in my hearing spoken of taking Dumfriesshire on your road ; on the contrary, when I spoke to you of Loch Luichart, you said : ' Oh, that was a great way off ! and you shouldn't be going back by land at all ! ' Then the letter, forwarded to Alderley from Chelsea, written in the belief I was still at home, made no allusion whatever to any intention of taking Dumfriesshire on your road home. You could not remain there longer, without work, and, to get on with your work, you must be ' beside your reservoir of books at Chelsea.' Read that letter yourself— Mary Austin has got it (I sent it to her as my valid excuse for breaking my engagement to come, and as a valid excuse she accepted it)—and say if I was committing any ' huge error,' or error at all, in supposing it in the highest degree probable that you would sail straight from Thurso to London ? And granting that high probability, there was but one course for me, under the circumstances (the curtains ; the keys, which you could never have known one from another ! the imbecile ' Old Jane ; ' the new servant to come, &c. &c.)—but one course : to go south again instead of north, on the day when my

Alderley visit was to terminate : unless, after my resolution was taken, and everybody warned not to expect me in Dumfriesshire, and the new woman who had been put off warned that she must now immediately render herself at Cheyne Row—unless, after all that, I was to unsettle everything over again at the very last hour, when there was no longer time to warn anybody. On the receipt of the two little letters, which came together, taking them as an exposition of your voluntary plans, not of plans which you had been forced to adopt voluntarily by the knowledge of mine—by the dread of going home to a comfortless house, and, simultaneously with that, a kind desire not to interfere with any arrangements of mine by which my health might be benefited. No! I could not be quite certain that, were I at Chelsea instead of half-way to Scotland, you might not still wish to avoid the ' horror of railways,' and to get back to your ' reservoir of books.' At all events, you should have your free choice, and now you have had it, and I learn, *through Mr. Neuberg*, that it is to be ' in no hurry.' I am very glad of that, as I shall be in better trim for you here than had you come straight.

As to my ' starting again ' (on any long expedition at least), you couldn't believe Mr. Neuberg or any-one else could persuade me to do it ! I am not ' able at all,' which does not mean, however, that I am ill. My three days at Alderley, before the letter came, did me all the good which I was likely to get from change of scene;—after the letter came, my sleep was no better than at Chelsea. When I am worried about anything, no air nor surroundings can put me to sleep. At present your curtains are come home and put up. The bricklayers have mended the broken tiles on your dressing closet. That dreadful old woman is to be got handsomely rid of next Wednesday; and I feel rather quiet, and am getting to sleep better, and mean to lead a pleasant life in my solitude—taking these ' little excursions so long talked of.'

Lady Stanley was to write to you, the day I left, to tell you I was despatched safely south. My own letter, to say I was going home on Tuesday, would reach you last Monday I suppose. You will write when the ' unborn generations' can spare you for half an hour.

The only news I have to tell is, that the poor ' little darling '[1] has lost the use of an arm and hand by paralysis. He came himself to tell me, with his arm in a sling, and repeatedly broke down into tears, and made me cry too. ' Oh!' he said, ' how I do miss my poor dear!'—I thought he was going to say wife—she died two years since; but, no, it was

---

[1] Her name for a neat and good old gardener that used to work for us.

‘ arm ! ’　‘ Oh, how I miss my poor dear arm ! ’
He didn’t need money, wouldn’t even be paid what
was owing him.　It was the helplessness that was
breaking his heart.

All good be with you.

Yours ever,

JANE WELSH CARLYLE.

Don’t expect another letter for a long time, even
should I know the address ; writing is very bad for
me, and I hate it at present.

LETTER 226.

T. Carlyle, Thurso Castle.

5 Cheyne Row, Chelsea : Monday, Sept. 3, 1860.

Two letters from you this morning—one re-
directed from Alderley.　But I must let the long
letter I wrote yesterday go, as it is all the same !
It is too much writing to throw away, after having
given myself a headache over it.　Besides, after
having read your two letters of this morning, I feel
none the less called upon to defend myself against
the charge of ‘ huge error,’ ‘ rashness,’ ‘ precipitancy,’
‘ folly,’ and so on !　I maintain that, however unfortunate my course may have been, I could not, under
the circumstances, have rightly taken any other !
So the letter of yesterday had best go !　Nor do I
deign to accept the very beggarly apology you

make for my 'infatuated conduct,' that I had myself lost heart for the Dumfriesshire visits, and was glad of any excuse to be off from them ; that tortuous style of thing is not at all in my line.   Had I lost heart I would have said so.   On the contrary, feeling myself at Alderley, half-way—all the hateful preparatory lockings up and packings well over—nothing to do but go north at Crewe instead of south, and Mary Austin and Mrs. Russell promising me the very warmest welcome, far from losing heart, I had for the first time gained heart for the further enterprise ; the 'interest' had 'not fallen but risen,' I assure you, and I turned south with real mortification !   There ! you have provoked that out of me, which, if 'well let alone,' I should never have said.

As for your indignation at my not writing, I don't quarrel with that—only beg to remind you that ' the reciprocity is not all on one side ! ' I also have been feeling myself extremely neglected—for what shall I say ? ' unborn generations ? '   Let us hope so, and not for just nothing at all !

Ever yours,
J. W. C.

LETTER 227.

Mrs. Russell, Holm Hill, Thornhill.

5 Cheyne Row, Chelsea : Sept. 7, 1860.

Dearest Mary,—I am so sorry that letter should have arrived to mislead you, for, alas ! I have had no thought of starting again, since I found, on my return home, that Mr. C. had made a perfectly wrong impression on me as to his plans! When he talked of ' sailing ' by such a steamer, how could I imagine he only meant sailing to Aberdeen, and afterwards making visits in Scotland ? He had always declared the attraction of Thurso, for him, to be the possibility of getting there and back by sea, without any horror of ' railwaying.' And he had never once spoken of returning through Dumfriesshire! My error was quite natural, almost inevitable. But that doesn't make it the less mortifying for myself and others.

If I had ordinary powers of locomotion I should, on perceiving the real state of the case, have streamed off again—this time straight to the Gill. But indeed, my dear, I have no such thing as ordinary strength. When I told my doctor that Mr. C. urged me to do this, he fairly swore, though a very mild man by nature ! It was not merely the ground to be gone over, but the fuss and flurry of so much travelling for me, that he entirely protested against. ' Quiet, quiet, quiet ' was what I needed above everything else—no change could do me good that involved fatigue or fret of mind. I know he is right in that, and that no purer air nor change of scene could do me good if bought with a new unsettling of myself, and the hurry of mind inseparable from the travelling, especially railway travelling, for a person whose nervous system is in such a preterna-tural state of excitability as mine is. I should never have had courage to think of going to you at all but for the week's rest in the middle of the journey, offered in the visit to Alderley. It has been a real dis-appointment to me, having had to turn back, and a great provocation to find my turning back unnecessary. But, now that I am here, I must make the best of it.

I will write you a long letter soon, and tell you several things about my household affairs which will throw more light for you on the supposed necessity for my abrupt return.

God bless you, dear.

Your ever affectionate
JANE W. CARLYLE.

LETTER 228.

' I did it, sir.'—Blusterous pedagogue, a Welsh Arch-deacon Williams, head of the Edinburgh New Academy (who used to call at Comely Bank, reporting to us his dreadful illness he once had, illness miserable and fatal ' unless you can dine for three weeks without wine '—' and I did it, sir ! '—T.C.

T. Carlyle, Scotsbrig.

5 Cheyne Row, Chelsea : Sunday night, Sept. 10, 1860.

Oh, my dear ! was there ever such a game at cross-purposes as this correspondence of ours ? It reminds me of nothing so much as the passages between ' the wee wifie, who lived in a shoe,' and her bairns, so many ' that she didn't know what to do ! '

> 'She went to the market to buy them some bread ;
> When she came back they were all lying dead !
> She went to the wright's to get them a coffin ;
> When she came back they were all sitting laughing !'

Not one letter you have written to me since you went away has hit the right state of things ! Do the best that ever you could, your 'sheep's head' and your 'coffin' have been equally out of time ! Such being, I suppose, the natural result of going where an answer to one's letters cannot be received in less than six days, in a world where nothing keeps still.

Your last letter, received on Saturday morning, expressing your relief from anxieties about me, found me a more legitimate object of anxiety than I had been at all since your departure !—at least found me thinking myself so ! For, thank God, this attack, if very violent while it lasted, has passed off unexpectedly soon. I suppose if I had followed Mr. Barnes's directions about lying down in the middle of the day, instead of yielding to popular clamour about 'change of air,' the thing would have been avoided altogether. On Friday morning down came Geraldine, having had a letter from you, and insisted that we should make one of those 'excursions' I had talked of. I had my 'sickness' (as I call it) worse than usual that morning, and begged to be off from any adventure ; but 'a breath of Norwood air would do me so much good!' 'It would take off the sickness to sit on the hillside,' &c., &c. I didn't feel that it would, but foolishly yielded to 'reason' rather than instinct. The movement made me sicker, and sicker; still I had fortitude to order dinner (a nice little roasted chicken, and a bottle of soda-water) at the best hotel, and to force myself to eat some of it too, at an open bow-window, with such a 'beautiful view.' But, oh, how I wished myself in my bed at home, with no view to speak of! for I had grown all burning-hot and ice-cold, not a square inch of me at the same temperature, and 'my head like a mall!'

I got home, better or worse, and went to bed, and lay, or rather tossed about, all night in a high fever, with a racking headache, severe sickness, and, most questionable of all, a bad sore throat. I only waited for Mr. Barnes being up to send for him, though he had given me up as a patient. Without having had a wink of sleep, however, or anything to do me good, my fever abated of itself as the morning advanced; and, after having had some tea in bed, between seven and eight, 'all very comfortable,' from the new woman, I felt so much better that I should have 'held my hand from sending for a doctor if it hadn't been for the sore throat, which continued very bad, and frightened me from its unusual nature. Mr. Barnes was out, and didn't come in to get the message till three o'clock, by which time I had transferred myself to the drawing-room sofa.

Meanwhile, long before this, being still in bed, but washed and combed, and the room tidied up in expectation of Mr. Barnes, there was sent up to me the card of Madame ——! two hours after I had read your wish that I should call for her! And I heard her voice in the passage! I sent down polite regrets in the first instance; then, thinking you would be vexed at my not admitting her, I called Charlotte ('Charlotte' the second) back, and said, to tell the lady, if she wouldn't dislike coming to me in my bedroom, that I should be glad to see her 'for a minute.' If I had known that she was to flop down on the bed, and cover my face with kisses (!) the first thing, I should have thought twice of admitting her, with the sore throat I had! However, the thing was done! So I didn't say a word of sore throat to put infection in her head, and indeed I hoped it mightn't be of an infectious nature. As for the 'minute,' she prolonged it to an hour; talking with an emphasis, and an exaggeration, and a velocity, and cordiality, which left me little to do but listen, and not scream! I will tell you all I remember of her talk when we meet. She will be again in London towards the end of October. She went off with the same, or rather redoubled, embracings and kissings; I, purposely, holding in my breath ; and when the door had closed, didn't I fall back on my pillows with a sense of relief!

Mr. Barnes looked into my throat, and said it was bad ; but if I had ' courage to swallow the very ugliest, most extraordinary looking medicine I had ever seen in this world, he thought he could cure it in a day or two ; ' and there came a bottle containing apparently bright blue oil-paint ! ! It did need courage, and faith, to take the first dose of that ! But ' I did it, sir ! ' and positively, as if by magic, my throat mended in half an hour ! I had a good night ; the throat was a little sore only in the morning. The second dose had the same magically sudden effect, and now, after three half-glassfuls of that magical blue oil-paint, my throat is perfectly mended, and I am as well as before I knocked myself up.

Monday.—For the rest, all that has been said and written about my turning back and about my not starting again is kindly meant, but being said or written in total or in partial ignorance of the subject, quite overshoots or undershoots the mark ; is, in fact, perfect nonsense, setting itself up for superior sense ! ' Why not have left you to " fen " for yourself, if you had come home in my absence ? ' your sister Jane asks ; ' if she had been me, she would have done that.' And I would have done it if I had been she perhaps.

Ever yours,
J. W. C.

LETTER 229.

T. Carlyle, The Gill.

5 Cheyne Row, Chelsea : Monday, Sept. 17, 1860.

You will open this, prepared to hear that I went to Forster's,[1] and have been very ill in consequence. If there be a choice betwixt a wise thing and a foolish one, a woman is always expected to do the foolish. Well, I didn't! Very ill I have been, but not from going out to dinner. By one o'clock that day I was quite ill enough to care no more for Fuz's wrath than for a whiff of tobacco! I had taken the influenza, and no doubt about it ! So I despatched a message to Montagu Square, and another to Mr. Barnes; went to bed, and have not slept till within the last hour! So provoking ! I had been so much better, and hoped to be quite flourishing on your return. *Howsomdever* an influenza properly treated, and an influenza allowed to treat itself, like all my former ones, is a very different affair I find. It has not been allowed to settle down on my chest at all, this one ; and, after only three days of sharp suffering, here I am in the drawing-room, looking forward with some interest to the sweet bread I am to dine on, and writing you a letter better or worse.

The new woman is a good nurse, very quiet and kindly, and with sense to do things without being

---

[1] Alluding to close of last letter, omitted.

told. I have not had my clothes folded neatly up, and the room tidied, and my wants anticipated in this way since I had no longer any mother to nurse me. In ordinary circumstances I should have felt it horrid to be lying entirely at the mercy of an utter stranger; but, being as she is, I have wished none else to come near me. Even you I rather hope may not come this week. It would worry me so, not to be able to run about when you come, and I must be cautious for some days yet—'Mrs. Prudence,' as Mr. Barnes calls me in mockery. The girl is to come to-morrow, but I don't feel to trouble my head about her. Charlotte (2nd) can be trusted to direct her in the way she should go till I am well enough to meddle. Besides, I have every reason to believe her a nice girl. The old Charlotte, poor foolish thing! is still hanging on at her 'mother's,' just as untidy in her person, with nothing to do, as she used to be in her press of work. She has been much about me, and I don't know what I should have done without her, to cook for me, and show me some human kindness, when I was ill under 'Old Jane.' But I am glad at the same time that I had fortitude to resist her tears, and her request to be taken back as cook. I told her some day I might take her back; but she had much to learn and to unlearn first. Still it is gratifying to feel that one's kindness to the girl has not been all lost on her, for she really loves both of us passionately—only that passionate loves, not applied to practical uses, are good for so little in this matter-of-fact world.

Kindest love to dear Mary. Tell her I will make out that visit some day, on my own basis; it is only postponed. 'Thanks God,' you can't get any clothes.

Yours,

J. W. C.

LETTER 230.

I seem to have got home again, September 22. Halted at Alderley a couple of days; of Annandale, the Gill, or Dumfries I remember nothing whatever, except the last morning at the Gill (which is still vivid enough), and my wandering about in manifold sorrowful reflections, loth to quit that kindly, safe *tugurium*; and also privately my making resolution (seeing the fitness of it), not to revisit Scotland till the unutterable Frederick were done—resolution sad and silent, which I believe was kept.—T. C.

Mrs. Austin, The Gill, Annan.

5 Cheyne Row, Chelsea: Thursday, Oct. 19, 1860.

My dear Mary,—The box arrived last night, ' all right.' Many thanks, Mary dear. The things from Dumfries are also all right; but I will write to tell Jane about them to-morrow. Mr. C. doesn't seem to have benefited from his long sojourn by the sea-side so much as I had hoped, and at first thought. He still goes on waking up several times in the night—when he bolts up, and smokes, and sometimes takes a cold bath ! And all that is very dismal for him, to whom waking betwixt lying down and getting up is a novelty.   For me, my own wakings up some twenty or thirty times every night of my life, for years and years back, are nothing compared with hearing him jump out of bed overhead, once or sometimes twice during a night. Before he went to Thurso, that sound overhead used to set my heart a-thumping to such a degree that I couldn't get another wink of sleep—and I was on the brink of a nervous fever when he left.[1] Now that my nerves have had a rest, and that I am more ' used to it,' I get to sleep again when I hear all quiet, but God knows how long I may be up to that! And when he has broken sleep, and I no sleep at all, it is sad work here, I assure you.

You will have heard of my setting up a second servant, and think perhaps that I must be more comfortable now, with two people to work and run for us ; but I would much rather have made less working and less running do, and kept to my accustomed one servant.   I have never felt the house my own since my maid-of-all-work was converted into a ' cook ' and ' housemaid,' and don't feel as if I should ever get used to the improvement.   It is just as if one had taken lodgers into one's lower story.   Often in the dead of night I am seized with a wild desire to clear the house of these new-comers, and take back my one little Charlotte, who is still hanging on at her

----

[1] Poor loving soul!

mother's, in a wild hope that one or other of them, or both, may break down, and she be reinstated in her place.   Poor little Charlotte ! if I had seen how miserable she was to be at leaving us, I couldn't have found in my heart to put her away, though she was so heedless, and ' thro' other,'[1] with a grain of method she could have done all the two do, as well or better than they do it, she was so clever and willing.

The new tall Charlotte (the cook) said to me one day ' little Charlotte' had been here: ' What a fool that girl is, ma'am ! I said to her to-day, " You seem to like being here ! " and, says she, " Of course I do ; I look upon this as my home."   " But," says I, " you are a nice-looking, healthy girl, you will easily get another place if you try." " Oh," says she, " I know that.   I may get plenty of places ; but I shall never get another home ! "   What a poor spirit the girl has ! If anybody had been dissatisfied with me, it's little that I should care about leaving them.' ' I can well believe that,' said I, with a strong disposition to knock her down. But I have no pretext for putting the woman away—although I don't like her. She is a good servant as servants go, and I can't put her away merely for being vulgar-minded, and totally destitute of sentiment ; and, after all, the faults for which I parted with little Charlotte after twelve months of considering won't have been cured, but rather have

---

[1] *Durcheinander* (German) as an adjective.

been aggravated by three months' muddling at her mother's. Heigh-ho! I feel just in the case of the 'Edinburgh meat-jack:' 'Once I was happ-happ-happ-y! but now I am mee-e-scrable!' If one's skin were a trifle thicker, all these worries would seem light. But one's skin being just no skin 'to speak of,' no wonder one falls into the meat-jack humour. God bless you and all your belongings. Kind regards to your husband.

Ever affectionately yours,
JANE W. CARLYLE.

LETTER 231.

To Miss Margaret Welsh, Auchtertool Manse.

Chelsea: December 8, 1860.

Dearest Maggie,—Having made no sign of myself for the last month, you may be fancying I have succumbed to the general doom; seeing that it has been 'the gloomy month of November, in which the people of England hang and drown themselves!' But I am neither hanged nor drowned yet (in virtue perhaps of being born in Scotland); only, all my energies having been needed to stave off suicide, I had none left for letter writing. It is now December, and the suicidal mania should have passed off; but I can't see much difference between this December and the gloomiest November on record! the fog, and the mud, and the liquid soot (called rain in the language of flattery), have not abated; and the blood in one's veins feels so thick and dirty! But, shame of my silence must serve instead of inspiration, impossible under the circumstances ; and you, dear, good little soul as you are, will not be critical!

In the first place you will be glad to hear I am 'about' anyhow. Except for one week that I had to lie on the sofa on my back, with neuralgia (differing in nothing, so far as I can see, from the old-fashioned 'rheumatiz'), I have not been laid up since you heard of me ; and I have had a great fret taken off me, in the removal of that vulgar, conceited woman, and the restoration of little Charlotte. Upon my word, I haven't been as near what they call 'happy' for many a day as in the first flush of little Charlotte! She looked so bursting with ecstasy as she ran up and down the house, taking possession, as it were, of her old work, and as she showed in the visitors (not her business, but she would open the door to them all the first time, to show herself, and receive their congratulations), that it was impossible not to share in her delighted excitement! Most of the people shook hands with her! and all of them said they were 'glad to see her back'! I had trusted that she would in time humanise the other girl, and that the two would be good friends, when the other girl got over the prejudices the woman who had left had inspired her with! But it needed no time at all. Sarah was humanised, and the two sworn friends in the first half-hour! In the first half-hour Sarah had confided to Charlotte that, if I hadn't given the tall Charlotte warning, she (Sarah) would have given me warning, she disliked ' tall Charlotte ' so much!

It is now three weeks since the new order of things; mistress and maid have subsided out of the emotional state into the normal one, but are still very glad over one another; and if the work of the house does not get done with as much order and method as under the tall Charlotte, it is done with more thoroughness, and infinitely more heartiness and pleasantness; and the ' bread-puddings ' are first rate. Sarah's tidiness and method are just what were wanted to correct little Charlotte's born tendency to muddle; while little Charlotte's willingness and affectionateness warm up Sarah's drier, more selfish nature. It is a curious establishment, with something of the sound and character of a nursery. Charlotte not nineteen till next March, and Sarah seventeen last week. And they keep up an incessant chirping and chattering and laughing; and as both have remarkably sweet voices, it is pleasant to hear. The two-ness is no nuisance to me now. As neither can awake of themselves, I don't know what I should have done about that, hadn't Charlotte's friends come to the rescue. An old man who lodges with Charlotte's ' mother ' (aunt), raps on the kitchen window till he wakes them, every morning at six, on his way to his work; and Charlotte's ' father ' (uncle) raps again on the window before. seven, to make sure the first summons had been attended to! to say nothing of an alarum, which runs down at six, at their very bed-head, and never is heard by either of these fortunate girls! So I daresay we shall get on as well as possible in a world where perfection is not to be looked for. I shall be glad to hear that your domesticities are in as flourishing a state!

I hope we shall go to the Grange by-and-by, and make a longer visit than last year. It is such a good break in the long, dreary, Chelsea winter, and stirs up one's stagnant spirits, and rules up one's manners! But Mr. Carlyle won't stay anywhere if he can't get work done; and though Lady Ashburton says he shall have every facility afforded him for working, I don't know how that will be when it comes to be tried. I never saw any work done in that house! Meanwhile, I have sent an azure blue *moire*, that Lady Sandwich gave me last Christmas Day, to be made, in case.

My dear, beautiful Kate Sterling (Mrs. Ross) was buried last week at Bournemouth, where she had been taken for the winter. I had long been hopeless of her recovery, but did not think the end so near, and that I should never see her sweet face again. Julia came to see me yesterday on her return, looking miserably ill. Poor Mr. Ross wrote me a sad, kind letter. I am very sorry for him; and none of the family treat him as if he had anything to do with their loss. He was not a man one would ever have wished Kate to marry, but he has been the most devoted husband, and tenderest nurse to her; and she said to her sister Lotta, the day before her death, that she had repented doing many things in her life, but she had never for one moment repented her marriage! Surely that should have made them all less hard for him! But, no!

Kindest love to Walter and Star.

Your affectionate
J. W. CARLYLE.

LETTER 232.

Mrs. Russell, Thornhill.

5 Cheyne Row, Chelsea: Dec. 31, 1860.

Dearest Mary,—If there were no other use in a letter from me just now, it will serve the purpose of removing any apprehensions you may have as to the frost having put an end to my life! ' Did you ever?' 'No, I never,'—felt such cold! But then, there being no question for me of ever crossing the threshold, and my time thrown altogether on my hands (my visitors being mostly away, keeping their Christmas in country houses, or, like myself, shut up with colds at home, or too busy with ' the festivities of the season ' to get as far as Chelsea, and my two maids leaving me nothing earthly to do in the business of the house), I have time, enough and to spare, for adopting all possible measures to keep myself warm. To see the fires I keep up in the drawing-room and my bedroom! An untopographical observer might suppose we lived within a mile of a coal pit, instead of paying twenty-eight shillings a cart-load for coals! Then I wear all my flannel petticoats at once, and am having two new ones made out of a pair of Scotch blankets! And Lady Sandwich has sent me a seal-fur pelisse (a luxury I had long sighed for, but, costing twenty guineas, it had seemed hopeless!), and a Greek merchant[1] has sent me the softest grey Indian shawl. And if all that can't warm me, I lie down under my coverlet of racoon skins! (My dear! if you are perishing, act upon my idea of the Scotch blankets; no flannel comes near them in point of warmth.) My doctor told me, in addition to all this outward covering, to drink 'at least three glasses of wine a day'! But I generally shirk the third. And the cough, and faceache, which I had the first week of the frost, is gone this week, at any rate.

Have you seen that Tale of Horror, which ran through the newspapers, about the Marquis of Downshire? Everybody here believed for some days that the Marquis of Downshire had really found the skipper of his yacht kneeling at the side of Lady Alice (his only daughter, a lovely girl of seventeen), and really

---

[1] Dilberoglue.

pitched him into the sea, and so there was an end of him! I was dreadfully sorry, for one. Lord D. is such a dear, good, kind-hearted savage of a man; and it seemed such a fatality that he should be always killing somebody!! He had killed a school companion, without meaning it; and afterwards (they say) a coalheaver, who was boxing with him! The fact is, he is awfully strong, and his strokes tell, as he doesn't expect. But if you knew what a simple, good man he is, you wouldn't wonder that I felt sorrier for him than the skipper, who, after all, had no business to be 'kneeling' there surely! And the little darling daughter, that her young life should be clouded at the outset with such a scandal! I made all sorts of miserable reflections about them all. And the story, all the while, a complete fabrication—equal to the proverbial story of the 'six black crows'! The story was told to Azeglio (the Sardinian Ambassador), who, to give himself importance, said, 'Oh, yes! it had been officially communicated to him from Naples.' And the man he said it to, being Secretary of Legation, made an official despatch of the story to Lord Cowley at Paris!! Then it flew like wild-fire, and people couldn't help believing it; and, of course, all sorts of details were added—that Lady Alice was 'struggling and screaming, that Lord D. wouldn't let a boat be lowered to pick the man up,' &c. &c. One knows how a story gathers like a snowball. They went the length of stating that Lord D. was being brought home to be tried by the Peers, 'the offence having been committed on the high seas!!!!' The talk now is all of prosecution of certain newspapers, and certain people. But I shouldn't wonder if it all end in Lord Downshire's giving somebody a good thrashing.

Please to give my good wishes 'of the season' to all my friends at Thornhill and about, and to attend to the old women on New Year's Day. I send a cheque this time. The Japanese trays are for the new drawing-room, if you think them worth a place in it. I took them as far as Alderley on the road in autumn. They are a popular drawing-room ornament here at present. Kindest regards to the Doctor.

Your ever affectionate

JANE CARLYLE.

LETTER 233.

To Miss Barnes, King's Road, Chelsea.

5 Cheyne Row : Sunday, April 26, 1861.

Carina,—I was going to you to-day, having been hindered yesterday ; but a thought strikes me. You are a Puseyite, or, as my old Scotch servant writes it, a 'Puisht,' and I am a Presbyterian ; would it be proper for you to receive me, or for me to pay a visit on Sunday ? I don't quite know as to you ; but for me it is a thing forbidden certainly. So I write to say that if you could have gone to the gorillas to-morrow, the gorillas would have been 'not at home.' On consulting my order of admission I find it is for all days except just the two I successively fixed upon, Saturdays and Mondays. My order is available through all the month of May, so it will still be time when you return, provided you do not indefinitely extend your programme, as you are in the habit of doing. I shall fix with the others for Tuesday, 28th, early—say to start between eleven and twelve. Will that do?

Your affectionate

JANE CARLYLE.

LETTER 234.

Mrs. Russell, Holm Hill.

5 Cheyne Row, Chelsea : Thursday, July 3, 1861.

Decidedly, dearest Mary, I am in a run of bad luck, and entertaining for a moment any idea of pleasure seems to be the signal with me for some misfortune to plunge down.

The longer I thought of it, the more it seemed to me fair and feasible that, since Mr. C. was minded to go nowhere this summer, I should go for two or three weeks by myself where I had been so unreasonably disappointed of going last August. Mr. C. himself said I might, 'if I thought it would be useful to me;' and there could be no question about its being 'useful to me' to have a breath of Scotch air and a glimpse of dear Scotch faces. So, when I had read your cordial letter, I felt my purpose strong to carry itself out, and only delayed answering till I had seen the baking difficulty overcome, and could say, positively, that I would come as soon as you pleased after your visitor had departed. Two visitors at one time is too much happiness, I think, for any not over strong mistress of a house, who gives herself so much trouble as you do to make everything comfortable and pleasant about one.

And, in the meantime, here is what has befallen. My nice trustworthy cook, who inspired me with the confidence to leave Mr. C., being certain, I thought, to keep him all right, and the house all right, and the young girl all right, in my absence; this treasure of a cook, my dear, who was to be the comfort of my remaining years, and nurse me in my last illness (to such wild flights had my imagination gone), turns out to have come into my service with a frightful neglected disorder—what the doctors call ‘strangulated hernia,’ making her life (my doctor says) ‘not safe for a day’! He could do nothing with it, he said; she must go to St. George’s Hospital, and what was possible to do for her would be done there. But I have no hope that the woman will ever be fit for service again. And what she could mean in going into a new service with such a complaint I am at a loss to conceive. And I am also dreadfully at a loss what I am to do with her.

She is such a good creature, and hasn't a relation in the world to depend upon. If the doctors take her as an in-patient, of course it would settle the question of her leaving here; but if they don't—! Oh, my gracious, how unlucky it is! In any case, I see no chance for me now of getting to you.

Unless, indeed, she could be cured sufficiently to go on at service. I shall know more about it when she comes back from the hospital, or when I have spoken with one of the surgeons there whom I know. But unless the case is much less grave than Mr. Barnes seemed to consider it, we shall be all at sea again. And the best arrangement I can think of, for the moment, would be to put my new housemaid into the kitchen, for which she is better suited than for her present place, only that she would have the cooking all to learn!—and to take another nice girl I know of for housemaid. But fancy the weeks and months it will take to get even that most feasible scheme to work right, and all the while I must be standing between Mr. C. and new bother, and looking after these girls that they may be kept in good ways! I declare I could take a good cry, or do a little good swearing! I will stop now till the poor woman comes back from the hospital; and then tell you the news she brings.

No Matilda come yet, and I must take the letters

myself now to the post-office, having nobody to send.

I will write soon.

Your much bedevilled, but always loving,

J. CARLYLE.

LETTER 235.

Mrs. Russell, Holm Hill.

5 Cheyne Row, Chelsea: Tuesday, July 16, 1861.

Dearest Mary,—Mr. Dunbar's[1] book was from you, was it not? I used to be able to swear to your handwriting; but latterly one or two people have taken to writing exactly like you, and I need the post-mark to verify the handwriting, and the post-mark was illegible on that book-parcel. Whether from you or not, I am glad of the little book, which I am sure I shall read with pleasure; I like that mild, gentlemanly man so much.

But I am still as far as when I last wrote from sitting down quietly to read a pleasant book. Everything is at sixes and sevens still! My treasure of a servant, who was to ' soothe my declining years,' and enable me to go to Scotland this year, is still lying in St. George's Hospital, certain to lie there ' for some months,' and not certain to be fit for service, even of the mildest form, when the months are over! Mr. ——, the Head Surgeon, found immediately

---

[1] I don't recollect.

that she had got ulceration of the spine, and the rupture proceeded from that. He says she 'may get over it; but it will be a tedious affair.' I don't think that, even if she were cured nominally, I should like to have her for kitchen servant again; I should live in perpetual terror of her hurting herself at every turn. Meanwhile I have been puddling on with my old 'going-out-to-cook-woman,' coming daily to cook the dinner, and teach the Welsh housemaid, whom I have decided to make kitchen-woman, getting another girl for housemaid. A safe housemaid is so much easier to get here than a cook, who doesn't drink, nor steal, nor take the house to herself! This Welsh girl[1] has, I think, more the shaping of a good cook than of a housemaid, not being good at needlework, and utterly incapable of reading the titles on Mr. C.'s books, so that she can't bring him a book when he wants it. The girl I am getting is more accomplished, whatever else !

The present state of affairs is wretched; for Mr. C., being a man, cannot understand to exact the least bit less attendance, when we are reduced to one servant again, than he had accustomed himself to exact from the two. So I have all the valeting, and needle-womaning, and running up and down to the

---

[1] *Irish* in reality; a little, black, busy creature, who did very well for some time; but, &c. &c. (some mysterious love-affair, I think)—and went to New Zealand out of sight.

study for books, &c. &c. &c. to do myself, besides having to superintend the Welsh girl, and to go to St. George's (two miles off) almost every day in my life, to keep up the heart of poor Matilda, who, lying there, with two issues in her back, and nobody but myself coming after her, and her outlooks of the darkest, naturally needs any cheering that I can take her.

Mercifully the plentiful rain keeps things cooler and fresher here than is usual in summer; and I am nothing like so sick and nervous as I was last year at this time. So I am more able to bear what is laid on me—to bear amongst the rest the heavy disappointment of having to give up my visit to you, and stay here at my post, which is a rather bothering one,

God bless you. It does me good anyhow to think that, if I could have gone, the kind Doctor and you would have been so kind to me.

Your ever affectionate
J. W. CARLYLE.

LETTER 236.

T. Carlyle, Esq., Chelsea.

Mrs. Stokes's, 21 Wellington Crescent, East Cliff, Ramsgate:
Sunday, August 4, 1861.

That is the address, if there be anything to be addressed! Fortune favours the brave! Had one talked, and thought, and corresponded, and investigated about lodgings for a month before starting, I doubt if we could have made a better business of it than we have done. Certainly in point of situation there is no better in Ramsgate or in the world: looking out over a pretty stripe of lawn and gravel walk on to the great boundless Ocean! You could throw a stone from the sitting-room window into the sea when the tide is up! Then there is not the vestige of a bug in our white dimity beds! For the rest, I cannot say it is noiseless! Geraldine says her room looking on the sea is perfectly so; but I consider her no judge, as she sleeps like a top. However, the rooms looking on the sea cannot but be freer from noise than those to the back, looking on roofs, houses, stables, streets, &c. ; but the bedrooms to the back are much larger, and better aired. With no sensibilities except my own to listen to them with, I can get used (I think) to the not extravagant amount of crowing and barking, and storming with the wind, and even to occasional cat-explosions on the opposite roofs! If I can't, I can exchange beds with Geraldine; and there I can only have the noise of the sea (considerable!), the possibilities of occasional carriages passing (I have none to-day, but it is Sunday), and ' rittle-tippling ' of Venetian blinds! With a great diminution of room, however, and alarming increase of glare. The people of the house are civil and honest-looking and slow. Oh, my! But we are not come here, Geraldine and I, to be in a hurry! For us the place will answer extremely well for a week, that we had to engage it for, and the sea air and the ' change ' will overbalance all the little disagreeables, as well as the *cha-arge*, which is considerable.

If my advice were of any moment, I would strongly advise you to come one day during the week, and see the place under our auspices, and stay one night. I could sleep on the sofa in the drawing-room; and you would not mind any trifling noises with the knowledge that it was only for one night. The mere journey and a sight of the sea and a bathe would do you good.

I am going to seek out the Bains after church. I feel much less tired to-day than I have done for weeks, months back; and though I was awake half the night, first feeling for bugs, which didn't come! and then taking note of all the different sounds far and near, which did come!

Margaret will do everything very well for you, if you will only tell her distinctly what you want; I mean not elaborately, but in few plain words.

Ever yours,

JANE W. C.

LETTER 237.

T. Carlyle, Esq., 5 Cheyne Row.

Wellington Crescent, Ramsgate: Tuesday, August 6, 1861.

[1] Very charming doesn't that look, with the sea in front as far as eye can reach ? And that seen (the East Cliff), you needn't wish to ever see more of Ramsgate. It is made up of narrow, steep, confused streets like the worst parts of Brighton. The shops look nasty, the people nasty, the smells are nasty! (spoiled shrimps complicated with cesspool!) Only the East Cliff is clean, and genteel, and airy ; and would be perfect as sea-quarters if it weren't for the noise! which is so extraordinary as to be almost laughable.

Along that still-looking road or street between the houses and gardens are passing and repassing, from early morning to late night, cries of prawns, shrimps, lollipops—things one never wanted, and will never want, of the most miscellaneous sort; and if that were all! But a brass band plays all through our breakfast, and repeats the performance often during the day, and the brass band is succeeded by a band of Ethiopians, and· that again by a band of female fiddlers! and interspersed with these are individual barrel-organs, individual Scotch bagpipes, individual French horns! Oh, it is 'most expensive !' And the night noises were not to be

---

[1] Written on Ramsgate note-paper, with a print of the harbour, &c.

estimated by the first night! These are so many
and frequent as to form a sort of mass of voice;
perhaps easier to get some sleep through than an
individual nuisance of cock or dog. There are hun-
dreds of cocks! and they get waked up at, say, one in
the morning by some outburst of drunken song or of
cat-wailing! and never go to sleep again (these cocks)
but for minutes! and there are three steeple clocks
that strike in succession, and there are doors and
gates that slam, and dogs that bark occasionally, and
a saw mill, and a mews, &c.—in short, everything
you could wish not to hear! And I hear it all and am
getting to sleep in hearing it! the bed is so soft and
clean, and the room so airy; and then I think under
every shock, so triumphantly, ' Crow away,' ' roar
away,' ' bark away,' ' slam away; you can't disturb
Mr. C. at Cheyne Row, that can't you!' and the
thought is so soothing, I go off asleep—till next
thing! I might try Geraldine's room; but she has
now got an adjoining baby! Yesterday we drove to
Broadstairs—a quieter place, but we saw no lodgings
that were likely to be quiet, except one villa at six
guineas a week, already occupied.

I sleep about, in intervals of the bands, on sofas
during the day; and am less sick than when I left
home, and we get good enough food very well
cooked, and I don't repent coming, on the whole;
though I hate being in lodgings in strange places.

I found the Bains; and saw Mrs. George [1] before she left.

Wednesday, Aug. 7, 1861.

I had just cleared my toilet table, and carried my writing-things from the sitting-room to my bedroom window, where there was no worse noise for the moment than carpet beating and the grinding of passing carts, whereas the sitting-room had become perfectly maddening with bagpipes under the windows, and piano-practice under the floor (a piano hired in by 'the first floor' yesterday)! All which received an irritating finishing touch from the rapid, continuous scrape, scraping of Geraldine's pen (nothing more irritating, as you know, than to see 'others' perfectly indifferent to what is driving oneself wild). Had just dipped the pen in the ink when—a 'yellow scoundrel,' the loudest, harshest of yellow scoundrels, struck up under my bedroom window! And here the master power of Babbage has not reached! Indeed, noise seems to be the grand joy of life at Ramsgate. If I had come to Ramsgate with the least idea of writing letters, or doing anything whatever with my head, I might go back at once. But I came to swallow down as much sea air as possible, and that end is attained without fatigue; for lying on the sofa with our three windows wide open on the sea, we are as well aired as if we

---

[1] Welsh; her uncle's wife.

were sailing on it ; and the bedroom is full of sea air all night too. It is certainly doing me good, though I can't ever get slept many minutes together for the noises. I get up hungry for breakfast, and am hungry again for dinner—and a fowl does not serve Geraldine and me two days !! I do hope you are getting decently fed. It won't be for want of assiduous will on Margaret's part if things are not as you like them.

We called for the Bains last night and invited them to tea to-night, which they thankfully accepted. They seem entirely occupied in studying their mutual health. Indeed, what else would any mortal stay here for ! Mrs. Bain is quite the female of that male, —clear and clever, and cold and dry as tinder ! They have ' the only quiet house in Ramsgate.' Mrs. Bain is troubled with nothing but the bleating of sheep to the back ; after to-day, however, there will be crying babies in the house, and it is nothing like so airy a situation as ours. What a mercy you did not try Ramsgate !

My compliments to the maids, and say I hope to find them models of virtue and activity when I come on Saturday. Geraldine is clear for staying another week ; but I had better have gone to Scotland than that.

Yours,
J. W. C.

LETTER 238.

Mrs. Russell, Holm Hill.

5 Cheyne Row, Chelsea : Tuesday, Aug. 30, 1861.

Darling! I want to hear about you ; and that is lucky for you, if you be at all wanting to hear about me! For I'll be hanged if mere unassisted sense of duty, and that sort of thing, could nerve me to sit down and write a letter in these days, when it takes pretty well all the sense and strength I have left to keep myself soul and body together, doing the thing forced into my hands to do, and answering when I am spoken to. A nice woman I am! But I know you have been in such depths yourself occasionally, and will have sympathy with me, instead of being contemptuous or angry, as your strong-minded, able-bodied women would be ; and accordingly strong-minded, able-bodied women are my aversion, and I run out of the road of one as I would from a mad cow. The fact is, had there been nobody in the world to consider except myself, I ought to have ' carried out ' that project I had set my heart on of streaming off by myself to Holm Hill, and taking a life-bath, as it were, in my quasi-natural air, in the scene of old affections, not all past and gone, but some still there as alive and warm, thank God, as ever! and only the dearer for being mixed up with those that are dead and gone.

Ah, my dear, your kindness goes to my heart, and

makes me like to cry, because I cannot do as you bid me. My servants are pretty well got into the routine of the house now, and if Mr. C. were like other men, he might be left to their care for two or three weeks, without fear of consequences. But he is much more like a spoiled baby than like other men. I tried him alone for a few days, when I was afraid of falling seriously ill, unless I had change of air. Three weeks ago I went with Geraldine Jewsbury to Ramsgate, one of the most accessible sea-side places, where I was within call, as it were, if anything went wrong at home. But the letter that came from him every morning was like the letter of a Babe in the Wood, who would be found buried with dead leaves by the robins if I didn't look to it. So, even if Ramsgate hadn't been the horridest, noisiest place, where I knew nobody, and had nothing to do except swallow sea air (the best of sea air indeed), I couldn't have got stayed there long enough to make it worth the bother of going. I had thought, in going there, that if he got on well enough by himself for the few days, I might take two or three weeks later, and realise my heart's wish after all. But I found him so out of sorts on my return that I gave it up, with inward protest and appeal to posterity.

Again a glimmer of hope arose. Lady Sandwich had taken a villa on the edge of Windsor Forest for a month, and invited us to go with her there. Mr. C. is very fond of that old lady, partly for her own sake, and partly for the late Lady Ashburton's (her daughter). He can take his horse with him there, and his books, and if he miss his sleep one night he can come straight home the next. So, on the whole, after much pressing, he consented to go. And the idea came to me, if he were all right there, might not I slip away meanwhile to you. Before however it had been communicated, he said to me one day : ' What a poor, shivering, nervous wretch I am grown ! I declare if you were not to be there to take care of me, and keep all disturbance off me, nothing would induce me to go to that place of Lady Sandwich's, though I dare say it is very necessary for me to go somewhere.' Humph ! very flattering, but very inconvenient. And one can't console oneself at my age for a present disappointment with looking forward to next year one is no longer so sure of one's next year.

One thing I can do, and you can do—we can write oftener. It is a deal nicer to speak face to face from heart to heart. But we might make our correspondence a better thing than it is, if we prevented the need of beginning our letters so often with an apology for silence.

Thanks for all your news. Every little detail about Thornhill people and things is interesting to me. And, oh, many, many thanks for your kind messages to us all ! God bless you, dear, and love to the Doctor.

Affectionately yours,
JANE W. CARLYLE.

LETTER 239.

The good old dowager Lady Sandwich had this autumn engaged us to go out with her to a pretty little lodge she had hired for a while in Windsor Forest, to rusticate there. It struck us afterwards, she had felt that this was likely to be her last autumn in this world, and that we, now among the dearest left to her, ought to be there. She was a brave, airy, affectionate, and bright kind of creature; and under her Irish gaieties and fantasticalities concealed an honest generosity of heart, and a clear discernment, and a very firm determination in regard to all practical or essential matters. We willingly engaged, went punctually, and stayed, I think, some twelve or more days, which, except for my own continual state of worn-out nerves, &c., were altogether graceful, touching, and even pleasant. I rode out, and rode back (my Jeannie by railway both times). Windsor Forest sounded something Arcadian when I started, but, alas ! I found all that a completely changed matter since the days of Pope and his sylvan eclogues ; and the real name of it now to be Windsor Cockneydom unchained. The ride out was nowhere pleasant, in parts disgusting ; the ride back I undertook merely because obliged. During my stay I rode daily a great deal; but except within the park, where was a gloomy kind of solitude, very gloomy always to me, I had nowhere any satisfaction in the exercise, nor did Fritz seem to have. Alas! both he and I were getting very sick of riding ; and one of us was laden for a long while past and to come far beyond his strength and years. It seems by this letter I was at times a very bad boy ; and, alas! my repentant memory answers too clearly Yes. The lumbago, indeed, I have entirely forgotten, but I remember nights sleepless, and long walks, the mornings after which were courageous rather than victorious ! I remember the old lady's stately and courteous appearance at dinner, affecting to me, and strange, almost painful. This little scene even to the very name had vanished from me, and Harewood Lodge, when I read it here, reads a whole series of things to me; things sad—now sad as death itself, but good too, perhaps, almost great.

Miss Barnes, King's Road, Chelsea.

Harewood Lodge, Berks: Sept. 22, 1861.

Carina! Oh, Carina! 'Did you ever?' 'No, you never!' It has been an enchantment—a bad spell! the '*quelque chose plus fort que moi*' of French criminals! I don't think a day has passed since I got your letter—certainly not a day has passed since I came here—that I haven't thought of you; and meant to write to you: only I never did it! And why? Were I to assign the only reason which occurs to me for the moment, it would seem incredible to your well-regulated mind. You could never conceive how a woman 'born of respectable parents, and having enjoyed the advantages of a liberal education' (like Judge somebody's malefactor, who, 'instead of which, had gone about the country stealing turkeys!'), should be withheld from doing a thing by just the feeling that she *ought to!* Although if she had ought to *not to* she would have done it at the first opportunity! No! You have no belief in such a make of a woman, you! You are too good for believing in her! And one can't do better than believe all women born to a sense of duty 'as the sparks fly upwards' as long as one can.

For the rest, I should have enjoyed this beautiful place excessively if Eve hadn't eaten that unfortunate apple, a great many years ago ; in result of which there has, ever since, been always a something to prevent one's feeling oneself in Paradise! The ' something ' of the present occasion came in the form of lumbago! not into my own back, but into Mr. C.'s ; which made the difference so far as the whole comfort of my life was concerned! For it was the very first day of being here that Mr. C. saw fit to spread his pocket-handkerchief on the grass, just after a heavy shower, and sit down on it! for an hour and more in spite of all my remonstrances!! The lumbago following in the course of nature, there hasn't been a day that I felt sure of staying over the next, and of not being snatched away like Proserpine ; as I was from the Grange last winter! For what avail the ' beauties of nature,' the ' ease with dignity ' of a great house, even the Hero Worship accorded one, against the lumbago? Nothing, it would seem! less than nothing! Lumbago, my dear, it is good that you should know in time, admits of but one consolation— of but one happiness! viz : ' perfect liberty to be as ugly and stupid and disagreeable as ever one likes ! ' And that consolation, that happiness, that liberty reserves itself for the domestic hearth! As you will find when you are married, I daresay. And so, all the ten days we have been here, it has been a straining on Mr. C.'s part to tear his way through the social amenities back to Chelsea; while I have spent all the time I might have been enjoying myself in expecting to be snatched away!

To-morrow we go finally and positively, though the lumbago is almost disappeared, and we were to have stayed at least a fortnight. Where are you, then? If you are returned to 'the paternal roof,' no need almost of this letter. But I daresay you are gadding about on the face of the earth; 'too happy in not knowing your happiness' of having a paternal roof to stay under! If your father would take me home for his daughter, and pet me as he does you, would I go dancing off to all points of the compass as you do? No, indeed. God bless you, anyhow! If you are returned, this letter will be worth while, as enabling me to look you in the face more or less.

Yours affectionately,

JANE WELSH CARLYLE.

LETTER 240.

January 1, 1862. — 'First foot,' perhaps explained already, is a Scotch superstition about good or ill luck for the whole year being omened by your liking or otherwise of the first person that accosts you on New Year's morning. She well knew this to be an idle babble; but nevertheless it had got hold of her fancy in a sort, and was of some real importance to her, as other such old superstitions were.

Thus I have seen her, if anybody made or received a present of a knife, insist on a penny being given for it, that so it might become 'purchase,' and not cut the friendship in two. I used to laugh at these practices, but found them beautiful withal; how much more amiable than strong-mindedness (which has needed only deduction of fine qualities) in regard to such things!—T. C.

J. G. Cooke, Esq.

5 Cheyne Row: January 1, 1862.
Ach Gott!

My dear Friend,—What an adorable little proceeding on your part! I declare I can't remember when I have been as pleased. Not only a 'good first foot,' but salvation from any possibility of a 'bad first foot,' with which my highly imaginative Scotch mind (imaginative on the reverse side of things in my present state of physical weakness) had been worrying itself as New Year's Day drew near. I could hardly believe my ears when little Margaret glided to my bedside and said, 'Mr. Cooke, ma'am, with this letter and beautiful egg-cup (!) for you; but he wouldn't come up, as you were in bed!' That, too, was most considerate of Mr. Cooke! The 'egg-cup' ravished my senses with its beauty and perfect adaptation to my main passion. I think you must have had it made on purpose for me, it feels already so much a part of myself. And how early you must have risen to be here at that hour!

Dressed, perhaps, by candle-light! Good God! all that for me! Well, I am grateful, and won't forget this. A talismanic remembrance to stand between my faith in your kindness for me and any ' babbles ' (my grandfather's word) that may ever attempt, consciously or unconsciously, to shake it. And so God bless you! and believe me

Yours affectionately,
JANE WELSH CARLYLE.

LETTER 241.

Miss Barnes, King's Road, Chelsea.

5 Cheyne Row: January 24, 1862.

Oh, you agonising little girl! How could you come down upon me in that slap-dash way, demand of poor, weak, shivery me a positive ' yes ' or ' no,' as if with a loaded pistol at my head? How can I tell what I shall be up to on the 18th? After such a three months of illness, and relapses, how can I even guess? If I am alive, and able to stand on my hind legs, and to look like a joyful occasion, I shall be only too happy to attend that solemnity. But in my actual state it would be a tempting of Providence to suppress the *if* in my acceptance of your ' amiable invitation.'

As for Mr. C.—my dear, I must confide to you a small domestic passage. I told him what your father

had said weeks ago, and he expressed himself as
terrified—as was to be expected—at the idea of his
being included in anything joyful! and I thought he
had forgotten all about it, three or four days after,
when he came into my room with evidently something on his mind, and said, ' My dear, there is a
small favour I want from you. I want you to not let
me be asked to Miss Barnes's marriage, for it would
be a real vexation to me to refuse that bonnie wee
lassie what she asked, and to her marriage I could
not go ; it would be the ruin of me for three weeks !'
And that is no exaggeration, I can say, who know
his ways better than anyone else. He added that,
' the rational thing to be done ' was, that you should
' bring your husband, when you had married him, to
spend an evening with him (Mr. C.) in his own house,
among quiet things ' (me and the cat ?).

Your affectionate

JANE W. CARLYLE.

LETTER 242.

Mrs. Russell, Holm Hill.

5 Cheyne Row, Chelsea : Feb. 23, 1862.
Oh, my dear, what a horrid thing ! [1] It still makes
my flesh creep all over whenever I think of it ! and
I think of it a great deal oftener than there is occasion for, since, thank God, he is now on foot

---

[1] Some accident which had befallen Dr. Russell.

again! But I have seen that safe! I can appreciate to the full the crash of its lid, smack down on human fingers! Mercy! what a piece of capital good stuff the Doctor must have been made of originally, that his fingers should have stuck together through such an accident, instead of being all pounded into mush! That is not what surprises me most, however, in the business. What surprises me most is, that the Doctor being a doctor, and a good, skilful one, should have gone about after, braving such a hurt, as though he had never in his life heard of lockjaw, or gangrene, or fever! I don't wonder that you were terrified. I wonder rather that you are not, now when your nursing is no more needed, in a brain fever yourself. The longer I live, the more I am certified that men, in all that relates to their own health, have not common sense! whether it be their pride, or their impatience, or their obstinacy, or their ingrained spirit of contradiction, that stupefies and misleads them, the result is always a certain amount of idiocy, or distraction in their dealings with their own bodies! I am not generalising from my own husband. I know that he is a quite extravagant example of that want of common sense in bodily matters which I complain of. Few men (even) are so lost to themselves as to dry their soaked trowsers on their legs! (as he does) or swallow five grains of mercury in the middle of the day, and then walk or ride three hours under a plunge of rain! (as he does) &c. &c. But men generally, all of them I have ever had to do with— even your sensible husband included, you see—drive the poor women, who care for them, to despair, either by their wild impatience of bodily suffering, and the exaggerated moan they make over it, or else by their reckless defiance of it, and neglect of every dictate of prudence! There! You may tell the Doctor what I say! It won't do him the slightest good against next time; but it is well he should know what one thinks of him—that one does not approve of such costly heroism at all!

I have nothing new to tell you which is lucky; as the things that have happened this long time back have been of a disastrous sort.

I go out now occasionally for a drive—walking tires me too much. I have even been twice out at dinner last week, and was at a wedding besides! The two dinners were of the quietest: at the one (Miss Baring's), nobody but Lord Ashburton, who had come up from the Grange for a consultation; at the other (Lady Sandwich's), nobody but the Marchioness of Lothian, who, having lived thirty years in Scotland, is as good as a Scotchwoman. But the wedding [1] was an immense affair! It was my doctor's little daughter, who was being married,

---

[1] Barnes's.

after a three years' engagement ; and as soon as she
was engaged, she had made me promise to attend
her wedding. I had rather wished to see a marriage
performed in a church with all the forms, the eight
bridesmaids, &c. &c. But I had renounced all idea
of going to the church, for fear of being laid up
with a fresh cold ; and meant to attend only the
breakfast party after, in which I took less interest.
But imagine how good the people here are to me.
Our rector, in whose church (St. Luke's) the marriage
was to take place, being told by his wife I wished
to go, but durstn't for fear of the coldness of the
church, ordered the fires to be kept up from Sunday
over into Tuesday morning ! besides a rousing fire in
the vestry, where I sat at my ease till the moment
the ceremony began ! I was much pressed afterwards to acknowledge how superior the English way
of marrying was to the Scotch, and asked how I had
liked it. I said my feelings were very mixed.
'Mixed ? ' the rector asked, ' mixed of what ? '
' Well, ' I said, ' it looked to me something betwixt a
religious ceremony and a—pantomime ! ' So it is.
There were forty-four people at the breakfast !

Your ever affectionate
J. W. CARLYLE.

LETTER 243.

Mrs. Russell, Holm Hill.

5 Cheyne Row, Chelsea: Thursday, June 5, 1862.

Dearest Mary,—I cannot count the letters I have written to you in my head within the last six weeks, they have been so many; I have written them mostly before getting out of bed in the morning, or while lying awake at night. But in the day-time, with pen and ink at hand, I have been always, always, always too sick or too bothered to put them on paper, have indeed been writing to nobody, if that be any excuse for not writing to you. The beginning of warm weather is as trying for me, in a different way, as winter was, and so many sad things have happened.

Just when the freshness of one sorrow was wearing off, there has come another. First Elizabeth Pepoli, then Lady Sandwich, then Mrs. Twisleton:[1] the three people in all London whose friendship I had most dependence on. Nobody will believe the loss Lady Sandwich is to us. They say 'a woman of eighty! that is not to be regretted.' But her intimate friends know that this woman of eighty was the most charming companion and the loyallest, warmest friend; was the only person in London or in the

---

[1] A very beautiful and clever little Boston lady, wife of Hon. Edward Twisleton, and much about us for the six or seven years she lived here. I well remember her affecting funeral (old Fiennes Castle, in Oxfordshire), and my ride thither with Browning, &c.

world that Mr. C. went regularly to see. Twice a
week he used to call for her; and now his horse
makes for her house whenever he gets into the
region of Grosvenor Square, and does not see or
understand the escutcheon that turns me sick as I
drive past. Dear little Mrs. Twisleton, so young,
and beautiful, and clever, so admired in society and
adored at home, is a loss that everyone can appreciate!
And the strong affection she testified for me, through
her long terrible illness, has made her death a keener
grief than I thought it would be.

I should have been thankful to be away from
here—anywhere—at the bottom of a coal-pit, to
think over this in quiet, safe from the breaking in of
all the idlers ' come up ' to that great vulgar show of
an ' Exhibition,' and safe from the endless weary
chatter about it. Nothing could keep me here for
an hour but Mr. C.'s determination to stay;—since
at the top of the house he is safe enough from tiresome interruptions, simply refusing to see anybody,
which, alas! makes it all the more needful for me to
be civil. Here he will stay and work on; (what an
idea you have all got in your heads, that, having
published a third volume he must be at ease in Zion,
when two more volumes are to come, and one wholly
unwritten; and to leave him in the present state of
things is what I cannot make up my mind to. If I
go on in this way, however, I shall die, and just

before it comes to that extremity I shall probably muster the necessary resolution.

Mr. C.'s comfort under the confusion of the Exhibition is that 'It is to be hoped it will end in total bankruptcy.' They say the guarantees will be called on to pay twenty-five per cent.

Kindest love to the doctor; a hearty kiss to yourself.

Yours affectionately,

JANE W. CARLYLE.

LETTER 244.

We were with the Ashburtons, she first, for a week or more, then both of us for perhaps a week longer. *Ay de mi!* (October 29, 1869.)

To Thomas Carlyle, Chelsea.

West Cliff Hotel: Wednesday, July 2, 1862.

Thanks, dear! especially for telling me about Mrs. Forster. I had been so vexed at myself for not begging you to go again and send me word.

Lady A. came and sat awhile in my room last night, and, speaking of Miss Bromley's departure, I took occasion to say that, 'As she and I came on the same day, I felt as if I ought to have also gone on the same day.' The answer to which was a very cordial 'Nonsense, my dear friend!' I was expected to stay as long as they did, 'or' (when I shook my head at that) 'as long at all events as I could possibly make it convenient.' There was no doubt whatever about her present wish being to that effect. And then came up the old question as a new one, 'Did I think he would come? It would be such a pleasure to Bingham, now that he could move about.' I said, you might perhaps be persuaded to come for a very short visit, but, &c. &c. That was it! A short visit was evidently what she wanted, and she *does* want that; but she did not see her way through a long one, in the circumstances I could see, and I don't wonder. She would write herself to-day, and urge you to come on Saturday and stay till Monday—'You might surely do that!'

Now that is just what you must do. Even two days of sea will benefit you; and it can be had at little sacrifice of anything. You don't need to trouble about clothes; what you could bring in your carpet-bag would be enough; there is no elaborate dressing for dinner here; and the tide is convenient, and there is a horse! And Lady A. says she can give you 'a perfectly quiet room:'—indeed, mine is quiet as the grave from outside noises; not a cock nor a dog in all Folkestone I think! And the cookery, which is objected to as all too English, would suit you:—constant loins of roast mutton, and constant boiled chickens! Now pray take no counsel with flesh and blood, but come straight off on Saturday morning, according to the invitation that will reach you (I expect) along with this.   And in all likelihood we will go home together on Monday.

If you don't come, I will stay away as long as ever they will keep me, just to spite you !

Look up in your topographical book for Salt-wood Castle.   Lady A. asked, when we were there to-day, if I thought you would be able to tell us about it ; and I said, 'Of course you would :' Salt-wood Castle, near Folkestone.

There is here too a review of 'Frederick' in the 'Cornhill,' which would amuse you !   Adoring your genius, but absolutely horror-struck at your 'scorn,' which is 'become normal.'   How you dare to utter such blasphemy against Messrs. Leibnitz and Mauper-tuis ! !   I could not help bursting out laughing at the man's sacred horror, as if he had been speaking of Milton's Devil !

Yours ever,

J. W. C.

Horrible paper !   I have no other.

LETTER 245.

Mrs. Russell, Holm Hill.

5 Cheyne Row, Chelsea : July 20, 1862.

Dearest Mary,—When you wrote last you were going somewhere—to see your cousin, I think.   Is that visit paid ? and what other visits have you to pay ?   And how are you? I fear but poorly from your late letters; but are you well enough to feel any pleasure in—in—in seeing me if I should come?

Look here! I am not sure about it! But Mr. C. said something this morning that I am determined to view as permission for me to go away by myself—where I please and when I please for a very little while. We had got into words about an invitation to the Marquis of Lothian's, in Norfolk. I had written a refusal by his (Mr. C.'s) desire, and Lady Lothian had written to me a second letter, holding out as inducements for altering his mind that there was a wonderfully fine library at Blickling Park, and that Lord Lothian's health prevented company; and Mr. C., tempted a little by the library and the no company, had suggested I might write that if the weather got unbearable! and if he got to a place in his work where he could gather up some papers and take them with him! and if—if—if ever so many things, he might perhaps—that is, we might perhaps—come 'by and by'!!!! I had said 'by no means.' I have written a refusal by your desire; I shall gladly now write an acceptance by your desire; but neither yes nor no, or yes and no both in one, I can't and won't write; you must do that sort of thing yourself!' And then he told me, 'Since I was so impatient about it,' I had better go by myself. To which I answered that it wouldn't be there that I would go by myself, nor to the Trevelyans, nor the Davenport Bromleys;

but to Scotland to Mrs. Russell. 'Then go to Mrs. Russell—pack yourself up and be off as soon as you like.'

Now it wasn't a very gracious permission, still it was a permission—at least I choose to regard it as such ; and if I had been quite sure how you were situated—whether you were at home, without other visitor, well enough to be bothered with me, &c. &c. I should have said on the spot, 'Thanks ! I will go then on such a day !'

I know to my sorrow that, if I should be long absent, things would go to sixes and sevens, and I should find mischievous habits acquired in the kitchen department, which it would take months to reform—if ever. But my week at Folkestone with the Ashburtons passed off with impunity ;—and their (the servants') moralities might surely hold out for a fortnight or so ; which would give plenty of time to see you, and look about on the dear old places, and go round by Edinburgh for a kiss of old Betty.

You see how it is, however, for I have told you exactly what passed ;—and you see it is not a very settled question. Without further speech with Mr. C. I can't just say, 'I am coming if you will have me !' But if you say you will have me, can have me soon, without inconvenience ; then I will myself open the further speech and ascertain if he means to stand to his word, and look favourably on my going for a week or two.

I say forgive me coming to you, year after year, with these indecisions. Next to being undecided oneself the greatest misery is to be mixed up with undecided people. I myself know always mighty well what I want; and buts and ifs and possiblys are not words in my natural vocabulary, for all so often as I am obliged to use them. If I plague you with my uncertainties, believe me I plague myself quite as much or more.

Affectionately yours,
J. CARLYLE.

LETTER 246.

Mrs. Russell, Holm Hill.

5 Cheyne Row, Chelsea : Saturday, Aug. 2, 1862.

Dearest Mary,—Your letter of this morning had the same effect that a glass of port wine, administered in my babyhood, was recorded to have had on a less dignified organ : 'Port wine' (I was said to have said to my mother, with the suddenness of Balaam's ass) 'mak's inside a' cozy!' So indeed did your cordial letter mak' heart a' cozy. On the strength of the coziness, I said right out to Mr. C., sitting opposite : 'How long had you to wait at Carlisle for the train that put you down at the Gill at seven in the morning?' No opening could have been better. He was taken quite by surprise ; and, before he had time to consider my going as a question, he found himself engaged in considerations of the best way to go. After that he could not well go back upon his implied assent.[1] The only 'demurrer' he could put in, with a good grace, was to ask : 'What did I mean to do with my foot ?' I meant it to get well, I said, in a few days ; of course I shouldn't think of going from home on one leg. This related to a bruised, or sprained, or someway bedevilled foot, that I came by the very day I had written to you, as if, I almost felt, with a shudder at the time, it was the monition of Providence that I should go on no such journey. I was returning from Islington where I had been to ask after the lamed foot (!) of the little lady who was my honorary nurse [2] last winter. The Islington omnibus put me down within some eighth part of a mile of my own house. I had one rather dark street to pass through first— taking the shortest way—and it was near eleven o'clock at night. I didn't care for being alone so late ; but I didn't want to be seen by any of the low people of that street alone. So I stepped off the pavement to avoid passing close to a small group standing talking at a door ; when I had cleared these only people to be seen in the whole street, I was

---

[1] Alas! how little did I ever *know* of these secret wishes and necessities—now or ever !

[2] Mrs. Dilberoglue (?).

stepping back on to the pavement, when, the curbstone being higher than I noticed in the shadow, I struck the side of my right foot violently against it and was tripped over, and fell smack down, full length on the pavement.[1]

Considering how easily I might have broken my ribs, it is wonderful that the fall did me no harm. I scrambled up directly ; but the foot I had struck on the curbstone before falling was dreadfully sore, and it was made worse, you may believe, by having to use it, after a sort, to get myself home. How I got home at all, even in holding on to walls and railings, I can't think. But once at home on a chair, I couldn't touch the ground with it on any account. Mr. C. had to carry me to bed, at the imminent risk of knocking my head off against the lintels. So I wouldn't be carried by him any more, my head being of more consequence to me than my foot. It was dreadfully swelled for a couple of days ; but to-day, though I still cannot get a shoe on, or walk, it is so much better, that I am sure it will be all right presently. In a few days I hope to be able to write that I am road-worthy, and I will only wait for that. It is a most provoking little accident, for delays are so dangerous. I should have wished after my experiences of late summers to go to you at once, before any ' pigs ' have time to ' run through.'

<hr>

[1] I remember, and may well.

And now I needn't be saying more but that God grant nothing may prevent our meeting this time.

Love to the doctor.

Affectionately yours,

JANE CARLYLE.

LETTER 247.

To Thomas Carlyle, Esq., Chelsea.

Holm Hill, Thornhill: August 13, 1862.

Oh, my dear, I wish they hadn't started that carpet-lifting and chimney-sweeping process so immediately, but left you time to recover my loss (if any) in the usual 'peace and quietness'! That chimney in my bedroom had to be swept, however, before winter came; and no time so good as when I was on my travels. You don't complain: but your few lines this morning make the impression on me of having been written under 'a dark brown shadd!' I told Maria if she observed you to be mismanaging yourself, and going off your sleep and all that sort of thing, to tell me, and I should be back like a returned sky-rocket.

For myself, I am all right. I was in bed before eleven o'clock struck, with a stiff little tumbler of whisky toddy in my head, and I went to sleep at once, and slept on, with only some half-dozen awakenings, till the maid brought in my hot-water at eight o'clock! My foot, as well as my 'interior,' is benefited by the good night. It was too lame for anything yesterday. But there was no temptation

to use it much yesterday; it rained without intermission. To-day is very cloudy, but not wet as yet;
and we are going for a drive in the close carriage.
Dr. Russell has both an open and a close carriage,
the lucky man! Indeed he has as pretty and well-
equipped a place here as any reasonable creature
could desire. But Mrs. Russell has never ceased to
regret the tumble-down old house in Thornhill,
'where there was always something going on!'
'Looking out on the trees and the river here makes
her so melancholy,' she says, that she feels sometimes
as if she should lose her senses! The wished-for,
as usual, come too late! Ease with dignity, when
the habits of a lifetime have made her incapable of
enjoying it!

Would you tell Maria to put a bit of paper round
the little long-shaped paste-board box, in my little
drawer next the drawing-room, containing the two
ornamental hair-pins, and send them to me by post;
—they are quite light; I want them to give away.
Also if you were to put a couple of good quill-pens
of your own making in beside the hair-pins, 'it would
be a great advantage.' I had written to say a word
expressly about the tobacco. Oh, please, do go to
bed at a reasonable hour, and don't overwork yourself, and consider you are no longer a child!

Faithfully yours,
J. W. C.

LETTER 248.

To Mrs. Austin, The Gill, Annan.

Holm Hill, Thornhill, Dumfries: Thursday, Aug. 14, 1862.

Oh, my little woman, how glad I was to recognise your face through the glass of the carriage window, all dimmed with human breath! And how frightened I was the train would move, while you were clambering up like a school-boy to kiss me! And how I grudged the long walk there and back for you, and the waiting. Still you did well to come, for it (your coming) quite brightened up my spirits for the last miles of my journey, which are apt to be mortally tiresome. I had meant to wave my handkerchief from the window when we passed the Gill, but I found no seat vacant except the middle one; and disagreeable women, on each side of me, closed the windows all but an inch, so to make any demonstration had been impossible. The more my gladness to catch sight of your very face. And Jane and her husband and daughter were waiting for me at Dumfries, having heard of my coming from Dr. Carlyle. 'So the latter end of that woman' (meaning me) 'was better than the beginning.'

Dr. Russell was waiting for me—had been waiting more than an hour, like everyone else—with his carriage, in which I was conveyed through ways, happily for me, clothed in darkness, so that the first object I saw was Mrs. Russell at the door of their new home. It is a most beautiful house and place they have made of old Holm Hill. And I do not see Templand from the windows as I feared I should. The trees have grown up so high.

The first night I couldn't sleep a bit for agitation of mind, far more than fatigue of body. The next night I slept; last night again not. So to-day I feel rather ghastly. Then it has rained pretty much without intermission. Yesterday we took a very short drive between showers, and that was the only time I have crossed the threshold; besides the bad weather I brought away with me a recently sprained foot, which makes walking both painful and imprudent.

Under these circumstances I have not yet formed any plan for my future travels; but shall tell you in a few days whether I will pay you a little visit on the road home, or run down from here, and back again. I will certainly not let that brief meeting stand for all, unless you forbid me to come. But I have all along looked to be guided by circumstances in this journey.

My stay is to be determined by the accounts I get of Mr. C. from himself, and (still more dependably) from my housemaid Maria; and my road back, whether as I came or by Edinburgh, to be decided on when I shall have heard from Lady Stanley and another English friend on the North Western line. But I would not leave you wondering what was become of me, or if it had been really me or my wraith you had seen.

In a few days, then, you will hear further. Meanwhile

Your affectionate
J. W. C.

LETTER 249.

To Mrs. Austin, The Gill, Annan.

Holm Hill : Saturday, Aug. 30, 1862.

My dear, ever kind Mary,—In the first place, God bless you and yours. Secondly, I am ' all right,' or pretty nearly so. Thirdly, I forward the proof-sheet of Mrs. Oliphant's book which I promised, and something else which was not promised—a photograph of my interesting self, taken by a Thornhill hairdresser, and not so very bad, it strikes me, as photographs go. This last blessed item of my sending is intended as a present to your husband, ' all to himself,' as the children say.

A letter from Mr. C. to me was forwarded from Scotsbrig to the Doctor, and given to me at the station, and another letter from Mr. C. awaited me at Thornhill ; a very attentive Mr. C. really !

I have no time to spare for writing more than the absolutely needful. Six letters by post this morning, most of them needing immediate answer, and we are to drive to Morton Castle before dinner.

God keep you all, well and mindful of me till I come again.   Yours affectionately,

JANE CARLYLE.

LETTER 250.

To T. Carlyle, Esq., Chelsea.

Craigenvilla: Tuesday, Sept. 2, 1862.

Oh, you stupid, stupid Good! not to know my handwriting when you see it at this time of day. It was I who directed that photograph and posted it at Thornhill. I just turned my handwriting a little back, and sent it, without a word, to puzzle you, forgetting that the post-mark would betray where it came from. It was done by a Thornhill hairdresser; Mrs. Russell and I got taken one day for fun, and if I had dreamt of coming out so well I would have dressed myself better, and turned the best side of my face.

My departure from Nithsdale was like the partings of dear old long ago, before one had experienced what ' time will teach the softest heart, unmoved to meet, ungrieved to part,' as the immortal Mr. Terrot once wrote. And then the journey through the hills to that little lonely churchyard[1]—all that caused me so many tears, that to-day my eyes are out of my head, and I am sick and sore. And, of course, sleep was out of the question after such a day of emotion —when so ill to be caught at the best of times—and

---

[1] Crawford, where her mother's grave is.

I have had just one hour of broken slumber (from five till six), and I was up at six yesterday morning. So I mustn't go after Betty to-day; she would be too shocked with my looks. Grace and I will take a short drive in an omnibus (for a change). Neither must I sit writing to you, in detail, for my head spins round, and I could tell you nothing worth the effort of telling it. I left a letter to be posted at Thornhill yesterday.

So Garibaldi—or, as a man in the carriage with me last evening was calling him, Garri-Bauldy—is wounded and captured already—luck, I should say, to the poor fellows he was leading to destruction! Mazzini will be thankful he must have reached Garibaldi; it is to be hoped he is not taken also, but he went with his eyes perfectly open to the madness.

Grace was waiting at the train for me, and instantly found me under my hat and feather in the dark. She said it was by a motion of my hand.

They are all most kind. Elizabeth not so poorly as I expected to find her; Grace and Ann younger-looking than last time—hair raven black, far blacker than mine. Good-bye! I hope to sleep to-night; for I will have a dose of morphia now that I am near Duncan and Flockhart, and then I will be up to a better letter than this. I have left Grace to make out the 'old goose,'[1] and tell me the needful.

Your ever

J. W. C.

---

[1] Some foolish letter to me.

LETTER 251.

Mrs. Russell, Holm Hill, Thornhill.

Craigenvilla, Morningside: Tuesday, Sept. 2, 1862.

My darling!—Nature prompts me to write just a line, though I am not up to a letter to-day, at least to any other letter than the daily one to Mr. C., which must be written dead or alive. Imagine! after such a tiring day, I never closed my eyes till after five this morning! and was awake again for good, or rather for bad, before six struck! My eyes are almost out of my head this morning; and tell the Doctor, or rather don't tell him, I will have a dose of morphia to-night!—am just going in an omnibus to Duncan and Flockhart's for it. It will calm down my mind for once—generally my mind needs no calming, being sunk in apathy. And this won't do to go on!

Mr. C. writes this morning that he had received a letter in the handwriting of Dr. Russell (!) (my own handwriting slightly disguised), and ' had torn it open in a fright!! thinking that the Doctor was writing to tell I was ill! and found a photograph of me, really very like indeed,' but not a word ' from the Doctor ' inside! He took it as a sign that I was off! (why, in all the world, take it as that?) ' but it would have been an additional favour had the Doctor written just a line!'

Grace was waiting at the station for me, much to my astonishment; and discovered me at once, under the hat and feather, actually! She said by 'a motion of my hand'! The drains are all torn up at Morningside, and she was afraid I would not get across the rubbish in my cab without a pilot. They are all looking well, I think—even Elizabeth. Many friendly inquiries about you, and love to be sent.

Oh, my dear, my dear! My head is full of wool! Shall I ever forget these green hills, and that lonely churchyard, and your dear, gentle face!

Oh, how I wish I had a sleep!

Your own friend,

JANE CARLYLE.

The roots are all in the garden.

LETTER 252.

To T. Carlyle, Esq., Chelsea.

Craigenvilla, Morningside (Edinburgh): Thursday, Sept. 4, 1862.

'Two afflictions make a consolation'—of a sort! The disappointment of not receiving the usual good words from you this morning comforted my conscience at least for having failed in my own writing yesterday. I could figure you eating your breakfast at Cheyne Row, without any letter from me, with no particular pang of remorse; when I was eating my breakfast here with only the direction on 'Orley Farm' for a relish to my indifferent tea! It was partly the morphia that hindered me yesterday, and partly the rain. The morphia, which answered the end capitally, and procured me the only really sound sleep I have had since I went on my travels, made me feel too listless for writing before going to Betty's; and the walk through the rain to the cab when we returned made me too tired for writing after in time for the Morningside post.

Well, I have seen Betty, and Betty has seen me. Poor dear! It wasn't so 'good a joy' as it might have been; for Ann and Grace in their kindness would not let me go by myself, and the three of us were too many for the wee house and for Betty's nerves, which aren't what they were. But she made the best of that as of everything else. 'It's weel they're so kind to ye, dear; and it's richt,' she said, during a minute we were alone together. She gave me the 'stockns' (beautiful fine white ones), and a little packet of peppermint lozenges were lying beside them, 'in case I ever cam'.' Dear, kind soul! her heart is the same warm loyal heart; but these seven years of nursing have made terrible alterations in her: her hair is white as snow, and her face is so fined away that it looks as if one might blow it away like powder. I don't think she can stand much longer of it. George (poor patient 'Garg'!) is neither better nor worse; his mind not weakened at all, I think (which is wonderful). Old Braid keeps himself in health by much working in his garden, which is prolific. 'Sic a crapp o' gude peas, dear! Oh, if I could have sent Mr. Carlyle a wee dish o' them to cheer him up when he was alane, poor man!' 'Oh, dear!' she said, again catching my arm excitedly, 'wad onybody believe it? He—yer gudeman—direcks "Punch" till us every week, his ain sell, to sic as us!' Mr. Braid did not know me when I went in at the door the first; and when I taxed him with it he said, 'How should I ken ye? Ye lookit like a bit skelt o' a lassie, wi' that daft wee thing a-tap o' yer heed!'

I mean to get home, please God, at the beginning of next week. I cannot fix the day just yet, being 'entangled in details' with the Auchtertool people. I have seen nobody here but the Braids—indeed, there is nobody I much care to see. A most uninteresting place Edinburgh is become. I would like to spend an hour at Haddington in the dark! But I 'don't see my way' to that. I was glad to hear that Scotsbrig Jenny was getting over her bad fit. Grace has just come in, and sends her regards.

Yours ever,

JANE CARLYLE.

LETTER 253.

To T. Carlyle, Chelsea.

Craigenvilla (Edinburgh): Friday, Sept. 5, 1862.

Thanks, dear; here is a nice little letter this morning, which has had the double effect of satisfying my anxieties and delivering me from 'prayers.' I ran up to my room with it, and shut myself in, and when I issued forth again, prayers were over! What luck! My aunts are as kind to me as they can be—all three of them—and they exert themselves beyond their strength, I can see, to make my visit pleasant to me; but still I am like a fish out of water in this element of religiosity, or rather like a human being *in* water, and the water hot.

I am glad you have heard from my lady at last. I was beginning to not understand it; to fear either you or I must have in some way displeased her. If you could bring yourself to go to the Grange at once I shouldn't at all mind your being away when I arrived; should rather like to transact my fatigues and my acclimatising 'in a place by mysell.' And we might still have the 'sacred week' of idling and sightseeing (an exceptional week in our mutual life, it would be) after your return.

I find I cannot get off from Auchtertool. I shouldn't dislike a couple of days there (though many days couldn't be endured) if it weren't for that 'crossing.'   But, like it or not, I must just ' cross and recross '!   Maggie is returned.   Walter has put off joining Alexander at Crawford ; they are all expecting me, and the only expedient by which I could have avoided visiting them without giving offence to their kind feelings, viz., inviting them all to spend a day with me here, cannot be ' carried out ' —for ' reasons it may be interesting not to state.' After all I have no kinder relative or friend in the world than poor Walter.   Every summer, when invitations were not so plenty, his house, and all that is his, has been placed at my disposal.   It is the only house where I could go, without an invitation, at any time that suited myself ; and, considering all that, I must just ' cross ' to-morrow, in the intention, however, of staying only two days.   I should have gone to-day but for a letter of Walter's—' mis-sent to Liberton '—and so not reaching me in time.

I am now going off to town with Grace, to get her photograph taken—'for Jeannie's book,' she says; but I doubt the singleness of the alleged motive.   I shall call for Mrs. Stirling—who else ?   Alas, my old friends are ' all wed away '![1]

I return the letter, which seems to me perfectly serious and rather sensible; only what of Shakespeare ?   Shakespeare ' never did the like o't ! '

[1] *Flowers of the Forest.*

Address here; I shall find it (the letter) on my return from Auchtertool, if I am not here before it. It was thunder and lightning and waterspouts yesterday; terrible for laying the crops, surely.

Yours ever,

JANE W. CARLYLE

LETTER 254.

Mrs. Russell, Holm Hill.

Auchtertool Manse: Monday, Sept. 8, 1862.

So long as I am in Scotland, my darling, I cannot help feeling that my head-quarters is Holm Hill! though I go buzzing here and there, like a ' Bumbee' in the neighbourhood of its hive. Everywhere that I go I am warmly welcomed, and made much of; but nowhere that I go do I feel so at home, in an element so congenial to me, as with you and the Doctor! At Craigenvilla, though treated as a niece, and perhaps even a favourite niece, I am always reacting against the self-assumption, and the religio sity (not the religion, mind!); and here, though I am ' cousin'—their one cousin, for whom their naturally hospitable and kindly natures are doubly hospitable and kindly—still I miss that congeniality which comes of having mutually suffered, and taken one's suffering to heart! I feel here as if I were ' playing' with nice, pretty, well-behaved children! I almost envy them their light-hearted capacity of being engrossed with trifles! And yet, not that! there is a deeper joy in one's own sorrowful memories surely, than in this gaiety that comes of 'never minding'! Would I, would you, cease to regret the dear ones we have lost if we could? Would we be light-hearted, at the cost of having nothing in one's heart very precious or sacred? Oh, no! better ever such grief for the lost, than never to have loved any-one enough to have one's equanimity disturbed by the loss!

I came here on Saturday; was to have come on Friday, but had to wait for a letter of Walter's 'mis-sent to Liberton.' I go back to Morningside to-morrow forenoon, unless it 'rains cats and dogs!' And then to London after one day's rest! And after all my haste—at least haste after leaving Holm Hill— the chances are I shall find Mr. C. just gone to the Grange. He had 'partly decided on going next Tuesday (to-morrow).' And, if I wasn't home in time to go with him, he had engaged I would join him there! Don't he wish he may get me! He will have to stay considerably longer than the 'one week' he talks of, before I shall feel disposed to 'take the road' again! In fact, I should greatly like a few days 'all to myself,' to sleep off my fatigues, and get acclimatised, before having to resume my duties as mistress of the house.

Alex. Welsh came to Crawford the 'next day,' as

predicted; but 'his Reverence' never joined him there. And Alex., finding the fishing as bad as possible, went on to spend a few days with the Chrystals in Glasgow, before returning to Liverpool.

God keep you, dearest friend; after the Doctor, there is nobody you are so precious to as to me! I will write from Chelsea.

Your loving
J. CARLYLE.

LETTER 255.

Mrs. Russell, Holm Hill.

5 Cheyne Row: Tuesday night, Sept. 30, 1862.

Dearest of Friends,—I am writing two lines at this late hour, because I don't want the feeling of closeness that has outlived the precious three weeks we were together to die out through length of silence. For the rest, I am not in good case for writing a pleasant letter, having had no sleep last night, and the bad night not having been compensated, as my bad nights at Holm Hill were, strangely enough, by a good day. And I am bothered, too, with preparations for a journey to-morrow. What a locomotive animal I have suddenly become! Yes, it is a fact, my dear, that to-morrow[1] I am bound for Dover, to stay till Monday with that lady we call ' the flight of Skylarks,'[2] who was wanting me to come home by her

---

[1] Went October 1.

[2] Miss Davenport Bromley; her great-grandfather at ' Wooton,' in Staffordshire, was the ' Mr. Davenport ' who gave shelter to Rousseau.

place in Derbyshire. She is now at Dover, in lodgings, for the benefit of sea air ; and has invited me there since I wouldn't go to Wooton Hall, and Mr. C., who thought I ought to have come home by her, wishes me to go. And I am sure I have no objections ; for I like her much, and I like the sea much. But I 'am not to be staying away this time,' he says, 'and leaving him long by himself again.' No fear ! I must return to London on Monday, or I should not see Charlotte Cushman (who is now in Liverpool and returns here on Thursday) before her departure for Rome. Indeed, charming as I think the 'flight of Skylarks,' I should not be unsettling myself again if only I had kept the better health and spirits I brought back from Scotland. It was too much to hope, however, that I could keep all that long. The clammy heavy weather we have had for the last week has put me all wrong somehow. I am sick at stomach, or at heart (I can't tell which), and have a continual irritation in my bits of 'interiors,' and horrid nights, for all which, I daresay, the sea is the best medicine. I shall tell you how it has answered when I come back.

Love to the Doctor.

Your own
J. W. C.

LETTER 256.

T. Carlyle, Esq., Chelsea.

1 Sidney Villas, Dover: Wednesday afternoon, Oct. 1, 1862.

I may take a reasonable sheet of paper, dear! for, besides being not 'too tired for writing,' I have abundance of time for writing, 'the Larks'[1] being all far up out of sight, beyond the visible sky! looking for me there. My journey was successful, and I stepped out at Dover worth half a dozen of the woman I left Chelsea. Curious what a curative effect a railway journey has on me always, while you it makes pigs and whistles of! Is it the motion, or is it the changed air? 'God knows!'

The first thing that befell me at Dover was a disappointment—no Larks waiting! not a feather of them to be discovered by the naked eye. The next thing that befell me was to be deceived and betrayed and entirely discomfited by—a sailor. After looking about for the Larks some ten minutes, and being persecuted as long by pressing proposals from cabmen and omnibus conductors, I was asking a porter how far it was to Sidney Villas. The porter not knowing the place, a sailor came forward and said he knew it, that it 'was just a few steps; I would be there in a minute if I liked to walk, and he would carry my trunk for me.' And, without waiting to have the question debated, he threw my trunk over his shoulder and walked off.

[1] See note, p. 123.

I followed, quite taken by assault. And we walked on and on, and oh, such a distance!—certainly two miles at least, the sailor pretending to not hear every time I remonstrated, or assuring me 'I couldn't find a prettier walk in all Dover than this.' At last we reached Sidney Villas ; and when I accused my sailor of having basely misled me that he might have a job, he candidly owned, 'Well, things are dear just now, and few jobs going,' wiping the sweat from his brow at the same time, and looking delighted with the shilling I gave him. I thought it was all gone to the devil together when the man who answered the bell denied that Miss Bromley was there. On cross-questioning, however, he explained that she did reside there, but was not at home—was 'gone to the railway to meet a lady '—and his eye just then squinting on my portmanteau, he exclaimed, with sudden cordiality, 'Perhaps you are the lady?' I owned the soft impeachment, and was shown to the bedroom prepared for me, and have washed and unpacked. Meanwhile Miss B.'s maid, who had gone to one station while Miss B. went to the other to make sure of me, returned and gave me a cup of tea, and then went off to catch the poor dear Larks, who was waiting for me at the wrong station. There being a third station (the one at which I landed), it hadn't occurred to either mistress or maid to ask at which of the three stations the three o'clock train stopped.

Larks come with feathers all in a fluff. 'So dreadfully sorry,' &c. &c. Dinner not till seven, and to be enlivened by the presence of Mr. Brookfield, whom she had met while looking for me. 'Seven!' and I had only one small cup of tea and one slice of etherial bread and butter. But we 'must make it *do*.'

This house is within a stone-cast of the sea, and also, alas! of the pier; so that there is as much squealing of children at this moment as if it were Cheyne Row. Nothing but a white blind to keep out the light of a large window. But with shutters and stillness, and all possible furtherances, I was finding sleep impossible at home; so perhaps it may suit the contradictory nature of the animal to sleep here without them.

Now, upon my word, this is a fairly long letter to be still in the first day of absence. It will, at least, show that I am less ghastly sick and with less worry in my interior than when I left in the morning.

Yours anyhow,

J. W. Carlyle.

LETTER 257.

T. Carlyle, Esq., Chelsea.

1 Sidney Villas, Dover: Friday, Oct. 3, 1862.

Oh, my dear! I 'did design' to write you a nice long letter to-day. But 'you must just excuse us' again. I am the victim of 'circumstances over which

I have no control.'   I must put you off with a few lines, and lie down on the sofa of my bedroom, and try to get warm, or it will be the worse for me. You see I am taking every day a warm sea-bath, hoping to derive benefit from it—'cha-arge' half-a-crown.   But, never mind, if I can stave off an illness at the beginning of winter, I shall save in doctor's bills!   Well, my bath to-day made me excessively sleepy, and I lay down to sleep, and in five minutes I was called down to luncheon, and after luncheon I must go with Miss Bromley to call for Lady Doyle, with whom Miss Wynne, just arrived from Carlsbad, had been yesterday—might still be to-day.   Our call executed, it was proposed we should drive on to Shakespeare's Cliff, and when there, we were driven away 'over the heights'—a most alarming road—all this time in an open carriage; and now that we are come in there is not a fire anywhere—never is any fire to warm myself at—and so I am not at all in right trim for letter-writing.   And common prudence requires I should lie down and get into heat.

For the rest it is all right.   I have slept very fairly both nights in spite of—'many things!'   Miss B. is kind and charming, the place is 'delicious,' and I am certainly much better for the change.   But, for all that, I am coming home without fail at the time I fixed; not from any 'puritanical' adherence to my word given, but that by Monday I shall have had enough of it and got all the good to be got. Miss B. has pressed me earnestly to stay till Monday week ; but no need to bid *me*—' be firm, Alicia ! '

What a pity about poor Bessy ! She says she ' was always a worshipper of genius, and recollects one day in particular when Mr. Carlyle poured out such a stream of continuous eloquence that she was forcibly reminded of the lady who spoke pearls and diamonds in the fairy tale.' She is very proud of her book and photograph. That absurd corkmaker sends me his photograph. I will bring his letter for you ; inclosed in mine it is over-weight.

[No room to sign] ' J. W. C.'

LETTER 258.

Mrs. Russell, Holm Hill.

5 Cheyne Row, Chelsea : Monday, October 20, 1862.

Now Mary, dear ! pray don't let the echoes of your voice die out of my ears, if you can help it ! It makes the difference betwixt feeling near and feeling far away ; the difference betwixt writing off-hand, as one speaks, and writing cramped apologies. You may not have anything momentous to tell ; but I am not difficult to interest, when it is you who are writing. Just fill a small sheet with such matter as you would say to me, if I were sitting opposite you, and I shall be quite content.

Neither have I myself anything momentous to

tell, except, I was going to say, that I had got a new
bonnet, or rather my last winter's bonnet transformed
into a new one; but it suddenly flashes over me, that
is by no means the most momentous thing I have to
tell; a new bonnet is nothing in comparison to a
new—maid! Ah, my dear! Yes, I am changing
my housemaid; I have foreseen for long, even when
she was capering about me, and kissing my hands
and shawl, that this emotional young lady would not
wear well; and that some fine day her self-conceit
and arrogance would find the limits of my patience.
Indeed, I should have lost patience with her long
ago, if it hadn't been for her cleverness about Mr.
C.'s books, which I fancied would make him extremely averse to parting with her, as cleverness of
that sort is not a common gift with housemaids.
But not at all—at least not in prospect; he says she
is ' such an affected fool,' and so heedless in other
respects that it is quite agreeable to him ' that she
should carry her fantasticalities and incompetences
elsewhere!'   She had calculated on being indispensable, on the score of the books, and was taking,
since soon after my return from Scotland, a position
in the house which was quite preposterous—domi-
neering towards the cook, and impertinent to me!
picking and choosing at her work—in fact, not
behaving like a servant at all, but like a lady, who,
for a caprice, or a wager, or anything except wages

and board, was condescending to exercise light func-
tions in the house, provided you kept her in good
humour with gifts and praises.

When Mr. C.'s attention was directed to her procedure, he saw the intolerableness as clearly as I did;
so I was quite free to try conclusions with the girl—
either she should apologise for her impertinence and
engage (like Magdalen Smith) 'to turn' over a new
leaf,' or she should (as Mr. C. said) 'carry her
fantasticalities and incompetences elsewhere!' She
chose, of course, the worser part; and I made all
the haste possible to engage a girl in her place, and
make the fact known, that so I might protect myself
against scenes of reconciliation, which, to a woman
as old and nervous as I am, are just about as tiresome as scenes of altercation. All sorts of scenes
cost me my sleep, to begin with; and are a sheer
waste of vital power, which one's servant at least
ought really not to cost one!

I am going to try a new arrangement—that of
keeping two women (experienced, or considering
themselves so) to do an amount of work between
them which any good experienced servant could do
singly having hitherto proved unmanageable with
me. I have engaged a little girl of the neighbourhood (age about fifteen) to be under the Scotchwoman. She is known to me as an honest, truthful,
industrious little girl. Her parents are rather superior

people in their station. The father is a collector on the boats. She is used to work, but not at all to what Mr. C.'s father would have called the 'curiosities and niceties' of a house like this. So I shall have trouble enough in licking her into shape But trouble is always a bearable thing for me in comparison with irritation. The chief drawback is that the mother is sickly, and this child has been her mainstay at home; and though both parents have willingly sacrificed their own convenience to get their child into so respectable a place, my fear is that after I have had the trouble of licking her into shape, the mother, under the pressure of home difficulties, may be irresistibly tempted to take her home again. Well, there is an excellent Italian proverb, 'The person who considers everything will never decide on anything!' Meanwhile, Elizabeth looks much more alive and cheerful since she had this change in view; and I shall be delivered from the botheration of two rival queens in the kitchen at all events. That I shall have to fetch the books, and do the sewing myself, will perhaps— ' keep the devil from my elbow.'

I had a letter from my Aunt Ann the other day, the first I have had from any of them since I was at Craigenvilla, in spite of entreaties and remonstrances on my part. She tells me that the maidservant whom Grace 'converted' some years ago is still praying earnestly for Mr. Carlyle. She has been at it a long while now, and must be tired of writing to my aunts to ask whether they had heard if anything had happened through her prayers.' I will send you Ann's letter ; burn it before, or having read it—as you like. Does it amuse you to read letters (good in their way) not addressed to yourself? Tell me that ; for if it does, I could often, at the small cost of an extra stamp, send you on any letter that has pleased myself, without putting you to the trouble of returning them. I am afraid you will not have so many visitors to enliven you in the winter ; and then you will take to thinking it was livelier at Thornhill, with your window looking on the street. Oh my dear! I wonder how the Doctor is so angelically patient with your hankering after the old house, when he has made the new one so lovely for you. Yet I can understand all that about the old house. I can, who am a woman !

LETTER 250.

To Mrs. Austin, The Gill, Annan.

5 Cheyne Row, Chelsea : Thursday, October 23, 1862.

Blessings on you, dear! These eggs have been such a deliverance. Can you believe it of me? I have been in such a worry of mind of late days, that were it asked of me, with a loaded pistol at my breast, whether or not I had written again after receiving your letter, I could not tell ! So in case I did not, I write to-night, while I have a little breathing-time.

Lord Ashburton, whom we had been led to suppose out of danger, made no progress in convalescence and then began to sink. Lady A., who has had the news of her mother's death since his illness, was alone to nurse him day and night. Her sister, who had gone to her at Paris, was obliged to hurry back to London, to attend to her own husband, who is confined to bed. She told me I was the only other person whom her sister (Lady A.) would like to have beside her. Would I write and ask if I might come? It was a serious undertaking for me, at this season, who had never crossed the Channel, and suffering so from sailing, and whose household affairs were in such a muddle; a servant to go away and no one yet found to replace her—but what else could I do but go to her if she would have me? Mr. C., too, thought I could do nothing else. So I wrote and offered to come immediately, and you may think if I have not been perfectly bewildered while waiting her answer— 'seeing servants,' as the phrase is, all the while. This morning I had a few hurried lines from her—No—I was not to come, 'it could do her no good and would knock me up ;' for the rest, she was 'past all human help,' she said, 'and past all sympathy.' And the poor dear soul had drawn her pen through the last words. So like her, that she might not seem unkind, even in her agony of grief and dread she thought of that.

Their doctor's last two letters to me were very despondent, and neither to-day nor yesterday has there been any word from him, as there would have surely been, could he have imparted a grain of hope. We dread now that the next post will bring the news of our dear Lord Ashburton's death. Carlyle will lose in him the only friend he has left in the world, and the world will lose in him one of the purest-hearted, most chivalrous men that it contained. There are no words for such a misfortune.

Meanwhile one's own poor little life struggles on, with its daily petty concerns, as well as its great ones. About these eggs, which mustn't be neglected, if the solar system were coming to a stand—I do not think, dear, it was the fewness of the eggs that kept them safe so much as the plentifulness of the hay. Depend on it, your woman's plan of making the eggs all touch each other was a bad one. We have still eggs for a week—and then? I know of two hens in the neighbourhood that have begun to lay, but they do it so irregularly, so I mustn't trust to them. I don't think it would be safe to send the butter and eggs in the same box; a coarse basket would do as well as a box for the eggs—the difficulty of getting them sent doesn't seem to be the carriage so much as things to pack them in. If we were but nearer, I might send what the Addiscombe gardener calls the empties back again at trifling cost. I must inquire what it would cost to send empty baskets, as it is; I could take them myself to the office.

Oh dear me! what a pleasure it is when one is away from home and has no servants to manage, and no food to provide. Mr. C. gets more and more difficult to feed, and more and more impatient of the imperfections of human cooks and human housewives. I sometimes feel as if I should like to run away. But the question always arises, where to?

Kind regards to Jamie and the girls. What a pleasant time I had with you all, those nice evening drives!—Carlaverock Castle! How like a beautiful dream it all is, when I look back on it from here!

Your affectionate

JANE CARLYLE.

LETTER 260.

Mrs. Russell, Holm Hill.

5 Cheyne Row, Chelsea: Thursday, Nov. 21, 1862.

Dearest Mary,—The last of the four notes I inclosed, which had come a few hours before I wrote to you, made us expect the worst; and as the day went on, we could not help expecting the worst with more and more certainty. The same night we were talking very sadly of Lord Ashburton, almost already in the past tense; Mr. C. saying, 'God help me! since I am to lose him, the kindest, gentlest, friendliest man in my life here! I may say the one friend I have in the world!' and I, walking up and down in the room, as my way is when troubled in mind, had just answered, 'It's no use going to bed and trying to sleep, in this suspense!' when the door opened and a letter was handed me. It was from Paris, a second letter that day! I durstn't open it. Mr. C. impatiently took it from me but was himself so agitated that he couldn't read it, when he had it. At last he exclaimed, '"Better!" I see the one word "better," nothing else! look there, is not that "better"?' To be sure it was! and you may imagine our relief! and our thankfulness to Lady A. and Mrs. Anstruther for not losing a moment in telling us! The letters go on more and more favourable. The doctors say 'they cannot understand it.' When do these grand doctors understand anything? But no matter about them, so that he is recovering, whether they understand it or not!

I may now tell you of my household crisis, which has been happily accomplished. Maria has departed this scene, and little 'Flo' (!) has entered upon it; not a little dog, as you might fancy from the name, but a remarkably intelligent, well-conditioned girl between fourteen and fifteen, who was christened 'Florence'—too long and too romantic a name for household use! She is so quick at learning that training her is next to no trouble. And Mr. C. is so pleased with the clever little creature, that he has been much less aggravating than usual under a change. Maria wished to make me a scene at parting (of course). But I brutally declined participating in it, so she rushed up to the study with her tears to Mr. C., who was 'dreadfully sorry for the poor creature.' The 'poor creature' had been employing her mind latterly in impressing on Elizabeth, who is weak enough to believe what mischief-makers tell her, rather than the evidence of her own senses, that she was going to be overworked (!) with only an untrained girl instead of a fine lady housemaid for fellow-servant, and in making herself so charming and caressing for Elizabeth that her former tyrannies were forgotten; and Elizabeth, who had looked quite happy at the idea of Maria's going ' and a girl under her,' turned suddenly round into wearing a sullen look of victimhood, and declining silently to give me the least help in training the girl! All the better for the girl; and perhaps also all the better for me!

But it is a disappointment to find that my Scotch blockhead is no brighter for having her ' Bubbly Jock ' taken off her! Such a woman to have had sent four hundred miles to one! Mr. C. always speaks of her as ' that horse,' 'that cow,' 'that mooncalf!' But upon my honour, it is an injustice to the horse, the cow, and even the mooncalf! For sample of her procedure: there is a glass door into the back court consisting of two immense panes of glass; the cow has three several times smashed one of these sheets of glass, through the same careless-ness, neglecting to latch it up! three times, in the six months she has been here! and nobody before her ever smashed that door! Another thing that nobody before her ever did, in all the twenty-eight or nine years I have lived in the house, was to upset the kitchen table! and smash, at one stroke, nearly all the tumblers and glasses we had, all the china breakfast things, a crystal butter-glass (my mother's), a crystal flower vase, and ever so many jugs and bowls! There was a whole washing-tub full of broken things! Surely honesty, sobriety, and steadi-ness must have grown dreadfully scarce qualities, that one puts up with such a cook; especially as her cooking is as careless as the rest of her doings. No variety is required of her, and she has been taught how to do the few things Mr. C. needs. She can do them when she cares to take pains; but every third day or so there comes up something that provokes him into declaring, 'That brute will be the death of me! It is really too bad to have wholesome food turned to poison.' But I suppose she understands herself engaged by the half-year, though I never had any explanation with her, as to the second half year. And so, Heaven grant me patience!

What a pack of complaints! but, my dear, there
is nobody but you that I would think of making
them to! and it is a certain easing of nature to utter
them ; so forgive the mean details.

Love to the Doctor.

Your ever affectionate

JANE CARLYLE.

LETTER 261.

To Mrs. Austin, The Gill, Annan.

5 Cheyne Row, Chelsea : Nov. 1862.

Dearest Mary,—The box of eggs came yesterday,
Another perfect success ; not a single egg broken or
cracked !   The barrel arrived to-day ; and Mr. C.
has already eaten a quarter of one of the fowls, and
found less fault with his dinner than he is in the
habit of doing now.   In fact, I look forward to his
dinner-time with a sort of panic, which the event for
most part justifies.   How I wish this long, weary
book were done, for his own sake and for everybody's near him.   It is like living in a madhouse on
the days when he gets ill on with his writing.

I have a new woman coming as cook next
Tuesday, and intense as has been Mr. C.'s abhorrence
of the present ' mooncalf,' ' cow,' ' brute-beast,' I look
forward with trepidation to having to teach the new-
comer all Mr. C.'s things, which every woman who
comes has to be taught, whether she can cook in a

general way or not. If the kitchen were only on the same floor with the room! but I have to go down three pairs of stairs to it, past a garden-door kept constantly open in all weathers; and at this season of the year, with my dreadful tendency to catch interminable colds, running up and down these stairs teaching bread-making, and Mr. C.'s sort of soup, and Mr. C.'s sort of puddings, cutlets, &c., &c., is no joke. My one constant terror is lest I should fall ill and be unable to go down to the kitchen at all. I dream about that at nights. Really

> If I were dead,
> And a stone at my head,
> I think I should be *be*-tter.[1]

There is the anxiety about dear Lord Ashburton too; that has been going on now some five weeks; sometimes relieved a little, then again worse than ever. I have a note in my pocket at this moment which Mr. C. does not know of, leaving scarce a hope of his recovery. As it was not from the doctor, but from Lady A.'s niece, who expresses herself very confusedly, and might have made the case worse than it is, I decided not to unsettle Mr. C. at his writing with a sight of it; and it has felt burning in my pocket all day; and every knock at the door

---

[1] Old beggar's rhyme on entering:

> ' I'm a poor helpless craiture,
> If I were &c. . . . . better (baiture!) '

makes my heart jump into my throat, for it may be news of his death.

As this letter won't reach you any sooner for being posted to-night, I will keep it open till to-morrow in case of another from Paris. And if I have more to say I had better keep that till to-morrow too. I write with such a weight on my spirits to-night.

But always

Most affectionately yours,

JANE CARLYLE.

A note has just come from Lady Ashburton's sister in London, forwarding a telegram just received: 'My Lord has passed a better night. Dr. Quain thinks him no worse.' So there is still hope—for those who have a talent for hoping.

LETTER 262.

To Mrs. Russell.

5 Cheyne Row: December 15, 1862.

I should not be at all afraid that after a few weeks my new maid would do well enough if it weren't for Mr. C.'s frightful impatience with any new servant untrained to his ways, which would drive a woman out of the house with her hair on end if allowed to act directly upon her! So that I have to stand between them, and imitate in a small, humble way the Roman soldier who gathered his arms full of the enemy's spears, and received them all into his own breast.[1] It is this which makes a change of servants, even when for the better, a terror to me in prospect, and an agony in realisation—for a time.

LETTER 203.

Mrs. Braid, Edinburgh.

5 Cheyne Row, Chelsea : Christmas Day, 1862.

Dearest Betty,—Here we are, you and I, again at the end of a year. Still alive, you and I, and those belonging to us still alive, while so many younger, healthier, more life-like people, who began the year with us, have been struck down by death. Can we do better, after thanking God that we are still spared, than embrace one another across the four hundred miles that lie between, in the only fashion possible, that is on paper.

'Merry Christmases,' and 'Happy New Years,' are words that produce melancholy ideas rather than cheerful ones to people of our age and experience. So I don't wish you a 'mirth,' and a 'happiness,' which I know to have passed out of Christmas and New Year for such as us for evermore; passed out of them along with so much else; our gay spirits, our bright hopes, living hearts that loved us, and the fresh, trusting life of our own hearts. It is a

[1] Oh heavens, the comparison! it was too true.

thing too sad for tears, the thought how much is past and gone, even while there is much to be cared for. And that is all the dismals I am going to indulge in at this writing.

For the rest, we have been in great anxiety about Lord Ashburton. It is six weeks past on Monday that he has been hanging betwixt life and death, at an hotel in Paris, where he was taken ill of inflammation of the lungs, on his way to Nice ; and all the time I have been receiving a letter from Lady A.'s sister by her directions, or from their travelling physician, Dr. Christison (son of that Robert Christison, who used to visit at my uncle Benjamin's in your time), every day almost, sometimes two letters in one day ; such constant changes there have been in the aspect of his illness ! The morning letter would declare him ' past all human help,' and in the evening would come news of decided ' improvement,' so that we couldn't have been kept in greater suspense if we had been in the same house with him. The last three days there has been again talk of ' a faint hope,' ' a bare possibility of recovery.' And their London physician, who has been five times telegraphed for to Paris, called here to-day immediately on his return, directed by Lady A., to go and tell us of his new hopes. When I was told Dr. Quain was in the drawing-room, I went in to him with my heart in my mouth, persuaded he had been sent to break

the news of Lord A.'s death. My first words to him
(he had never been in the house before) were, ' Oh,
Dr. Quain, what has brought you here?'—a reception so extraordinary that he stood struck speechless,
which confirmed me in my idea, and I said, violently,
'Tell me at once! you are come to tell me he is
dead?' 'My dear lady, I am come to tell you no
such thing, but quite the contrary! I am come by
Lady Ashburton's desire to explain to you the changes
which again have raised us into hope that he may
recover.' Then, in the reaction of my fright, I began
to cry. What a fool that man must have thought
me! Poor Lady A., who is devotedly attached to
her husband, has nursed him day and night, till she
is so worn out that one could hardly recognise her
(her sister writes). Next to her and their child, it is
to us, I believe, that he would be the greatest loss.
He is the only intimate friend that my husband has
left in the world—his dearest, most intimate friend
through twenty years now.

I told you in my last—did I not?—that I had got
a little girl of fifteen in place of my fine-lady housemaid; and that the East Lothian woman, instead of
coming out in a better light when left to her own
inspirations, was driving Mr. C. out of his senses with
her blockheadisms and carelessness; and that, much
as I disliked changes in the dead of winter, there was
no help for it, but to send that woman back to a part

of God's earth where she had been ' well thought of'
(Jackie Welsh had said), and where she 'could get
plenty of good places' (the Goose herself said).   A
sorry account of the style of service now going in
East Lothian, I can only say.

I hope I shall be more comfortable now—for a
while, at least.   The little girl is extremely intelligent,
and active, and willing; is a great favourite with her
master, thank Heaven! and has never required a
cross word from me during the six weeks or so that
she has been in the house.   The other is a girl of
twenty-four, with an excellent three years' character,
whom I confess I chose out of some dozen that offered,
more by character than outward appearance; she is
only on a month's trial as yet.   I rather hope she will
do; but it is too soon to make up my mind in the
four days she has been with me.

I inclose a post-office order for a sovereign to
buy what you need most, and wear it for the sake of
your loving

JANE W. CARLYLE.

Best regards to your husband and dear George.

LETTER 264.

Dr. Russell, Holm Hill.

5 Cheyne Row, Chelsea: Jan. 6, 1863.

My dear Dr. Russell,—At last I send you the
promised photograph.   It goes along with this note.

You were meant to have it on New Year's Day; but I needed to go out for the sheet of millboard, and then to cut it to the proper size; and all that, strange to say, took more time than I had at my disposal. You wonder, perhaps, what a woman like me has to take up her time with. Here, for example, is one full day's work, not to say two. On the New Year's morning itself, Mr. C. 'got up off his wrong side,' a by no means uncommon way of getting up for him in these overworked times! And he suddenly discovered that his salvation, here and hereafter, depended on having, 'immediately, without a moment's delay,' a beggarly pair of old cloth boots, that the street-sweeper would hardly have thanked him for, 'lined with flannel, and new bound, and repaired generally!' and 'one of my women'—that is, my one woman and a half—was to be set upon the job! Alas! a regular shoemaker would have taken a whole day to it, and wouldn't have undertaken such a piece of work besides! and Mr. C. scouted the idea of employing a shoemaker, as subversive of his authority as master of the house. So, neither my one woman, nor my half one, having any more capability of repairing 'generally' these boots than of repairing the Great Eastern, there was no help for me but to sit down on the New Year's morning, with a great ugly beast of a man's boot in my lap, and scheme, and stitch, and worry over it till night;

and next morning begin on the other! There, you
see, were my two days eaten up very completely, and
unexpectedly ; and so it goes on, ' always a something ' (as my dear mother used to say).

The accounts from Paris continue more favourable. But they sound hollow to me somehow.

Love to Mary.

Your ever affectionate

JANE CARLYLE.

LETTER 265.

The following letter has been forwarded to me by a
gentleman who modestly desires that his name may not be
mentioned.—J. A. F.

To J. T.

5 Cheyne Row, Chelsea: Feb. 11, 1863.

I wish, dear sir, you could have seen how your
letter brightened up the breakfast-time for my husband
and me yesterday morning, scattering the misan-
thropy we are both given to at the beginning of the
day, like other nervous people who have ' bad nights.'
I wish you could have heard our lyrical recognition
of your letter—its ' beautiful modesty,' its ' gentleness,' and ' genuineness ; ' above all I wish you could
have heard the tone of real feeling in which my
husband said, at last, ' I do think, my dear, that is
the very nicest little bit of good cheer that has come

our way for seven years!' It might have been thought Mr. C. was quite unused to expressions of appreciation from strangers, instead of (as is the fact) receiving such almost every day in the year—except Sundays, when there is no post. But, oh, the difference between that gracious, graceful little act of faith of yours, and the. intrusive, impertinent, presumptuous letters my husband is continually receiving, demanding, in return for so much 'admiration,' an autograph perhaps! or to read and give an opinion on some long, cramped MS. of the writer's; or to—find a publisher for it even! or to read some idiotic new book of the writer's [that is a very common form of letter from lady admirers]—say a translation from the German (!) and 'write a review of it in one of the quarterlies!' 'It would be a favour never to be forgotten!' I should think so indeed.

Were I to show you the 'tributes of admiration' to Mr. C.'s genius, received through the post during one month, you, who have consideration for the time of a man struggling, as for life, with a gigantic task —you, who, as my husband says, are 'beautifully modest,' would feel your hair rise on end at such assaults on a man under pretence of admiring him; and would be enabled perhaps, better than I can express it in words, to imagine the pleasure it must have been to us when an approving reader of my husband's books came softly in, and wrapped his wife in a warm, beautiful shawl, saying simply—'There! I don't want to interrupt you, but I want to show you my good-will; and that is how I show it.'

We are both equally gratified, and thank you heartily. When the shawl came, as it did at night, Mr. C. himself wrapped it about me, and walked round me admiring it. And what think you he said? He said, 'I am very glad of that for you, my dear. I think it is the only bit of real good my celebrity ever brought you!'

Yours truly,
JANE W. CARLYLE.

The letter which called out so many praises was this:—

'Mrs. Thomas Carlyle. Madam,—Unwilling to interrupt your husband in his stern task, I take the liberty of addressing you, and hope you will accept from me a woollen long shawl, which I have sent by the Parcel Delivery Co., carriage paid, to your address. If it does not reach you, please let me know, and I shall make inquiries here, so that it be traced and delivered. I hope the pattern will please you, and also that it may be of use to you in a cold day.

'I will also name to you my reason for sending you such a thing. My obligations to your husband are many and unnameably great, and I just wish to acknowledge them. All men will come to acknowledge this, when your husband's power and purpose shall become visible to them.

'If high respect, love, and good wishes could comfort him and you, none living command more or deserve more.

'You can take a fit moment to communicate to your

husband my humble admiration of his goodness, attainments,
and great gifts to the world; which I wish much he may be
spared to see the world begin to appreciate.

'I remain, &c.,

'J. T.'

LETTER 266.

To Mrs. Austin, The Gill, Annan.

5 Cheyne Row: Thursday, Feb. 26, 1863.

I promised you a voluntary letter, Mary dear;
and after all the waiting you are going to get a
begging letter, which is nothing like so pleasant for
either the writer or the receiver. But those London
hens! they are creatures without rule or reason. I
had just made an arrangement with a grocer, who
keeps a lot of them, to let me have at least seven
new-laid eggs a week; and the very day the bargain
was concluded the creatures all struck work again,
'except one bantam!' So we are eating away at
yours, without any hope of reinforcement from this
neighbourhood. Jane, in a letter to Mr. C., kindly
offered to send a second supply from Dumfries! but,
as she does not lay them 'within herself' (as an old
lady at Haddington used to say), it seems more
natural that I should apply to you who do! We
have still enough to last about a week. There! I
have done my begging at the beginning of my letter,
instead of reserving it for a postscript, the common

dodge, which deceives nobody. And now my mind is free to tell any news I may have.

You would hear of my incomparable small housemaid having turned out an incomparable small demon. People say these wonderfully clever servants, whether old or young, are always to be suspected. Perhaps ; still a little cleverness is much nicer than stupidity to start with. Anyhow I don't need to live in vague apprehensions about either of my present servants on the ground of cleverness.

But I am well enough content with them as servants go. I have arranged things on a new footing, which I am in hopes ('hope springing eternal in the human mind') may work better than the old one ; I have made the cook, who came in place of the Scotch one, a general or upper servant ; she does all the work upstairs, the valeting, &c., besides the cooking ; and the new girl is a sort of kitchenmaid under her. On this plan there cannot be the same room for jealousies and squabbles for power, which have tormented me ever since I kept two.

I had a visit the other day which turned me upside down with the surprise of it ! I was putting on my bonnet to go out early in the day, when Mary came to say there was ' a lady at the door, who would like if I would see her for a few minutes.' The hour being unusual for making calls, and the message being over-modest for a caller, I thought it

might be some ' good lady ' with a petition, a sort of
people I cannot abide, so I asked : ' Is she a lady, do
you think ? ' ' Well—no, ma'm—I think hardly ; '
said Mary. ' She wouldn't give her name ; but she
said she came from fishshire, or something like
that ! ' ' Fishshire ?—could it be Dumfriesshire ? ' I
said with a veritable inspiration of genius. ' Show
her up,' and I heard a heavy body passed into the
drawing-room. I hastened in and saw, standing in
the middle of the floor, a figure like a haystack,
with the reddest of large fat faces, the eyes of which
were straining towards the door. The woman was
dressed in decent country clothes and bore no
resemblance to any ' lady ' ' in the created world,'
but looked well-to-do. I stared ; I didn't know the
woman from Adam (as the people here say) !

But she spoke—' Eh ! ! ' she said ; ' Lord keep me !
Is that you ? '—and there was something strangely
familiar in the voice. I stared again and said—
' Nancy ? '—' Atweel and it's just Nancy,' answered
the haystack ! and then followed such shaking of
hands, as if we had been the dearest friends. Do
you know who it was ? Not the little Nancy we used
to call ' piggy ' at Craigenputtock, but the great
coarse Nancy with the beard. She who said she
' never kenned folk mak sic a wark aboot a bit lee
as we did ! ' She left Craigenputtock to marry an
old drunken butcher at Thornhill, who, happily for

her, died in a few years, and then (as she phrased it) she ' had another chance,' and she just took it, as she ' thocht it might be her last,' that is, she married again a very respectable man of her own age, who is something in the Duke's mines at Sanquhar. She bore him one son, who is well educated, and clerk in the Sanquhar bank. He had been at Holm Hill on some bank business just before I was there last year, and Mrs. Russell had him to tea, and said he was a ' nice gentlemanly lad.' Well done, Nancy, beard and all the rest of it! Her man had been married before, as well as herself, and had a son, who is a haberdasher ' on his own account ' in this neighbourhood, and he had married, and his wife was being confined ; and Nancy had been sent for up to ' take care of her.' She met one of the Miss W——s on the road before leaving home, and made her ' put down my address on a bit of paper ; ' and so there she was—the first day she crossed the threshold after being in London five weeks! I was really glad to see the creature! she looked so glad to see me; except for the shock my personal appearance manifestly was to her! I gave her wine and cake, and a little present, and she went away in a transport.

I slept away from home last night. I had gone to a place called Ealing, some seven miles out of London, to visit Mrs. Oliphant—she who wrote the ' Life of Edward Irving '—and it was too far to come back at night; indeed I never go out after sunset at this season. She is a dear little homely woman, who speaks the broadest East Lothian Scotch, though she has lived in England since she was ten years old! and never was in East Lothian in her life, except passing through it in a railway carriage!!! But her mother was an East Lothian woman. I wish to heaven I had any place out of London, near hand, that I could go to when I liked; I am always so much the better for a little change. Life is too monotonous, and too dreary in the valley of the shadow of Frederick the Great! I wonder how we shall live, what we shall do, where we shall go, when that terrible task is ended.

Kindest regards to Jamie and the bonnie lassies.

Your affectionate
JANE WELSH CARLYLE.

LETTER 267.

To Miss Grace Welsh, Edinburgh.

5 Cheyne Row, Chelsea: Monday, March 2, 1863.

My dear Grace,—You say you have sent me 'them,' and you have only sent me *it*; and you say 'the head' is thought a good likeness, and I have got only a standing figure. Was it an involuntary omission on your part, or did you fall away from your good intention to send 'them'? Revise it if you did, for I want very much to see the likeness of the young man which is considered the best. I should like much to see the young man himself; for me as for you, a certain melancholy interest attaches to the last of so large and so brave a family.[1] Don't wait till you have time and heart to write me another nice long letter; but put ' the head ' in an envelope, and send it at once.

Mr. C. was again laid hold of by Mr. A—— the other day, in the King's Road, and escorted by him all the way to Regent Street. 'Really a good, innocent-hearted man! very vulgar, but he can't help that, poor fellow!' I have never once met him in the street since I made up my mind to speak to him, and invite him to call for me, which Mr. C. hadn't the grace to do. I used never to walk out without meeting him; but this winter I have taken my walk early in the forenoon—when he is busy, I suppose; just once I saw him pass the butcher's door when I was giving him directions about a piece of beef. He had a pretty young lady with him, on whom he was ' beaming ' benevolence and all sorts of things.

I was away a day and night last week at Ealing, visiting Mrs. Oliphant. Even that short ' change of air and scene ' did me good. On the strength I got by it I afterwards went to a dinner party at the

----

[1] Robert Welsh's second son: he too is dead; died shortly before her own departure out of vale of sorrow.

Rectory, and am to dine out again to meet Dickens, and nobody else. The people send their carriage for me, and send me home ; so in this mild weather the enterprise looks safe enough.

Such a noise about that 'Royal marriage!' I wish it were over. People are so woefully like sheep—all running where they see others run, and doing what they see others do. Have you heard of that wonderful Bishop Colenso? Such a talk about him too. And he isn't worth talking about for five minutes, except for the absurdity of a man making arithmetical onslaughts on the Pentateuch, with a bishop's little black silk apron on!

Dear love to you all.

Your affectionate

JEANNIE W. CARLYLE.

LETTER 208.

*Miss Grace Welsh, Craigenvilla, Morningside,
Edinburgh.*

5 Cheyne Row, Chelsea: March 17, 1863.

My dear Grace,—I am wanting to know if your pains keep off. I hardly dare to hope it in these trying east winds, which are the worst sort of weather for that sort of ailment. The last ten days have been horrid with us ; all the worse for coming after such a summery February. My own head has been in a very disorganised state indeed. The cold first came into my tongue, swelling it, and making it raw on one side, so that for days I had to live on slops, and restrict my speech to monosyllables; then it got into my jaws and every tooth in my mouth; and that is the present state of me. I am writing with my pocket-handkerchief tied over my lower face, and my imagination much overclouded by weary gnawing pain there. Decidedly a case for trying your remedy, and I mean to; have been thinking of realising some chlorodyne all the week. But either it has been too cold for me to venture up to the druggist's in Sloane Square, or I have had to go somewhere else.

It is a comfort to reflect, anyhow, that I have not brought these aches on myself by rushing ' out for to see ' the new Princess, as the rest of the world did, or to see the illuminations. I had an order sent me from Paris for seats for myself and ' a friend ' in the balcony erected at Bath House—the best for seeing in the whole line of the procession. But, first, I have no taste for crowds; and, secondly, I felt it would be so sad, sitting there, when the host and hostess were away in such sickness and sorrow; and, thirdly, I was somewhat of Mr. C.'s opinion: That this marriage, the whole nation was running mad after, was really less interesting to every individual of them than setting a hen of one's own on a nest of sound eggs would be!

The only interest I take in the little new Princess is founded on her previous poverty and previous humble, homely life. I have heard some touching things about that from people connected with the Court. When she was on her visit to the Queen after her engagement, she always wore a jacket. The Queen said, ' I think you always wear a jacket; how is that?' ' Oh,' said little Alexandra, ' I wear it because it is so economical. You can wear it with any sort of gown ; and you know I have always had to make my own gowns. I have never had a lady's-maid, and my sisters and I all made our own clothes ; I even made my bonnet.' Two or three days after the marriage she wrote to her mother : ' I am so happy ! I have just breakfasted with Bertie' (Albert, her husband); 'and I have on a white muslin dressing-gown, beautifully trimmed with pink ribbon.' Her parents were not so rich as most London shopkeepers ; had from seven hundred to a thousand a year. That interests me ; and I also feel a sympathy with her in the prospect of the bother she will have by-and-by.

You have never found the missing photograph ? I am so sorry about it. Please write, ever so little ; but I want to know if you keep free of pain. I am not up to a long letter. I am glad you are going to the Bridge of Allan. It will do Ann good for certain, and you probably ; and you will be able to judge of

Grace's[1] health with your own eyes, which are better than other people's reports.

I have seen nothing of Mrs. George[2] lately, though, of course, she would be in at the show. Love to you all.

Your affectionate
JANE W. CARLYLE.

LETTER 269.

Mrs. Russell, Holm Hill.

5 Cheyne Row, Chelsea: Friday, March 21, 1863.

Yes, my dear, the Doctor was right; the cold in my mouth was symptomatic of nothing but just cold in the mouth! I was afraid myself, for some days, it might turn to a regular influenza; the only time I ever had the same sort of thing as bad before being in the course of that dangerous influenza I had a good many years ago, when I had first to call in Mr. Barnes. But I have got off with the ten days of sore tongue and faceache, which is almost cured by the west wind we have had for the last two days.

My aunt Grace has ' suffered martyrs ' (as a French friend of mind used to express it) from faceache, and pains of the head, during this last winter; and cured herself (she believes) in a day by the new pet medicine chlorodyne. She was in an agony that could no longer be borne, and invested half-a-crown in a

---

[1] One of Robert Welsh's daughters who also died.
[2] Welsh (of Richmond).

small bottle of chlorodyne; and took ten drops every two hours, till she had taken as many as fifty; and then fell into a refreshing sleep, and (when she wrote) had had no return of the pain for three weeks. I haven't much faith in medicines that work as by miracle; and am inclined to believe that her pain, having reached its height, had been ready to subside of itself when the chlorodyne was taken. Still, as there might be some temporary relief, more or less, in the thing, I, too, invested in a small phial, and took ten drops when I was going to bed one night; and the only effect traceable in my case was a very dry dirty mouth next morning. To the best of my taste, it was composed of chloroform, strong peppermint, and some other carminatives. Has the Doctor used it? The apothecary here told me it was not sold much by itself, but that a great deal was used in the doctors' prescriptions.

Did I tell you that Mr. C.'s horse came down with him one day, and cut its knees to the bone, and had been sold for nine pounds! It cost fifty, and was cheap at that. My aunt Grace writes, that 'Mrs. Fergusson is still praying diligently for Mr. C., and that perhaps it was due to her prayers that Mr. C. was not hurt on that occasion!!'

Your ever affectionate

J. W. CARLYLE.

LETTER 270.

Mrs. Braid, Green End, Edinburgh.

5 Cheyne Row, Chelsea : May 22, 1863.

My own Betty,—I am wearying for some news of you. I never could lay that proverb ' No news is good news ' sufficiently to heart. Whenever I am feeling poorly myself (and I should be almost ashamed to say how often that is the case), I fall to fancying that you are perhaps ill, and nobody to tell me of it, and I so far away! It is so stupid of Ann and Grace, who take so much fatigue on themselves, in visiting about in their ' district,' and attending all sorts of meetings, that they don't take a walk out of their district now and then to see how you are going on, and tell me when they write. Some news of Betty would make a letter from them infinitely more gratifying than anything they can say about Dr. Candlish, and this and the other preacher and pray-er ; and would certainly inspire me with more Christian feelings. But, once for all, it is their way, and there is no help for it.

When I came in from a drive one day lately, I was told ' a person ' was waiting for me ; and, on opening the dining-room door, where the ' person ' had been put to wait, I saw, sitting facing me, Helen D——, the Sunny Bank housemaid. It was such a surprise ! I never liked Helen so well as Marion, the cook ; but

anyone from dear old Sunny Bank was a welcome
sight to me now. She has been for some years in
charge of some children at a clergyman's in Hampshire, and was passing through London with the
children and their father, who was returned from
India, on their way to an aunt's near Peebles. She
would go on to Haddington, she said, 'just to look
in on them all, but she wouldn't like to stay there
now—oh, no!' She was grown very stout and con-
sequential. I took her into my bedroom to show her
my picture of Sunny Bank, which hangs there, and
another of the Nungate Bridge; and, while looking
about, she suddenly exclaimed, 'I declare there is
Mrs. Braid!' You, too, are framed in a gilt frame,
and hung on the wall. The likeness must be very
good that she knew you at once, for she had only
seen you twice, she said, 'when you came to breakfast.' Her fine talk will astonish the Haddington
people when she 'looks in upon them.' She spoke
very respectfully of Miss Donaldson; 'Miss Jess,' she
said, 'hadn't the same balance of mind that Miss
Donaldson had!' But she was no favourite with
Miss Jess, and knew it.

Poor Jackie Welsh has lost her aunt, who had
been more than a mother to her all her life; and she
seems quite crushed to the earth with her grief. No
wonder; she is so much in need of some one to
sympathise with her and nurse her in her frequent

illnesses; and that one aunt was the only person on earth that she felt to belong to, and that belonged to her. Her mother is still alive; but her mother has never done anything for her but what she had better have left alone—brought her into being! And now she (the mother) is past being any good to anybody —quite frail and stupefied.

Oh, Betty! do you remember the little green thing that I left in your care once while I was over in Fife? And when I returned you had transplanted it into a yellow glass, which I have on my toilet-table to this hour, keeping my rings, &c., in it. Well! I must surely have told you long ago that the little thing, with two tiny leaves, from my father's grave, had, after twelve months in the garden at Chelsea, declared itself a gooseberry-bush! It has gone on flourishing, in spite of want of air and of soil, and is now the prettiest round bush, quite full of leaves.[1] I had several times asked our old gardener if there was nothing one could do to get the bush to bear, if it were only one gooseberry; but he treated the case as hopeless. 'A poor wild thing. No; if you want to have gooseberries, ma'am, better get a proper gooseberry-bush in its place.' The old Goth! He can't be made to understand that things can have any value but just their garden value. He once, in

---

[1] It still stands thêre, green and leafy, and with berries; how strange and memorable to me now!

spite of all I could beg and direct, rooted out a nettle I had brought from Crawford Churchyard, and with infinite pains got to take root and flourish. But, I was going to tell you, one day Lizzy, my youngest maid, came running in from the garden to ask me had I seen the three little gooseberries on the goose-berry-bush? I rushed out, as excited as a child, to look at them. And there they were—three little gooseberries, sure enough! And immediately I had settled it in my mind to send you one of them in a letter when full grown. But, alas! whether it was through too much staring at them, or too much east wind, or through mere delicacy in 'the poor wild thing,' I can't tell; only the result, that the three bits of gooseberries, instead of growing larger, grew every day less, till they reached the smallness of pin-heads, and then dropped on the ground! I could have cried when the last one went.

You remember my little Charlotte? I had a visit from her yesterday; and she looks much more sedate and proper than when I had to put her away. She is ' third housemaid at the Marquis of Camden's,' and lives in the country, which is good for her. She sent her compliments to ' Betty.'

My present pair of girls go on very peaceably. They are neither of them particularly bright; but they are attentive, and willing, and well behaved. I often look back with a shudder over the six months of that East Lothian Elizabeth! Her dinners blackened to cinders! her constant crashes of glass and china! her brutal manners! her lumpish insensibility and ingratitude! And to think that that woman must have been considered above the average of East Lothian servants, or Jackie Welsh wouldn't have sent her to me. What an idea it gives one of the state of things in East Lothian!

And now good-bye, Betty, dear. There is a long letter for you; which will, I hope, soon draw me a few lines from you in return. I am anxious to know how yourself, and your husband, and George have stood these cold spring weeks. My kind regards to them.

Your ever affectionate
JANE WELSH CARLYLE.

LETTER 271.

Mrs. Russell, Holm Hill.

5 Cheyne Row, Chelsea: June 3, 1863.

I had something to tell you which did not find room in my last letter. The name of Mrs. Oliphant's publisher is Blackett; and he has a smart wife, who came with him to dinner at Mrs. Oliphant's when I was there. They were very (what we call in Scotland) 'up-making' to me, and pressed me to visit them at Ealing, which I hadn't the least thought of doing. Well, some weeks ago, Mr. C. was just come in from his ride, very tired, and, to do him justice, very ill-humoured, when Mary put her head in at the drawing-room door and said, ' Mrs. Blackett wished to know if she could see me for a few minutes?' I went out hurriedly, knowing Mr. C.'s temper wouldn't be improved by hearing of people he didn't want coming after me. I told Mary to take the lady into the dining-room (where was no fire), and before going down myself put a shawl about me, chiefly to show her she mustn't stay. On entering the room, the lady's back was to me ; and she was standing looking out into the (so-called) garden ; but I saw at once it wasn't the Mrs. Blackett I had seen. This one was very tall, dressed in deep black, and when she turned round, she showed me a pale beautiful face, that was perfectly strange to me! But I was no stranger to her seemingly, for she glided swiftly up to me like a dream, and took my head softly between her hands and kissed my brow again and again, saying in a low dreamlike voice, ' Oh, you dear! you dear! you dear! Don't you know me?' I looked into her eyes in supreme bewilderment. At last light dawned on me, and I said one word—'Bessy?' 'Yes, it is Bessy!' And then the kissing wasn't all on one side, you may fancy. It was at last Bessy—not Mrs. Blackett, but Mrs. B——, —who stood there, having left her husband in a cab at the door, till she had seen me first. They were just arrived from Cheshire,

where they had gone to see one of his sons, who
had been dangerously ill, and were to start by the
next train for St. Leonards. They had only a quarter
of an hour to stay. He is a good, intelligent-looking
man ; and while he was talking all the time with
Mr. C., Bessy said beautiful things about him to me,
enough to show that if he wasn't her first love, he
was at least a very superior being in her estimation.
They pressed me to come to them at St. Leonards,
and I promised indefinitely that I would.

About a fortnight ago, Bessy walked in one
morning after breakfast. She 'had had no peace
for thinking about me; I looked so ill, she was sure
I had some disease! Had I?' I told her 'None that
I could specify, except the disease of old age, general
weakness, and discomfort.' Reassured on that head,
she confided to me that 'I looked just as Mrs. B——
had looked when she was dying of cancer!!'
And she had come up, certain that I had a cancer,
to try and get me away to be nursed by her, and
attended by her husband. Besides she had heard
there was so much small-pox in London ; 'and if I
took it, and died before she had seen me again, she
thought she would never have an hour's happiness
in the world again!' Oh, Bessy, Bessy! just the
same old woman—an imagination morbid almost to
insanity! 'Would I go back with her that night
anyhow?' 'Impossible!' 'Then when would I come?

and she would come up again to fetch me !' That I would not hear of; but I engaged to go so soon as it was a little warmer. And to-day I have written that I will come for two or three days on Monday next. She is wearing mourning for the mother and eldest brother of her husband, who have both died since her marriage.

And now I mustn't begin another sheet.

Your ever affectionate
J. W. CARLYLE.

LETTER 272.

To Mrs. Austin, The Gill, Annan.

5 Cheyne Row, Chelsea: Sunday, July 5, 1863.

My dear little woman,—Every day, since I got your letter, I have put off answering it till the morrow, in hope always that the morrow would find me more up to writing an answer both long and pleasant. But, alas! I had best not wait any longer for ' a more convenient season,' but just write a stupid little note, according to my present disability; as a time when my head will be clearer, and my heart lighter, and my stomach less sick, is not to be calculated on.

I went some three weeks ago to St. Leonards, the pleasantest place I know ; and stayed from Monday to Saturday, in circumstances the most favourable to health that could be desired. The finest sea air in the world—a large, airy, quiet house close on the shore; a carriage to drive out in twice a day; a clever physician for host, who dieted me on champagne and the most nourishing delicacies; and for hostess, a gentle, graceful, loving woman, who, besides being full of interest for me as a heroine of romance, has the more personal interest for me of having been my—servant, about thirty years ago; and of having been sincerely mourned by me as—dead!

Well, I returned from that visit quite set up; and the improvement lasted some two or three days. Then I turned as sick as a dog one evening, and had to take to bed; and the sickness not abating after two days, during which time, to Mr. C.'s great dismay, I could eat nothing at all (nothing in the shape of illness ever alarms Mr. C. but that of not eating one's regular meals), Mr. Barnes was sent for, who ordered mustard blisters to my stomach, and unlimited soda-water 'with a little brandy in it.' In about a week I was on foot again—but weak as a dishclout! And that is my condition to the present hour. I don't see much chance of bettering it here —and Mr. C. seems determined to stick to his 'work' all this summer and autumn, as he did the last. It is very bad for him, and very bad for the work. He would get on twice as fast if he would give himself a holiday. But there is no persuading him, as you know; 'vara obstinate in his own wae!'[1] And as

---

[1] Cumberland man's account of the Scotch.

I was away last autumn a whole month by myself, I cannot have the face to leave him again this year, unless for a few days at a time, when I am hardly missed till I am back again. Besides, the present servants are not adapted to being left to their own devices. They do very well with overlooking and direction ; and the week I was at St. Leonards nothing went wrong ; but, for that long, they could have their orders for every day; and as I did not tell them for certain what day I should be back, there was a constant wholesome expectation of my return.

Mr. Carlyle has got his tent up in the back area, and writes away there without much inconvenience, as yet, from the heat. He has changed his dinner hour to half-past three instead of seven ; then he sleeps for an hour, and then goes for his ride in the cool of the evening.

The horse Lady Ashburton sent him is a pretty, swift little creature, and very sure-footed, which is the first quality for a horse whose rider always goes at a gallop. But Mr. C. draws many plaintive comparisons between this horse and poor old Fritz, as to moral qualities. This one ' shows no desire to please him whatever ; only goes at its best pace when its head is turned towards its own stable ! Fritz was always endeavouring to ascertain his wishes and to gain his approbation ; it was a horse of very superior sense and sensibility, and had a profound regard for him.'

Kindest love to you all.

Your ever affectionate

JANE CARLYLE.

LETTER 273.

Mrs. Russell, Holm Hill.

5 Cheyne Row, Chelsea: Wednesday night, Sept. 16, 1863.

How absurd of you, my dearest Mary, to make so many apologies about a trifling request like that! Why, if you had asked for twenty autographs, Mr. C. would have written them in twenty minutes, and would have written them for you with pleasure. Certainly, my dear, as I have often said before, faith is not your strong point!

Well, we have done our 'outing,' as the people here call going into the country; and it is all the 'outing we are likely to do till next summer (if we live to see next summer), unless Lord Ashburton should be well enough, and myself well enough, to make another expedition to the Grange during the winter.

I had some idea of going to Folkestone, where Miss Davenport Bromley has a house at present, and pressed me to come and take some tepid sea-water baths. But my experience of the wretchedness of being from home, with this devilry in my arm, has decided me to remain stationary for the present. In spite of the fine air and beauty of the Grange, and Lady Ashburton's superhuman kindness, I had no enjoyment of anything all the three weeks we stayed: being in constant pain, day and night, and not able to comb my own hair, or do anything in which a left arm is needed as well as a right one! I think I told you I had had pain more or less in my left arm for two months before I left London. It was trifling in the beginning; indeed, nothing to speak of, when I did not move it backwards or upwards. I did not think it worth sending for Mr. Barnes about it at first, and latterly he was away at the sea-side for some weeks, having been ill himself. There was nobody else I liked to consult; besides, I always flatter myself that anything that ails me more than usual is sure to be removed by change of scene, so I bore on, in hope that so soon as I got to the Grange the arm would come all right. It did quite the reverse, however; for it became worse and worse, and I was driven at last to consult Dr. Quain, when he came down to see Lord A. He told me, before I had spoken a dozen words, that it wasn't rheumatism I had got, but neuralgia (if any good Christian would explain to me the difference between these two things I should feel edified and grateful). It had been produced, he said, by extreme weakness, and that I must be stronger before any impression could be

made on it.   Could I take quinine?   I didn't know;
I would try; so he sent me quinine pills from London,
to be taken twice a day if they gave me no headache,
which they don't do, and an embrocation of opium,
aconite, camphor, and chloroform (I tell you all this
that you may ask your Doctor if he thinks it right, or
can suggest anything else); moreover, I was to take
castor oil every two or three days.   I have been following these directions for a fortnight, and there is
certainly an improvement in my general health.   I
feel less cowardly and less fanciful, and feel less disgust at human food; but although the embrocation
relieves the pain while I am applying it, and for a
few minutes after, it is as stiff and painful as ever
when left to itself.

Yours ever affectionately,
JANE CARLYLE.

Of all these dreary sufferings and miseries, which had been
steadily increasing for years past, I perceive now, with pain
and remorse, 1 had never had the least of a clear notion;
such her invincible spirit in bearing them, such her constant
effort to hide them from me altogether.   My own poor existence, as she also well knew, was laden to the utmost pitch
of strength, and sunk in perpetual muddy darkness, by a
task too heavy for me—task which seemed impossible, and as
if it would end me instead of I it.   I saw no company, had
no companion but my horse (fourteen miles a day, winter
time, mainly in the dark), rode in all, as I have sometimes
counted, above 30,000 miles for health's sake, while writing
that unutterable book.   The one bright point in my day—

was from half an hour to twenty minutes' talking with her, after my return from those thrice dismal rides, while I sat smoking (on the hearthrug, with my back to the jamb, puffing firewards—a rare invention !) and sipping a spoonful of brandy in water, preparatory to the hour of sleep I had before dinner. She, too, the dear and noble soul, seemed to feel that this was the eye of her day, the flower of all her daily endeavour in the world. I found her oftenest stretched on the sofa (close at my right hand, I between her and the fire), her drawing-room and self all in the gracefullest and most perfect order, and waiting with such a welcome; ah, me ! ah, me ! She was weak, weak, far weaker than I understood ; but to me was bright always as stars and diamonds ;— nay, I should say a kind of cheery sunshine in those otherwise Egyptian days. She had always something cheerful to tell me of (especially if she had been out, or had had visitors) ; generally something quite pretty to report (in her sprightly, quiet, and ever-genial way). At lowest, nothing of unpleasant was ever heard from her ; all that was gloomy she was silent upon, and had strictly hidden away. Once, I remember, years before this, while she suffered under one of her bad influenzas (little known to me how bad), I came in for three successive evenings, full of the ' Battle of Molwitz ' (which I had at last got to understand, much to my inward triumph), and talked to her all my half-hour about nothing else. She answered little ('speaking not good for me,' perhaps); but gave no sign of want of interest—nay, perhaps did not quite want it, and yet confessed to me, several years afterwards, her principal thought was, ' Alas, I shall never see this come to print ; I am hastening towards death instead ! ' These were, indeed, dark days for us both, and still darker unknown to us were at hand. One evening, probably the 1st or 2nd of October, 1863—but for long years I had ceased writing in my note-books, and find nothing marked on that to me most memorable of dates—on my return from riding, I learned rather with satisfaction for her sake that she had ventured on a drive to the General Post Office to see her cousin, Mrs. Godby, 'matron' of that establishment; and would take tea there. After sleep and dinner, I was still without her; 'Well, well, I thought, what a nice little story will she have to tell me soon!' and lay quietly down on the sofa, and comfortably waited—still comfortably, though the time (an hour or more) was longer than I had expected. At length came the welcome sound of her wheels; I started up—she rather lingered in appearing,—I rang, got no clear answer, rushed down, and, oh, what a sight awaited me! She was still in the cab, Larkin speaking to her (Larkin lived next door, and for him she had sent, carefully saving me!) Oh, Heavens! and, alas! both Larkin and I were needed. She had had a frightful street-accident in St. Martin's, and was now lamed and in agony! This was the account I got by degrees.

Mrs. Godby sent a maid-servant out with her to catch an omnibus; maid was stupid, unhelpful, and there happened to be some excavation on the street which did not permit the omnibus to come close. Just as my poor little darling was stepping from the kerbstone to run over (maid merely looking on), a furious cab rushed through the interval; she had to stop spasmodically, then still more spasmodically try to keep from falling flat on the other side, and ruining her poor neuralgic arm. In vain, this latter effort; she did fall, lame arm useless for help, and in the desperate effort she had torn the sinews of the thigh-bone, and was powerless to move or stand, and in pain unspeakable. Larkin and I lifted her into a chair, carried her with all our steadiness (for every shake was misery) up to her bed, where, in a few minutes, the good Barnes, luckily found at home, made appearance with what help there was. Three weeks later, this letter gives account in her own words.

The torment of those first three days was naturally horrible; but it was right bravely borne, and directly thereupon all things looked up, she herself, bright centre of them, throwing light into all things. It was wonderful to see how in a few days she seemed to be almost happy, contented with immunity from pain, and proud to have made (as she soon did) her little bedroom into a boudoir, all in her own likeness. She sent for the carpenter, directed him in everything, had cords and appliances put up for grasping with and getting good of her hand, the one useful limb now left. It was wonderful what she had made of that room, by carpenter and housemaid, in a few hours—all done in her own image, as I said. On a little table at her right hand, among books and other useful furniture, she gaily pointed out to me a dainty little bottle of champagne, from which, by some leaden article screwed through the cork, and needing only a touch, she could take a spoonful or teaspoonful at any time, without injuring the rest: 'Is not that pretty? Excellent champagne (Miss Bromley's kind gift), and does me good, I can tell you.' I remember this scene well, and that, in the love of gentle and assiduous friends, and their kind little interviews and ministrations, added to the hope she had, her sick room had comparatively an almost happy air, so elegant and beautiful it all was, and her own behaviour in it always was. Not many evenings after the last of these two letters, I was sitting solitary over my dreary Prussian books, as usual, in the drawing-room, perhaps about 10 P.M., room perhaps (without my knowledge) made trimmer than usual, when suddenly, without warning given, the double door from her bedroom went wide open, and my little darling, all radiant in graceful evening dress, followed by a maid with new lights, came gliding in to me, gently stooping, leaning on a fine Malacca cane, saying *silently* but so eloquently, 'Here am I come back to you, dear!' It was among the bright moments of my life—the picture of it—still vivid with me, and will always be. Till now I had not seen her in the drawing-room, had only heard of those tentative pilgrimings thither with her maid for support. But now I considered the victory as good as won, and everything fallen into its old course again or a better. Blind that we were! This was but a gleam of sunlight, and ended swiftly in a far blacker storm of miseries than ever before.

That 'bright evening' of her re-entrance to me in the drawing-room must have been about the end of October or beginning of November, shortly following these two letters, 'Monday evening, November 23' (as I laboriously make out the date); 'the F——s,' F—— and his wife, the pleasantest, indeed almost the only pleasant evening company we now used to have; intelligent, cheerful, kindly, courteous, sincere (they had come to live near us, and we hoped for a larger share of such evenings, of which probably this was the first? Alas, to me, too surely it was in effect the last!) Cheerful enough this evening was; my darling sat latterly on the sofa, talking chiefly to Mrs. F——; the F——s gone, she silently at once withdrew to her bed, saying nothing to me of the state she was in, which I found next morning to have been alarmingly miserable, the prophecy of one of the worst of nights, wholly without sleep and full of strange and horrible pain. And the nights and days that followed continued steadily to *worsen*, day after day, and month after month, no end visible. It was some ten months now before I saw her sit with me again in this drawing-room—in body weak as a child, but again composed into quiet, and in soul beautiful as ever, or more beautiful than ever, for the rest of her appointed time with me, which indeed was brief, but is now blessed to look back upon, and an unspeakable favour of Heaven. I often think of that last evening with the F——s, which we hoped to be the first of a marked increase of such, but which to me was essentially the last of all; the F——s have been here since, but with her as hostess (in my presence) never more, and the reflex of that bright evening, now all pale and sad, shines, privately incessant, into every meeting we have.

Barnes, for some time, said the disease was 'influenza, merely accidental cold, kindling up all the old injuries and maladies,' and promised speedy amendment; but week after week gave dismally contrary evidence. 'Neuralgia!' the doctors then all said, by which they mean they know not in the least what; in this case, such a deluge of intolerable pain, indescribable, unaidable pain, as I had never seen or dreamt of, and which drowned six or eight months of my poor darling's life as in the blackness of very death; her recovery at last, and the manner of it, an unexpected miracle to me. There seemed to be pain in every muscle, misery in every nerve, no sleep by night or day, no rest from struggle and desperate suffering. Nobody ever known to me could more nobly and silently endure pain; but here for the first time I saw her vanquished, driven hopeless, as it were looking into a wild chaotic universe of boundless woe— on the horizon, only death or worse. Oh, I have seen such expressions in those dear and beautiful eyes as exceeded all tragedy! (one night in particular, when she rushed desperately out to me, without speech; got laid and wrapped by me on the sofa, and gazed silently on all the old familiar objects and me). Her pain she would seldom speak of, but, when she did, it was in terms as if there were no language for it; 'any honest pain, mere pain, if it were of cutting my flesh with knives, or sawing my bones, I could hail that as a luxury in comparison!'

And the doctors, so far as I could privately judge, effected approximately to double the disease. We had many doctors, skilful men of their sort, and some of them (Dr. Quain, especially, who absolutely would accept no pay, and was unwearied in attendance and invention) were surely among the friendliest possible; but each of them—most of all each new one—was sure to effect only harm, tried some new form of his opiums and narcotic poisons without effect; on the whole I computed, 'Had there been no doctors, it had been only about half as miserable.' Honest Barnes admitted in the end, 'We have been able to do nothing.' We had sick-nurses, a varying miscellany, Catholic 'Sisters of Mercy' (ignominiously dismissed by her third or fourth night, the instant she found they were in real substance Papist propagandists. Oh, that '3 A.M.,' when her bell awoke me too, as well as Maggie Welsh, and the French nun had to disappear at once, under rugs on a sofa elsewhere, and vanish altogether when daylight came!) Maggie Welsh had come in the second week of December, and continued, I think, at St. Leonards latterly, till April ended. December was hardly out till there began to be speech among the doctors of sea-side and change of air: the one hope they continued more and more to say; and we also thinking of St. Leonards and our Dr. B—— and bountiful resources there, waited only for spring weather, and the possibility of flight thither. How, in all this tearing whirlpool of miseries, anxieties, and sorrows, I contrived to go on with my work is still an astonishment to me. For one thing, I did not believe in these doctors, nor that she (if let alone of them) had not yet strength left. Secondly, I always counted 'Frederick' itself to be the prime source of all her sorrows as well as my own; that to end it was the condition of new life to us both, of which there was a strange dull hope in me. Not above thrice can I recollect when, on stepping out in the morning, the thought struck me, cold and sharp, 'She will die, and leave thee here!' and always before next day I had got it cast out of me again. And, indeed, in all points except one I was as if stupefied more or less, and flying on like those migrative swallows of Professor Owen, after my strength was done and coma or dream had supervened, till the Mediterranean Sea was crossed! But the time altogether looks to me like a dim nightmare, on which it is still miserable to dwell, and of which I will after this endeavour only to give the dates.—T. C.

LETTER 274.

To Miss Grace Welsh, Edinburgh.

5 Cheyne Row, Chelsea: Tuesday, Oct. 20, 1863.

Thank you a thousand times, dearest Grace, for your long, most moving letter. It is not because of it that I write to-day, for I was meaning to write to-day at any rate; indeed, it rather makes writing more difficult to me: I have cried so over it, that I have given myself a bad headache in addition to my other lamings. But a little letter I will write by to-day's post, and a bigger one when I am more able.

I wrote a few lines to Mrs. Craven, in answer to her announcement of that dear girl's angel death. I told her of my accident, and was trusting to her telling you; but as I told her I had kept you in ignorance of it in the beginning, lest Elizabeth and you and Ann,[1] with your terrible experience of such

---

[1] Poor Elizabeth had slipped and fallen on the street; dislocated her thigh-bone; got it wrong set; then, after long months of misery, undergone a setting of it 'right'—but is lame to this day.

an accident, might be alarmed and distressed for me more than (I hoped) there would prove cause for ; she thought, perhaps, I wished you to remain unaware of it, even when I reported myself progressing more favourably than could have been predicted. I need not go into the *how* of the fall ; I will tell you all ' particulars ' when I gain more facility in writing ; enough to say that exactly this day three weeks I was plashed down on the pavement of St. Martin-le-Grand (five miles from home) on my left side (the arm of which couldn't break the fall), and hurt all down from the hip-joint so fearfully, and on the already lamed shoulder besides, that I couldn't stir ; but had to be lifted up by people who gathered round me (a policeman among them) and put into a cab. Elizabeth can fancy my drive home (five miles), and the getting of me out of the cab and upstairs to bed ! Wasn't I often thinking of her all the time ?

' My ' doctor came immediately, and found neither breakage of the leg nor dislocation ; but the agony of pain, he said, would have been less had the bone broken : I thought of Elizabeth, and doubted that ! Still, for three days and three sleepless nights it was such agony as I had never known before ; after that, the pain went gradually out of the leg, unless when I moved it, for some bed operations, &c., &c. But the arm, with its complication of sprain and neuralgia, has given me a sad time, till these last two days that it has returned almost to the state it was in before the fall. A week ago Mr. Barnes made me get out of bed for fear of ' a bad back,' and *sit on end* on a sofa in my bedroom, like Miss Biffin (the little egg-shaped woman that used to be shown); and two days ago he compelled me to walk a few steps, supported with his arms, and to do the same thing at least twice a day. It has been a case of ' lacerated sinews ; ' and he said the tendency of the muscles was to contract themselves after such a thing, and if I did not force myself to put down my foot now and then, I should never be able to walk at all ! Such a threat, and his determined manner, enable me to make the effort, which *costs*, I can tell you. But, at whatever cost of pain and nervousness, I have to-day passed through the door of my bed-room (which opens into the drawing-room luckily), using one of the maids as a crutch ; so you see I am already a good way towards recovery, for which I feel, every moment, deep thankfulness to God. To have experienced such agony, and to be delivered from it comparatively, makes one feel one's depend-ence as nothing else does.

For the rest, as dear Betty is always saying, ' I have mony mercies.' My servants have been most kind and unwearied in their attentions ; my friends more like sisters or mothers than commonplace friends. Oh, I shall have such wonderful kindnesses to tell you of when I can write freely! My third cousin, Mrs. Godby, and several others, wished to stay with me; but the 'nursing' I needed was of quite a menial sort; I should still have sought it from my servants, and a lady-nurse would only have given them more to do, and been dreadfully in the way of Mr. C. My great object, after getting what waiting on I absolutely needed, has been that the usual quiet routine of the house should not be disturbed around Mr. C., who thinks, I am sure, that he has been victimised enough in having to answer occasional letters of inquiry about me. And now I must conclude for the present. I am so sorry for poor Robert's fingers. Be sure to send me the copy of Grace's [1] words to her mother. Oh, poor souls! what woe, and what mercy!

Your loving niece,
JANE W. CARLYLE.

LETTER 275.

Mrs. Russell, Holm Hill, Thornhill.

5 Cheyne Row, Chelsea: Monday, Oct. 26, 1863.

Dearest Mary,—Though I still write to you in pencil I have progressed. I walk daily from my bedroom to the drawing-room, after a fashion; my sound arm round Mary's neck, and her arm round my waist.

---

[1] The poor niece's.

I think there is more nervousness than pain in the difficulty with which I make this little journey. For the rest, I don't lie much on my sofa, but sit on end. I cannot, however, sit up at table to write with pen and ink; I must write with cushions at my back, and with the paper on my knees; in which circumstances a pencil is less fatiguing than pen and ink, as well as less destructive to my clothes.

The unlucky leg will in a week or two, I hope, be all right. I have no pain whatever in it now, except when I try to use it; and then the pain is not great, and gets daily a trifle less. But my arm is still a bad business; especially at night I suffer much from it. It spoils my sleep, and that again reacts upon it and makes it worse. I cannot satisfy myself how much of the pain I am now suffering is the effect of the fall—how much that of the old neuralgia; and Mr. Barnes can throw no light on that for me, or suggest any remedy: at least he doesn't. It seems to me he regards my leg as his patient, and my arm as Dr. Quain's patient, which he has nothing to do with; and he is rather glad to be irresponsible for it, seeing nothing to be done! He did once say in a careless way that plain bark and soda, 'one of the most nauseous mixtures he knew of in this world,' was better than ' my quinine;' but when I asked, 'would it have as good an effect on my spirits as the quinine had had, he said, ' Oh, I can't promise you that; it would probably make you sick and low; better keep to your ladylike quinine!'

Ask the Doctor if he sees any superiority in plain bark and soda? I don't care how nauseous a medicine is if it do me good.

Another of my uncle Robert's daughters has died of consumption. Grace (my aunt) has written me a long, minute account of her death-bed—one of the saddest things I ever read in my life. It quite crushed down the heart in one for days. The poor young woman's sufferings, and the deaf mother's, and, oh, such a heap of misery is set before one so vividly; and then the consolation! It is a comfort to know that the dying girl was supported through her terrible trial by her religious faith and hope; a comfort, and the only comfort possible, conceivable—if it had stopped there. But you know my feelings about religious excitement—ecstatics; I cannot regard that as a genuine element of religion. Was not Christ Himself, on the cross, calm, simple? Did He not even pray that, if it were possible, the cup might pass from Him? Was there ever in the whole history of His life a trace of excitement? The fuss and excitement that seem to have gone on about this poor young deathbed, then, jars on my mind; the working up of the sufferer herself, and the working up of themselves (the onlookers) into a sort of hysterical ecstasy is almost as painful to me as the rest of the sad business; I feel it to be a getting-up of a death-bed scene to be put into a tract! And in the heart of it all such an amount of real terrible anguish; and the grand solemn faith that could bear all, and triumph over all, harassed by earthly interference and excitations! I will send the letter; perhaps you will find all this wrong in me; we could never agree about the ' revivals.' Never mind; we love one another all the same.

My kindest regards to the Doctor.

Your affectionate
JANE CARLYLE.

Send back Grace's letter.

LETTER 276.

To Miss Margaret Welsh, Liverpool.

Chelsea: November 2, 1863.

Dearest Maggie,—The very sight of your letter was a relief to me, for I knew that unless dear Jackie had been a little better you couldn't have written as much! Next time do write a mere bulletin, or I can't press you to ' be quick!' From the account you give, I draw far better hope about him than, I dare say, you meant to give in writing it. But there seems to be so much vitality in the poor little fellow; his caring to be read to, his little speech, all that sounds as if there were a good basis of life at the bottom of all this illness. God grant he may soon be pronounced convalescent !

I am very convalescent ! I can move about the room with a stick, and the pain in my arm has been considerably less for the last few days, when I make no attempt to move it more than it likes. I attribute the improvement to a new medicine, recommended to me by Carlyle's friend, Mr. Foxton, who had been cured by it. Before taking it I asked the advice of Dr. B—— at St. Leonards (a man of real ability), and he sent me a proper prescription, and directions about using it. It is called Iodide of Potash, and is taken with quantities of fluid; and along with it have to be taken pills of Valeriate or Quinine. If it cures me, and you ever need curing, you shall have the prescription.

In the beginning of the arm-business, some four months ago now, I fancied I had given my arm an unconscious sprain, as the pain in attempting to move it preceded any aching or shooting, independent of attempting to move it. The Doctor persuaded me ' it was all neuralgia.' Since my accident that sprained feeling has been dreadful, till within the last few days. And though Mr. Barnes always declared ' it was all rheumatism,' it has been impossible to persuade me that the same blow received on my shoulder and hip-joint at the same time, and damaging the sinews in my thigh, would not damage the sinews in my arm also. 'That stands to reason' (as old Helen used to say).

Of course, if rheumatism is about in one, it will gather to any strained part; and so there has been plenty of rheumatic pain, besides the pain from the hurt. But I am certain it is more than rheumatism that hinders me from lifting my arm. And having a faculty of remembering things long after date, I remembered the other day that I took to using the dumb-bells for two or three days, to make myself stronger *par vive force*, when I was feeling so weak and ill early in summer (it must have been just before I noticed the stiffness of my arm), and that I left them off because my arms felt too weak to use them, and ached after. It would be a comfort to my weak mind to be assured that I, then and there, sprained some sinew in my arm, and all the rest would have followed in the course of nature; and I might give up vague terrors about angina pectoris, paralysis, disease of the spine, &c. &c. Best stop.

Yours affectionately,

J. W. C.

LETTER 277.

Mrs. Simmonds, Oakley Street, Chelsea.

5 Cheyne Row: Nov. 3, 1863.

My darling,—I am so thankful that you are all right. And to think of your writing on the third day after your confinement the most legible—indeed, the only legible—note I ever had from you in my life!

Now about this compliment offered me, which you are pleased to call a ' favour ' (to you), I don't know what to say. I wish I could go and talk it over; but, even if I could go in a cab one of these next dry days, I couldn't drive up your stairs in a cab! I should be greatly pleased that your baby bore a name of mine. But the Godmotherhood? There seems to me one objection to that, which is a fatal one—I don't belong to the English Church ; and the Scotch Church, which I do belong to, recognises no Godfathers and Godmothers. The father takes all the obligations on himself (serves him right !). I was present at a Church of England christening for the first time, when the Blunts took me to see their baby christened, and it looked to me a very solemn piece of work; and that Mr. Maurice and Julia Blunt (the Godfather and Godmother) had to take upon them-selves, before God and man, very solemn engage-ments, which it was to be hoped they meant to fulfil! I should not have liked to bow and murmur, and undertake all they did, without meaning to fulfil it according to my best ability. Now, my darling, how could I dream of binding myself to look after the spiritual welfare of any earthly baby? I, who have no confidence in my own spiritual welfare ! I am not wanted to, it may perhaps be answered—you

mean to look after that yourself without interference.
What are these spoken engagements then?   A mere
form ; that is, a piece of humbug.   How could I, in
cold blood, go through with a ceremony in a church,
to which neither the others nor myself attach a grain
of veracity ?   If you can say anything to the purpose.
I am very willing to be proved mistaken ; and in that
case very willing to stand Godmother to a baby that
on the third day is not at all red !

Yours affectionately,

JANE CARLYLE.

LETTER 278.

Mrs. Simmonds, 82 Oakley Street, Chelsea.

5 Cheyne Row : Friday, Nov. 27, 1863.

Dear Pet,—I am not the least well, and should
just about as soon walk overhead into the Thames as
into a roomful of people !   At the same time, I wish
to pay my respects to the baby on this her next
grand performance after getting herself born, and to
place in her small hands a talisman worthy of the
occasion, and suitable to a baby born on ' All Saints'
Day ' (whatever sort of day that may be).   As I
shouldn't at all recommend running a long pin into
the creature, I advise you to wear the brooch in its
present form till the baby is sufficiently hardened,
from its present pulpy condition, to bear something
tied round its throat, without fear of strangulation !

And then you may remove the pin, and attach the talisman to a string in form of a locket. But what is it? 'What does it do?' (as a servant of mine once asked me in respect of ' a lord.') What it is, my dear, is an emblematic mosaic, made from bits of some tomb of the early Christians, and representing an early Christian device: the Greek cross, the palm leaves, and all the rest of it. Worn by the like of me, I daresay it would have no virtue to speak of; but worn by a baby born on All Saints' Day! it must be a potent charm against the devil and all his works one would think, for it is a perfectly authentic memorial of the early Christians.

I hope you didn't go and drop the 'Jane' after all! Bless you and it.

Affectionately yours,
JANE BAILLIE WELSH CARLYLE.

LETTERS 279-282.

FOUR SHORT LETTERS.

About the beginning of January (1864) there were thought to be perceptible some faint symptoms of improvement or abatement; which she herself never durst believe in; and indeed to us eager on-lookers they were faint and uncertain —nothing of real hope, except in getting to St. Leonards so soon as the season would permit.

Early in March, weather mild though dim and wettish, this sad transit was accomplished by railway; I escorting, and visiting at every stage ; Maggie Welsh and our poor patient in what they called a ' sick carriage,' which indeed took her up at this door, and after delays and haggles at St. Leonards, put her down at Dr. B——'s ; but was found otherwise inferior to the common arrangement for a sick person (two window-seats, with board and cushion put between), though about five or six times dearer, and was never employed again. She was carried downstairs here in the bed of this dreary vehicle (which I saw well would remind her, as it did, of a hearse, with its window for letting in the coffin) ; she herself, weak but clear, directed the men. So pathetic a face as then glided past me at this lower door I never saw nor shall see ! And the journey—and the arrival. But of all this, which passed without accident, and which remains to myself unforgetable enough, and sad as the realms of Hades, I undertook to say nothing.

Her reception was of the very kindest ; her adjustment, with Maggie and one of our maids (in fine, airy, quiet rooms, in the big house, with the loving and skilful hosts), I saw in a few hours completed to my satisfaction, far beyond expectation. She herself said little ; but sat, in her pure, simple dress, &c., looking, though sorrowful, calm and thankful. At length I left the house (or indeed they almost pushed me out, ' not to miss the last train,' which I saved only by half a moment by hot speed and good luck), and got home in a more hopeful mood than I had come away. Solely, in my last cab (from Waterloo Station), I had stuck my cap (a fine black velvet thing of *her* making) too hurriedly into my pocket, and it had hustled out, and in the darkness been left. Loss irrecoverable, not noticed till next morning, and which I still regret. ' Oh, nothing !' said she, cheerily and yet mournfully, at our next meeting. ' I will make you a new cap when I am able to sew again.' But I think, in effect, she never sewed more.

Maggie's daily bulletin was indistinct and ambiguous, but strove always to be favourable, or really was so. I sat busy here; generally wrote to my poor darling some daily line; got from her now and then some word or two, but always on mere practical or household matters; seldom or never any confirmation of Maggie's reading of the omens. In the last week of March (as covenanted) I made my first visit (Friday till Monday, I think). Forster and Mrs. F. went with me, but did not see her. I stayed at Dr. B——'s, they at a hotel, where was dining, &c. Whether this was my first visit to her there I strive to recollect distinctly, but cannot. I seem to have even seen but little of her, and certainly learned nothing intimate; as if she rather avoided much communication with me, unwilling to rob me of the doctor's confident prognostications, and much unable to confirm them. Her mood of fixed quiet sorrow, with no hope in it but of enduring well, was painfully visible. I had just got rid of my vol. v., deeply disappointed latterly on finding that there must be a sixth. Hades was not more lugubrious than that book too now was to me; and yet there was something in it of sacred, of Orpheus-like (though I did not think of 'Orpheus' at all, nor name my darling an 'Eurydice'!) and the stern course was to continue—what else?

In the end of April brother John came to me. Before this it had been decided (since the B——s, who at first pretended that they would, now evidently would not, accept remuneration from us) that a small furnished house should be rented, and a shift made thither; which was done and over about the time John came. I was to remove thither with my work (so soon as liftable). He by himself made a preliminary visit thither; then perhaps another with me; and at his return I could notice (though he said nothing) that he meant to try staying with us there ; which he did, and surely was of use to me there.

Early in May this (Chelsea) house was left to Larkin's care (who at last came into it, letting his own); and all of us had reassembled in the poor new hospice ('117 Marina, St. Leonards'), studious to try our best and utmost there. Maggie Welsh had to return to Liverpool (to nurse a poor little child-nephew who was dying). I did not find Maggie at St. Leonards ; but the good Mary Craik (Professor's Mary, from Belfast), by my Jeannie's own suggestion, was written to, came directly, and did as well ; perhaps more quietly, and thus better.

In those seven or eight months of martyrdom (October 1863—May 1864) there is naturally no record of the poor dear martyr's own discoverable ; nothing but these small, most mournful notes written with the left hand, as if from the core of a broken heart, and worthy to survive as a voice *de profundis.* Maggie's part, which fills the last two pages, I omit. The address is gone, but still evident on inference.

T. Carlyle, Esq., Chelsea.

St. Leonards : Friday, April 8, 1864.

Oh, my own darling ! God have pity on us ! Ever since the day after you left, whatever flattering accounts may have been sent you, the truth is I have been wretched—perfectly wretched day and night with that horrible malady. Dr. B. knows nothing about it more than the other doctors. So, God help me, for on earth is no help !

Lady A. writes that Lord A. left you two thousand pounds—not in his will, to save duty—but to be given you as soon as possible. 'The wished for come too late!' Money can do nothing for us now.

Your loving and sore suffering
JANE W. CARLYLE.

To-day I am a little less tortured—only a little; but a letter having been promised, I write.

T. Carlyle, Esq., Chelsea.

St. Leonards: April 19, 1864.

It is no 'morbid despondency;' it is a positive physical torment day and night—a burning, throbbing, maddening sensation in the most nervous part of me ever and ever. How be in good spirits or have any hope but to die! When I spoke of going home, it was to *die* there; here were the place for *living*, if one could! It was not my wish to leave here. It was the B——s' own suggestion and wish that we should get a little house of our own.

Oh, have pity on me! I am worse than ever I was in that terrible malady.

I am,
Yours as ever,
JANE CARLYLE.

T. Carlyle, Esq., Chelsea.

St. Leonards-on-Sea: April 25, 1864.

Oh, my husband! I am suffering torments! each day I suffer more horribly. Oh, I would like you beside me! I am terribly alone. But I don't want to interrupt your work. I will wait till we are in our own hired house; and then if am no better, you must come for a day.

Your own wretched
J. W. C.-

To the Misses Welsh, Edinburgh.

St. Leonards-on-Sea:[1] end of April, 1864.

My own dear Aunts,—I take you to my heart and kiss you fondly one after another. God knows if we shall ever meet again; and His will be done! My doctor has hopes of my recovery, but I myself am not hopeful; my sufferings are terrible.

The malady is in my womb—you may fancy. It is the consequence of that unlucky fall; no disease there, the doctors say, but some nervous derangement. Oh, what I have suffered, my aunts! what I may still have to suffer! Pray for me that I may be enabled to endure.

Don't write to myself; reading letters excites me too much. And Maggie tells me all I should hear. I commit you to the Lord's keeping, whether I live or die. Ah, my aunts, I shall die; that is my belief!

JANE CARLYLE.

---

[1] Probably still in Dr. B——'s house there. The next letter is expressly dated from the new hired house. Maggie still there, but just about to leave.

LETTER 283.

With a violent effort of packing and scheming (e.g., a box of books with cross-bars in it, and shelves which were to be put in, and make the box a press, &c. &c.), in all which Larkin and Maggie Welsh assisted diligently, I got down to Marina on one of the first days of May. Dreary and tragic was our actual situation there, but we strove to be of hope, and were all fixedly intent to do our best. The house was new, clean, light enough, and well aired; otherwise paltry in the extreme—small, misbuilt every inch of it; a despicable, cockney, scamped edifice; a rickety bandbox rather than a house. But that did not much concern us, tenants only for a month or two—nay, withal there were traces that the usual inhabitants (two old ladies, probably very poor) had been cleanly, neat persons, sensible, as we, of the sins and miseries of their scamped, despicable dwelling-place, poor, good souls!

In a small back closet, window opposite to door, and both always open, I had soon got a table wedged to fixity, had set on end my book-box, changing it to a book-press, and adjusted myself to work, quite tolerably all along, though feeling as if tied up in a rack. One good bedroom there was in the top story, looking out over the sea—this was naturally hers; mine below and to rearward was the next best, and, by cunning adjustments curtains improvised out of rugs and ropes were made to exclude the light in some degree and admit freely the air currents. We made with our knives about a dozen little wedges as the first thing to keep the doors open or ajar at our will, their own being various in that respect! To put up with the house was a right easy matter, almost a solacement, in sight of the deep misery of its poor mistress, spite of all her striving.

The first day she was dressed waiting my arrival, and

came painfully resolute down to dinner with us, but could hardly sit it out; and never could attempt again. With intellect clear and even inventive, her whole being was evidently plunged in continual woe, pain as if unbearable, and no hope left; in spite of our encouragements no steady hope at all. On the earth I have never seen so touching a sight! She drove out at lowest three or four times a day— ultimately long drives (which John took charge of to Battle, to Bexhill regions seeking new lodgings—alas, in vain!). Her last daily drive from four to half-past five was always with me, my day's work now done. She was evidently thankful, but spoke hardly at all; or, if she did for my sake, on some indifferent matter, naming to me some street oddity, locality, or the like; those poor efforts now in my memory are the saddest of all, beautiful to me, and sad and pathetic to me beyond all the rest. On setting her down at home I directly stepped across to the livery stable, and mounted for a rapid obligato ride of three hours: rides unlike any I have ever had in the world; more gloomy and mournful even than the London ones, though by no means so abominable even, one's company here being mainly God's sky and earth, not cockneydom with its slums, enchanted aperies and infernalries. I rode far and wide, saw strange old villages (a pair of storks in one), saw Battle by many routes (and even began to understand the Harold-William duel there. Strange that no English soldier, scholar, or mortal ever yet tried to do it). Battle, town and monastery, in the calm or in the windy summer gloaming, was a favourite sight of mine; only the roads were in parts distressing (new cuts, new cockney scamped edifices, and railways and much dust). Crowhirst and its yew, that has seen (probably) the days of Julius Cæsar as well as William the Conqueror's, and ours. But that is not my topic. In the green old lanes with their quaint old cottages, good old cottagers, valiant, frugal,

patient, I could have wept.   In the disastrous, dust-covered,
cockneyfying parts my own feeling had something of rage in
it, rage and disgust.   It was usually after nightfall when I
got home.   Tea was waiting for me ; and silently my Jeannie
(as I at length observed) to preside over it (ah, me ! ah, me !),
directly after which she went up to bed.   Hastings, St.
Leonards, Battle, Rye, Winchelsea, Beachy Head, intrinsically all a beautiful region (when not cockneyfied, and turned
to cheap and nasty chaos and the mortar tubs), and yet in
the world is no place I should so much shudder to see
again.

We had various visitors—Forster, Twisleton, Woolner—
and none of these could she see; not even Miss Bromley,
who came twice for a day or more, but in vain—except the
last time, just one hurried glimpse.   Nothing could so in-
dicate to what a depth of despair the ever-gnawing pain and
boundless misery had sunk this once brightest and openest
of human souls.   The B——s continued with unwearied
kindness doing, and hoping, and endeavouring; but that
also, even on the Doctor's part, much more on her own, began to seem futile, unsuccessful; good old Barnes came once
(fast falling into imbecility and finis, poor man), said :
' Hah ! intrinsically just the same; however, the disease
will burn itself out ! '

About the middle of June (lease was to end with that
month, and her own house, especially her own room there, had
grown horrible to her thoughts) she moved that we should
engage the house till end of July; which was done.   But,
alas! before June ended things had grown still more intolerable; sleep more and more impossible, and she wished
to be off from the July bargain—would the people have
consented ? (which they would not)—so that the question
what to do became darker and darker.   ' If your room at
Chelsea had a new paper ? ' somebody suggested ; and Miss

Bromley had undertaken to get it done. This of the 'new paper' went into my heart as nothing else had done, 'so small, so helpless, faint;' and to the present hour it could almost make me weep! It was done, however, by-and-by; and under changed omens. Thank God.

But in the meanwhile, hour by hour, things were growing more intolerable. Twelve successive nights of burning summer, totally without sleep; morning after the eleventh of them she announced a fixed resolution of her own, and the next morning executed it. Set off by express train, with John for escort, to London; would try Mrs. Forster's instead of her own horrible room; but would go (we could all see) or else die. Miss Bromley, who had again come, she consented to see in passing into the train; one moment only, a squeeze of the hand, and adieu. With a stately, almost proud step, my poor martyred darling took her place, John opposite her, and shot away.

At the Forsters' she had some disturbed sleep, not much; and next morning ordered John to make ready for the evening train to Dumfries (to sister Mary's, at the Gill), and rushed along all night, 330 miles at once—a truly heroic remedy of nature's own prescribing, which did by quick steps and struggles bring relief.

The Gill, sister Mary's poor but ever kind and generous *human* habitation, is a small farmhouse, seven miles beyond Annan, twenty-seven beyond Carlisle, eight or ten miles short of Dumfries, and, therefore, twenty-two or twenty-four short of Thornhill, through both of which the S.W. Railway passes. Scotsbrig lies some ten miles northward of the Gill (road at right angles to the Carlisle and Dumfries Railway): passes by Hoddam Hill, even as of old—and at Eccleféchan, two miles from Scotsbrig, crosses the Carlisle, Moffat, or Caledonian Railway—enough for the topography of these tragic things.—T. C.

T. Carlyle, Esq., 117 Marina, St. Leonards-on-Sea.

The Gill: July 15, 1864.

Oh, my dear, I am quite as amazed as you to find myself here, so promiscuous! I had given up all idea of Scotland when I left St. Leonards; felt neither strength nor courage for it; but postponed projects till I saw what lay for me at Palace-Gate House. I found there much kindness, and much state, and a firm expectation that I was merely passing through! And if they had wanted me ever so much to stay, there was not a bed in the house fit to be slept in from the noise point of view! Cheyne Row full of Larkins; and my old room in the same state: horrible was the idea to me! The Blunts perhaps out of town; London very hot! I did sleep some human sleep in my luxurious bedroom, all crashing with wheels; but only the having had no sleep the night before made me so clever! I could not have slept a second night. No, there was nothing to be done but what I did—turn that second night to use, travel through it, and not try for any sleep until there was some chance of getting it; that night on the road was nothing like so wretched as those nights at Marina. I drank four glasses of champagne in the night! and took a good breakfast at Carlisle. John was dreadfully ill-tempered: we quarrelled incessantly, but he had the grace to be ashamed of himself after, and apologise. On the whole, it was a birthday of good omen. My horrible ailment kept off as by enchantment.

Mary is all that one could wish as hostess, nurse, and sister. She has had something of the sort herself, and her sympathy is intelligent.

I am gone in for milk diet: took porridge and buttermilk in quantity last night, and slept, with few awakenings, all night; had a tumbler of new milk at eight, and got up to breakfast at nine. I am very shaky, you will see, but, oh, so thankful for my sleep and ease—would it but last! John went to Dumfries yesterday afternoon; and all who had been about me being gone, I felt like a child set down out of arms, but am contriving to totter pretty well so far. John was to be here to-day some time.

I am very sorry for you with those idiot servants. Mary[1] proved herself of no earthly use to me, besides being sulky and conceited. Mary Craik is your only present stay; kiss her for me, dear, kind, good girl. I will write to her next. I am so sorry at having had to leave her in such a mess.

James Austin had already got a nice carriage for Mary to drive me about in. Oh, they are so kind, and so polite!

Your own

J. W. C.

---

[1] Servant now (privately) in a bad way, as turned out!

EXTRACTS FROM LETTERS.

Mrs. Carlyle's letters, during the remainder of the summer, are a sad record of perpetually recurring suffering. The carriage broke down in her second drive with her sister-in-law, and she was violently shaken. Mrs. Austin gave her all the care that love had to bestow; but in a farmhouse there was not the accommodation which her condition required, and her friend Mrs. Russell carried her off to Holm Hill, where she would be under Dr. Russell's immediate charge. A series of short extracts from the letters to her husband will convey a sufficient picture of her condition in body and mind. The most touching feature in them is the affection with which she now clung to him. Carlyle's anxiety, at last awake, had convinced her that his strange humours had not risen from real indifference. John Carlyle, the doctor, with whom she had travelled, had been rough and unfeeling.—J. A. F.

To T. Carlyle.

Holm Hill, July 23, 1864.—I have arrived safe. They met me at the station, and are kind, as so many are. John offered to accompany here, but I declined. Fancy him telling me in my agony yesterday that if I had ever done anything in my life this would not have been; that no poor woman with work to mind had ever such an ailment as this of mine since the world began![1] Oh, my dear, I think how near my mother I am! How still I should be

---

[1] Poor John! well-intending, but with hand unconsciously rough, even cruel, as in this last instance, which she never could forget again.

laid beside her.[1]   But I wish to live for you, if only I could live out of torment.

July 25.—Mary Craik will go to-day, and you will be alone with town maids ; and if I were there I could but add to your troubles. We are sorely tried, and God alone knows what the end will be. It is no wonder if my stock of hope and courage is quite worn out.

July 27.—I could not write yesterday ; I was too ill and desperate. Again, without assignable cause, I had got no wink of sleep. I am terribly weak. If I had not such kind people beside me I should be wretched indeed. I do not feel so agitated by the sights about here as I used to do. I seem already to belong to the passed-away as much as to the present ; nay, more.

God bless you on your solitary way.

July 28.—When will I be back? Ah, my God ! when ? for it is no good going back to be a trouble to you and a torment to myself. I must not look forward, but try to bear my life from day to day, thankful that for the present I am so well cared for.

August 2.—I am cared for here as I have never been since I lost my mother's nursing ; and everything is good for me : the quiet airy bedroom, the new milk, the beautiful drives ; and when all this fails to bring me human sleep or endurable nervous-

[1] Oh, Heaven !

ness, can you wonder that I am in the lowest spirits about myself. So long as I had a noisy bedroom or food miscooked even, I had something to attribute my sleeplessness to; now I can only lay it to my diseased nerves, and at my age such illness does not right itself.

August 5.—Except for this wakefulness I am better than when I left Marina, and it is unaccountable that I should be so well in spite of getting less sleep than I ever heard of anyone, out of a medical book, getting and living with. I was weighed yesterday, and found a gain of five pounds since April. If sleep would come I think I should recover—the first time I have had this hope seriously; but if it won't come I must break down sooner or later, being no Dutchman nor Jeffrey;[1] and I fear not for my life, but for my reason. It is almost sinfully ungrateful, when God has borne me through such prolonged agonies with my senses intact, to have so little confidence in the future; but courage and hope have been ground out of me. Submission! Acknowledgment that my sufferings have been no greater than I deserved is just the most that I am up to.

Oh, my dear, I am very weary! My agony has lasted long! I am tempted to take a long cry over myself—and no good will come of that.

---

[1] In Cabanis, case of a Dutch gentleman who lived twenty years without sleep! which I often remembered for my own sake and hers. Jeffrey is Lord Jeffrey; sad trait of insomnia reported by himself.

August 22.—I have no wholly sleepless nights to report now. I don't sleep well, by any means ; but to sleep at all is such an improvement. I continue to gain flesh. A—— declares that in the last ten days I have gained four pounds ! But that must be nonsense.

August 26.—Walking is hardly possible for me at present, the change of the weather having produced rheumatic pains and stiffness in my knees. I did the best I could for myself in buying a good supply of woollen under-garments—not new dresses, not a single new dress, nor anything for the outside. The mercury of my mental thermometer has not risen to care for appearances, only to the hope of living long enough to need new flannels. I did once turn over the idea of a new bonnet, the one I have having lasted me three years ! But I sent it to the daughter of your old admirer, Shankland the tailor, and she took out the ' clures ' and put in a clean cap for tenpence !

August 29.—The thought of how I am ever to make that long journey back which I made here in the strength of desperation, troubles me night and day ; and what is to become of me when I am back, with my warm milk and my nursing and my doctoring taken away ? Oh, I am frightened—frightened ! a perfect coward am I become—I, who was surely once brave ! But I cannot, must not, stay on here

through the winter. Besides the unreasonableness
of inflicting such a burden on others, it would be too
cold and damp for me here in the valley of the Nith.
So, dear, though I would fain spare you this and all
troubles with me, I must go to the subject of the paper-
ing [of her room in Cheyne Row], and you must forgive what may strike you as weakly fanciful in my
desire to have ' a new colour about me.' You must
consider that I was carried out of those rooms to be
shoved into a sort of hearse, and (to my own feelings) buried out of that house for ever ; and that I
have not had time yet, nor got strength enough yet,
to shake off the associations that make those rooms
terrible for me. To give them somewhat of a different appearance is the most soothing thing that
can be done for me.[1]

August 30.—No sleep at all last night ; had no
chance of sleep, for the neuralgic pains piercing me
from shoulder to breast like a sword. I am pro-
foundly disheartened. Every way I turn it looks
dark, dark to me. I had dared to hope, to look
forward to some years of health—no worse, at least,
than I had before. I cannot write cheerfully. I am
not cheerful.

September 6.—Oh, that it was as easy to put
tormenting thoughts out of one's own head as it is for

---

[1] Poor, forlorn darling! All this was managed to her mind—all this
yet stands mournfully here, and shall stand.

others to bid one do that! I wish to heaven you were delivered from those paper-hangers. I did not think it would have been so long in the wind. I, the unlucky cause, am quite as sorry for the bother-ation to you as —— expresses herself, though I have more appreciation of the terrible half-insane sensi-tiveness which drove me on to bothering you. Oh, if God would only lift my trouble off me so far that I could bear it all in silence, and not add to the troubles of others!

September 7.—I cannot write. I have passed a terrible night. Sleeplessness and restlessness and the old pain (worse than it has ever been since I came here); and, in addition to all that, an inward black-ness of darkness. Am I going to have another winter like the last? I cannot live through another such time: my reason, at least, cannot live through it. Oh, God bless you and help me!

September 9.—I am very stupid and low. God can raise me up again; but will He? Oh, I am weary, weary! My dear, when I have been giving directions about the house then a feeling like a great black wave will roll over my breast, and I say to myself, whatever pains be taken to gratify me, shall I ever more have a day of ease, of painlessness, or a night of sweet rest, in that house, or in any house but the dark narrow one where I shall arrive at last.

September 16.—Oh, if there was any sleep to be got in that bed wherever it stands! [alluding to a change in the position of her bed at Chelsea.]   But it looks to my excited imagination, that bed I was born in, like a sort of instrument of red-hot torture ; after all those nights that I lay meditating on self-destruction as my only escape from insanity.   Oh, the terriblest part of my suffering has not been what was seen, has not been what could be put into human language !

September 26, 1864.—Oh, my dear ! I thank God I got some little sleep last night ! for I had been going from bad to worse, till I had reached a point that seemed to take me back to the time just before I left Marina, and to give to that time additional poignancy. I had the quite recent remembrance of some weeks of such comparative ease and well-ness ! Oh, this relapse is a severe disappointment to me, and, God knows, not altogether a selfish disappointment ! I had looked forward to going back to you so much improved, as to be, if not of any use and comfort to you, at least no trouble to you, and no burden on your spirits ![1]   And now God knows how it will be ! Sometimes I feel a deadly assurance that I am progressing towards just such another winter as the last ! only what little courage and hope supported me in the beginning, worn out now, and ground into dust, under long fiery suffering !

[1] Oh, my poor martyr darling !

Dr. Russell says, as Dr. B—— said, that the special misery will certainly wear itself out in time ; if I can only eat and keep up my strength, that it may not wear out me ! But how keep up my strength without sleep?

Oh, dear ! you cannot help me, though you would ! Nobody can help me ! Only God : and can I wonder if God take no heed of me when I have all my life taken so little heed of Him ?

John is coming to-day to settle about the journey. When I spoke so bravely about going alone, I was much better than I am at present. I am up to nothing of the sort now, and must be thankful for his escort, the best that offers. He says Saturday is the best day. But I don't incline to arriving on a Sunday morning, so I shall vote for Friday night. But you will hear from me again and again before then.

Your ever affectionate

J. W. CARLYLE.

LETTER 284.

Thomas Carlyle, Chelsea, London.

Holm Hill : Wednesday, Sept. 28, 1864.

Again a night absolutely sleepless, except for a little dozing between six and seven. There were no shooting pains to keep me awake last night, although I felt terribly chill, in spite of a heap of blankets that kept me in a sweat; but it was a cold sweat.

I am very wretched to-day. Dr. Russell handed me the other night a medical book he was reading, open at the chapter on ' Neuralgia ' that I might read, for my practical information, a list of ' counter-irritants.'

I read a sentence or two more than was meant, ending with ' this lady was bent on self-destruction.' You may think it a strange comfort, but it was a sort of comfort to me to find that my dreadful wretchedness was a not uncommon feature of my disease, and not merely an expression of individual cowardice.

Another strange comfort I take to myself under the present pressure of horrible nights. If I had continued up till now to feel as much better as I did in the first weeks of my stay here, I should have dreaded the return to London as a sort of suicide. Now I again want a change—even that change! There lies a possibility, at least, of benefit in it; which I could not have admitted to myself had all gone on here as in the beginning.

I am very sorry for Lady Ashburton, am afraid her health is irretrievably ruined. Pray do write her a few lines.[1]

It has been a chill mist from the water all the morning, but the sun is trying to break through.

God send me safe back to you, such as I am.

Ever yours,

J. W. C.

[1] Is again in vigorous health.

LETTER 285.

Thomas Carlyle, Chelsea, London.

Holm Hill: Thursday, Sept. 20, 1864.

This, then, is to be my last letter from here. Where will the next letter be from, or will there be a next? Blind moles! with our pride of insight too! we can't tell even that much beforehand.

If I had trusted my power of divination yesterday I should have renounced all hope of seeing you this week. I had to go to bed at five in the afternoon, in a sort of nervous fever from want of sleep. The irritation, too, unbearable! That clammy, deathly sweat, in which I had passed the previous night, as if I had been dipped in ice-water, then placed under a crushing weight of frozen blankets, seemed to have taken all warm life out of me. So I gave up and went to bed. At night I took one of Dr. B——'s blue pills (the larger dose had ceased to be beneficial) and about twelve I fell asleep, thank God! and went on sleeping and waking till half-past seven. It was healing sleep, besides being a good deal of it. My first reflection this morning was: ' And there are beggars—nay, there are blackguards, or both in one— who get every night of their lives far better sleep than even this, which is such an unspeakable mercy to me. • *Ach!* it is no discovery that much in this world quite surpasses one's human comprehension.

I have been thrown out of my reckoning. I had calculated that on the principle of a bad night, and a less bad, the less bad would fall to-night; and that I should have some sleep in me to start with. But two waking nights coming together changes the order; and to-night, in the course of nature (second nature), no rest is to be expected.

Tell Mary I now take coffee to breakfast (John takes tea); and to have a little cream in the house that one may fall soft.

And now good-bye till we meet. Oh, that I had been a day and night (and the night a good one) in the house! No mortal can imagine the thoughts of my heart in returning there, where I was *buried* from! and my life still unrenewed! only the hope, often overcast, that it is in the way of being renewed.

Your ever affectionate

JANE CARLYLE.

My little maid asked me this morning, when about to draw on my stockings: 'What d'ye think? wouldn't it be a good thing to hae the taes (toes) clippet again, afore ye gang away?' I shall so miss that kind, thoughtful girl!

LETTER 286.

Saturday, October 1, 1864, a mild, clear (not sunny) day. John brought her home to me again to this door—by far the gladdest sight I shall ever see there, if gladness were the name of any sight now in store for me. A faint, kind, timid smile was on her face, as if afraid to believe fully; but the despair had vanished from her looks altogether, and she was brought back to me, my own again as before.

During all this black interval I had been continuing my ' comatose flight' without intermission, and was not yet by four months got to land. To extraneous events my attention was momentary, if not extinct altogether; for months and years I had not written the smallest letter or note except on absolute compulsion. But here was an event extraneous to ' Frederick,' which could not be extraneous to ' Frederick's ' biographer, never so worn out and crushed into stupefaction. This again awoke me into life and hope, into vivid and grateful recognition, and was again a light, or the sure promise of a light from above on my nigh desperate course. (Oh, what miserable inapplicable phrasing is this! or why speak of myself at all ?)

My poor martyred darling continued to prosper here beyond my hopes—far beyond her own ; and in spite of utter weakness (which I never rightly saw) and of many fits of trouble, her life to the very end continued beautiful and hopeful to both of us—to me more beautiful than I had ever seen it in her best days. Strange and precious to look back upon, those last eighteen months, as of a second youth (almost a second childhood with the wisdom and graces of old age), which by Heaven's great mercy were conceded her and me. In essentials never had she been so beautiful to me ; never in my time been so happy. But I am unfit to speak of these things, to-day most unfit (August 12, 1869), and will leave the little series of letters (which were revised several days ago) to tell their own beautiful and tragical story.

Mrs. Russell, Holm Hill, Thornhill, Dumfriesshire.

5 Cheyne Row, Chelsea: Monday, Oct. 3, 1864.

Oh, my darling! my darling! God for ever bless you—you and dear Dr. Russell, for your goodness to me, your patience with me, and all the good you have done me! I am better aware now how much I have gained than I was before this journey; how much stronger I am, both body and mind, than I was on my journey to Scotland. I felt no fatigue on the journey down, but I made up for it in nervous excitement! On the journey up, all my nervousness was over when I had parted with you two. Even when arrived at my own door (which I had always looked forward to as a most terrible moment, remembering the hearse-like fashion in which I was carried away from it) I could possess my soul in quiet, and meet the excited people who rushed out to me, as gladly as if I had been returned from any ordinary pleasure excursion!

Very excited people they were. Dr. C. had stupidly told his brother he might look for us about ten, and, as we did not arrive till half after eleven, Mr. C. had settled it in his own mind that I had been taken ill somewhere on the road, and was momentarily expecting a telegram to say I was dead. So he rushed out in his dressing-gown, and kissed me, and wept over me as I was in the act of getting down out of the cab (much to the edification of the neighbours at their windows, I have no doubt); and then the maids appeared behind him, looking timidly, with flushed faces and tears in their eyes; and the little one (the cook) threw her arms round my neck and fell to kissing me in the open street; and the big one (the housemaid) I had to kiss, that she might not be made jealous the first thing!

They were all astonished at the improvement in my appearance. Mr. C. has said again and again that he would not have believed anyone who had sworn it to him that I should return so changed for the better. Breakfast was presented to me, but though I had still Holm Hill things to eat, I had not my Holm Hill appetite to eat them with. All Saturday there was nothing I cared to swallow but champagne (Lady Ashburton had sent me two dozen, first-rate, in the winter); so I took the B—— blue pill that first night, as Dr. Russell had advised. And, oh, such a heavenly sleep I had! awoke only twice the whole night! It is worth while passing a whole night on the railway to get such blessed sleep the night after. Last night, again, I slept; not so well as the first night, of course, but wonderfully well for me; and this morning my breakfast was not contemptible. But it is a great hardship to have lost my warm milk in the morning. I thought by paying an exorbitant price it might have been obtained; but no; the stuff offered me yesterday at eight o'clock it was impossible to swallow. And my poor 'interiors,' perfectly bewildered by all the sudden changes put on them, don't seem to have any clear ideas left; so I am driven back into the valley of the shadow of pills!

I had a two-hours' drive yesterday in Battersea Park and Clapham Common. When one hasn't the beauties of nature, one must content one's self with the beauties of art. To-day my drive must be townward; so many things wanted at the shops! There is hardly a kitchen utensil left unbroken; all broken by 'I can't imagine who did it!' Still, it might have been worse; there seems to have been no serious mischief done.

Wasn't it curious to have your eternal 'Simpson' given me for fellow-traveller?

Oh, my darling, if I might continue just as well as I am now! But that is not to be hoped. Anyhow, I shall always feel as if I owed my life chiefly to your husband and you, who procured me such rest as I could have had nowhere else in the world.

Your own

JANE W. C.

LETTER 287.

Mrs. Russell, Holm Hill, Thornhill, Dumfriesshire.

5 Cheyne Row, Chelsea: Thursday, Oct. 6, 1864.

Dearest,—At Holm Hill, at this hour, I should have just drunk my glass of wine, and been sitting down at the dining-room table to write the daily letter to Mr. C. The likest thing I can do here is to sit down at the drawing-room table and write to you. I feel the same sort of responsibility for myself to you, as to him, and to you only, of all people alive! and feel, too, the same certainty of being read with anxious interest. Oh, my dear Mary, it is an unspeakable blessing to have such a friend as you are to me! Often, when I have felt unusually free from my misery of late, it has seemed to me that I could not be grateful enough to God for the mercy; unless He inspired me with a spiritual gratitude, far above the mere tepid human gratitude I offered Him! And just so with you: I feel as if I needed God's help to make me humanly capable of the sort of sacred thankfulness I ought to feel for such a friend as yourself! I wanted to say to you and your dear husband something like this when I came away, but words choked themselves in my throat at parting.

I have been wonderfully well since I came home; have slept pretty well—not as on the first night (that was sleep for only the angels, and for the mortal who had travelled from three to four hundred miles through the night!), but quite tolerably for me, every night till the last. The last was very bad. But I had the comfort of being able to blame something for it, and that was my own imprudence.

I wearied myself putting pictures to rights, which were hung up all crooked (Dr. Russell will sympathise with me), and then worried myself with the shortcomings of my large beautiful housemaid, who justifies (and more) all Mr. C.'s tirades against her! This creature, with her goosishness, and her self-conceit, is unendurable after little Mary.

Only think! I get my new milk again, at eight, as usual!! Our Rector's wife keeps a cow for her children, and I have a key to her grounds; and, going through that way, it is not three minutes' walk for my cook to take a warm tumbler and fetch it back full of real milk, milked into it there and then. I get plenty of cream, quite good, paying for it exorbitantly; but no matter, so that I get it. My eight stones eleven-and-a-half would soon have had a hole made into it without the milk and cream.

I go out in a nice brougham, with a safe swift horse, whom I know, every day from one till three. And, when I come in, I have added your little tumbler full of excellent champagne to the already liberal allowance of drink ! ! !   It is to make up for the difference in the purity of the air !!

The letters Dr. Russell forwarded were from Dr. B—— and Maria (the maid).   I send them back, the doctor's for Dr. Russell, and Maria's for you, to amuse you with the girl's presumption !   My 'eternal good.'   Help us ! if Maria is to preach to me !   Here is a letter from Grace Welsh, too.   Everybody 'praying for me.'   Burn them all—I mean the letters —when you have done with them.

God bless my darling.

JANE W. CARLYLE.

LETTER 288.

'Curiosities and niceties of a civilised house.'—Old phrase of my father's.

'Elise's.'—Madame Elise, she often told me, was an artist and woman of genius in her profession ; and of late years there had sprung up a mutual recognition, which was often pleasant to my dear one.—T. C.

Mrs. Russell, Holm Hill, Thornhill, Dumfriesshire.

5 Cheyne Row, Chelsea : Monday, Oct. 10, 1864.

Dearest,—Nature prompts me to begin the week with writing to you, though I have such a pressure of work ahead as I can't see daylight through, with no help in putting to rights ; for my large, beautiful housemaid is like a cow in a flower-garden amongst

the ' curiosities and niceties ' of a civilised house ! Oh,
thank God, for the precious layer of impassivity which
that stone weight of flesh has put over my nerves !
I am not like the same woman who trembled from
head to foot, and panted like a duck in a thunderstorm, at St. Leonards whenever a human face
showed itself from without, or anything worried
from within. Indeed, my nerves are stronger than
they have been for years. Just for instance, yesterday, what I went through without having the irritation increased, or my sleep worsened ! As soon as I
was in the drawing-room George Cooke came—the
same who wrote to tell you of my accident. Now
this George Cooke is a man between thirty and forty ;
tall, strong, silent, sincere ; has been a sailor, a soldier,
a New Zealand settler, a ' man about town,' and a
stockbroker ! The last man on earth one would have
expected to make one ' a scene.' But, lo ! what happened ? I stood up to welcome him, and he took me in
his arms, and kissed me two or three times, and then
he sank into a chair and—burst into tears! and sobbed
and cried for a minute or two like any schoolboy.
Mercifully I was not infected by his agitation ; but it
was I who spoke calmly, and brought him out of it !
He accompanied me in my drive after, and when I
had come home, and was going to have my dinner, a
carriage drove up. Being nothing like so polite and
self-sacrificing as you, I told Helen to say I was tired,

and dining, and would see no one. She returned
with a card. 'Please, ma'm, the gentleman says he
thinks you will see him.' The name on the card was
Lord Houghton, a very old friend whom you may
have heard me speak of as Richard Milnes. 'Oh,
yes! he might come up.' Nobody could have predicted sentiment out of Lord Houghton! but, good
gracious! it was the same thing over again. He
clasped me in his arms, and kissed me, and dropped
on a chair—not crying, but quite pale, and gasping,
without being able to say a word.

When the emotional stage was over, and we were
talking of my stay at Holm Hill, I mentioned the
horrid thing that befell just when I was leaving—the
death of Mrs. ——. 'Where?' said Lord Houghton.
'At —— Hall.' He sprang to his feet as if shot,
and repeated, 'Dead? dead? dead?' till I was quite
frightened. 'Oh, did you know her?' I asked. 'I
am sorry to have shocked you.' 'Know her? I have
known her intimately since she was a little girl! I
was to have gone to visit her this month.'

He told me she had had a romantic history. She
was granddaughter to a brother of the —— who
was Secretary of State at Naples. The family got
reduced, but struggled bravely to keep up their rank
in Naples; chiefly helped by this girl, who was 'most
brave and generous.' They afterwards came to
England, and here, too, it was a struggle. 'The

girl' went on a visit, and at her friend's house Mr. —— saw her, fell in love with her, and proposed to her. 'The girl' shuddered at him. He was a coarse, uncultivated man, perfectly unlike her, and she would not hear of such a marriage; but the father and mother gathered round her, and implored, and reasoned, and impressed on her that with so rich a husband she would be able to lift them out of all their difficulties, and make their old age comfortable and happy, till at length she gave in. Having once married the man, Lord H. said, she made him a good wife and he was a good husband.

After these two enthusiastic meetings, I was sure I should get no sleep. But I slept much as usual during the last week; not at all as I slept the first night, but better than my fraction of sleep during the last weeks with you.

My bedroom is extremely quiet; my comfort well attended to by—myself. I miss little Mary for more things than 'the clipping o' the taes,' bless her! I was at Elise's, to get the velvet bonnet she made me last year, stripped of its finery. White lace and red roses don't become a woman who has been looking both death and insanity in the face for a year. I told her (Elise) that I had seen two of her bonnets on a Mrs. H—— in Scotland. 'Oh, yes, she has every article she wears from here!' 'You made her court dress, didn't you, that was noticed in the " Morning

Post."?' 'Yes, yes, I dressed the whole three. Mrs. H——'s dress cost three hundred pounds! but she doesn't mind cost.'

Dear love to the Doctor.

Your affectionate
J. CARLYLE.

LETTER 289.

John Forster, Esq., Palace-Gate House, Kensington.

5 Cheyne Row, Chelsea : October 1864.

Dearest Mr. Forster,—Now that Mr. C. has me here before his eyes, in an upright posture, he considers it not only my business, but my wifely duty to answer all inquiries about me, myself. I have then the melancholy pleasure of informing you and dear 'Small Individual' that I am returned to this foggy scene of things with no intentions of further travels for the present. I not only 'stood' the long night journey (they always bid me travel by night) very well, but, as on the journey down, it procured me one night of heavenly sleep ; and, as nervous illness is more benefited by change than anything else, I felt, for the first week after my return, even better than in the first weeks of my stay in Scotland. The almost miraculous improvement is now wearing off. I have again miserable nights, and plenty of pain intermittently. Still I am a stone heavier (!); and, in every way, an improved woman from what I was when you *did not* see me at Marina. But you will soon be here to take a look at me, and judge for yourself. I hope you won't be so shocked as my carpenter, who told me yesterday : 'I am very sorry indeed, ma'am, to see you fallen so suddenly into infirmity! There is a sad change since I saw you last!' And me a stone heavier!

Best love to her.

Yours ever affectionately,
JANE CARLYLE.

LETTER 290.

To Mrs. Austin, The Gill, Annan.

5 Cheyne Row: Tuesday, Oct. 18, 1864.

Oh, little woman! you will come to our aid, if possible; but if impossible, what on earth are we to do for eggs? At this present Mr. C. is breakfasting on shop-eggs, and doesn't know it; and I am every morning expecting to hear in my bed an explosion over some one too far gone for his making himself an illusion about it. All the people who kept fowls round about have, the maids say, during my absence ceased to keep them, and the two eggs from Addiscombe three times a week are not enough for us both ; I, ' as one solitary individual,' needing three in the day—one for breakfast, one in hot milk for luncheon, and one in my small pudding at dinner. When I left Holm Hill, Mrs. Russell was in despair over her hens; thirty of them yielded but three eggs a day. Yours, too, may have struck work; and in that case never mind. Only if you could send us some, it would be a mercy.

Only think of my getting here every morning a tumbler of milk warm from the cow, and all frothed up, just as at the Gill and at Holm Hill, to my infinite benefit. The stable-fed cow does not give such delicious milk as those living on grass in the open air; but still it is milk without a drop of water or anything in it, and milked out five minutes before I drink it. Mr. C. says it is a daily recurring miracle. The miracle is worked by our Rector's wife, who keeps two cows for her children, and she has kindly included me as 'the biggest and best child;' and with a key into their garden my cook can run to their stable with a tumbler and be back at my bedside in ten minutes. Indeed, it is impossible to tell who is kindest to me; my fear is always that I shall be stifled with roses. They make so much of me, and I am so weak. The Countess of Airlie was kneeling beside my sofa yesterday embracing my feet, and kissing my hands! A German girl[1] said the other day, 'I

---

[1] Reichenbach's daughter, probably.

think, Mrs. Carlyle, a many many peoples love you very dear!' It is true, and what I have done to deserve all that love I haven't the remotest conception. All this time I have been keeping better— getting some sleep, not much nor good; but some, better or worse, every night, and the irritation has been much subsided. Yesterday afternoon and this afternoon it is troubling me more than usual. Perhaps the damp in the air has brought it on, or perhaps I have been overdone with people and things; I must be more careful. I have always a terrible consciousness at the bottom of my mind that at any moment, if God will, I may be thrown back into the old agonies. I can never feel confident of life and of ease in life again, and it is best so.

I cannot tell you how gentle and good Mr. Carlyle is! He is busy as ever, but he studies my comfort and peace as he never did before. I have engaged a new housemaid, and given warning to the big beautiful blockhead who has filled that function here for the last nine months; this has been a worry too. God bless you all.

Your affectionate
JANE W. CARLYLE.

Ever so few eggs will be worth carriage.

LETTER 291.

For years before this there had been talk from me of a brougham for her; to which she listened with a pleased look, but always in perfect silence. Latterly I had been more stringent and immediate upon it; and had not I been so smothered under 'Frederick,' the poor little enterprise (finance now clearly permitting) would surely have been achieved. Alas, why was not it? That terrible street accident, for instance, might have been avoided. But she continued silent when I spoke or proposed, with a noble delicacy all her own; forbore to take the least step; would not even by a shake of the head, or the least twinkle of satire in her eyes, provoke me to take a step. Those 'hired flys,' so many per week, which were my lazy *succedaneum*, had to be almost forced upon her, and needed argument. It was in vain that I said (what was the exact truth), 'No wife in England deserves better to have a brougham from her husband, or is worthier to drive in it. Why won't you go and buy one at once?' After her return to me the propriety and necessity was still more evident; but her answer still was (and I perceived would always be) that fine, childlike silence, grateful, pleased look, and no word spoken.

Whereupon at length—what I ever since reckon among the chosen mercies of Heaven to me—I did at last myself stir in the matter, and in a week or little more (she also, on sight of this, skilfully co-operating, advising me, as she well could) the long talked of was got done. God be for ever thanked that I did not loiter longer! She had infinite satisfaction in this poor gift; was boundlessly proud of it, as her husband's testimony to her; believed it to be the very saving of her, and the source of all the health she had, &c. &c.

The noble little soul! So pitiful a bit of tribute from me, and to her it was richer than kingdoms.

Oh, when she was taken from me, and I used in my gloomy walks to pass that door where the carriage-maker first brought it out for her approval, the feeling in me was (and at times still is) deeper than tears; and my heart wept tragically loving tears, though my gloomy eyes were dry! And her mare, named 'Bellona!' There is a bitter-sweet in all that, and a pious wealth of woe and love that will abide with me till I die. No more of it here (August 14, 1869).—T. C.

Mrs. Russell, Holm Hill, Thornhill, Dumfriesshire.

5 Cheyne Row, Chelsea: Monday, Oct. 31, 1864.

Dearest,—I am not tied to two hours now for my drive, which was long enough to stay out in a 'fly,' costing, as it did, six shillings! I have now set up a nice little Brougham, or Clarence (as you call it), all to myself, with a smart grey horse and an elderly .driver (in Mr. C.'s old brown surtout)! I was at half-a-dozen coachmakers' yards seeking that carriage, examining with my own eyes, on my own legs! Of course, I took advice as to the outside quality. Mr. Farie and the livery-stable man, who has kept Mr. C.'s horse these dozen years, both approved my choice, and considered it a great bargain. Sixty pounds, and perfectly new, and handsome in a plain way.

It needs no unbleached linen to protect it, being dark blue morocco and cloth inside, which won't dirty in a hurry; and it is all glass in front like Mrs. Ewart's, so you will see finely about you when I drive you to see the lions here. That prospect is one of my pleasures in the new equipage. I have nothing to show you like the drive to Sanquhar; but the parks here are very beautiful, and I never drive through them now without fancying you at my side and seeing them with your fresh eyes. Mr. C. expects to actually finish his book about New Year, and then—please God that I keep well enough for it—we go to Lady Ashburton's, at a new place she has got in Devonshire, where it will be warmer than here, and evidently I can't have too much change! When we come back, and the weather is fit for the journey, the Doctor and you must come.

It has been moist, even rainy, of late; and damp seems to suit me worst of anything. My appetite defies quinine to bring it back, and the *irritation* has been more distressing. Still, I am no worse, on the whole, than when I left you; and I force myself to take always the new milk and the custard at twelve. There is a weighing-machine at our greengrocer's, at the bottom of the street, but I dare not get myself weighed.

I don't like that photograph of Mary at all. The crinoline quite changes her character and makes

her a stranger for me. I want the one that is,
as I have always seen her, a sensible girl with no
crinoline. I would like her, if she would get herself
done for me, as she is on washing mornings—in the
little pink bed-gown and blue petticoat. I send a
shilling in stamps for the purpose, but don't force her
inclinations in the matter.

My friend Mr. Forster was at Müller's trial the
last day—saw him receive his sentence, and said he
behaved very well. When the sentence was pronounced he bowed to the judge, and walked away
with the turnkey. But at the little door leading
down from the court he stopped, and said to the
turnkey that he wished to say a few words to the
judge; and the turnkey led him back; and he said
something which could not be heard, on account of
his keeping his hand at his mouth to steady it.
Forster said the only sign of emotion he had given,
all through the business, was a quivering of his lips.
When told to speak out he removed his hand, and
said courteously to the judge: 'I have had a most
fair trial! but I cannot help saying some of the worst
things said by the witnesses against me are gross
falsehoods.' Then he seemed to break down, and
hurried out. I am certain, had it not been that every
juryman felt his personal safety on the railway com-
promised by the acquittal of this man, he would not
have been condemned to death on the evidence. It

is clear to everybody he had no premeditation of murder, and that Mr. Briggs threw himself out of the carriage, and probably caused his own death thereby. The poor wretch, returning from his visit to his ' unfortunate,' having taken a second-class ticket, had seen Mr. Briggs with his glittering watch-chain get into the first-class carriage, and jumped in after him, thinking the chain would take him to America. It was to take him to a far other land! Curious that he got off, that night, without the discovery of his ticket being second-class. The train had been very late, and, contrary to all use and wont, the tickets were not asked for in the carriages.

I send you a nice letter from Thomas Erskine, the author of many religious books—which I never read, except the first ('Evidences of Christianity'). He is a fine old Scotch gentleman, such as are hardly to be found extant now. Also one from Lady A.

Love to the Doctor. Has the ' young man ' from Laich been to call for you?

Tell me about the poor woman in Thornhill who was to have the operation. Mrs. Beck, was that the name?

Kind regards to Mrs. Ewart, and compliments to —— Mrs. Macgowan.

Your loving
JANE CARLYLE.

Dr. Carlyle left for Lancashire this morning. He will be back in Dumfries shortly, and said he would go up to tell you about me.

LETTER 292.

Mrs. Russell, Holm Hill, Thornhill, Dumfriesshire.

5 Cheyne Row, Chelsea: Saturday, Nov. 12, 1864.

Dearest Mary,—At the beginning of this cold, during the time I was constantly retching, and could swallow nothing, I got a moral shock which would, I think, have killed me at St. Leonards; and all it did to me, I think, was to astonish and disgust me. I told you I was parting with my big beautiful housemaid because she was an incorrigible goose, and destructive and wasteful beyond all human endurance. As a specimen of the waste, figure three pounds of fresh butter at twenty pence a pound regularly consumed in the kitchen, and half a pound of tea at four shillings made away with in four days! Then, as a specimen of the destruction—figure all, every one of my beautiful, fine, and some of them quite new, table napkins actually 'worn out' of existence! Not a rag of them to be found; and good sheets all in rags; besides a boiler burst, a pump-well gone irrecoverably dry, a clock made to strike fourteen every hour, and all the china or crockery in the house either disappeared or cracked! To be sure, the housemaid was not alone to bear the blame of all the mischief, and the cook was to be held responsible for the waste of victuals at least. But Mary—the one who attended me at St. Leonards—though the slowest and stupidest of servants, had so impressed me with the idea of her trustworthiness, and her devotion to me, that I could accuse her of nothing but stupidity and culpable weakness in allowing the other girl, seven years her junior, to rule even in the larder! Accordingly I engaged an elderly woman to be cook and housekeeper, and Mary was to be housemaid, and wait on me as usual. Helen (the housemaid) meanwhile took no steps about seeking a place, and when I urged her to do so, declared she couldn't conceive why I wanted to part with her. When I told her she was too destructive for my means, she answered excitedly: 'Well! when I am out of the house, and can't bear the blame of everything any longer, you will then find out who it is that makes away with the tea, and the butter, and all the things!' As there was nobody else to bear the blame but Mary, and as I trusted her implicitly, I thought no better of the girl for this attempt to clear herself at the expense of nobody knew who; especially as she would not explain when questioned. When I told slow, innocent Mary, she looked quite amazed, and said: 'I don't think Helen knows what she is saying sometimes; she is very strange!'

Well, Mary asked leave to go and see her family in Cambridgeshire before the new servant came home, and got it, though very inconvenient to me. When she took leave of me the night before starting, she said in her half-articulate way: 'I shall be always wondering how you are till I get back.' She was to be away nearly a week. Mrs. Southam, who sat up at night with me last winter, my Charlotte's mother, came part of the day to help Helen. She is a silent woman, never meddling; so I was surprised when she said to me, while lighting my bedroom fire, the day my cold was so bad: 'Helen tells me, ma'am, you are parting with her?' 'Full time,' said I; 'she is a perfect goose.' 'You know best, ma'am,' said the woman; 'but I always like ill to see the innocent suffering for the guilty!' 'What do you mean?' I asked; 'who is the innocent and who is the guilty?' 'Well, ma'am,' said the woman, 'it is known to all the neighbours round here; you will be told some day, and if I don't tell you now, you will blame me for having let you be so deceived. Mary is the worst of girls! . . . . and all the things you have been missing have been spent on her man and her friends. There has been constant company kept in your kitchen since there was no fear of your seeing it; and whenever Helen threatened to tell you, she frightened her into silence by threats of poisoning her and cutting her own throat!'

Now, my dear, if you had seen the creature Mary you would just as soon have suspected the Virgin Mary of such things! But I have investigated, and found it all true. For two years I have been cheated and made a fool of, and laughed at for my softness, by- this half-idiotic-looking woman; and while she was crying up in my bedroom—moaning out, 'What would become of her if I died?' and witnessing in me as sad a spectacle of human agony as could have been anywhere seen; she was giving suppers to men and women downstairs; laughing and swearing— oh, it is too disgusting!

God bless you, dearest.

JANE CARLYLE.

LETTER 293.

Mrs. Russell, Holm Hill, Thornhill, Dumfriesshire.

5 Cheyne Row, Chelsea: Monday, Dec. 20, 1864.

Dearest Friend,—If it is as cold, and snows as hard, there as here, you will be fancying me broken down if I don't write and tell you I am taking all that very easily; driving out every day from two to three hours, as usual. The cold is not so trying for me as the damp, I find. My horse has not stood it nearly so well! I had him roughened the first day of the frost and snow, but nevertheless he managed to get a strain in one of his hind legs, and is now in great trouble, poor beast, with a farrier attending him, and his leg 'swollen awful!' He is a beautiful grey horse, given me, whether I would or no, by Lady Ashburton; but young, and, I am afraid, too sensitive for this world! 'Whenever he is the least put out of his way, he goes off his food,' the groom says. Nobody can say when he will be fit for work again—if ever. Meanwhile I get a horse from the livery stables.

The most spirited thing I have done since you last heard of me was driving to Acton with—Madame Elise! to see her beautiful place there, and take a dinner-tea with her, and back with her, arriving at home as late as six o'clock! It was a pleasant little excursion. Elise, as a woman, with a house and children, is charming. It is a magnificent house, with a dining-room about three times the size of the Wallace Hall dining-room, and a drawing-room to match; both rooms fitted up with the same artist-genius she displays in her dresses! It is an old manor house, with endless passages; and at every turn of the passage there is a bust—Lord Byron, Sir Walter Scott, Pope, Milton, Locke.

The drawing-room opens into a conservatory that

would take Mrs. Pringle's into a small corner of it. There is an immense garden round the house, with greenhouses, and a great green field beyond the garden, with sheep in it—clean sheep! A middle-aged, ladylike governess took charge of the three children: perfect little beauties! and the nurse and other maids had the air of a 'great family' about them. They all treated 'Madame' as if she had been a princess! A triumph of genius!

The only drawback to my satisfaction was a dread of catching cold. The immense rooms had immense fires in them. But their size, and the knowledge that they were only lived in from Saturday till Monday in a general way, gave me a sense of chill; and then being abroad so late at this season was very imprudent. I went to bed with a pain in my shoulder and much self-upbraiding; but got some sleep, and no harm was done.

Do you know that bottle of whisky you gave me has been of the greatest use! Things affect one so differently at different times? Whisky seemed to fever me at Holm Hill. Here it calms me, and helps me to sleep. I take a tablespoonful raw when I get desperate about sleeping, and invariably, hitherto, with good effect. I take no quinine, nor other medicine, at present, except the aperient pills. Half a one I have to take every night. The potash-water

I like very much with my wine and my milk, and take from one to two bottles of it every day.

I have not been weighed again ; but I don't think I can have lost any more, as I eat better since the new cook took me in hand. She continues to be a most comfortable servant : such courtesy ! such equability of temper ! such obligingness ! and all that so cheap ! for the weekly bills are less than when I had ignorant servants. The housemaid is also a good servant, but not so agreeable a one. The droop at the corners of her mouth, indicating a plaintive, even peevish, nature, does not belie her I think. When Mr. C. finds fault, instead of going to do what he wants, she cries and sulks. When are you going to give me little Mary? My compliments to her and to Lady Macbeth.

My grateful and warm love to your husband. To yourself a hundred kisses. I will write soon again.

Your true friend,

JANE CARLYLE.

LETTER 294.

Mrs. Russell, Holm Hill, Thornhill, Dumfriesshire.

5 Cheyne Row, Chelsea : Dec. 27, 1864.

Oh, darling, I have been wanting to write to you every day for a week, but the interruptions have been endless, and the unavoidable letters many. On Christmas Day I thought I should have a quiet day for writing, Mr. C. being to dine at Forster's. But a young German lady of whom I am very fond 'could not let me be left alone,' and came at eleven in the morning and stayed till nine at night; and then our Rector—bless him!—came when he left church and sat with me till eleven.

I wonder how you would have taken a thing that befell me last Wednesday? I was waiting before a shop in Regent Street for some items of stationery; and a young woman, black-eyed, rosy-cheeked, with a child in her arms, thrust herself up to the carriage window and broke forth in a paroxysm of begging: refusing to stand aside even when the shopman was showing me envelopes. Provoked at her noise and pertinacity, I said: 'No, I will give you not a single penny as an encouragement to annoy others as you are annoying me.' If there be still such a thing as the evil eye, that beggar-woman fixed the evil eye on me, and said slowly, and hissing out the words: 'This is Wednesday, lady; perhaps you will be dead by Christmas Day, and have to leave all behind you! Better to have given me a little of it now!' and she scuttled away, leaving me with the novel sensation of being under a curse.

Would you have minded that after the moment? I can't say I took it to heart. At the same time, I was rather glad when, Christmas Day being over, I found myself alive and just as well as before.

Dr. B—— writes that his wife had been dreaming about me again. Bessy is a most portentous dreamer. If I had been told this between the Wednesday and Christmas Day, it would really have frightened me, I think.

My dear, I have got five drops of my heart's blood congealed and fastened together to encircle your wrist, as a memorial of my last visit and as a New Year's blessing. I am hesitating whether to send it by post or by railway. I never lost, or knew personally of anything being lost by post except the Whigham butterfly, so I had best risk it ; there is such confusion of parcels by rail at this time of year. Only I will not register it, as I always think that just points out to the covetous postman what is worth stealing.

Please to send a single line or an old newspaper by return of post, that I may be sure the thing has not misgone.

Ever your affectionate
JANE CARLYLE.

LETTER 295.

Sunday night, January 5, 1865, went out to post-office—with my last leaf of 'Frederick' MS. Evening still vivid to me. I was not joyful of mood; sad rather, mournfully thankful, but indeed half killed, and utterly wearing out and sinking into stupefied collapse after my ' comatose ' efforts to continue the long flight of thirteen years to *finis.* On her face, too, when I went out, there was a silent, faint, and pathetic smile, which I well felt at the moment, and better now! Often enough had it cut me to the heart to think what she was suffering by this book, in which she had no share, no interest, nor any word at all; and with what noble and perfect constancy of silence she bore it all. My own heroic little woman! For long months after this I sank and sank into ever new depths of stupefaction and dull misery of body and mind; nay, once or twice into momentary spurts of impatience even with her, which now often burn me with vain remorse: Madame Elise, e.g.—I sulkily refused to alight at the shop there, though I saw and knew she gently wished it (and right well deserved it); Brompton Museum (which she took me to, always so glad to get me with her, and so seldom could). Oh, cruel, cruel! I have remembered Johnson and Uttoxeter, on thought of that Elise cruelty more than once; and if any clear energy ever returned to me, might some day imitate it.—T. C.

To Mrs. Austin, The Gill, Annan.

5 Cheyne Row, Chelsea: Feb. 1865.

My dear,—The box is come, and this time the eggs have been a great success, not a single one broken! Neither were the cakes broken to any inconvenient degree. Already they are half eaten, by myself. Mr. C. wouldn't take a morsel because ' there was butter in them—a fatal mistake on the part of poor Mary!' I told him I believed it was not butter but cream, and no ' mistake ' at all; as the cakes you made for me in that way at the Gill

R 2

agreed with me quite well. It was so kind of you to take immediate note of my longing! My dear little woman, you not only do kind things, but you do them in such a kind way! Many a kind action misses the grateful feelings it should win by the want of graciousness in the doing.

I continue improving; but a week of terrible pain has given me a good shake, and I don't feel in such good heart about the Devonshire visit as I did. Still it stands settled at present that we go on the 20th, God willing. For how long will depend on how Mr. C. gets on with his sleep, &c.

I shall take my housemaid with me as lady's-maid; for I shudder at the notion of being at the mercy of other people's servants when I am so weak and easily knocked down. She is a very respectable woman, the new housemaid, and both she and Mrs. Warren (the cook) were as kind to me as kind could be when I was laid up. I never was so well cared for before, and with so little fuss, since I left my mother's house. It is a real blessing to have got good, efficient, comfortable servants at last, and I may say I have earned it by the amount of bad servants I have endured.

I have a great deal to do to-day, and little strength; so good-bye. I will write soon again.

Affectionately yours,
JANE CARLYLE.

LETTER 296.

Mrs. Braid, Green End, Edinburgh.

5 Cheyne Row, Chelsea: Feb. 14, 1865.

My own dear Betty! Oh, I am sorry for you! sorrier than I can say in words! I know what a crushing sorrow this will be for you. I, who know your affectionate, unselfish heart, know that the consolations, which some would see for you in poor suffering George's death, will be rather aggravations of the misery! That you should have found at last rest from the incessant, anxious, wearing cares, that have been your lot for years and years— oh, so many years—will be no relief, no consolation to you! This rest will be to you, at first and for long, more irksome, more terrible than the strain on body and mind that went before. He that is taken from you was not merely your own only son, but he was too the occupation of your life, and that is the hardest of all losses to bear up under! Oh, Betty darling, I wish I were near you! If I had my arm about your neck, and your hand in mine, I think I might say things that would comfort you a little, and make you feel that, so long as I am in life, you are not without a child to love you. Indeed, indeed, it is the sort of love one has for one's own mother that I have for you, my dearest Betty! But here I am, four hundred miles away; and with so little power of locomotion compared with what I once had!　And the words fall so cold and flat on paper!

I have been dangerously ill; about three weeks ago I got a chill, at least so the doctor said, and the result was inflammation of the bowels. I was in terrible agony for some days, and confined to bed for a week. I am still very feeble even for me; but there is no return of the miserable nervous illness, which kept me so ruined for more than a year. I cannot write much.

Give my thanks to Mrs. Duncan,[1] who seems a most kind, nice woman. I will write to her when I am a little more able. My kind regards to your husband.

Your own bairn,
JEANNIE WELSH CARLYLE.

LETTER 207.

Seaforth (near Seaton, Devonshire) is the Dowager Lady Ashburton's pretty cottage, who waited for us at the station that Wednesday evening, and was kindness itself. It was Wednesday, March 8, 1865, when we made the journey. The day was dry and temperate; we had a carriage to ourselves, and she (though far weaker than I had the least idea of—stupid I!) made no complaint, nor, indeed, took any harm; though at the end (Lady Ashburton having brought an open carriage

---

[1] Not known to me.

unfit for the coldish evening of a day so bright, we had to wrap our invalid in quite a heap of rugs and shawls, covering her very face and head; in which she patiently acquiesced, nor did she suffer by it afterwards.

I think we stayed above a month; and in spite of the noise, the exposure, &c., she did really well, slept wonderfully, and was charming in her cheerful weakness. She drove out almost or altogether daily. Sir Walter and Lady Trevelyan were close neighbours, often fellow-guests. Sir Walter and I rode almost daily, on ponies; talk innocent, quasi-scientific even, but dull, dull! My days were heavy laden, but had in them something of hope. My darling's well-being helped much. Ah, me! ah, me! We drove to Exeter one day (Lady A., a Miss Dempster, and we two); how pretty and cheery her ways that day! Lady A. came up to London with us. From a newspaper we learned the death of Cobden (which may serve to date if needed).— T. C.

Mrs. Russell, Holm Hill.

Seaforth Lodge, Seaton, Devonshire: March 10, 1865.

Dearest,—I was to have written before I went on my travels, but adverse circumstances were too powerful. First, the nausea, which I think I complained of in my last letter, kept increasing, so that I had no heart to do anything that could be let alone till the last possible moment; and my last days were crammed full of shopping, and packing, and leave-taking, and settling with workmen about repairs, and white-washing to be done in my absence; so that any moment left me to bless myself in was devoted to lying quite done on the sofa, rather than letter-writing.

When we started on Wednesday morning, with, on my part, no sleep ' to speak of,' and five hours of railway before us, besides a carriage drive after, my mood was of the blackest. But George Cooke was at the station to look after our luggage; and, halfway, the sun broke out, and it was new country for me part of the way, and very beautiful. And the sheep, bless them, were not only white as milk, but had dear wee lambs skipping beside them ! And the river, that falls into the sea near here, was not muddy and sluggish, like all the rivers (very few indeed) I had seen since I left dear Nith—but clear as crystal, and bright blue. And, at the end, such a lovely house, on a high cliff overlooking the bluest sea. And such a lovely and loveable hostess ! So truly ' the latter end of that woman was better than the beginning.' I am glad to find the insane horror I conceived of the sea, all in one night at St. Leonards, has quite passed away. I love it again as I had always done till then; and rather regret that no sound of it reaches over the cliff.

But there is something I want to say to you, more interesting to me than the picturesque—something that my heart is set on—about your coming to see London. I know you would make no difficulty for my sake, if for nothing else. It is that calmly obstinate husband of yours, who carries his love of home to such excess, that is the ' lion in the way ' for my imagination. Yet, if he knew how much good I expect to get of having you in London with me, and what efforts I will make to repay him for his efforts, he, who is so kind, so obliging to the poorest old women of the country-side, will surely not resist my entreaties. You are 'to understand that, besides the pleasure of the thing to me, your coming at the time I ask would be doing me a real service; Mr. C. is going on his travels shortly after our return to London from this place—some two or three weeks hence, if all goes right here, and I am to be left alone at Chelsea. Accompanying him would not suit me at all; indeed, several of the houses he is going to could not receive us both at a time, as we need two bedrooms. And then I should prefer doing my out-ing (as the Londoners call it) in autumn. So I shall be alone, needing company; and of all company, I should like best the Doctor's and yours. Then, when he is away, I have plenty of house-room, which is not the case when he is at home, seeing that he occupies two floors of the house ' all to himself!' And I have my time all to myself to show you about London, and my carriage to take you wherever you liked. Oh, my dear, it would be so nice! I have heard

you say the Doctor could leave the bank [1] for a fortnight whenever he liked.   Well! if he could not
stay longer than a fortnight, he might bring you up ;
and see and do all that could be seen and done in
one fortnight, and then leave you for a good while
longer.   You would have no difficulty in going back
along the road you had come ; or I might find some-
one going that direction to take charge of you ; or,
if you were very good, and stayed long enough, I
would go and take charge of you myself, and stay,
not three months next time (!) but a week or two.
Oh, my darling, it would make me so glad!   Surely,
surely, you and the Doctor will not refuse me.   Mr.
Carlyle spoke of writing to you himself to press your
staying with us till he returns.[2]

[Not signed] J. W. C.

LETTER 298.

Mrs. Russell, Holm Hill.

5 Cheyne Row: May 4, 1865.

Darling,—When I came in to-day, and saw a
letter from you on the table, I felt myself make as
near an approximation to a blush as my sallow
complexion is capable of.   It was a little ' coal of

---

[1] Dr. Russell's special employment for years back was superintendence
of a country bank; but his gratis practice of *medicine,* and of every
helpful thing in that region, continued and continues (1860).

[2] Alas! they never came.

fire' heaped on my head! For days back I had been thinking how neglectful I must seem to you, making no answer to that kindest of letters and of invitations, written, too, when you were ailing, and 'looking at the dark of things!' You had still managed to look at the bright of *me*, since you could believe that my presence would 'cheer you' instead of boring you. But it was not that I was really not caring to write, nor yet that I was giving way to physical languor (though that has been considerable). It was that for the last week or two I have been kept in a whirl of things which made it out of the question for me to sit down quietly, and make up my mind what to say.

Mr. C. has been sitting to Woolner for his bust; and it seems he 'is as difficult to catch a likeness of' as a flash of lightning' is; so that it is a trying business for both sitter and sculptor. I have had to drive up to Woolner's every two or three days, and climb steep endless stairs to tell what faults I see. And in connection with this bust, there has been such a sitting to photographers as never was heard of! Woolner wants a variety of photographs to work from, and the photographer wants a variety to sell! and Mr. Carlyle yields to their mutual entreaties. And then, when they have had their will of him, they insist on doing me (for my name's sake). And Mr. C. insists too, thinking always the new one may be

more successful than former ones ; so that, with one
thing and another, I have been worried from morning
till night, and postponed writing till I should have
got leisure to think what was to be written. But I
must not put off any longer, since you are getting
uneasy about me.

I am not worse—indeed, as to the sickness and
the sleeplessness I am rather better in both respects
—but I am weak and languid, have little appetite,
and am getting thinner. The best thing for me
would be to get away ; and away to you, rather than
anywhere else ! I know that well enough in both
my heart and my head ; but one cannot do just what
one likes best, and even what is best for one. I
could not go with Mr. C. for several reasons. First,
having made up his mind to go off ' at his own sweet
will,' and having understood that I was to stay
behind, he would now find it a great incumbrance to
take me with him. Second, I have invited Dr.
B—— and Bessy to pay me a visit so soon as I
have a bedroom for them ; and they have promised
to come for a few days.[1] About the end of May is
the doctor's leisurest time at St. Leonards. Third,
Mr. C. wants the dining-room papered, and fitted up
with bookcases from the study at the top of the
house ; which is too long a climb for him now that
' Frederick ' is done. That he expects me to ' see to '

---

[1] They never came.

in his absence. And how long it will take me to
' see to it ' will depend on the workmen.

For the rest, I am uncertain how long he will be
away ; if ' months' (as he speaks of), there might still
be time for me, after I had finished my business here,
to rush off to Holm Hill, and stay as many weeks with
you as I stayed *months* last year. I should so like it !
And Mr. C. wouldn't object, though he would find it
very absurd to be taking such a long journey so soon
again. I put out a *feeler* the other night ; Miss
Dempster was pressing him to visit her when he
should be in Forfarshire (he is going to Linlathen
amongst other places), and I said : ' I shall perhaps
be nearer you than he will be ! Lady Airlie was
pressing me so hard to-day to come to Cortachy
Castle, that there is no saying but I will follow him
north.' ' Indeed ! ' he said, not with a frown, but
a smile. And I added, ' If he stays away long I
may at least get the length of Dumfriesshire.' But
till I get my workmen out of the house, and know
something definite of Mr. C.'s plans, I can determine
nothing. Will you let me leave it open ? I like so
ill to say positively, and absolutely, ' No, I cannot
come this year ! ' Because, you see, having a character for standing by my word to keep up, I could
not, after an absolute ' no ' said now, avail myself of
any facilities for going to you which may turn up
later. So may I leave the question open ?

How absurd! In telling you on the other sheet how I was bodily, I quite forgot to mention my most serious ailment for the last six weeks. My right arm has gone the way that my left went two years ago, gives me considerable pain, so that I cannot lie upon it, or make any effort (such as ringing a bell, opening a window, &c. &c.) with it; and if anyone shakes my hand heartily, I—shriek! Geraldine Jewsbury is always asking, 'Have you written to Dr. Russell yet about your arm?' But what could any-one do before for the other arm? All that was tried was useless except quinine; and quinine destroys my sleep. I must just hope it will mend of itself as the other did.

Your ever-attached friend,
Jane W. Carlyle.

LETTER 299.

To-day (August 9, 1866) I have discovered in drawers of pedestal these mournful letters of my darling in 1865. They had lain torn in my writing-case, till their covers were all lost, and there is now no correct dating of them. I have tried to save the sequence and be as correct as I could. Here are the cardinal dates. About May 20 I went to Dumfries, thence to the Gill; and she, here at home (courageous little soul!), began doing this room (the very beauty of which now pains and amazes me).

Beginning of May her right arm took ill, as her left had done last year, and she painfully went and came between

Streatham and here for some time (perhaps near a fort-night), writing with her left hand. June 17, she passed me (little guessing of her in the rail) and went to Holm Hill; very ill then too, still left hand; and thence in July to Nithbank, and after about ten or twelve days (middle or farther of July) went home somewhat better; got her room done, recovered her right hand, and went to Folkestone to Miss Bromley's for a few days (which proved her last visit, little as I then anticipated). Her beautiful figure and presence welcoming me home (end of August) will never leave my memory more.—T. C.

T. Carlyle, Esq., The Hill, Dumfries.

5 Cheyne Row, Wednesday, May 24, 1865.

I wonder if you will get this letter to-morrow, should it be put in the pillar to-night? Dear! dear! should no word reach you till Friday morning, you will be ' vaixed,' and perhaps frightened besides.

The figure I cut on Monday morning was not encouraging. When I had cried a very little at being left by myself, I lay on the sofa till mid-day, not sleeping, but considering what to do for the best with this arm, which had got to a pitch, and was reducing me to the state of last year in point of sleep. And the result of my considerations was, first, a note to Dr. B——, urging him and Bessy to keep their promise of spending a couple of days with me as soon as possible; and next, in the meantime, a call at Quilter's to order the old quinine pills and a bottle of castor oil. If I am to be kept awake all night at any rate by the pain, I may as well have recourse to the only prescription which did any good to the other arm—even at the cost of sleep. That first day I also called at the carpenter's, to *lever* himself, for he 'had great things to do.' Then on to luncheon at the Gomms'. Do you remember I was engaged to luncheon there? They have a beautiful, large, old-fashioned, cool house. And the luncheon was a sonnet done into dainties. I brought away Lord Lothian's book on America, but have not yet read a word of it, nor of anything else—not even of Mrs. Paulet's novel, nor my own 'Daily Telegraph.' On my return, I came upon Geraldine in Cheyne Row; and she 'could not leave me' till ten at night, I 'looked such a ghost.'

On Tuesday I had to take Mrs. Blunt to make calls at Fulham; and then I 'did the civil thing' to Mrs. F——. F—— was in, and talked much of your 'gentleness and tenderness of late,' and the 'much greater patience you had in speaking of everybody and everything.' And I thought to myself, 'If he had only heard you a few hours after that walk with him, in which you had made such a lamb-like impression!' He expressed a wish to read Mrs. Paulet's novel, and I have sent it to him. A very curious, clever, 'excessively ridiculous, and perfectly unnecessary' book is Mrs. Paulet's novel, so far as I have read in the first volume. And Mrs. Paulet herself I don't know what to make of, for I have seen her. In my saintly forgiveness and beautiful pity I left a card for her yesterday; and she came a few hours after; and Geraldine, too, came; and I was not left alone till half-past ten, when it was too late to write.

This morning (I don't know by what right) I expected a letter from you, which did not come till the afternoon. And positively I was almost well pleased there was no letter—to answer, for I had 'indulged in a cup' of castor oil, and was—oh, so sick; and besides, that matter had unexpectedly taken to 'culminating' again. Last night there had come from Jessie Hiddlestone a very nice letter, not accepting my rejection on the score of the 'situation' being 'too dull for her,' but assuring me that she would not 'be the least dull and discontented,' and 'altogether' throwing a quite different and rosier colour on the project. I will inclose the letter, and you will read it, and tell me if you think I was right in being moved thereby to engage her; for that is what I have done this forenoon, in the middle of my sorrows of castor oil!

For the rest I have no doubt you will get better, and do well there for a time. Perhaps I shall take flight myself if my terrible nights continue too long for endurance and this wearing pain lasts. It is pulling me down sadly; and neuralgia has such an effect on the spirits.

One thing I have to say, that I beg you will give ear to. I have not recovered yet the shock it was to me to find, after six months, all those weak, wretched letters I wrote you from Holm Hill 'dadding about' in the dining-room; and should you use my letters in that way again I shall know it by instinct, and not write to you at all! There!

Please return Jessie Hiddlestone's letter.

Your ever affectionate

JANE W. CARLYLE.

LETTER 300.

To T. Carlyle, Esq., The Hill, Dumfries.

5 Cheyne Row, Chelsea: Saturday, May 27, 1865.

I think, dear, you must have lost a day this week —must have—stop! No! I should have said— gained a day! You bid me 'not bother myself writing to-morrow, but send a word on Saturday.' And the to-morrow is Saturday. This day on which I am not to 'bother myself writing' is Saturday. I posted a letter to you yesterday at the right time. That night post is later than you think. It was past nine when Fanny put in the pillar the letter you received the following evening at eight.

My quinine and castor oil have quite failed of

doing the good to my right arm which they formerly did to my left. The pain gets more severe and more continuous from day to day. Last night it kept me almost entirely awake. I often wonder that I am able to keep on foot during the day, and take my three hours' drives, and talk to the people who come to relieve my loneliness, with that arm always in pain, as if a dog were gnawing and tearing at it! But anything rather than the old nervous misery, which was not to be called pain at all! positive natural pain I can bear as well as most people. But I wish Dr. B—— would come! Perhaps he can deal with a reality like this, though he could 'do nothing against hysterical mania!'[1] I got the thing he mentioned, Veratrine lineament, yesterday, from Quiller; and Geraldine rubbed it in for an hour last night. But, as I said, last night was the worst!

George Cooke said you desired him to 'come often, and look after me!' 'Perfectly unnecessary;' I mean the desiring! Couldn't you fetch up Noggs[2] to Dumfries. So much walking in such hot weather must be tiring.

All good be with you,
Yours ever,
J. W. C.

---

[1] His phrase to me one day at St. Leonards—in that desperate time.
[2] My saucy little Arab (gift of Lady Ashburton).

LETTER 301.

T. Carlyle, Esq., The Gill.

Thursday, June 1, 1865.

Dearest,—' You must excuse us the day.' I really cannot use my hand without extreme pain; and Geraldine has not come in to write for me.

I am just going off to Dr. Quain; since Dr. B—— is postponed into the vague. I have been quite wild with the pain, the last two nights and days. To-morrow I will go to these good Macmillans whom you sneered at as my ' distinguished visitors.' None of the more ' distinguished ' have come to me with such practical help and sympathy. They are just the right distance off. I can have my carriage come and take me home any day to look after the house; and for a drive as usual.

I think you will be better at the Gill than the Hill, in spite of the grand house, if you can only sleep through the railway; and do not indulge too far in curds and cream for dinner.

God bless you.

Your lamed

GOODY.

LETTER 302.

T. Carlyle, Esq., The Gill.

Streatham Lane:[1] Saturday, June 3, 1865.

Dearest,—You are so good about writing that you deserve to be goodly done by ; so I write a few lines to-day 'under difficulties,' though you gave me an excuse for putting off, in saying you could not hear till Tuesday. But I must study brevity, the soul of wit, for the cost of physical pain at which I write is something you can hardly conceive!

When I got your letter telling me to hold my hand, it was too late! I had set my heart on doing one more stroke of work (my sort of work), fitting up one more room before I died![2] It was all very well to say ' give the room a good cleaning.' But no amount of mere cleaning could give that room a clean look, with that *oory*, dingy paint and paper. To put clean paper without fresh paint would only have made the dirtiness of the paint more flagrant. And if the painting was not done whilst you were away, when was there a chance of doing it? I knew I couldn't sleep in wet paint; but I looked to finding a bed somewhere : and the offer of one here came most opportunely.

The day before leaving home I went to Dr. Quain,

---

[1] Mr. Macmillan's house (fine old-fashioned suburban villa there).
[2] Alas, and this was it : often have I remembered that word.

who did me at least the good of being extremely kind, and eager to help me. He said I had ' much fever ; ' and gave me a prescription for that, and two other prescriptions. And when I returned from here, I was to tell him, and he would ' run over.' I said to him that Dr. B—— had declared I had no organic disease, but only a strong predisposition to gout! ' Quite right,' he said, ' that is the fact.' ' Then,' I asked, ' perhaps this affair in my arm, so much more painful than what I had in the left arm, is gout?' 'I have not the least doubt that it is!!' was his answer. Pleasant!

Well! I came here about five yesterday ; and the good simple people welcomed me most honestly ; and Mr. Macmillan sang Scotch songs, which would have charmed you, all the evening, the governess playing an accompaniment. At eleven I retired to my beautiful bedroom, the largest, prettiest, freshest bedroom I ever was put to sleep in ! And then they left me to the society of a watchdog, chained under my window !!! It barked and growled and howled in the maddest manner till they set it loose at seven in the morning. Of course I never closed my eyes for one minute all the night! and I got up in the morning a sadder and a wiser woman! How to get away without hurting feelings? I was the wretchedest woman till I got it settled softly, that when the carriage comes for me to-day to take me home for an inspection of the work, it should not bring me back, but leave me to sleep or wake in my own quiet bed; and to come out to-morrow to spend the day, and sleep here or there after, as I liked best. The dog to be 'removed to a greater distance.' So address to Cheyne Row.

Dr. Quain said I must go as soon as possible to Scotland, 'as it had agreed so well with me last year.' I said I shuddered at the length of the journey; he reminded me that I had done it with impunity last year when I was weaker than now. I suppose it will come to that before long! I need have no doubt about my welcome.

Since you are not disturbed by that railway which drove me mad, you will do well at Mary's; she is so kind and unfussing. But you must not exceed in milk diet &c.! You must have mutton!

And oh, take care with Noggs on these hilly roads! Oh, my dear, I am not up to more; my arm is just as if a dog had got it in its teeth, and were gnawing at it, and shaking at it furiously.

Love to Mary.

Your ever affectionate
JANE CARLYLE.

LETTER 303.

T. Carlyle, Esq., The Gill.

5 Cheyne Row, Chelsea: Wednesday, June 7, 1865.

Dear Mr. Carlyle,—You will be disappointed to see my handwriting, instead of Jane's; but to-day it is not a matter of choice, but of necessity; for the pain and swelling in her hand and fingers make them entirely helpless; and she has to feed herself with the left hand. She has just come in from Mrs. Macmillan's; and has been selecting a paper for the dining-room. She incloses the three patterns, which we all think the prettiest of those submitted to us; and she says, Will you please to say which of the three *you* like the best? I think Jane is a shade better than when she went last Friday; but still to-day she is very poorly, and pulled down by the pain, which seems to increase. She would sleep if it were not for that; she does manage to sleep a little. Everything, she says, is most charmingly comfortable; and the dog has been reduced to silence.

My great hope is in Scotland; and she seems to look forward to going, which in itself is a good thing. Please to address your next letter to Streatham Lane, as they are delayed by coming here first.

I am, dear Mr. Carlyle,

Yours very respectfully,

GERALDINE E. JEWSBURY.

LETTER 304.

In pencil, with the left hand, and already well done.—T. C.

T. Carlyle, Esq., The Gill.

Streatham: Monday, June 12, 1865.

Dearest,—I will write before returning home. There will be neither peace nor time there. Thanks! I never needed more to be made much of. I must tell you about my hand: you think the swelling more important than it is; the two middle fingers were much as now for some weeks before you left, but with the thumb and forefinger I could still do much; now the forefinger is as powerless and pained as the other two; that is all the difference, but a conclusive one, for one can do nothing with only a thumb! I could sometimes sit down and cry. The pain—the chief pain—that which wakes me from my sleep is in the shoulder and forearm. Even hopeful Dr. Quain does not tell me I shall soon get back my hand, only tells me blandly I must learn to write with my left; and it was he who told me to take a black-lead pencil. I went to him on Friday by appointment when I had finished the antifebrile powders. I think they have quieted me. He gave me a bumper of champagne; was kind as kind could be; desired me to try the quinine once more; said Dr. B——'s prescription was an ' admirable suggestion, and well worth my trying, but, as it would cause me a good deal of pain and feverishness, I had better wait till after my journey to Scotland.' He does me real good by his kindness.

My visit here has been a great success, so far as depended on my host and hostess; and I am certainly better in my general health for all the nourishing things they have put into me by day and by night. It is a place you might fly to in a bilious crisis. Quiet as heaven, when the dog is in the wash-house.

Bellona (my mare) has given me a fine fright. You would never believe she was not safe to be left. It has been the nearest miss of herself and the carriage being all smashed to pieces! She has escaped miraculously without scratch. The carriage has not been so fortunate. I am not up to writing the narrative to-day.

Love to my dear kind Mary.

Your loving but unfortunate

J. W. C.

LETTER 305.

T. Carlyle, Esq., The Gill.

Railway Hotel, Carlisle: Saturday, June 17, 1865.

Here I am! as well as could be expected, after travelling all night, choked in dust—an unprotected female with one arm! It is no sudden thought striking me! My mind has been made up to 'try a change,' ever since my last interview with Dr. Quain, and to try it with as little delay as possible. But I would not tell you I was coming; because it was important that I should travel by night; and for you to meet me at Carlisle would have necessitated your sleeping there (an impossibility!) or else your starting from the Gill at an unearthly hour. Kindest not to place you in the dilemma!

Up to the last moment, I schemed about taking the Gill on my road to Dumfries and appointing you to meet me. But I was sure to be awfully tired, just every atom of strength needed to carry me on to Thornhill without increasing my fatigues by the smallest demand, or by any avoidable 'emotion of the mind.' To stay here a couple of hours, and have breakfast and rest; and then on past Cummertrees, with shut eyes, to the place of my destination, seemed the wisest course. To this, since my arrival here, has been added the sublime idea to throw out a note for you, and a sixpence at Cummertrees; as it had suddenly flashed on me that no letter from me could reach you by post till Tuesday. So soon as I am rested, I will make an appointment with you to meet at Dumfries, if you would rather not come on to Holm Hill.

To think that I shall fly past within a quarter of a mile of you presently; and you will have no perception of my nearness!

Yours ever.

A kiss to Mary.

J. W. C.

LETTER 306.

The 'Saturday' in this letter must refer to the visit she proposed making us at the Gill. Jamie of Scotsbrig particularly invited. Mournfully I ever recollect the day: bright and sunny; Jamie punctually there; I confidently expecting. Fool! I had not the least conception of her utter feebleness, and that she was never to visit 'The Gill' more! Train passed. I hung about impatiently till the gig should return from Cummertrees Station—with her, I never doubted. It came with John instead, to say she had been obliged to stop at Dumfries, and I must come thither by the next train: 'be exact; there will be a two and a half or three hours for us there still.' I went (with John, Jamie regretfully turning home). She was so pleasant, beautifully cheerful, and quiet, I enjoyed my three hours without misgiving. Fool! fool!—and yet there was a strange infinitude of sorrow and pity encircling all things and persons for me —her beyond all others, though being really myself as if crushed flat after such a 'flight' of twelve or thirteen years, latterly on the Owen 'comatose' terms. I was stupefied into blindness! The time till her train should come was beautiful to me and everybody. Cab came for her, I escorting (the rest walked, for it was hardly five minutes off). Train was considerably too late. An old and good dumb 'Mr. Turner,' whom she recognised and remembered kindly after forty years, was brought forward at her desire by brother John. Her talk with Turner (by slate and pencil, I writing for her)—ah me! ah me! It was on the platform-seat, under an awning; she sat by me; the great, red, sinking sun flooding everything: day's last radiance, night's first silence. Grand, dumb, and unspeakable is that scene now to me. I sat by her in the railway carriage (empty otherwise) till the train gave its third signal, and she vanished from my eyes.—T. C.

T. Carlyle, Esq., The Gill.

Holm Hill, Wednesday, June 28, 1865.

I cannot make it Friday, dear—at least, could not without rudeness to a nice woman who has always been kind to me. I am engaged to dine with my sort of a cousin, Mrs. Hunter, on Friday, having been invited for Thursday, and asked to have the day changed to Friday. And last year, when she had got up a dinner for me, I had to send an excuse at the last hour, being too ill. To-morrow you will now be hardly expecting me. So let us say Saturday; if that does not suit there will be time to tell me. ' The wine I drink?' Oh, my! That it should be come to that. But surely you ought not to be without wine, setting aside me.

Don't be bothering, making plans embracing me. The chief good of a holiday for a man is just that he should have shaken off home cares—the foremost of these a wife. Consider that, for the present summer, you have nothing to do with me, but write me nice daily letters, and pay my bills. I came on my own hook, and so will I continue, and so will I go! To be living *in family* in some country place is just like no holiday at all, but like living at home ' under diffi-culties.' Shall I ever forget ' the cares of meat ' at Auchtertool House ? [1] ever forget the maggots gene-rated by the sun in loins of mutton on the road from

---

[1] In 1859 : ' Cares of bread.'—Mazzini's phrase.

Kirkcaldy, and all the other squalid miseries of that time, for which I, as housewife, was held responsible, and had my heart broken twenty times a day? Well, my worried arm is pain enough for the present, without recalling past griefs. To-day, however, I feel rather easier. And I had more and better sleep last night. Thanks to exhaustion! for the preceding night I had not closed my eyes at all.

It is such a pity but I could have a little bodily ease. For I was never more disposed to be content with ' things in general.' I could really feel ' happy,' if it were not for my arm, and the perfectly horrid nights it causes me.

Jessie Hiddlestone is in Thornhill, awaiting my orders—the most promising-looking servant we have had since her mother. I am greatly pleased with her, and so glad I had faith in breed and engaged her. Many were eager to have her. But she was ' prood to go back to the family!' 'The family?' Where are they?

My dear, your observation of handwritings is perfectly amazing. You take Geraldine's writing for mine, Mr. Macmillan's for Geraldine's. And now I send you a charming, witty, grateful little letter of Madame Venturi's, with vignette[1] of Venturi sawing; and you seem to have taken it for, Mrs. Paulet's. You could not possibly have read the letter, or you

---

[1] Maid's writing begins.

could not have made such a mistake ; so I advise you to read it now, with a key : 'The Gorilla' means George Cooke, 'M.' stands for Mazzini, the sawer Venturi.

Since you wish to know, I have gone back to sherry. And now good-bye till Saturday, unless I hear to the contrary. My left hand had taken the cramp, so this is the writing of the housemaid, who takes the opportunity to assure you that she means to be a very good girl, and try to please you, for the sake of her mother, who liked you so well.

J. CARLYLE.

[Madame Venturi had been Miss Ashurst, of a well-known London parentage. She had (and has) fine faculties, a decidedly artistic turn, which led her much to Italy, &c. Venturi was a Tyrolese Venetian (ex-Austrian military cadet, and also Garibaldist to the bone, consequently in a bad Italian position), who had fallen in love at first sight, &c., &c. ; and was now fitting up a modest English house for wife and self. Within a year he died tragically—as will be seen.—T. C.]

LETTER 307.

T. Carlyle, Esq., The Gill, Annan.

Nith Bank, Thornhill: Tuesday.

Dearest,—A regular wet day. No drive possible. Well, the image of driving you have just set before my imagination—you driving me with Noggs in London—is quite enough for one day. It melts the marrow in my bones! Nor is there much relief in turning to that other picture — little Mary flying through the air in one of his 'explosions' and breaking her skull! If you were to put an advertisement in the newspapers that the horse of Thomas Carlyle was for sale, there would be competition for the possession of it.

The housemaid, while combing my hair this morning, fell to telling me of 'ever so many young drapers, an' the like,' that of her knowledge had 'run frae Thornhill to the station to get a bare look o' Mr. Carlyle! And when Mr. Morrison' (the minister of Durrisdeer) 'cam' to his dinner yesterday, the first word oot o' his heed, on the very door-steps, was: "Is Mrs. Carlyle still here?" He never asket for Mrs. Ewart or the ither ladies, but only for you, mem!' I endeavoured to inform her mind by telling her, 'Yes; people liked to see any lady much spoken of, whether for good or ill. If Dr. Pritchard [1] had been at the station, all Thornhill together would have run to see him.' 'Oddsake!' said the girl, 'I daresay they would; I daresay ye're richt; but I never thocht o' that afore.'

Geraldine writes that never was such 'emotion' excited by a speech as by this of Mill's. 'Public Opinion' came addressed to you at Nith Bank in Mrs. Warren's [2] hand. How she came to know the name Nith Bank I am puzzled to know.

---

[1] Glasgow poisoner in those weeks.   [2] Servant here.

I took the quinine and iron yesterday twice, and slept rather sounder than otherwise. But I had a badish headache all morning. Nevertheless I took another dose before breakfast, as Dr. Russell had ordered, and the headache is wearing off.

I adhere to the intention of Dumfries for Friday, if it suit you and Mary.

Affectionately,
JANE.

LETTER 308.

Monday, July 24.—Early in the forenoon I was waiting at Dumfries for her train Londonward ; got into her carriage (empty otherwise), and sate talking and encouraging as I could to Annan (which would hardly be an hour). Servant Jessie was in the same train ; also Jamie Aitken, junior, for Liverpool. I felt in secret extremely miserable ; agitated she, no doubt, and even terrified, but resolute—and *the lid shut down.* I little thought it would be her last railway journey.—T. C.

T. Carlyle, Esq.

5 Cheyne Row, Chelsea : Thursday, July 27, 1865.

All goes well still, dearest, and this time nothing serious is *manquing.* The second night, as I expected, I slept ' beautiful.' Three hours without a break, to begin with. When I woke from that, I not only didn't know where I was, but didn't know who I was ! As I got out of bed (by force of habit) to look at my watch, I was saying to myself, ' It can't be me that has made this fine sleep. It must be somebody else.' It was a full minute, I am sure, before I could satisfy myself that I hadn't been changed into somebody else. Then I slept piecemeal till seven o'clock, when I was startled erect by what seemed the house falling. Jessie came at my call, looking very guilty, and explained that it was she, who had been coming downstairs very softly, for fear of waking me, and, having new shoes on, had ' slid and sossed down on her back,' just opposite my bed-head. Luckily she was none the worse for the fall. A greater contrast than that young woman is to Fanny cannot be figured. So quick, so willing, so intelligent; never needs to be told a thing twice; and so warmly human ! My only fear about her is that she will be married-up away from me. Mrs. Warren calls her ' my dear,' and they get on charmingly together.

The person who addressed the newspaper to you at ' Coming Trees ' was Fanny, who had called to ask if I would ' see a lady ' for her, and Mrs. Warren being busy asked her to address the newspaper.

On Tuesday Bellona, who had been warned a week before, came round at one ; and after some shopping I called at Grosvenor Street, and found Miss Bromley at home—a satisfaction which I owed to the youngest of the three pugs, ' Jocky,' who was ' suffering from the heat.' She was delighted to see me ; most anxious I should come to her at

Folkestone; and told me, to my great joy, that Lady A. had not started on the 21st; wasn't going till Thursday (to-day); was staying at Bath House, but gone that morning to Bath for one day. I left a card and message at Bath House on the road home. Yesterday (Wednesday) I drove to Bath House, the first thing when I went out at one, and found the lady looking lovely in a spruce little half-mourning bonnet; and she would, 'if it was within the bounds of possibility,' come to me in the evening 'between ten and eleven;' and I went in her carriage with her (my own following) to Norfolk Street (Mrs. Anstruther's) to see baby, who is going with her mother to Germany after all. I left her there, and got into my own carriage, and went and bought my birthday present with the sovereign—at least, I paid out fifteen shillings of it. On what? My dear, the thing I bought was most appropriate, and rather touching. I drove to the great shop in Conduit Street, where the world is supplied with 'trusses,' 'laced stockings,' and mechanical appliances for every species of human derangement, and bought a dainty little sling for my arm. The mere ribbon round my neck hurt my neck, and drew my head down. This fastens across the back, and is altogether a superior contrivance. I don't believe in Dr. Russell's prediction any more than you do. At all rates, there was no call on him to state so hopeless a view of the question when I was not asking his opinion at all. It could do no harm to leave me the consolation of hope. But I will hope in spite of him. Indeed, it seems to me that ever since he said I should never get the use of my hand, nor get rid of the pain there, that a spirit of protest and opposition has animated the poor hand, and set it on trying to do things it had for some time ceased from doing.

Lady A. did come last night—came at half after eleven, and stayed till near one! Mrs. Anstruther was left sitting in the carriage, and sent up to say 'it was on the stroke of twelve;' and then, with Lady A.'s permission, I invited her up; and if it hadn't been for her I don't think Lady A. would have gone till daylight! She said in going, 'My regards—my—what shall I send to him?' (you). 'Oh,' I said, 'send him a kiss!' 'That is just what I should like,' she said; 'but would he not think it forward?' 'Oh, dear, not at all!' I said. So you are to consider yourself kissed. I am going up to Bath House now. She goes at night.

Lady Stanley writes to ask how I am, and to beg that you will come that way.

What a long letter! I ought to have said that all this did not give me a bad night. Of course I did not sleep as on the preceding night, but better than

I ever did at Holm Hill; and the pain in my arm is really less since I came home.

Yours affectionately,

JANE CARLYLE.

LETTER 309.

T. Carlyle, Esq.

5 Cheyne Row, Chelsea: Sunday, July 30, 1865.

I will write to-night, dearest, while the way is open to me. To-morrow I shall be busy from the time I get up till Bellona comes for me; and after driving there is no time, as I take the three hours at least every day. It is such 'a privilege' (as Maria's mother would say) to have a carriage and a Bellona ' all to oneself,' independent of all agricultural operations. I don't feel it too warm a bit when I haven't to walk on the hot pavement, though they are celebrating the thermometer at 85° in the shade. But anyhow Miss Bromley is irresistibly pressing; and I have promised to go to her about the twelfth, whether my work here is done or not. She will write to you, to urge your joining me, which you will do—won't you?—if I, on surveying the premises, can promise you a tolerably quiet bedroom. Of course I shall take Jessie, as I can't put my clothes off and on yet without help. I think of staying about a fortnight.

I am sorry you gave up the sailing and Thurso.

Sailing agrees with you, and you had good sleep at
Thurso. 'The good, the beautiful, and the true'
came last evening, to inquire how I was after my
journey, and to tell me, who knew nothing and cared
less, how he had written letters of introduction for
Dr. Carlyle, and sent them to the captain of some
steamer, &c. &c., and how his wife had set her heart
on having a lock of your hair and mine set in a
brooch, and he had promised her to try and complete her wishes. And it ended—for happily everything does end—in his begging and receiving the last
pen you used, to be kept under a glass case. I have
seldom seen a foolisher hero-worshipper. But the
greatest testimony to your fame seems to me to be
the fact of my photograph—the whole three, two of
them very ugly (Watkins's)—stuck up in Macmichael's
shop-window. Did you ever hear anything so preposterous in your life? And what impertinence on
the part of Watkins! He must have sent my three
along with your nine to the wholesale man in Soho
Square, without leave asked. But it proves the interest or curiosity you excite; for being neither a
'distinguished authoress,' nor 'a celebrated mur-
deress,' nor an actress, nor a 'Skittles' (the four
classes of women promoted to the shop-windows),
it can only be as Mrs. Carlyle that they offer me for
sale.

I continue to sleep on the improved principle,

and my arm continues less painful, and my hand, if not more capable, is at least more venturesome.

I saw Dr. Quain on Saturday, and he 'approved highly of my present course of treatment—that is, taking neither quinine nor anything else.' I told him what Dr. Russell had said, and his answer was, 'How could he know? That is what nobody could say but God Almighty.'

I drove to Streatham Lane to-day, and saw the Macmillans; also Mr. and Mrs. George Craik.[1] Mr. Macmillan is greatly delighted with him as a junior partner. They did not look at all ill-matched. His physical sufferings have made up in looks the ten years of difference. He has got an excellent imitation leg, and walks on it much better than American James.

God keep you.

Your affectionate
JANE.

LETTER 310.

Mrs. Russell, Holm Hill.

5 Cheyne Row: Aug. 7, 1865.

Dearest,—Just a line to say that all goes well with my health. I continue to sleep better—almost to sleep well; and the pain is greatly gone out of my

---

[1] Miss Mulock once, now a current authoress of *John Halifax,* &c. &c.

arm, and I use my hand a little; this charming penmanship is from my right hand.

But I have no time for elaborate writing. I was never busier in my life; about three thousand volumes have had to pass through my hands, and be arranged on the shelves by myself; nobody else could help me. The new room is getting finished, and will strike Mr. C. dumb with admiration when he comes.

Yours affectionately,

JANE CARLYLE.

LETTER 311.

Brother John and I, as I now recollect, were in and about Edinburgh, Stowe, Newbattle (I *solus* for a call); then Linlathen both, for some days; whence to Stirling of Keir (dreary rail journey, dreary all, though in itself beautiful and kind); thence to Edinburgh (John's bad lodging there, &c.), after which back to Dumfriesshire—to Scotsbrig, I suppose. Before this I had been three days at Keswick with my valued old friend, T. Spedding; walked to *Bassenthwaite Ha's*. (Seen five-and-forty years ago and not recognisable!) Nothing could exceed my private weariness, sadness, misery, and depression. Little thought it was, within few months, to be all sharpened into poignancy and tenderest woe, and remain with me in that far exceeding if somewhat nobler form.—T. C.

T. Carlyle, Esq.

5 Cheyne Row, Chelsea: Friday, Aug. 12, 1865.

Dearest,—It all came of you being moving, and me sitting still! I didn't know exactly when and where a letter would find you, and was occupied enough to avail myself of the shabby excuse for spending no time in writing. Besides, the time is always much longer for the person on his travels than for the one at home. And your right address did not reach me in time for that day's post. It came to hand at tea-time, as did yesterday's newspaper. So I could only answer at night to be ready for the post of yesterday. To-day I send a line or two, remembering that Sunday you can get nothing.

Jessie and I are alone just now, Mrs. Warren having petitioned for 'her holiday.' No age exempts people here from the appetite for holidays. She left on Wednesday afternoon, and does not return till Sunday, in time to see me off on Monday. As that new journey comes near, I shudder at it considerably. '*Stava bene!*'

If you cannot be at the trouble to go out to Betty's, do send her a line, telling where and when she can come to you. She will read in the newspapers that you are in Edinburgh, and break her poor old heart over it if she gets no sight of you.[1] She has already had one bad disappointment in not seeing me when I was so near.

We had a great thunderstorm last evening, and the air to-day is delightfully fresh. I had poor little Madame Reichenbach at tea with me, and her husband came late to take her home; and the thunder

---

[1] I did go.

burst, and the rain fell; and the lamp was burning dim; and the dingy little countess from time to time made little moaning speeches in English—unintelligible, 'upon my honour!'—and Reichenbach, as usual, sat with crossed arms, and knitted brows, silent as the tombs! And to let them walk home in such pouring wet seemed too cruel; and they had no shilling to take a cab; and I would gladly have paid a cab for them, but, of course, dared not! And, 'altogether, the situation was rather exquisite!'[1]

And now I must conclude, and prepare for Bellona. That poor beast behaves quite well at present. Of course, old Silvester never quits the box. I couldn't have the heart to complain about his having grown old.

I will send my address—or stop! 'Tuesday next!' —perhaps better send it now:

'Care of Miss Davenport Bromley,

'4 Langhorne Gardens, West Cliff, Folkestone.'

Yours lovingly,

JANE CARLYLE.

LETTER 312.

T. Carlyle, Esq., Scotsbrig.

Folkestone: Saturday, Aug. 19, 1865.

Dearest,—It will be surest to direct to Scotsbrig; one might easily fail of hitting you on the wing at

---

[1] 'Pang which was exquisite.' Foolish phrase of Godwin's in his *Life of Mary Wollstonecraft.*

Edinburgh! But I wish you could have brought yourself to go for a few days to the Lothians ;[1] their patience and perseverance in asking you deserved a visit! And it is rather perverse, this sudden haste to get home while I am not there to receive you! Don't you think it is? For your own sake, however, I do entreat you to break the long journey by either stopping at Alderley, or making out that visit to Foxton.[2] Alderley, which you know, and are sure of a fine quiet bedroom at, would be best. It is such a pity to arrive at home entirely fevered, and knocked up with that journey, as always happens ; and then you take it to be 'London' that is making you ill!

Then, if you stayed a few days at Alderley, I could stay out the fortnight I undertook for here, and be home in time to give you welcome. I should go home on Monday week (Monday, 28th) in the course of nature. I suppose this place is good for me ; I have slept so much—more than in any other week for the last three years! But I don't feel stronger for all this sleep, nor more able to eat, or to walk. One day that I tried walking, about as far as from Cheyne Row to the hospital, I had to come home ignominiously in a donkey-cart. But the drives don't tire me, especially since Miss Bromley has had her own carriage and horses sent down.

[1] To Newbattle, where I spent a day.

[2] Frederic, my old German fellow-tourist: his cottage 'near Rhayader' was of route too intricate for me.

Nor need there be any reflections for want of 'simmering stagnation!' There is not a human creature to speak to out of our own house; and in it, the pugs have the greatest share of the conversation to themselves!

I cannot forgive Thomas Erskine for taking up and keeping up with such a woman as that Mrs. ——. Letting you be driven out by Mrs. —— !

I am so glad you went to see dear Betty; it will be something good for her to think of for a year to come!

Do write distinctly the when, and the how, of your home-coming. What do you think? I have exactly two sovereigns in the world! enough to pay the servants here, and my railway fare home, and no more!! Yet I have not been extravagant that I am aware of. I had to pay Silvester before I went to Scotland sixteen pounds eleven shillings and four pence; and to ditto after my return five pounds seventeen shillings. And Freure[1] couldn't get on without 'something towards the work;' and I paid him ten pounds.

£	*s.*	*d.*
16	11	4
10	0	0
5	17	0
32	8	4

making up in all one half of my house-money. Then

[1] The Chelsea carpenter.

your being away makes no difference in the rent, taxes, servants' wages, keep, &c. And for my being away myself, I certainly have to pay to other people's servants more than it would cost me for individual ' living's cares ! '

I had indeed, besides the house-money, my own fifteen pounds, of which the two sovereigns above mentioned are the sad remains. But, when these pounds came to hand, I owed for my summer bonnet and cloak ; and I had some little presents to buy, to take with me to Scotland, besides a gown for myself. The only part of my own money I can be said to have spent needlessly was a guinea and a half for— you would never guess what!—for a miniature of you ! ! Such a beauty ! Everyone who sees it screams with rapture over it—even Ruskin !

But my hand will do no more.

Miss Bromley bids me say, ' that fourfooted animal sends his respects ' (' and put that in inverted commas, please ! '). She is good as possible to me.

Yours lovingly,

JANE CARLYLE.

LETTER 313.

Mrs. Russell, Holm Hill.

4 Langhorne Gardens, Folkestone : Aug. 23, 1865.

I am going to make an attempt at putting on paper the letter that has been in my head for you, dear, ever since I came to this place. I had even begun to write it two or three days ago, when at the first words my conscience gave me a smart box on the ear, reminding me that I hadn't written one word to Mrs. Ewart since I left her, after all her kindness to me, whereas to you I had written once and again; so my pen formed, quite unexpectedly for myself, the words 'Dear Mrs. Ewart,' instead of 'Dearest Mary.' To be sure there have been leisure hours enough since. Life here is made up of 'leisure hours'; but just the less one does, as I long ago observed, the less one can find time to do. I get up at nine, and it takes me a whole mortal hour to dress, without assistance. At ten we sit down to breakfast, and talk over it till eleven. Then I have to write my letter to Mr. Carlyle; then I make a feeble attempt at walking on the cliff by the shore, which never fails to weary me dreadfully, so that I can do nothing after, till the first dinner (called luncheon), which comes off at two o'clock; then between three and four we go out for a drive in an open barouche, with a pair of swift horses, and explore the country for three or four hours. On coming home we have a cup of tea, then rest, and dress for the second dinner at eight (nominally, but in reality half-past eight). At eleven we go to bed, very sleepy generally with so much open air. There is not a soul to speak to from without. But Miss Bromley and I never bore one another : when we find nothing of mutual interest to talk about, we have the gift, both of us, of being able to sit silent together without the least embarrassment. She is adorably kind to me, that ' fine lady ! ' and in such an unconscious way, always looking and talking as if it were I that was kind to her, and she the one benefited by our intimacy. And then she has something in her face, and movements, and ways, that always reminds me of my mother at her age.

I am sorry that Mr. Carlyle, after all his objections to my returning to London in August, should have taken it in his head to return to London in August himself. I find it so pleasant here; and am sleeping so wonderfully, that I feel no disposition to go back to Chelsea already ; Miss Bromley having taken her house for five weeks, and being heartily desirous I should stay and keep her company. But a demon of impatience seems to have taken possession of Mr. C., and he has been rushing through his promised visits as if the furies were chasing him. Everything right, seemingly, wherever he went; the people all kindness for him ; the bedrooms quiet and airy ; horses and carriages at his command ; and, behold, it was impossible to persuade him to stay longer than three days with Mr. Erskine, of Linlathen ; ditto with Stirling, of Keir ; and just three hours (for luncheon) at Newbattle with the Lothians ; and by this time he is back at Scotsbrig (if all have gone right), to

stay ' one day or at most two,' preparatory for starting for Chelsea. It is really so unreasonable, this
sudden haste—after so much dawdling—that I do
not feel it my duty to rush home ' promiscuously ' to
receive him. I promised to stay here a fortnight at
the least, and the fortnight does not complete itself
till Monday next; so I have written to him that I
will be home on Monday—not sooner—and begging
him to break the journey, and amuse himself for a
couple of days at Alderley Park, and then he would
find me at home to receive him; since he won't do as
Miss Bromley and I wish—come here for a little sea-
bathing to finish off with.

It really is miraculous how soundly I have slept
here, though I take two glasses of champagne, besides
Manzanilla, every day at the late dinner. It couldn't
have been sound, that champagne of poor, kind
Mrs. ——'s, or it wouldn't have so disagreed with me.
Here it always does me good. And the pain is entirely gone out of my arm; I can't move it any better
yet, but that is small matter in comparison. I can do
many things with my hand : write (as you see)—knit
—I have knitted myself a pair of garters—I can play
on the piano a little, and do a few stitches with a
very coarse needle.

Kindest love to the Doctor.

Your ever affectionate
Jane Carlyle.

LETTER 314.

To Miss Welsh, Edinburgh.

5 Cheyne Row, Monday: Oct. 1865.

My dear Elizabeth,—I am very glad indeed of the photograph, and grateful to you for having had it done at last, knowing how all such little operations bore you. It is very satisfactory as a portrait too— very like and a pleasant likeness—' handsome and ladylike' (the epithets that used to be bestowed on you in old times). Photography is apt to be cruel on women out of their teens; but this one is neither old-looking nor cross-looking. So thank you again with all my heart.

We have had a severe time of it with heat since our return to London. Plenty of people found it ' delicious,' but Mr. C. and I—and, indeed, the whole household, not excepting the cat—suffered in our stomachs, and even more in our tempers. It was quite curious to hear the cat squabbling with her cat companions in the garden—just as the cook and housemaid squabbled in the kitchen, or Mr. C. and I in the ' up stairs;' a general overflow of bile producing the usual results of irritability and disagreement. Now the weather is again favourable to the growth of the domestic virtues, and also, sad to say, to the development of rheumatism.

I paid a visit the other day, which interested me,

to ' Queen Emma.'   She is still in the house of Lady Franklin (the widow of that ' Sir John ' that everybody used to sail away to ' seek '). When Lady Franklin made a journey to the Sandwich Islands, amongst other out-of-the-way places, she was received with great kindness by the ' royal family,' and is now repaying it by having ' the Queen ' and her retinue to live with her; though *our* Queen has placed *her* apartments at Clarges' Hotel at the Sandwich Island Queen's disposition.   We (Geraldine Jewsbury and I) were taken by Lady Franklin into the garden where the Queen was sitting writing, and ' much scandalised to receive us in a little hat, instead of her widow's cap,' which she offered to go in and put on.   She is a charming young woman, in spite of the tinge of black—or rather green.   Large black, beautiful eyes, a lovely smile, great intelligence, both of face and manner, a musical, true voice, a perfect English accent.   Lady Franklin introduced me as ' the wife of Mr. Carlyle, a celebrated author of our country.'   ' I know him, I have read all about him, and read things he has written,' answered the Queen of the Sandwich Islands !   In fact, the young woman seemed remarkably informed on ' things in general.' The funniest part of the interview, for me, was to hear Geraldine addressing Queen Emma always as ' Your Majesty,' in a tone as free and easy as one would have adopted to one's cat.

Do you remember Joseph Turner who was deaf and dumb? I saw him on the platform at Dumfries and spoke to him, and he has written to me—such a nice letter. I will send it when I have answered it. I cannot conceive how he should have known my father, he was too young.

I hope Ann has gone or is going to Dumfriesshire. It always does her good, that trip; and many people are glad of her coming. I saw her old friend Mrs. Gilchrist at Thornhill. How changed from the time she helped me to make woollen mattresses at Craigenputtock! The history she gave me of her accidents was most pitiful. I didn't like the daughter's looks much; but she had the room as clean as a pin, and spoke kindly enough, though roughly, to her mother.

Good-bye, dear Elizabeth!

Yours affectionately,
JANE W. CARLYLE.

LETTER 315.

To Mrs. Austin, The Gill, Annan.

5 Cheyne Row: Wednesday, Oct. 11, 1865.

My dear little woman,—It is ' a black and a burning shame' that I should not have told you before now that the butter is good, very good! And Mr. C. eats it to his oat-cakes in preference to the Addiscombe fresh butter, which is the best in the world. The girl—or I should say young woman (her age being thirty)—whom I brought from Thornhill is an admirable hand at oat-cakes, and is fond of being praised, as most of us are when we can get it! so is willing to do the cake-making of the family, though it isn't ' in her work.' And I seldom eat loaf-bread now, having taken it into my head that the oat-cakes do instead of rhubarb pills. She is a capital servant, that Jessie; and pleases Mr. Carlyle supremely, attending to all his little ' fykes and manœuvres ' (as she calls it in her private mind) with a zeal and punctuality that leaves him nothing to wish. But to me she leaves a good deal to wish. Not in her work : she is clever and active, and has an excellent memory ; but, as a woman, I might wish her different in some respects. With a face that captivates everyone by its ' brightness and sweetness,' she is, I find, what the clergyman at Morton, who had known her from a child, told me she was, and I would not believe him till I tried, ' a—*vixen.*' And when Mrs. Russell told me she was—' Oh, well, about that, I should say she was as truthful as the generality of servants nowadays ! ' even that mild account was stretching a point in her favour. But as long as Mr. C. finds her all right, the rest don't signify. He has been off his sleep again, listening for ' railway whistles,' which have been just audible—nothing more —for years back ; but he never discovered them till his experiences at Dumfries made him morbidly sensitive to that sound. The last week he has slept better ; and in other respects he is better, I think, than before he went to Scotland ; can walk further, and looks stronger.

For me, my neuralgia continues in abeyance—no pain in my arm, or hand, or anywhere. And though a certain stiffness remains, I can do myself, without help, almost everything I need to do, and some things not needed. For example, I made myself yesterday a lovely bonnet ! My sleep has been greatly improved ever since my return from Scotland ; for the bad nights I have had lately were not my own fault, but produced by listening to Mr. C. jumping up to smoke, to thump at his bed, and so on.[1]

God bless you, dear. Kind regards to them all.

Your affectionate

JANE W. CARLYLE.

LETTER 316.

Some wretched people who had settled next door had brought poultry and other base disturbances ; against which, for my sake, the noble soul heroically started up (not to be forbidden), and with all her old skill and energy gained victory, complete once more. For me—for me ! and it was her last. The thought is cuttingly painful while I live.

The omnibus at Charing Cross. Oh, shocking ! How well do I remember all this, and how easily might I have avoided it !—T. C.

---

[1] Alas, alas ; watchful for two ! How sad, sad that now is to me !

To Mrs. Austin, The Gill, Annan.

5 Cheyne Row: Wednesday, Dec. 1865.

Oh, my dear! I am so vexed that you should not have had your kind sending acknowledged sooner. It arrived when I was under a cloud, last Saturday, confined to bed in a perfect agony of sick headache!

I had had nothing of that sort for many years, and it was really strange to me, the thought, how many such days I had passed formerly without being killed by them! But I am sure I couldn't live through many such at the present date. The headache and sickness lasted only one day and night, but the effects of it have not yet passed. I am as weak and nervous as if I had just come through a course of mercury! And that is why I have let several posts pass without returning you our thanks; but expressing them meanwhile in an approving consumption of the eggs and fowls. One was boiled on Monday (excellent!), the other is to be roasted to-day, according to my views about variety of food being requisite to the welfare of the human stomach— a consideration which Mr. C. makes light of, but exemplifies in his own person very convincingly the truth of.

I could very well account for that crisis the other day; several things had conspired to throw me on my back. First, my black mare, who enjoys the most perfect health generally, got her foot hurt by a run-away cart, and has had to remain in the stable for more than a week, in a state of continual poultices! Not choosing to pay for another horse, I agreed to go for exercise in an omnibus with Mr. C.—the first time I had entered an omnibus since the evening I had my fall—the beginning of all my woes! I felt very nervous at the notion, but I was to go to the end of the line and sit still while the horses were changed, and then come back again, so as to avoid any walking or hanging about in the streets. But Mr. C., as usual, dawdled till we found ourselves too late for going the whole way, and I had to get down at Charing Cross in a busy thoroughfare—and Mr. C. had to run after omnibuses to stop them—and I was like to cry with nervousness to find myself left alone in an open street—and couldn't run after him as he kept calling to me to do—couldn't run at all! and was besides paralysed at the sight of carriages so near me, so that I was terribly flurried, and felt quite ill when I had to go out to dinner with Mr. C. the same evening. Then I am sure the champagne they gave us was bad—that is, poisonous; and for two nights before, I had had next to no sleep, owing to a terrible secret on my mind. One morning, when I looked out of my dressing-room window to see what sort of day it was, imagine the spectacle that met my eyes : a rubbishy hen-hutch, erected over night, in the garden next to ours—next! think of that!—and nine large hens and one very large cock sauntering under our windows !!! I should have fainted where I stood had I been in the habit of fainting; but that I never was. As Mr. C. said nothing, I could not guess whether he had made the discovery or not. The crowing which occurred several times during the night, as well as abundantly in the morning, certainly did not awake him, his mind being, at present, intent on 'railway whistles.' But when he should have once opened his eyes to the thing, and as the days should lengthen, the crowing would increase. Ah! my heaven, what then?—no wonder that I lay awake thinking 'What then?' I have not time to give a detailed account of all that followed. Enough to say the poultry is all to evacuate the premises at Christmas, and meanwhile the cock is shut up in a dark cellar from darkening till after our breakfast. And Mr. C. clasped me in his arms and called me his 'guardian angel;' and all I have to pay for this restoration of peace and quietness is giving a lesson three times a week, in syllables of two letters, to a small Irish boy ! Rhyme that if you can !

Excuse this ill-written letter. I am not quite recovered from the crush of that poultry affair on my mind, although the secret load is removed.

I will write soon when more up to writing. This

is merely thanks and a kiss for the fowls and eggs.
Oh, if one never saw a fowl but like these—dead!

Love to them all.

Your ever affectionate
JANE W. CARLYLE.

Jessie, the Thornhill girl, is going on quite satis-
factorily, since I ceased treating her too kindly—
snubbing, and riding with a curb-bridle, is what she
needs. All her former mistresses warned me of that,
but I wouldn't believe them, the girl looked so sweet
and affectionate—the humbug! Mercifully, Mr. C.
sees no fault in her.

[Remainder, a small fragment, is lost.]

LETTER 317.

Nothing nobler was ever done to me in my life than the
unseen nobleness recorded in this letter. When I look out
on that garden, all so trim and quiet now (old rubbish
tenants gone for ever), and think what she looked out on,
and resolved to do—oh, these are facts that go beyond
words! Praise to thee, darling! praise in my heart at least,
so long as I continue to exist.—T. C.

Mrs. Russell, Holm Hill.

5 Cheyne Row: Dec. 25, 1865.

Dearest Mary,—I was unwilling to leave your
husband's letter unanswered for a single day, or I
wouldn't have chosen Friday morning for writing to

him, when I was busy packing your box, and had besides to write a business letter to the Haddington lawyer,[1] and to give a lesson in syllables of two letters to a small boy,[2] all before one o'clock, when I should go for my drive. After my return, between four and five, there is no time to catch the general post, which closes for Chelsea at half-past four. So, having so much to do in haste, I could only do it all badly.

Then you may be perplexed by the four pieces of cork. My dear, Mr. Carlyle has admirers of all sorts and trades ; and one of them, a very ardent.admirer, is by trade a cork-cutter, and he sent me, as a tribute of admiration, a box containing some dozens of bottle-corks, large and small, and half-a-dozen pairs of cork soles, to put into my shoes, when shaped with a sharp knife. It is not by many, or any, chances that I have to wet my feet; so there is small generosity in bestowing two pairs on you or the Doctor.

I hope you read that tale going on in the ' Fortnightly '—'The Belton Estate' (by Anthony Trollope) It is charming, like all he writes ; I quite weary for the next number, for the sake of that one thing ; the rest is wonderfully stupid.

When I wrote to the Doctor, ' my interior ' (as

---

[1] About some trifle of legacy from poor 'Jackie Welsh,' I think (*supra*).

[2] Part of her task with those new neighbours, and their noises and paltriuesses. Good Heaven !

Mr. C. would say) was in wild agitation, not severe but annoying, and reminding me of the inflammatory attack I had last winter. Nevertheless, I took my daily three hours' drive, and some tea after, and put on my black velvet gown, and went to 'Lady William's'[1] eight o'clock dinner. I hadn't dined with her for some three weeks, so I must be getting better when I could muster spirit for such a thing. Rolled up in fur, and both windows up, and warm water to my feet, I caught no cold, and it is always pleasant there, and I always sleep well after. I met the man who is said to have made the Crimean war, Lord Stratford de Redcliffe, and found him a most just-looking, courteous, agreeable, white-headed, old gentleman.

When I told you I had been off my sleep, I told you—did I not?—that I had been worried off it. Better when one can put one's finger on the cause of one's sleeplessness. The cause this time, or rather the causes, were: first, a bilious fit on the part of Mr. Carlyle, who was for some days ' neither to hold nor to bind '—a condition which keeps my heart jumping into my mouth when it should be composing itself to rest. Then it happened that in these nervous days I had Agnes Veitch, my old Haddington playmate (Mrs. Grahame) coming to dinner, and seeing that he had made up his mind to find her dreadfully in his

---

[1] Lady William Russell, who much liked and admired her.

way, I ordered my brougham at eight o'clock to take her home to St. John's Wood, and that she mightn't think it was sending her off too early, I went along with her, to give her another hour of my company. Prettily imagined, you will allow. Having deposited her safely at her own door, I was on my way back, crossing Oxford Street, when I saw a mad or drunk cart bearing down upon me at a furious rate, and swerving from side to side, so that there was no escaping. My old coachman is a most cautious, as well as skilful driver; but this was too much. I shut my eyes, and crossed my arms tight, and awaited the collision. Instead of, as I expected, running into the carriage, the wild thing ran into the black mare, threw her round with a jerk that broke part of the harness, and then rushed on. Men gathered round, and Silvester descended from his box, to knot up the broken straps; my beautiful Bellona (so named for her imputed warlike disposition) standing the while as quiet as a lamb. Then we went on our way again, thanking God it was no worse. But it was found, on reaching the stables, that poor Bellona had got her foot badly hurt. The mad wheel seemed to have bruised it and snipped out a piece of skin. She was not at all lame, and was quite willing to go out with me next day; but the next again, her leg was much swelled, and for more than a fortnight she had to be attended by the veterinary surgeon, who forbade her going out, and said if the bruise had been an inch nearer the hoof she would have been a ruined Bellona. Also, he said, 'a more sweet-natured horse he had never handled!' After much poulticing, the inward suppuration came outward; and she is now all right, being of an admirable constitution, this one; never, even through the poulticing time, losing her excellent appetite and excellent spirits. But it was worrying to not know when she could be taken out, and meanwhile to be putting Mr. C. to the cost of a livery-horse as well.

But the grand worry of all, that which perfected my sleeplessness, was an importation of nine hens, and a magnificent cock, into the adjoining garden! For years back there has reigned over all these gardens a heavenly quiet—thanks to my heroic exertions in exterminating nuisances of every description. But I no longer felt the hope or the energy in me requisite for such achievements. Figure then my horror, my despair, on being waked one dark morning with the crowing of a cock, that seemed to issue from under my bed! I leapt up, and rushed up to my dressing-room window, but it was still all darkness. I lay with my heart in my mouth, listening to the cock crowing hoarsely from time to time, and listening for Mr. C.'s foot stamping frantically, as of old, on the floor above. But, strangely enough, he gave no sign of having heard his enemy, his whole attentions having been, ever since his visit to Mrs. Aitken, morbidly devoted to— railway whistles.   So soon as it was daylight I looked out again, and there was a sight to see—a ragged, Irish-looking hen-house, run up over night, and sauntering to and fro nine goodly hens, and a stunning cock! I didn't know whether Mr. C. remained really deaf as well as blind to these new neighbours, or whether he was only magnanimously resolved to observe silence about them ; but it is a fact, that for a whole week he said no word to enlighten me, while I expected and expected the crisis which would surely come, and shuddered at every cock-crow, and counted the number of times he crowed in a night—at two! at three! at four! at five! at six! at seven! Oh, terribly at seven!

For a whole week I bore my hideous secret in my breast, and slept 'none to speak of.' At the week's end I fell into one of my old sick headaches. I used always to find a sick headache had a fine effect in clearing the wits. So, even this time, I rose from a day's agony with a scheme of operation in my head, and a sense of ability to ' carry it out.' It would be too long to go into details—enough to say my negotiations with ' next door ' ended in an agreement that the cock should be shut up in a cellar, inside the owner's own house, from three in the afternoon till ten in the morning ; and, in return, I give the small boy of the house a lesson every morning in his 'Reading made Easy,' the small boy being 'too excitable' for being sent to school ! It is a house full of mysteries—No. 6 ! I have thoughts of writing a novel about it. Meanwhile, Mr. C. declares me to be his 'guardian angel.' No sinecure, I can tell him. So I might fall to sleeping again if I could. But I couldn't all at once. Getting back to even that much sleep I had been having must be gradual, like the building of Rome.

Jessie is going on quite well since I decided to take the upper hand with her, and keep it. I don't think Mrs. Warren likes her any better, but I ask no questions. Best 'let sleeping dogs lie.' She (Jessie) is much more attentive to me since I showed myself quite indifferent to her attentions, and particular only as to the performance of her work. She is even kindly and sensitive with me occasionally. But she can't come over me ever again with that dodge. She let me see too clearly into her hard, vain nature that I should place reliance or affection on her again. I do not regret having taken her—not at all. As a servant, she is better than the average ; as a woman, I do not think ill of her ; but I mistook her entirely at the first, and see less good in her than perhaps there is, because I began by seeing far more good in her than she had the least pretension to. At my age, and with my experience, it would have well beseemed me to be less romantic. I have paid for it in the disappointment of the heartfelt hopes I had invested in my hereditary housemaid.

Good-bye, dear!

Your ever affectionate
JANE CARLYLE.

LETTER 318.

Mrs. Russell, Holm Hill, Thornhill, Dumfriesshire.

5 Cheyne Row, Chelsea: Saturday, Dec. 30, 1865.

Just a line, dearest, to inclose the poor little money-order. I have no time for a letter—indeed, my hurry is indescribable, for I have been fit for nothing this week, and all my New Year writing is choked into the last day of it.

Wrap up five shillings, please, and address it to John Hiddlestone, and give it or transmit it to Margaret, who will save you the trouble of seeking out himself. And you remember there was to be five shillings to that unlucky Mrs. Gilchrist—into her own hand. The other ten shillings please give where you see it most needed.

A woman who had had something from me through you (an old post-woman, Jessie said) came to Jessie, when she was coming away, and begged her to tell me that ' she had been sometimes at Templand, and had once taken tea with Mrs. Welsh in her own parlour, and if I would do something more for her, that being the case!' Jessie had properly told her that it was no business of hers to interfere, and that she could tell myself. No; I do not recognise the claim. Let her have what she has been used to have, and no more. She ought to have appealed to me through you, not through my prospective servant.

My sickness and my sleeplessness have culminated in a violent cold or influenza. Blue pill, castor oil, morphia—I have not been idle, I assure you; and now the evil thing is blowing over, and I expect to be able to keep my engagement to dine with Dr. Quain on the 3rd of January!

I hope you got my long letter—that it was not confiscated for the sake of the buttons! Will you tell me how you manage to get baskets all the way to our door without a farthing to pay? Nobody else can manage it. Even when the carriage is paid, there is still porterage from the station to the place of delivery, which cannot be prepaid—sixpence, or eightpence, or a shilling, according to the bulk. I really want to understand. Had you any porterage, from the station to Holm Hill, to pay for my box? A good New Year to the Doctor. I would be his ' first foot ' if I had a ' wishing carpet.'

Tell me how poor little Mrs. Ewart is.

Your ever affectionate
JANE CARLYLE.

LETTER 319.

To Miss Grace Welsh, Edinburgh.

5 Cheyne Row, Chelsea : Jan. 23, 1866.

My dear Grace,—Have you any more news of Robert?[1] I weary to hear how he is, though without hope of hearing he is better. From the first mention of his illness, I have felt that it was all over with the poor lad for this life!

One thinks it so sad that one's family should die out! And yet, perhaps, it is best (nay, of course it is best, since God has so ordered it!) that a family lying under the doom of a hereditary, deadly malady should die out, and leave its room in the universe to healthier and happier people! But, again, hereditary maladies are not the only maladies that kill; and plenty of mothers have, like Mrs. George and Mrs. Robert, seen their children, one after another, swept from the earth without consumption having anything to do with it. It is hard, hard to tell by what death, slow or swift, one would prefer to lose one's dearest ones, when lose them one must!

Figure what has just befallen that dear, kind Dr. B——, who saved my life (I shall always consider) by taking me under his care at St. Leonards. Of all his sons, the most promising was Captain P——

---

[1] Uncle Robert's only surviving son, who had returned from sea in a dangerous state of health.

B——, risen to be naval captain while still very young. Oh, such a handsome, kindly, gallant fellow! He had married a beautiful girl with a little fortune, and they were the happiest pair! A year ago he was made 'Commander'—a signal honour for so young a man! and just three weeks ago his wife was confined of her second baby, in her mother's house at St. Leonards, the captain being away to bring home a ship from somewhere in the West Indies. Well! four days ago, in reading his morning newspaper, Dr. B—— read the 'Death of that distinguished officer, Captain P—— B——, from fever, after three days' illness!' It is too terrible to try to conceive the feelings of a warm-hearted, proud father under a shock like that! Not a word of warning!

I think that going down of the 'London' has sent all the blood from my heart! Ever since I read its touching details I have felt in a maze of sadness, have had no affinity for any but sorrowful things, and can find in my whole mind no morsel of cheerful news to tell you! Perhaps I am even more stupid than sad ; and no shame to me, with a cold in my head, dating from before Christmas! It is the only illness I have had to complain of this winter, and is no illness ' to speak of;' but, none the less, it makes me very sodden and abject; and, instead of having thoughts in my head, it (my head) feels to be filled with wool! Fuzzly is the word for how I feel, all through! But I continue to take my three hours' drive daily, all the same. Since I returned from Folkestone in September, I have only missed two days! the days of the snowstorm a fortnight ago; when it was so dangerous for horses to travel, that the very omnibuses struck work. And besides the forenoon drive, I occasionally, with this wool in my head, go out to dinner!!! With a hot bottle at my feet, and wrapt in fur, I take no hurt, and the talk stirs me up. Dr. Quain told me I ' couldn't take a better remedy, if only I drank plenty of champagne ' —a condition which I, for one, never find any difficulty in complying with!

My chief intimates have been away all this winter, which has made my life less pleasant—Lady Ashburton on the Continent, and Miss Davenport Bromley waiting in the country till the new paint smell should have gone out of her house. But there are always nice people to take the place of those absent. It made me laugh, dear, that Edinburgh notion, that because Mr. C. had been made Rector of the University, an office purely honorary, we should immediately proceed to tear ourselves up by the roots, and transplant ourselves there!

After thirty years of London, and with such society as we have in London, to bundle ourselves off to Edinburgh, to live out the poor remnant of our lives in a new and perfectly uncongenial sphere, with no consolations that I know of but your three selves, and dear old Betty! *Ach!* 'A wishing carpet' on which I could sit down, and be transported to Craigenvilla, for an hour's talk with you all, two or three times a week, and—back again!—would be a most welcome fairy gift to me! But no 'villa at Morningside' tempts me, except your villa! And for Edinburgh people—those I knew are mostly dead and gone; and the new ones would astonish me much if they afforded any shadow of compensation for the people I should leave here! No, my dear, we shall certainly not go 'to live in Edinburgh;' I only wish Mr. C. hadn't to go to deliver a speech in it, for it will tear him to tatters.

Love to you all.

Affectionately,
J. W. C.

LETTER 320.

To Mrs. Russell, Holm Hill.

5 Cheyne Row: January 29, 1866.

The town is no longer ' empty.' All my most intimate friends are come back, except Lady Ashburton, who, alas! will still remain on the Continent, and give no certain promise of return. Her rheumatism is better; but there are family reasons for her avoiding England at present, which she considers imperative, though her friends find them chimerical enough.

Miss Davenport Bromley is back; the Alderley Stanleys, the Airlies, the Froudes, &c. &c. We were much surprised by the Lothians coming to London some two or three weeks ago. They had not stirred from Newbattle Abbey for two years! The poor young Marquis came the whole journey in one day. Some hope of electricity had been put into his head, and they have been trying it on him. He said he 'did not think it had done him any harm as yet; but that was the most he could say.' He is the saddest spectacle I have seen for long. His body more than half dead, his face so worn with suffering, and the soul looking out of him as bright as in his best days. I had not seen him since before my own illness; and I was shocked with the change, especially in his voice, which, from being most musical, had become harsh and husky. She, poor soul, bears up wonderfully; but is so white and sad, that I cannot look at her without dreading for her the fate of her mother.

The house (ours) goes on peaceably enough on the whole; not without crises of ill temper, of course. But I have got Jessie pretty well in hand now. It is mortifying, after all my romantic hopes of her, to find that kindness goes for nothing with her, and that she is only amenable to good sharp snubbing. Well, she shall have it! At the same time, I make a point of being just to her and being kind to her, as a *mistress* to a *servant*. So she got the 'nice dress' at Christmas, along with Mrs. Warren; but I put no affection into anything I do for her, and let her see that I don't. It was a lucky Christmas for her. Mr. Ruskin always gives my servants a sovereign apiece at that season. 'The like had never happened to her before,' she was obliged to confess. She went to the theatre one night with some Fergussons, and has acquaintances enough. So I hope she is happy, though I don't like her.

Has the Doctor seen young Corson, who had to leave Swan and Edgar's with a bad knee? He came here several times to see Jessie. Love to the Doctor.

Yours ever,
J. C.

How is Mrs. Ewart?

LETTER 321.

Miss Ann Welsh, Edinburgh.

5 Cheyne Row: Monday, March 27, 1866

My dear Aunts,—It is long since I have written, and I have not leisure for a satisfactory letter even now; but I want you to have these two admissions in good time, in case you desire to hear poor Mr. C.'s address, and don't know how to manage it. If you don't care about it, or can't for any other reason use the admissions, or either of them, please return them to me forthwith; for the thing[1] comes off this day week and there is a great demand for them.

---

[1] Carlyle's address to the students as Lord Rector.—J. A. F.

Mr. C. was too modest, when asked by the University people how many admissions he wished reserved for himself, and required only twenty for men and six for women, or, as I suppose they would say in Edinburgh, 'ladies.' Four have been given away to ladies who have shown him great kindness at one time or other; and the two left he sends to you, in preference to some dozen other ladies who have applied for them directly or indirectly. So you see the propriety of my request to have one or both returned if you are prevented from using them yourselves.

I am afraid, and he himself is certain, his address will be a sad break-down to human expectation. He has had no practice in public speaking—hating it with all his heart. And then he does *speak*; does not merely read or repeat from memory a composition elaborately prepared—in fact, as in the case of his predecessors, printed before it was 'delivered'!

I wish him well through it, for I am very fearful the worry and flurry of the thing will make him ill. After speculating all winter about going myself, my heart failed me as the time drew near, and I realised more clearly the nervousness and pain in my back that so much fuss was sure to bring on. I did not dread the bodily fatigue, but the mental. We were to have broken the journey by stopping a few days at Lord Houghton's, in Yorkshire; and after giving up Edinburgh, I thought for a while I would still go as far as the Houghtons, and wait there till Mr. C. returned. But that part of the business I also decided against, only two days since, preferring to reserve Yorkshire till summer, and till I was in a more tranquil frame of mind.

Mr. C. is going to stay while in Edinburgh at Thomas Erskine's, our dear old friend; not, however, because of liking him better than anyone else there, but because of his being most out of the way of—railway whistles! It was worth while, however, to have talked of accompanying Mr. C., to have given so much enthusiastic hospitality an opportunity for displaying itself.

One of the letters of invitation I had quite surprised me by its warmth and eagerness, being from a quarter where I hardly believed myself remembered —David Aitken and Eliza Stoddart! They had both grown into sticks, I was thinking. But I have no time to gossip.

Do send me soon some word of Robert,[1] though I know too well there can no good news come.

Affectionately yours,

J. W. CARLYLE.

---

[1] Her dying cousin.

LETTER 322.

T. Carlyle, Esq., T. Erskine, Esq., Edinburgh.

Cheyne Row: Good Friday, March 30, 1866.

Dearest,—What with your being on the road, and what with the regulations of Good Friday, I don't know when this will reach you. Indeed I don't know anything about anything. I feel quite stupefied. I should have liked to have seen your handwriting this morning, though none the less obliged to Mr. Tyndall, who makes the best of your having had a bad night. What a dear, warm-hearted darling he is! I should like to kiss him! I did sleep *some* last night—the first wink since the night before you left. Last evening I felt quite smashed, so willingly availed myself of the feeble pen of Maggie,[1] who had walked in ' quite promiscuous.' She was back at Agnes Baird's, and had fixed to leave for Liverpool on Saturday. For decency's sake I asked her to come here instead and stay over Sunday, which she agreed to do. She will be company to James.[2] He didn't come back to sleep last night, having accepted an invitation from somebody (McGeorge?) at Islington, with whom he was going to spend Good Friday out of town somewhere. He had ' not quite' concluded about his office—' all

---

[1] Maggie Welsh.

[2] Aitken, now attempting business in the City.

but;' had failed in all attempts to find a lodging, but this McGeorge 'would help him in looking,' he thought. I pressed him to keep his bed here till he was suited, but he 'would be nearer his office at McGeorge's.' He is to come on Sunday morning, however, to spend the day; and I promised to take him to Richmond Park or somewhere before dinner. At parting, for the present, he tried to make a good little speech about 'my kindness to him.' Pity he is so dreadfully inarticulate, for his meaning is modest and affectionate, poor fellow.

The sudden intimation of Venturi's death, sleepless as I was at the time, stunned me for the rest of the day like a blow on the head. He was taken ill in the night at the house of Herbert Taylor,[1] but would not allow his wife to raise anyone, or to make any disturbance, and at five in the morning he was dead. There was an examination, that satisfied the doctors he had died of heart disease, and that he must have been suffering a great deal, while De Musset and other doctors of his acquaintance had treated any complaint of illness he made as 'imaginary, the result of his unsatisfactory life.' Poor Emilie is, as you may imagine, 'like death.' Mr. Ashurst was trying to prevent a coroner's inquest, but he feared it would have to be—to-day.

[1] John Mill's *step*son-in-law.

Good-bye! Keep up your heart the first three minutes, and after that it will be all plain sailing.

Ever yours,

J. C.

LETTER 323.

T. Carlyle, Esq., T. Erskine's, Esq., Edinburgh.

5 Cheyne Row, Chelsea: April 2, 1866.

Dearest,—By the time you get this you will be out of your trouble, better or worse, but out of it, please God. And if ever you let yourself be led or driven into such a horrid thing again, I will never forgive you—never!

What I have been suffering, vicariously, of late days is not to be told. If you had been to be hanged I don't see that I could have taken it more to heart. This morning, after about two hours of off-and-on sleep, I awoke, long before daylight, to sleep no more. While drinking a glass of wine and eating a biscuit at five in the morning, it came into my mind, 'What is *he* doing, I wonder, at this moment?' and then, instead of picturing you sitting smoking up the stranger-chimney, or anything else that was likely to be, I found myself always dropping off into details of a regular execution!—Now they will be telling him it is time! now they will be pinioning his arms and saying last words! Oh, mercy! was I dreaming or waking? was I mad or sane? Upon my word, I hardly know now. Only that I have been having next to no sleep all the week, and that at the best of times I have a too 'fertile imagination,' like 'oor David.'[1] .When the thing is over I shall be content, however it have gone as to making a good 'appearance' or a bad one. That you have made your 'address,' and are alive, that is what I long to hear, and, please God! shall hear in a few hours. My 'imagination' has gone the length of representing you getting up to speak before an awful crowd of people, and, what with fuss, and 'bad air,' and confusion, dropping down dead.

Why on earth did you ever get into this galley?

J. W. C.

LETTER 324.

T. Carlyle, Esq., Edinburgh.

5 Cheyne Row, Chelsea : Tuesday, April 3, 1866.

I made so sure of a letter this morning from some of you—and 'nothing but a double letter for Miss Welsh.' Perhaps I should—that is, ought—to have contented myself with Tyndall's adorable telegram, which reached me at Cheyne Row five minutes after six last evening, considering the sensation it made.

Mrs. Warren and Maggie were helping to dress me for Forster's birthday, when the telegraph boy gave his double-knock. 'There it is!' I said. 'I am

---

[1] A lying boy at Haddington, whom his mother excused in that way.

afraid, cousin, it is only the postman,' said Maggie. Jessie rushed up with the telegram. I tore it open and read, ' From John Tyndall' (Oh, God bless John Tyndall in this world and the next!) 'to Mrs. Carlyle.' ' A perfect triumph!' I read it to myself, and then read it aloud to the gaping chorus. And chorus all began to dance and clap their hands. ' Eh, Mrs. Carlyle!' Eh, hear to that!' cried Jessie. ' I told you, ma'am,' cried Mrs. Warren, ' I told you how it would be.' ' I'm so glad, cousin! you'll be all right now, cousin,' twittered Maggie, executing a sort of leap-frog round me. And they went on clapping their hands, till there arose among them a sudden cry for brandy! ' Get her some brandy!' ' Do, ma'am, swallow this spoonful of brandy; just a spoonful!' For, you see, the sudden solution of the nervous tension with which I had been holding in my anxieties for days—nay, weeks, past—threw me into as pretty a little fit of hysterics as you ever saw.

I went to Forster's nevertheless, with my telegram in my hand, and ' John Tyndall' in the core of my heart! And it was pleasant to see with what hearty good-will all there—Dickens and Wilkie Collins as well as Fuz—received the news; and we drank your health with great glee. Maggie came in the evening; and Fuz, in his joy over you, sent out a glass of brandy to Silvester! Poor Silvester, by-the-by, showed as much glad emotion as anybody on my telling him you had got well through it.

Did you remember Craik's paper? I am going to take Maggie to the railway for Liverpool. I suppose I shall now calm down and get sleep again by degrees. I am smashed for the present.

J. W. C.

LETTER 325.

T. Carlyle, Esq., Edinburgh.

5 Cheyne Row, Chelsea: Wednesday, April 4, 1866.

Well! I do think you might have sent me a 'Scotsman' this morning, or ordered one to be sent! I was up and dressed at seven; and it seemed such an interminable time till a quarter after nine, when the postman came, bringing only a note about— Cheltenham, from Geraldine! The letter I had from Tyndall yesterday might have satisfied any ordinary man or woman, you would have said. But I don't pretend to be an ordinary man or woman; I am perfectly extraordinary, especially in the power I possess of fretting and worrying myself into one fever after another, without any cause to speak of! What do you suppose I am worrying about now?— because of the 'Scotsman' not having come! That there may be in it something about your having fallen ill, which you wished me not to see! this I am capable of fancying at moments; though last evening

I saw a man who had seen you ' smoking very quietly at Masson's ; ' and had heard your speech, and—what was more to the purpose (his semi-articulateness taken into account)—brought me, what he said was as good an account of it as any *he* could give, already in ' The Pall Mall Gazette,' written by a hearty admirer of long standing evidently. It was so kind of Macmillan to come to me before he had slept. He had gone in the morning straight from the railway to his shop and work. He seemed still under the emotion of the thing ;—tears starting to his black eyes every time he mentioned any moving part ! !

Now just look at that ! If here isn't, at half after eleven, when nobody looks for the Edinburgh post, your letter, two newspapers, and letters from my aunt Anne, Thomas Erskine, and ' David Aitken besides.' I have only as yet read your letter. The rest will keep now. I had a nice letter from Henry Davidson yesterday, as good as a newspaper critic. What pleases me most in this business—I mean the business of your success—is the hearty personal affection towards you that comes out on all hands. These men at Forster's with their cheering—our own people—even old Silvester turning as white as a sheet, and his lips quivering when he tried to express his gladness over the telegraph : all that is positively delightful, and makes the success ' a good joy ' to me.

No appearance of envy or grudging in anybody ; but one general, loving, heartfelt throwing up of caps with young and old, male and female ! If we could only sleep, dear, and what you call *digest,* wouldn't it be nice ?

Now I must go ; I promised to try and get Madame Venturi out with me for a little air. She has been at her brother's, quite near Forster's, since the funeral. The history she herself gave me of the night of his death was quite excruciating. He took these spasms which killed him, soon after they went to bed ; and till five in the morning the two poor souls were struggling on, he positively forbidding her to give an alarm. Mrs. Taylor had a child just recovering from scarlet fever, and sent from home for fear of infecting the others. When Emilie would have gone to the Taylors' bedroom to tell them, he said, 'Consider the poor mother ! If you rouse her suddenly, she will think there has come bad news of her child ! It might do her great harm.' 'And I thought, dear, there was no danger,' she said to me. 'The doctors had so constantly said he had no ailment but indigestion.' It was soon after this that he 'threw up his arms as if he had been shot ; and fixed his eyes with a strange wondering look, as if he saw something beautiful and surprising ; and then fell to the floor dead !' I am so glad she likes me to come to her, for it shows she is not desperate.

Oh, dear, I wish you had been coming straight back ! [1] for it would be so quiet for you here just now : there isn't a soul left in London but Lady William, whom I haven't seen since the day you left I am afraid she is unwell.

Good-bye ! We have the sweeps to-day in the drawing-room, and elsewhere.

Affectionately yours,
JANE W. CARLYLE.

LETTER 326.

Read near Cleughbrae, on the road to Scotsbrig. Came thither, Saturday, April 7.

T. Carlyle, Esq., Scotsbrig.

5 Cheyne Row : Friday, April 6, 1866.

Dearest,—Scotsbrig, I fancy, will be the direction now.

I am just getting ready to start for Windsor, to stay a day and night, or two nights if the first be successful, with Mrs. Oliphant. Even that much ' change of air ' and ' schane ' [2] may, perhaps, break the spell of sleeplessness that has overtaken me. It is easier to go off one's sleep than to go on to it. I did rather better last night, however, after an eight o'clock dinner with the Lothians. The American,

---

[1] Oh, that I had—alas, alas !

[2] Old grandfather Walter's ' vaary the schane.'

Mason, was there—a queer, fine old fellow, with a touch of my grandfather Walter in him. Both Lord and Lady, and the beauty, Lady Adelaide, were so kind to me. It made me like to ' go off,' to hear the young Marquis declaring ' how much he wished he could have heard your speech.' He looked perfectly lovely yesterday, much more cheerful and bright than I have seen him since he came to London. They seemed to take the most affectionate interest in the business.

Lady William, too, charged me with a long message I haven't time for here. I found her in bed in the middle of newspapers, which she had been ' reading and comparing all the morning ; and had discovered certain variations in ! ' I am to dine with her on Sunday, after my return from Windsor. Miss Bromley is come back ; she came yesterday, and I am to dine with her on Tuesday. I needn't be dull, you see, unless I like !

Will you tell Jamie the astonishing fact that I have eaten up all the meal he sent me, and cannot live without cakes. *Ergo!* Also take good care of Betty's tablecloth ! [1] She writes me it was her mother's *spening*. She was awfully pleased at your visit. ' What am i, O der me, to be so vesated ! ' Here is an exuberant letter from Charles Kingsley.— Exuberant letters, more of them than I can ever

---

[1] A gift of poor Betty's—never to arrive.

hope to answer. Lady Airlie offers to come and
drink tea with me on Sunday night. 'Can't be
done'—must write in this hurry to put her off. Even
I have my hurries, you see. Kind love to Jamie and
the rest.

Yours ever,
J. W. C.

LETTER 327.

T. Carlyle, Esq., Scotsbrig.

5 Cheyne Row: Tuesday, April 10, 1866.

Alas, I missed Tyndall's call! and was 'vaixed!'
He left word with Jessie that you were 'looking well;
and everybody worshipping you!' and I thought to
myself, 'A pity if he have taken the habit of being
worshipped, for he may find some difficulty in keeping it up here!'

Finding the first night at Windsor (Friday night)
a great success, I gladly stayed a second night; and
only arrived at Cheyne Row in time for Lady
William's Sunday dinner. It couldn't be 'quiet'
that helped me to sleep so well at Mrs. Oliphant's;
for all day long I was in the presence of fellow-
creatures. The first evening, besides two Miss
Tullochs living in the house, there arrived to tea
and supper (!) a family of Hawtreys, to the number
of seven!—seven grown-up brothers and sisters!!
The eldest, 'Mr. Stephen,' with very white hair and

beard, is Master of Mathematics at Eton ; and has a pet school of his own—tradesmen's sons, and the like—on which he lays out three hundred a year of his own money. He complimented me on your ' excellent address,' which he said ' We read aloud to our boys.' I asked Mrs. Oliphant after, what boys he meant ? She said it would be the boys of his hobby school ; they were the only boys in the world for Mr. Stephen ! On the following day arrived Principal Tulloch, and wife, on a long visit. Mrs. Oliphant seems to me to be eaten up with long visitors. He (the Principal) had been at the ' Address,' and seen you walking in your wideawake with your brother, just as himself was leaving Edinburgh.

Frederick Elliot and Hayward (!) were at Lady William's. Hayward was raging against the Jamaica business—would have had Eyre cut into small pieces, and eaten raw. He told me *women* might patronise Eyre—that women were naturally cruel, and rather liked to look on while horrors were perpetrated. But no *man* living could stand up for Eyre now ! ' I hope Mr. Carlyle does,' I said. ' I haven't had an opportunity of asking him ; but I should be surprised and grieved if I found him sentimentalising over a pack of black brutes ! ' After staring at me a moment : ' Mr. Carlyle ! ' said Hayward. ' Oh, yes ! Mr. *Carlyle !* one cannot indeed swear what he will *not*

say! His great aim and philosophy of life being
" The smallest happiness of the fewest number!"'   —

I slept very ill again, that night of my return;
but last night was better, having gone to bed dead
weary of such a tea-party as you will say could have
entered into no human head but mine! Sartosina,[1]
Count Reichenbach, and James Aitken!! there was
to have been also Lady Airlie!!! You have no idea
how well Reichenbach and James suit each other!
They make each other quite animated, by the delight
each seems to feel in finding a man more inarticulate
than himself! They got towards the end into little
outbursts of laughter, of a very peculiar kind!

Yours ever,
JANE CARLYLE.

Send me a proof[2] as soon as you can.

LETTER 328.

I still in Edinburgh on that fated visit. I called on Mrs.
Stirling; the last time I have seen her. This letter was
dated only ten days before the utter *finis*.

The sudden death mentioned here, minutely and sympa-
thetically described in a letter to me, was that of Madame
Venturi's (born Ashurst's) Italian husband,[3] with both of
whom she was familiar.—T. C.

[1] A tailor's daughter, in the Kensington region, a modest yet ardent
admirer, whom, liking the tone of her letter, she drove to see, and
liked, and continued to like.

[2] *Correcting* to the Edinburgh printer of the Address. A London
pirate quite *forestalled* me and it.   [3] See page 321.

To Mrs. Stirling, Hill Street, Edinburgh.

5 Cheyne Row, Chelsea: Wednesday, April 11, 1866.

My dear Susan Hunter,—No change of modern times would have surprised me more disagreeably than your addressing me in any other style than the old one. The delight of you is just the faith one has —has always had—in your constancy. One mayn't see you for twenty years, but one would go to you at the end with perfect certainty of being kissed as warmly and made as much of as when we were together in the age of enthusiasm.

I was strongly tempted to accompany Mr. C. to Edinburgh and see you all once more. But, looked at near hand, my strength, or rather my courage, failed me in presence of the prospective demand on my 'finer sensibilities.' Since my long, terrible illness, I have had to quite leave off seeking emotions, and cultivating them. I had done a great deal too much of that sort of work in my time. Even at this distance I lost my sleep, and was tattered to fiddle-strings for a week by that flare-up of popularity in Edinburgh. To be sure the sudden death of an apparently healthy young man, husband of one of my most intimate friends, had shocked me into an unusually morbid mood; to say nothing of poor Craik struck down whilst opening his mouth to reprove a pupil. I had got it into my head that

the previous sleeplessness and fatigue, and the fuss
and closeness of a crowded room, and the novelty of
the whole thing, would take such effect on Mr. C.
that when he stood up to speak he would probably
drop down dead! When at six o'clock I got a telegram from Professor Tyndall to tell me it was over,
and well over, the relief was so sudden and complete,
that I (what my cook called) 'went off'—that is,
took a violent fit of crying, and had brandy given me.

I am very busy and cannot write a long letter;
but a short one, containing the old love and a kiss,
will be better than ' silence,' however 'golden.'

Your very affectionate

J. W. Carlyle.

LETTER 329.

T. Carlyle, Esq., Scotsbrig.

5 Cheyne Row: Thursday, April 12, 1866.

Dearest,—I sent you better than a letter yesterday—a charming 'Punch,' which I hope you received
in due course; but Geraldine undertook the posting
of it, and, as Ann said of her long ago, ' Miss can
write books, but I'm sure it's the only thing she's fit
for.' Well, there only wanted to complete your
celebrity that you should be in the chief place of
' Punch;' [1] and there you are, cape and wideawake,

---

[1] It came to Scotsbrig, with this letter, late at night; how merry it
made us all: oh, Heaven! 'merry!'

making a really creditable appearance. I must repeat what I said before—that the best part of this success is the general feeling of personal goodwill that pervades all they say and write about you. Even 'Punch' cuddles you, and purrs over you, as if you were his favourite son. From 'Punch' to Terry the greengrocer is a good step, but, let me tell you, he (Terry) asked Mrs. Warren—'Was Mr. Carlyle the person they wrote of as Lord Rector?' and Mrs. Warren having answered in her stage voice, 'The very same!' Terry shouted out ('Quite shouted it, ma'm!'), 'I never was so glad of anything! By George, I am glad!' Both Mrs. Warren and Jessie rushed out and bought 'Punches' to send to their families; and, in the fervour of their mutual enthusiasm, they have actually ceased hostilities—for the present. It seems to me that on every new compliment paid you these women run and fry something, such savoury smells reach me upstairs.

Lady Lothian was here the day before yesterday with a remarkably silly Mrs. L——. I was to tell you that she (Lady L.) was very impatient for your return—'missed you dreadfully.' I was to ' come some day before luncheon, and then we could go— somewhere.' To Miss Evans [1] is where we should go still, if you would let us.

Don't forget my oatmeal.

----

[1] Famous 'George Eliot' (or some such pseudonym).

There is a large sheet from the Pall Mall Bank, acknowledging the receipt of seventy pounds 'only.' I don't forward any nonsense letters come to you. This one inclosed has sex and youth to plead for it—so,

Yours ever,
J. W. C.

My kindest regards to Mary,[1] for whom I have made a cap, you may tell her, but couldn't get it finished before you left.

LETTER 330.

T. Carlyle, Esq., Scotsbrig.

5 Cheyne Row: Friday, April 13, 1866.

Oh, what a pity, dear, and what a stupidity I must say! After coming safely through so many fatigues and dangers to go and sprain your ankle, off your own feet! And such treatment the sprain will get! Out you will go with it morning and night, along the roughest roads, and keep up the swelling Heaven knows how long! The only comfort is that 'Providence is kind to women, fools, and drunk people,' and in the matter of taking care of yourself you come under the category of 'fools,' if ever any wise man did.

There came a note for you last night that will surprise you at this date as much as it did me,

---

[1] Sister.

though I daresay it won't make you start and give a little scream as it did me.[1] It—such a note!—is hardly more friendly than silence, but it is more polite. I wish I hadn't sent him that kind message. Virtue (forgiveness of wrong, 'milk of human kindness,' and all that sort of 'damned thing') being 'ever its own reward, unless something particular occurs to prevent,' which it almost invariably does.

There! I must get ready for that blessed carriage. I have been *redding up* all morning.

Ever yours,
J. W. CARLYLE.

It would be good to send back Mill's letter, that Reichenbach might tell Löwe[2] of it.

LETTER 331.

T. Carlyle, Esq., Scotsbrig.

5 Cheyne Row: Tuesday, April 17, 1866.

Oh, my dear, these women are too tiresome! Time after time I have sworn to send on none of their nonsense, but to burn it or let it lie, as I do all about ' ——,' and there is always 'a something' that touches me on their behalf. Here is this Trimnell! She was doomed, and should have been cast into outer darkness (of the cupboard) but for that poor

---

[1] A note from John Mill—response about some trifle, after long delay.

[2] Löwe (German, unknown to me) wanted to translate something of Mill's, and had applied, through Reichenbach, to me on the matter.

little phrase, 'as much as my weak brains will permit.' And the Caroline C——— (who the deuce is she that writes such a scratchy, illegible hand?) sends her love to Mrs. Carlyle, and proposes to 'talk to her about Amisfield and Haddington.' 'Encouraged by your brother to beg,' &c. &c., complicates the question still further. Yes, it is the mixing up of things that is 'the great bad.'[1]

I called at the Royal Institution yesterday to ask if Tyndall had returned. He was there; and I sat some time with him in his room hearing the minutest details of your doings and sufferings on the journey. It is *the* event of Tyndall's life! Crossing the hall, I noticed for the first time that officials were hurrying about; and I asked the one nearest me, 'Is there to be lecturing here to-day?' The man gave me such a look, as if I was *deeranged*, and people going up the stairs turned and looked at me as if I was *deeranged*. Neuberg ran down to me and asked, 'Wouldn't I hear the lecture?' And by simply going out when everyone else was going in I made myself an object of general interest. As I looked back from the carriage window I saw all heads in the hall and on the stairs turned towards me.

I called at Miss Bromley's after. She had dined at Marochetti's on Saturday, being to go with them to some spectacle after. The spectacle which she

---

[1] Reichenbach's phrase.

saw without any going was a great fire of Marochetti's studio—furnaces overheated in casting Landseer's 'great lion.'

How dreadful that poor woman's[1] suicide! What a deal of misery it must take to drive a working-woman to make away with her life! What does Dr. Carlyle make of such a case as that? No idleness, nor luxury, nor novel-reading to make· it all plain.[2]

Ever yours,
J. W. C.

LETTER 332.

T. Carlyle, Esq., Scotsbrig.

5 Cheyne Row, Chelsea: Thursday, April 19, 1866.

I read the Memoir[3] 'first' yesterday morning, having indeed read the 'Address' the evening before, and read it some three times in different newspapers. If you call that 'laudatory,' you must be easily pleased. I never read such stupid, vulgar janners.[4] The last of calumnies that I should ever have expected to hear uttered about you was this of your going about 'filling the laps of dirty children with comfits.' Idiot! My half-pound of barley-sugar made into such a legend! The wretch has even

---

[1] A poor neuralgic woman, near Scotsbrig—a daughter of old Betty Smail's (mentioned already ?—'head like a *mall*,' &c.).

[2] Alas! that was a blind, hasty, and *cruel* speech of poor, good John's!

[3] By London *pirate*.   [4] Capital Scotch word.

failed to put the right number to the sketch of the house—'No. 7!' A luck, since he was going to blunder, that he didn't call it No. 6, with its present traditions. It is prettily enough done, the house. I recollect looking over the blind one morning and seeing a young man doing it. 'What can he be doing?' I said to Jessie. 'Oh, counting the windows for the taxes,' she answered quite confidently; and I was satisfied.

I saw Frederick Chapman yesterday, and he was very angry. He had 'frightened the fellow out of advertising,' he said; and he had gone round all the booksellers who had subscribed largely for the spurious Address, and required them to withdraw their orders. By what right, I wonder? Difficulty of procuring it will only make it the more sought after, I should think. 'By making it felony, ma'am, yourselves have raised the price of getting your dogs back.'[1]

I didn't write yesterday because, in the first place I was very sick, and in the second place I got a moral shock,[2] that stunned me *pro tempore*. No time to tell you about that just now, but another day.

I have put the women to sleep in your bed to air it. It seems so long since you went away.

Imagine the tea party I am to have on Saturday[3]

---

[1] London dog-stealers pleaded so, on the Act passed against them.
[2] What I could never guess.
[3] Oh, Heaven!

night. Mrs. Oliphant, Principal Tulloch and wife and two grown-up daughters, Mr. and Mrs. Froude, Mr. and Mrs. Spottiswoode!

Did you give Jane the things I sent?[1] When one sends a thing one likes to know if it has been received safe.

Yours ever,

J. W. C.

LETTER 333.

The last words her hand ever wrote. Why should I tear my heart by reading them so often? They reached me at Dumfries, Sunday, April 22, fifteen hours after the fatal telegram had come. Bright weather this, and the day before I was crippling out Terregles way, among the silent green meadows, at the moment when she left this earth.

Spottiswoodes, King's Printer people. I durst never see them since. Miss Wynne, I hear, is dead of cancer six months ago.

'Very equal,' a thrifty Annandale phrase.

'Scende da carrozza' (Degli Antoni).

'Picture of Frederick.' I sent for it on the Tuesday following, directly on getting to Chelsea. It still hangs there; a poor enough Potsdam print, but to me priceless.

I am at Addiscombe in the room that was long 'Lady Harriet's;' day and house altogether silent, Thursday, August 5, 1869, while I finish this unspeakable revisal (reperusal and study of all her letters left to me). Task of about eleven months, and sad and strange as a pilgrimage through Hades.— —T. C.

[1] I did, and told her so in the letter *she* never received. Why should *I* ever read this again! (*Note of* 1866.)

T. Carlyle, Esq., The Hill, Dumfries.

5 Cheyne Row, Chelsea : Saturday, April 21, 1866.

Dearest,—It seems 'just a consuming of time' to write to-day, when you are coming the day after to-morrow. But 'if there were nothing else in it' (your phrase) such a piece of liberality as letting one have letters on Sunday, if called for, should be honoured at least by availing oneself of it! All long stories, however, may be postponed till next week. Indeed, I have neither long stories nor short ones to tell this morning. To-morrow, after the tea-party, I may have more to say, provided I survive it! Though how I am to entertain. 'on my own basis,' eleven people in a hot night 'without refresh-ment' (to speak of) is more than I 'see my way' through! Even as to cups—there are only ten cups of company-china ; and eleven are coming, myself making twelve! 'After all,' said Jessie, 'you had once eight at tea—three mair won't kill us!' I'm not so sure of that. Let us hope the motive will sanctify the end ; being 'the welfare of others!' an unselfish desire to 'make two Ba-ings happy :' Principal Tulloch and Froude, who have a 'great liking for one another! The Spottiswoodes were added in the same philanthropic spirit. We met in a shop, and they begged permission to come again ; so I thought it would be clever to get them over (handsomely with Froude and Mrs. Oliphant) before you came. Miss. Wynne offered herself, by accident, for that same night.

The Marchioness was here yesterday, twice; called at four when I hadn't returned, and called at five. She brought with her yesterday a charming old Miss Talbot, with a palsied head, but the most loveable babyish old face! She seemed to take to me, as I did to her ; and Lady Lothian stayed behind a minute, to ask if I would go with her some day to see this Miss Talbot, who had a house full of the finest pictures. You should have sent the Address to Lord Lothian or Lady. I see several names on the list less worthy of such attention.

Chapman is furious at Hotten ; no wonder! When he went round to the booksellers, he found that everywhere Hotten had got the start of him. Smith and Elder had bought five hundred copies from Hotten! And poor Frederick did not receive his copies from Edinburgh till he had 'telegraphed,' six-and-thirty hours after I had received mine!

I saw in an old furniture-shop window at Richmond a copy of the Frederick picture that was lent you—not bad ; coarsely painted, but the likeness well preserved. Would you like to have it ? I will, if so, make you a present of it, being to be had 'very equal.' . I 'descended from the carriage,' and asked,

'What was that?' (meaning what price was it).   The broker told me impressively, 'That, ma'am, is Peter the Great.' 'Indeed! and what is the price?' 'Seven-and-sixpence.' I offered five shillings on the spot, but he would only come down to six shillings.   I will go back for it if you like, and can find a place for it on my wall.

Yours ever,

J. W. C.

On the afternoon of the day on which the preceding letter was written, Mrs. Carlyle died suddenly in her carriage in Hyde Park. A letter of Miss Jewsbury's relating the circumstances which attended and followed her death has been already published in the 'Reminiscences.' I reprint it here as a fit close to this book.—J. A. F.

To Thomas Carlyle.

'43 Markham Square, Chelsea : May 26, 1866.

'Dear Mr. Carlyle,—I think it better to write than to speak on the miserable subject about which you told me to inquire of Mr. Silvester.[1] I saw him to-day. He said that it would be about twenty minutes after three o'clock or thereabouts when they left Mr. Forster's house; that he then drove through the Queen's Gate, close by Kensington Gardens, that there, at the uppermost gate, she got out, and walked along the side of the Gardens very slowly, about two hundred paces, with the little dog running, until she came to the Serpentine Bridge, at the southern end of which

---

[1] Mrs. Carlyle's coachman.

she got into the carriage again, and he drove on till they came to a quiet place on the Tyburnia side, near Victoria Gate, and then she put out the little dog to run along. When they came opposite to Albion Street, Stanhope Place (lowest thoroughfare of Park towards Marble Arch), a brougham coming along upset the dog, which lay on its back screaming for a while, and then she pulled the check-string; and he turned round and pulled up at the side of the footpath, and there the dog was (he had got up out of the road and gone there). Almost before the carriage stopped she was out of it. The lady whose brougham had caused the accident got out also, and several other ladies who were walking had stopped round the dog. The lady spoke to her; but he could not hear what she said, and the other ladies spoke. She then lifted the dog into the carriage, and got in herself. He asked if the little dog was hurt; but he thinks she did not hear him, as carriages were passing. He heard the dog squeak as if she had been feeling it (nothing but a toe was hurt); this was the last sound or sigh he ever heard from her place of fate. He went on towards Hyde Park Corner, turned there and drove past the Duke of Wellington's Achilles figure, up the drive to the Serpentine and past it, and came round by the road where the dog was hurt, past the Duke of Wellington's house and past the gate opposite St. George's. Getting no sign (noticing only the two hands laid on the lap, palm uppermost the right hand, reverse way the left, and all motionless), he turned into the Serpentine drive again; but after a few yards, feeling a little surprised, he looked back, and, seeing her in the same posture, became alarmed, made for the streetward entrance into the Park a few yards westward of gatekeeper's lodge, and asked a lady to look in; and she said what we know, and she addressed a gentleman who confirmed her fears. It was then fully a quarter past four;

going on to twenty minutes (but nearer the quarter); of this
he is quite certain. She was leaning back in one corner of
the carriage, rugs spread over her knees; her eyes were
closed, and her upper lip slightly, slightly opened. Those
who saw her at the hospital and when in the carriage speak
of the beautiful expression upon her face.

'On that miserable night, when we were preparing to
receive her, Mrs. Warren [1] came to me and said, that one time,
when she was very ill, she said to her, that when the last had
come, she was to go upstairs into the closet of the spare
room and there she would find two wax candles wrapt in
paper, and that those were to be lighted and burned. She
said that after she came to live in London she wanted to
give a party; her mother wished everything to be very
nice, and went out and bought candles and confectionery,
and set out a table, and lighted the room quite splendidly,
and called her to come and see it when all was prepared.
She was angry; she said people would say she was extravagant, and would ruin her husband. She took away two of
the candles and some of the cakes. Her mother was hurt
and began to weep. She was pained at once at what she
had done ; she tried to comfort her, and was dreadfully sorry.
She took the candles and wrapped them up, and put them
where they could be easily found. We found them and
lighted them, and did as she desired.

'G. E. J.'

What a strange, beautiful, sublime and almost terrible
little action ; silently resolved on, and kept silent from all
the earth for perhaps twenty-four years! I never heard a
whisper of it, and yet see it to be true. The visit must
have been about 1837 ; I remember the soirée right well ;
the resolution, bright as with heavenly tears and lightning,

---

[1] The housekeeper in Cheyne Row.

was probably formed on her mother's death, February 1842.—T. C.

Mrs. Carlyle was buried by the side of her father, in the choir of Haddington Church. These words follow on the tombstone after her father's name :—

HERE LIKEWISE NOW RESTS

JANE WELSH CARLYLE,

SPOUSE OF THOMAS CARLYLE, CHELSEA, LONDON.

SHE WAS BORN AT HADDINGTON, 14TH JULY, 1801, ONLY DAUGHTER OF THE ABOVE JOHN WELSH, AND OF GRACE WELSH, CAPLEGILL, DUMFRIESSHIRE, HIS WIFE. IN HER BRIGHT EXISTENCE SHE HAD MORE SORROWS THAN ARE COMMON; BUT ALSO A SOFT INVINCIBILITY, A CLEARNESS OF DISCERNMENT, AND A NOBLE LOYALTY OF HEART, WHICH ARE RARE. FOR FORTY YEARS SHE WAS THE TRUE AND EVER-LOVING HELPMATE OF HER HUSBAND, AND BY ACT AND WORD UNWEARIEDLY FORWARDED HIM, AS NONE ELSE COULD, IN ALL OF WORTHY, THAT HE DID OR ATTEMPTED. SHE DIED AT LONDON, 21ST APRIL, 1866; SUDDENLY SNATCHED AWAY FROM HIM, AND THE LIGHT OF HIS LIFE, AS IF GONE OUT.

LONDON : PRINTED BY
SPOTTISWOODE AND CO., NEW-STREET SQUARE
AND PARLIAMENT STREET

39 Paternoster Row, E.C.
London, *November* 1882.

GENERAL LISTS OF WORKS

PUBLISHED BY

Messrs. Longmans, Green & Co.

HISTORY, POLITICS, HISTORICAL MEMOIRS, &c.

History of England from the Conclusion of the Great War in 1815 to the year 1841. By Spencer Walpole. 3 vols. 8vo. £2. 14*s*.

History of England in the 18th Century. By W. E. H. Lecky, M.A. 4 vols. 8vo. 1700–1784, £3. 12*s*.

The History of England from the Accession of James II. By the Right Hon. Lord Macaulay.
Student's Edition, 2 vols. cr. 8vo. 12*s*.
People's Edition, 4 vols. cr. 8vo. 16*s*.
Cabinet Edition, 8 vols. post 8vo. 48*s*.
Library Edition, 5 vols. 8vo. £4.

The Complete Works of Lord Macaulay. Edited by Lady Trevelyan.
Cabinet Edition, 16. vols. crown 8vo. price £4. 16*s*.
Library Edition, 8 vols. 8vo. Portrait, price £5. 5*s*.

Lord Macaulay's Critical and Historical Essays.
Cheap Edition, crown 8vo. 3*s*. 6*d*.
Student's Edition, crown 8vo. 6*s*.
People's Edition, 2 vols. crown 8vo. 8*s*.
Cabinet Edition, 4 vols. 24*s*.
Library Edition, 3 vols. 8vo. 36*s*.

The History of England from the Fall of Wolsey to the Defeat of the Spanish Armada. By J. A. Froude, M.A.
Popular Edition, 12 vols. crown, £2. 2*s*.
Cabinet Edition, 12 vols. crown, £3. 12*s*.

The English in Ireland in the Eighteenth Century. By J. A. Froude, M.A. 3 vols. crown 8vo. 18*s*.

The English in America; Virginia, Maryland, and the Carolinas. By J. A. Doyle, Fellow of All Souls' College, Oxford. 8vo. Map, 18*s*.

Journal of the Reigns of King George IV. and King William IV. By the late C. C. F. Greville, Esq. Edited by H. Reeve, Esq. Fifth Edition. 3 vols. 8vo. price 36*s*.

The Life of Napoleon III. derived from State Records, Unpublished Family Correspondence, and Personal Testimony. By Blanchard Jerrold. With numerous Portraits and Facsimiles. 4 vols. 8vo. £3. 18*s*.

The Early History of Charles James Fox. By the Right Hon. G. O. Trevelyan, M.P. Fourth Edition. 8vo. 6*s*.

Selected Speeches of the Earl of Beaconsfield, K.G. With Introduction and Notes, by T. E. Kebbel, M.A. 2 vols. 8vo. Portrait, 32*s*.

The Constitutional History of England since the Accession of George III. 1760–1870. By Sir Thomas Erskine May, K.C.B. D.C.L. Seventh Edition. 3 vols. cr. 8vo. 18*s*.

Democracy in Europe; a History. By Sir Thomas Erskine May, K.C.B. D.C.L. 2 vols. 8vo. 32*s*.

Introductory Lectures on Modern History delivered in 1841 and 1842. By the late THOMAS ARNOLD, D.D. 8vo. 7s. 6d.

History of Civilisation in England and France, Spain and Scotland. By HENRY THOMAS BUCKLE. 3 vols. crown 8vo. 24s.

Lectures on the History of England from the Earliest Times to the Death of King Edward II. By W. LONGMAN, F.S.A. Maps and Illustrations. 8vo. 15s.

History of the Life & Times of Edward III. By W. LONGMAN, F.S.A. With 9 Maps, 8 Plates, and 16 Woodcuts. 2 vols. 8vo. 28s.

Historic Winchester; England's First Capital. By A. R. BRAMSTON and A. C. LEROY. Crown 8vo. 6s.

The Historical Geogra-phy of Europe. By E. A. FREEMAN, D.C.L. LL.D. Second Edition, with 65 Maps. 2 vols. 8vo. 31s. 6d.

History of England un-der the Duke of Buckingham and Charles I. 1624-1628. By S. R. GARDINER, LL.D. 2 vols. 8vo. Maps, price 24s.

The Personal Govern-ment of Charles I. from the Death of Buckingham to the Declaration in favour of Ship Money, 1628-1637. By S. R. GARDINER, LL.D. 2 vols. 8vo. 24s.

The Fall of the Monarchy of Charles I. 1637-1649. By S. R. GARDINER, LL.D. VOLS. I. & II. 1637-1642. 2 vols. 8vo. 28s.

A Student's Manual of the History of India from the Earliest Period to the Present. By Col. MEADOWS TAYLOR, M.R.A.S. Third Thousand. Crown 8vo. Maps, 7s. 6d.

Outline of English His-tory, B.C. 55–A.D. 1880. By S. R. GARDINER, LL.D. With 96 Woodcuts Fcp. 8vo. 2s. 6d.

Waterloo Lectures; a Study of the Campaign of 1815. By Col. C. C. CHESNEY, R.E. 8vo. 10s. 6d.

The Oxford Reformers—John Colet, Erasmus, and Thomas More; a History of their Fellow-Work. By F. SEEBOHM. 8vo. 14s.

History of the Romans under the Empire. By Dean MERIVALE, D.D. 8 vols. post 8vo. 48s.

General History of Rome from B.C. 753 to A.D. 476. By Dean MERIVALE, D.D. Crown 8vo. Maps, price 7s. 6d.

The Fall of the Roman Republic; a Short History of the Last Century of the Commonwealth. By Dean MERIVALE, D.D. 12mo. 7s. 6d.

The History of Rome. By WILHELM IHNE. 5 vols. 8vo. price £3. 17s.

Carthage and the Cartha-ginians. By R. BOSWORTH SMITH, M.A. Second Edition; Maps, Plans, &c. Crown 8vo. 10s. 6d.

History of Ancient Egypt. By G. RAWLINSON, M.A. With Map and Illustrations. 2 vols. 8vo. 63s.

The Seventh Great Ori-ental Monarchy; or, a History of the Sassanians. By G. RAWLINSON, M.A. With Map and 95 Illustrations. 8vo. 28s.

The History of European Morals from Augustus to Charlemagne. By W. E. H. LECKY, M.A. 2 vols. crown 8vo. 16s.

History of the Rise and Influence of the Spirit of Rationalism in Europe. By W. E. H. LECKY, M.A. 2 vols. crown 8vo. 16s.

The History of Philo-sophy, from Thales to Comte. By GEORGE HENRY LEWES. Fifth Edition. 2 vols. 8vo. 32s.

A History of Classical Latin Literature. By G. A. SIMCOX, M.A. Fellow of Queen's College, Oxford. 2 vols. 8vo. 32s.

A History of Classical Greek Literature. By the Rev. J. P. MAHAFFY, M.A. Crown 8vo. VOL. I. Poets, 7s. 6d. VOL. II. Prose Writers, 7s. 6d.

Witt's Myths of Hellas,

or Greek Tales Told in German. Translated into English by F. M. YOUNGHUSBAND. With a Preface by A. SIDGWICK, M.A. C.C. Coll. Oxon. Crown 8vo. *[Nearly ready.*

Zeller's Stoics, Epicureans, and Sceptics.

Translated by the Rev. O. J. REICHEL, M.A. New Edition revised. Crown 8vo. 15*s*.

Zeller's Socrates & the Socratic Schools.

Translated by the Rev. O. J. REICHEL, M.A. Second Edition. Crown 8vo. 10*s*. 6*d*.

Zeller's Plato & the Older Academy.

Translated by S. FRANCES ALLEYNE and ALFRED GOODWIN, B.A. Crown 8vo. 18*s*.

Zeller's Pre-Socratic Schools;

a History of Greek Philosophy from the Earliest Period to the time of Socrates. Translated by SARAH F. ALLEYNE. 2 vols. crown 8vo. 30*s*.

Epochs of Modern History.

Edited by C. COLBECK, M.A.

Church's Beginning of the Middle Ages, price 2*s*. 6*d*.
Cox's Crusades, 2*s*. 6*d*.
Creighton's Age of Elizabeth, 2*s*. 6*d*.
Gairdner's Lancaster and York, 2*s*. 6*d*.
Gardiner's Puritan Revolution, 2*s*. 6*d*.
——— Thirty Years' War, 2*s*. 6*d*.
——— (Mrs.) French Revolution, 2*s*. 6*d*.
Hale's Fall of the Stuarts, 2*s*. 6*d*.
Johnson's Normans in Europe, 2*s*. 6*d*.
Longman's Frederic the Great, 2*s*. 6*d*.
Ludlow's War of American Independence, price 2*s*. 6*d*.
M'Carthy's Epoch of Reform, 1830–1850. price 2*s*. 6*d*.
Morris's Age of Anne, 2*s*. 6*d*.
Seebohm's Protestant Revolution, 2*s*. 6*d*.
Stubbs' Early Plantagenets, 2*s*. 6*d*.
Warburton's Edward III. 2*s*. 6*d*.

Epochs of Ancient History.

Edited by the Rev. Sir G. W. Cox, Bart. M.A. & C. SANKEY, M.A.

Beesly's Gracchi, Marius and Sulla, 2*s*. 6*d*.
Capes's Age of the Antonines, 2*s*. 6*d*.
——— Early Roman Empire, 2*s*. 6*d*.
Cox's Athenian Empire, 2*s*. 6*d*.
——— Greeks & Persians, 2*s*. 6*d*.
Curteis's Macedonian Empire, 2*s*. 6*d*.
Ihne's Rome to its Capture by the Gauls, price 2*s*. 6*d*.
Merivale's Roman Triumvirates, 2*s*. 6*d*.
Sankey's Spartan & Theban Supremacies, price 2*s*. 6*d*.
Smith's Rome and Carthage, 2*s*. 6*d*.

Creighton's Shilling History

of England, introductory to 'Epochs of English History.' Fcp. 1*s*.

Epochs of English History.

Edited by the Rev. MANDELL CREIGHTON, M.A. In One Volume. Fcp. 8vo. 5*s*.

Browning's Modern England, 1820–1874, 9*d*.
Creighton's (Mrs.) England a Continental Power, 1066–1216, 9*d*.
Creighton's (Rev. M.) Tudors and the Reformation, 1485–1603, 9*d*.
Gardiner's (Mrs.) Struggle against Absolute Monarchy, 1603–1688, 9*d*.
Rowley's Rise of the People, 1215–1485, 9*d*.
——— Settlement of the Constitution, 1689–1784, 9*d*.
Tancock's England during the American and European Wars, 1765–1820, 9*d*.
York-Powell's Early England to the Conquest, 1*s*.

The Student's Manual of

Ancient History; the Political History, Geography and Social State of the Principal Nations of Antiquity. By W. COOKE TAYLOR, LL.D. Cr. 8vo. 7*s*. 6*d*.

The Student's Manual of

Modern History; the Rise and Progress of the Principal European Nations. By W. COOKE TAYLOR, LL.D. Crown 8vo. 7*s*. 6*d*.

BIOGRAPHICAL WORKS.

Reminiscences chiefly of

Oriel College and the Oxford Movement. By the Rev. THOMAS MOZLEY, M.A. Second Edition, with New Preface. 2 vols. crown 8vo. 18*s*.

Apologia pro Vitâ Suâ;

Being a History of his Religious Opinions by Cardinal NEWMAN. Crown 8vo. 6*s*.

Thomas Carlyle, a History of the first Forty Years of his Life, 1795 to 1835. By J. A. FROUDE, M.A. With 2 Portraits and 4 Illustrations. 2 vols. 8vo. 32*s.*

Reminiscences. By THOMAS CARLYLE. Edited by J. A. FROUDE, M.A. 2 vols. crown 8vo. 18*s.*

Life of Sir William Rowan Hamilton, Kt. LL.D. D.C.L. M.R.I.A. &c. Including Selections from his Poems, Correspondence, and Miscellaneous Writings. By the Rev. R. P. GRAVES, M.A. VOL. I. 8vo. 15*s.*

The Marriages of the Bonapartes. By the Hon. D. A. BINGHAM. 2 vols. crown 8vo. 21*s.*

Recollections of the Last Half-Century. By COUNT ORSI. With a Portrait of Napoleon III. and 4 Woodcuts. Crown 8vo. 7*s.* 6*d.*

Autobiography. By JOHN STUART MILL. 8vo. 7*s.* 6*d.*

Felix Mendelssohn's Let- ters, translated by Lady WALLACE. 2 vols. crown 8vo. 5*s.* each.

The Correspondence of Robert Southey with Caroline Bowles. Edited by EDWARD DOWDEN, LL.D. 8vo. Portrait, 14*s.*

The Life and Letters of Lord Macaulay. By the Right Hon. G. O. TREVELYAN, M.P.

LIBRARY EDITION, 2 vols. 8vo. 36*s.*
CABINET EDITION, 2 vols. crown 8vo. 12*s.*
POPULAR EDITION, 1 vol. crown 8vo. 6*s.*

William Law, Nonjuror and Mystic. By the Rev. J. H. OVERTON, M.A. 8vo. 15*s.*

James Mill; a Biography. By A. BAIN, LL.D. Crown 8vo. 5*s.*

John Stuart Mill; a Criticism, with Personal Recollections. By A. BAIN, LL.D. Crown 8vo. 2*s.* 6*d.*

A Dictionary of General Biography. By W. L. R. CATES. Third Edition. 8vo. 28*s.*

Outlines of the Life of Shakespeare. By J. O. HALLIWELL-PHILLIPPS, F.R.S. 8vo. 7*s.* 6*d.*

Biographical Studies. By the late WALTER BAGEHOT, M.A. 8vo. 12*s.*

Essays in Ecclesiastical Biography. By the Right Hon. Sir J. STEPHEN, LL.D. Crown 8vo. 7*s.* 6*d.*

Cæsar; a Sketch. By J. A. FROUDE, M.A. With Portrait and Map. 8vo. 16*s.*

Life of the Duke of Wel- lington. By the Rev. G. R. GLEIG, M.A. Crown 8vo. Portrait, 6*s.*

Memoirs of Sir Henry Havelock, K.C.B. By JOHN CLARK MARSHMAN. Crown 8vo. 3*s.* 6*d.*

Leaders of Public Opi- nion in Ireland. By W. E. H. LECKY, M.A. Crown 8vo. 7*s.* 6*d.*

Memoir of Augustus De Morgan, with Selections from his Letters. By his Wife, SOPHIA ELIZABETH DE MORGAN. 8vo. with Portrait, 14*s.*

MENTAL and POLITICAL PHILOSOPHY.

Comte's System of Posi- tive Polity, or Treatise upon Sociology. By various Translators. 4 vols. 8vo. £4.

De Tocqueville's Demo- cracy in America, translated by H. REEVE. 2 vols. crown 8vo. 16*s.*

Analysis of the Pheno- mena of the Human Mind. By JAMES MILL. With Notes, Illustrative and Critical. 2 vols. 8vo. 28*s.*

On Representative Go- vernment. By JOHN STUART MILL. Crown 8vo. 2*s.*

On Liberty. By John Stuart Mill. Crown 8vo. 1s. 4d.

Principles of Political Economy. By John Stuart Mill. 2 vols. 8vo. 30s. or 1 vol. crown 8vo. 5s.

Essays on some Unset- tled Questions of Political Economy. By John Stuart Mill. 8vo. 6s. 6d.

Utilitarianism. By John Stuart Mill. 8vo. 5s.

The Subjection of Wo- men. By John Stuart Mill. Fourth Edition. Crown 8vo. 6s.

Examination of Sir Wil- liam Hamilton's Philosophy. By John Stuart Mill. 8vo. 16s.

A System of Logic, Ratiocinative and Inductive. By John Stuart Mill. 2 vols. 8vo. 25s.

Dissertations and Dis- cussions. By John Stuart Mill. 4 vols. 8vo. £2. 6s. 6d.

A Systematic View of the Science of Jurisprudence. By Sheldon Amos, M.A. 8vo. 18s.

Path and Goal; a Discussion on the Elements of Civilisation and the Conditions of Happiness. By M. M. Kalisch, Ph.D. M.A. 8vo. price 12s. 6d.

Sir Travers Twiss on the Rights and Duties of Nations, considered as Independent Communities, in Time of War. Second Edition. 8vo. 21s.

A Primer of the English Constitution and Government. By S. Amos, M.A. Crown 8vo. 6s.

Fifty Years of the English Constitution, 1830-1880. By Sheldon Amos, M.A. Crown 8vo. 10s. 6d.

Francis Bacon's Promus of Formularies and Elegancies, illustrated by Passages from Shakespeare. By Mrs. H. Pott. With a Preface by the Rev. E. A. Abbott, D.D. 8vo. 16s.

Principles of Economical Philosophy. By H. D. Macleod, M.A. Second Edition, in 2 vols. Vol. I. 8vo. 15s. Vol. II. Part I. 12s.

Lord Bacon's Works, collected & edited by R. L. Ellis, M.A. J. Spedding, M.A. and D. D. Heath. 7 vols. 8vo. £3. 13s. 6d.

Letters and Life of Fran- cis Bacon, including all his Occasional Works. Collected and edited, with a Commentary, by J. Spedding. 7 vols. 8vo. £4. 4s.

The Institutes of Jus- tinian; with English Introduction, Translation, and Notes. By T. C. Sandars, M.A. 8vo. 18s.

The Nicomachean Ethics of Aristotle, translated into English by R. Williams, B.A. Crown 8vo. price 7s. 6d.

Aristotle's Politics, Books I. III. IV. (VII.) Greek Text, with an English Translation by W. E. Bolland, M.A. and Short Essays by A. Lang, M.A. Crown 8vo. 7s. 6d.

The Ethics of Aristotle; with Essays and Notes. By Sir A. Grant, Bart. LL.D. 2 vols. 8vo. 32s

Bacon's Essays, with Annotations. By R. Whately, D.D. 8vo. 10s. 6d.

An Introduction to Logic. By William H. Stanley Monck, M.A. Prof. of Moral Philos. Univ. of Dublin. Crown 8vo. 5s.

Picture Logic; an Attempt to Popularise the Science of Reasoning. By A. J. Swinburne, B.A. Post 8vo. 5s.

Elements of Logic. By R. Whately, D.D. 8vo. 10s. 6d. Crown 8vo. 4s. 6d.

Elements of Rhetoric. By R. Whately, D.D. 8vo. 10s. 6d. Crown 8vo. 4s. 6d.

The Senses and the In- tellect. By A. Bain, LL.D. 8vo. 15s.

The Emotions and the Will. By A. Bain, LL.D. 8vo. 15s.

Mental and Moral Science; a Compendium of Psychology and Ethics. By A. BAIN, LL.D. Crown 8vo. 10s. 6d.

An Outline of the Necessary Laws of Thought; a Treatise on Pure and Applied Logic. By W. THOMSON, D.D. Crown 8vo. 6s.

Essays in Political and Moral Philosophy. By T. E. CLIFFE LESLIE, Barrister-at-Law. 8vo. 10s. 6d.

On the Influence of Authority in Matters of Opinion. By the late Sir G. C. LEWIS, Bart. 8vo. price 14s.

Hume's Philosophical Works: Edited, with Notes, &c. by T. H. GREEN, M.A. and the Rev. T. H. GROSE, M.A. 4 vols. 8vo. 56s. Or separately, Essays, 2 vols. 28s. Treatise on Human Nature, 2 vols. 28s.

MISCELLANEOUS & CRITICAL WORKS.

Studies of Modern Mind and Character at Several European Epochs. By JOHN WILSON. 8vo. 12s.

Selected Essays, chiefly from Contributions to the Edinburgh and Quarterly Reviews. By A. HAYWARD, Q.C. 2 vols. crown 8vo. 12s.

Short Studies on Great Subjects. By J. A. FROUDE, M.A. 3 vols. crown 8vo. 18s. FOURTH SERIES, 8vo. 12s.

Literary Studies. By the late WALTER BAGEHOT, M.A. Second Edition. 2 vols. 8vo. Portrait, 28s.

Manual of English Literature, Historical and Critical. By T. ARNOLD, M.A. Crown 8vo. 7s. 6d.

Poetry and Prose; Illustrative Passages from English Authors from the Anglo-Saxon Period to the Present Time. Edited by T. ARNOLD, M.A. Crown 8vo. 6s.

The Wit and Wisdom of Benjamin Disraeli, Earl of Beaconsfield, collected from his Writings and Speeches. Crown 8vo. 6s.

The Wit and Wisdom of the Rev. Sydney Smith. Crown 8vo. 3s. 6d.

Lord Macaulay's Miscellaneous Writings :—
LIBRARY EDITION, 2 vols. 8vo. 21s.
PEOPLE'S EDITION, 1 vol. cr. 8vo. 4s. 6d.

Lord Macaulay's Miscellaneous Writings and Speeches. Student's Edition. Crown 8vo. 6s. Cabinet Edition, including Indian Penal Code, Lays of Ancient Rome, and other Poems. 4 vols. post 8vo. 24s.

Speeches of Lord Macaulay, corrected by Himself. Crown 8vo. 3s. 6d.

Selections from the Writings of Lord Macaulay. Edited, with Notes, by the Right Hon. G. O. TREVELYAN, M.P. Crown. 8vo. 6s.

Miscellaneous Works of Thomas Arnold, D.D. late Head Master of Rugby School. 8vo. 7s. 6d.

Realities of Irish Life. By W. STEUART TRENCH. Crown 8vo. 2s. 6d. Sunbeam Edition, 6d.

Evenings with the Skeptics; or, Free Discussion on Free Thinkers. By JOHN OWEN, Rector of East Anstey, Devon. 2 vols. 8vo. 32s.

Outlines of Primitive Belief among the Indo-European Races. By CHARLES F. KEARY, M.A. 8vo. 18s.

Language & Languages.

A Revised Edition of Chapters on Language and Families of Speech. By F. W. FARRAR, D.D. F.R.S. Crown 8vo. 6s.

Grammar of Elocution.

By JOHN MILLARD, Elocution Master in the City of London School. Second Edition. Fcp. 8vo. 3s. 6d.

Selected Essays on Language, Mythology, and Religion.

By F. MAX MÜLLER, M.A. K.M. 2 vols. crown 8vo. 16s.

Lectures on the Science of Language.

By F. MAX MÜLLER, M.A. K.M. 2 vols. crown 8vo. 16s.

Chips from a German Workshop;

Essays on the Science of Religion, and on Mythology, Traditions & Customs. By F. MAX MÜLLER, M.A. K.M. 4 vols. 8vo. £1. 16s.

India, What Can it Teach Us?

A Course of Lectures delivered before the University of Cambridge. By F. MAX MÜLLER, M.A. K.M. 8vo. [*In the press.*

The Essays and Contributions of A. K. H. B.

Uniform Cabinet Editions in crown 8vo.

Autumn Holidays, 3s. 6d.
Changed Aspects of Unchanged Truths, price 3s. 6d.
Commonplace Philosopher, 3s. 6d.
Counsel and Comfort, 3s. 6d.
Critical Essays, 3s. 6d.
Graver Thoughts. Three Series, 3s. 6d. each.
Landscapes, Churches, and Moralities, 3s. 6d.
Leisure Hours in Town, 3s. 6d.
Lessons of Middle Age, 3s. 6d.
Our Little Life, 3s. 6d.
Present Day Thoughts, 3s. 6d.
Recreations of a Country Parson, Three Series, 3s. 6d. each.
Seaside Musings, 3s. 6d.
Sunday Afternoons, 3s. 6d.

DICTIONARIES and OTHER BOOKS of REFERENCE.

English Synonymes.

By E. J. WHATELY. Edited by R. WHATELY, D.D. Fcp. 8vo. 3s.

Roget's Thesaurus of English Words and Phrases,

classified and arranged so as to facilitate the expression of Ideas, and assist in Literary Composition. Re-edited by the Author's Son, J. L. ROGET. Crown 8vo. 10s. 6d.

Handbook of the English Language.

By R. G. LATHAM, M.A. M.D. Crown 8vo. 6s.

Contanseau's Practical Dictionary

of the French and English Languages. Post 8vo. price 7s. 6d.

Contanseau's Pocket Dictionary,

French and English, abridged from the Practical Dictionary by the Author. Square 18mo. 3s. 6d.

A Practical Dictionary

of the German and English Languages. By Rev. W. L. BLACKLEY, M.A. & Dr. C. M. FRIEDLÄNDER. Post 8vo. 7s. 6d.

A New Pocket Dictionary

of the German and English Languages. By F. W. LONGMAN, Ball. Coll. Oxford. Square 18mo. 5s.

Becker's Gallus; Roman Scenes of the Time of Augustus.

Translated by the Rev. F. METCALFE, M.A. Post 8vo. 7s. 6d.

Becker's Charicles;

Illustrations of the Private Life of the Ancient Greeks. Translated by the Rev. F. METCALFE, M.A. Post 8vo. 7s. 6d.

A Dictionary of Roman and Greek Antiquities.

With 2,000 Woodcuts illustrative of the Arts and Life of the Greeks and Romans. By A. RICH, B.A. Crown 8vo. 7s. 6d.

**A Greek-English Lexi-
con.** By H. G. LIDDELL, D.D. Dean of Christchurch, and R. SCOTT, D.D. Dean of Rochester. Crown 4to. 36*s.*

**Liddell & Scott's Lexi-
con, Greek and English,** abridged for Schools. Square 12mo. 7*s.* 6*d.*

**An English-Greek Lexi-
con,** containing all the Greek Words used by Writers of good authority. By C. D. YONGE, M.A. 4to. 21*s.* School Abridgment, square 12mo. 8*s.* 6*d.*

**A Latin-English Diction-
ary.** By JOHN T. WHITE, D.D. Oxon. and J. E. RIDDLE, M.A. Oxon. Sixth Edition, revised. Quarto 21*s.*

**White's Concise Latin-
English Dictionary,** for the use of University Students. Royal 8vo. 12*s.*

M'Culloch's Dictionary
of Commerce and Commercial Navigation. Re-edited (1882), with a Supplement containing the most recent Information, by A. J. WILSON. With 48 Maps, Charts, and Plans. Medium 8vo. 63*s.*

Keith Johnston's General
Dictionary of Geography, Descriptive, Physical, Statistical, and Historical; a complete Gazetteer of the World. Medium 8vo. 42*s.*

The Public Schools Atlas
of Ancient Geography, in 28 entirely new Coloured Maps. Edited by the Rev. G. BUTLER, M.A. Imperial 8vo. or imperial 4to. 7*s.* 6*d.*

The Public Schools Atlas
of Modern Geography, in 31 entirely new Coloured Maps. Edited by the Rev. G. BUTLER, M.A. Uniform, 5*s.*

ASTRONOMY and METEOROLOGY.

Outlines of Astronomy.
By Sir J. F. W. HERSCHEL, Bart. M.A. Latest Edition, with Plates and Diagrams. Square crown 8vo. 12*s.*

The Moon, and the Con-
dition and Configurations of its Surface. By E. NEISON, F.R.A.S. With 26 Maps and 5 Plates. Medium 8vo. price 31*s.* 6*d.*

Air and Rain; the Begin-
nings of a Chemical Climatology. By R. A. SMITH, F.R.S. 8vo. 24*s.*

**Celestial Objects for
Common Telescopes.** By the Rev. T. W. WEBB, M.A. Fourth Edition, adapted to the Present State of Sidereal Science; Map, Plate, Woodcuts. Crown 8vo. 9*s.*

The Sun; Ruler, Light, Fire,
and Life of the Planetary System. By R. A. PROCTOR, B.A. With Plates & Woodcuts. Crown 8vo. 14*s.*

Proctor's Orbs Around
Us; a Series of Essays on the Moon & Planets, Meteors & Comets, the Sun & Coloured Pairs of Suns. With Chart and Diagrams. Crown 8vo. 7*s.* 6*d.*

Proctor's Other Worlds
than Ours; The Plurality of Worlds Studied under the Light of Recent Scientific Researches. With 14 Illustrations. Crown 8vo. 10*s.* 6*d.*

Proctor on the Moon;
her Motions, Aspects, Scenery, and Physical Condition. With Plates, Charts, Woodcuts, and Lunar Photographs. Crown 8vo. 10*s.*6*d.*

Proctor's Universe of
Stars; Presenting Researches into and New Views respecting the Constitution of the Heavens. Second Edition, with 22 Charts and 22 Diagrams. 8vo. 10*s.* 6*d.*

Proctor's New Star Atlas,

for the Library, the School, and the Observatory, in 12 Circular Maps (with 2 Index Plates). Crown 8vo. 5*s.*

Proctor's Larger Star

Atlas, for the Library, in Twelve Circular Maps, with Introduction and 2 Index Plates. Folio, 15*s.* or Maps only, 12*s. 6d.*

Proctor's Essays on Astronomy.

A Series of Papers on Planets and Meteors, the Sun and Sun-surrounding Space, Stars and Star Cloudlets. With 10 Plates and 24 Woodcuts. 8vo. price 12*s.*

Proctor's Transits of

Venus; a Popular Account of Past and Coming Transits from the First Observed by Horrocks in 1639 to the Transit of 2012. Fourth Edition, including Suggestions respecting the approaching Transit in December 1882; with 20 Lithographic Plates (12 Coloured) and 38 Illustrations engraved on Wood. 8vo. 8*s. 6d.*

Proctor's Studies of

Venus-Transits; an Investigation of the Circumstances of the Transits of Venus in 1874 and 1882. With 7 Diagrams and 10 Plates. 8vo. 5*s.*

NATURAL HISTORY and PHYSICAL SCIENCE.

Ganot's Elementary

Treatise on Physics, for the use of Colleges and Schools. Translated by E. ATKINSON, Ph.D. F.C.S. Tenth Edition. With 4 Coloured Plates and 844 Woodcuts. Large crown 8vo. 15*s.*

Ganot's Natural Philosophy

for General Readers and Young Persons. Translated by E. ATKINSON, Ph.D. F.C.S. Fourth Edition; with 2 Plates and 471 Woodcuts. Crown 8vo. 7*s. 6d.*

Professor Helmholtz'

Popular Lectures on Scientific Subjects. Translated and edited by EDMUND ATKINSON, Ph.D. F.C.S. With a Preface by Prof. TYNDALL, F.R.S. and 68 Woodcuts. 2 vols. crown 8vo. 15*s.* or separately, 7*s. 6d.* each.

Arnott's Elements of Physics

or Natural Philosophy. Seventh Edition, edited by A. BAIN, LL.D. and A. S. TAYLOR, M.D. F.R.S. Crown 8vo. Woodcuts, 12*s. 6d.*

The Correlation of Physical Forces.

By the Hon. Sir W. R. GROVE, F.R.S. &c. Sixth Edition, revised and augmented. 8vo. 15*s.*

A Treatise on Magnetism,

General and Terrestrial. By H. LLOYD, D.D. D.C.L. 8vo. 10*s. 6d.*

The Mathematical and

other Tracts of the late James M'Cullagh, F.T.C.D. Prof. of Nat. Philos. in the Univ. of Dublin. Edited by the Rev. J. H. JELLETT, B.D. and the Rev. S. HAUGHTON, M.D. 8vo. 15*s.*

Elementary Treatise on

the Wave-Theory of Light. By H. LLOYD, D.D. D.C.L. 8vo. 10*s. 6d.*

Fragments of Science.

By JOHN TYNDALL, F.R.S. Sixth Edition. 2 vols. crown 8vo. 16*s.*

Heat a Mode of Motion.

By JOHN TYNDALL, F.R.S. Sixth Edition. Crown 8vo. 12*s.*

Sound.

By JOHN TYNDALL, F.R.S. Fourth Edition, including Recent Researches. [*In the press.*

Essays on the Floating-

Matter of the Air in relation to Putrefaction and Infection. By JOHN TYNDALL, F.R.S. With 24 Woodcuts. Crown 8vo. 7*s. 6d.*

Professor Tyndall's Lectures

on Light, delivered in America in 1872 and 1873. With Portrait, Plate & Diagrams. Crown 8vo. 7*s. 6d.*

Professor Tyndall's Lessons in Electricity at the Royal Institution, 1875-6. With 58 Woodcuts. Crown 8vo. 2s. 6d.

Professor Tyndall's Notes of a Course of Seven Lectures on Electrical Phenomena and Theories, delivered at the Royal Institution. Crown 8vo. 1s. sewed, 1s. 6d. cloth.

Professor Tyndall's Notes of a Course of Nine Lectures on Light, delivered at the Royal Institution. Crown 8vo. 1s. swd., 1s. 6d. cloth.

Six Lectures on Physical Geography, delivered in 1876, with some Additions. By the Rev. SAMUEL HAUGHTON, F.R.S. M.D. D.C.L. With 23 Diagrams. 8vo. 15s.

An Introduction to the Systematic Zoology and Morphology of Vertebrate Animals. By A. MACALISTER, M.D. With 28 Diagrams. 8vo. 10s. 6d.

Text-Books of Science, Mechanical and Physical, adapted for the use of Artisans and of Students in Public and Science Schools. Small 8vo. with Woodcuts, &c.

Abney's Photography, 3s. 6d.
Anderson's (Sir John) Strength of Materials, price 3s. 6d.
Armstrong's Organic Chemistry, 3s. 6d.
Ball's Elements of Astronomy, 6s.
Barry's Railway Appliances, 3s. 6d.
Bauerman's Systematic Mineralogy, 6s.
Bloxam & Huntington's Metals, 5s.
Glazebrook's Physical Optics, 6s.
Goodeve's Mechanics, 3s. 6d.
Gore's Electro-Metallurgy, 6s.
Griffin's Algebra and Trigonometry, 3s. 6d.
Jenkin's Electricity and Magnetism, 3s. 6d.
Maxwell's Theory of Heat, 3s. 6d.
Merrifield's Technical Arithmetic, 3s. 6d.
Miller's Inorganic Chemistry, 3s. 6d.
Preece & Sivewright's Telegraphy, 3s. 6d.
Rutley's Study of Rocks, 4s. 6d.
Shelley's Workshop Appliances, 3s. 6d.
Thomé's Structural and Physical Botany, 6s.
Thorpe's Quantitative Analysis, 4s. 6d.
Thorpe & Muir's Qualitative Analysis, 3s. 6d.
Tilden's Chemical Philosophy, 3s. 6d.
Unwin's Machine Design, 6s.
Watson's Plane and Solid Geometry, 3s. 6d.

Experimental Physiology, its Benefits to Mankind; with an Address on Unveiling the Statue of William Harvey at Folkestone August 1881. By RICHARD OWEN, F.R.S. &c. Crown 8vo. 5s.

The Comparative Anatomy and Physiology of the Vertebrate Animals. By RICHARD OWEN, F.R.S. With 1,472 Woodcuts. 3 vols. 8vo. £3. 13s. 6d.

Homes without Hands; a Description of the Habitations of Animals, classed according to their Principle of Construction. By the Rev. J. G. WOOD, M.A. With about 140 Vignettes on Wood. 8vo. 14s.

Wood's Strange Dwellings; a Description of the Habitations of Animals, abridged from 'Homes without Hands.' With Frontispiece and 60 Woodcuts. Crown 8vo. 5s. Sunbeam Edition, 4to. 6d.

Wood's Insects at Home; a Popular Account of British Insects, their Structure, Habits, and Transformations. 8vo. Woodcuts, 14s.

Common British Insects, abridged from *Insects at Home.* By the Rev. J. G. WOOD, M.A. F.L.S. Crown 8vo. with numerous Illustrations.

Wood's Insects Abroad; a Popular Account of Foreign Insects, their Structure, Habits, and Transformations. 8vo. Woodcuts, 14s.

Wood's Out of Doors; a Selection of Original Articles on Practical Natural History. With 6 Illustrations. Crown 8vo. 5s.

Wood's Bible Animals; a description of every Living Creature mentioned in the Scriptures. With 112 Vignettes. 8vo. 14s.

The Sea and its Living Wonders. By Dr. G. HARTWIG. 8vo. with many Illustrations, 10s. 6d.

Hartwig's Tropical World. With about 200 Illustrations. 8vo. 10s. 6d.

Hartwig's Polar World;

a Description of Man and Nature in the Arctic and Antarctic Regions of the Globe. Maps, Plates & Woodcuts. 8vo. 10*s.* 6*d.* Sunbeam Edition, 6*d.*

Hartwig's Subterranean

World. With Maps and Woodcuts. 8vo. 10*s.* 6*d.*

Hartwig's Aerial World;

a Popular Account of the Phenomena and Life of the Atmosphere. Map, Plates, Woodcuts. 8vo. 10*s.* 6*d.*

A Familiar History of

Birds. By E. STANLEY, D.D. Revised and enlarged, with 160 Woodcuts. Crown 8vo. 6*s.*

Rural Bird Life; Essays

on Ornithology, with Instructions for Preserving Objects relating to that Science. By CHARLES DIXON. With Coloured Frontispiece and 44 Woodcuts by G. Pearson. Crown 8vo. 5*s.*

Country Pleasures; the

Chronicle of a Year, chiefly in a Garden. By GEORGE MILNER. Second Edition, with Vignette. Crown 8vo. 6*s.*

Rocks Classified and De-

scribed. By BERNHARD VON COTTA. An English Translation, by P. H. LAWRENCE, with English, German, and French Synonymes. Post 8vo. 14*s.*

The Geology of England

and Wales; a Concise Account of the Lithological Characters, Leading Fossils, and Economic Products of the Rocks. By H. B. WOODWARD, F.G.S. Crown 8vo. Map & Woodcuts, 14*s.*

Keller's Lake Dwellings

of Switzerland, and other Parts of Europe. Translated by JOHN E. LEE, F.S.A. F.G.S. With 206 Illustrations. 2 vols. royal 8vo. 42*s.*

Heer's Primæval World

of Switzerland. Edited by JAMES HEYWOOD, M.A. F.R.S. With Map, Plates & Woodcuts. 2 vols. 8vo. 12*s.*

The Puzzle of Life; a

Short History of Praehistoric Vegetable and Animal Life on the Earth. By A. NICOLS, F.R.G.S. With 12 Illustrations. Crown 8vo. 3*s.* 6*d.*

The Bronze Implements,

Arms, and Ornaments of Great Britain and Ireland. By JOHN EVANS, D.C.L. LL.D. F.R.S. With 540 Illustrations. 8vo. 25*s.*

The Origin of Civilisa-

tion, and the Primitive Condition of Man. By Sir J. LUBBOCK, Bart. M.P. F.R.S. Fourth Edition, enlarged. 8vo. Woodcuts, 18*s.*

Proctor's Light Science

for Leisure Hours; Familiar Essays on Scientific Subjects, Natural Phenomena, &c. 2 vols. cr. 8vo. 7*s.* 6*d.* ea.

Brande's Dictionary of

Science, Literature, and Art. Re-edited by the Rev. Sir G. W. Cox, Bart. M.A. 3 vols. medium 8vo. 63*s.*

Hullah's Course of Lec-

tures on the History of Modern Music. 8vo. 8*s.* 6*d.*

Hullah's Second Course

of Lectures on the Transition Period of Musical History. 8vo. 10*s.* 6*d.*

Loudon's Encyclopædia

of Plants; the Specific Character, Description, Culture, History, &c. of all Plants found in Great Britain. With 12,000 Woodcuts. 8vo. 42*s.*

Loudon's Encyclopædia

of Gardening; the Theory and Practice of Horticulture, Floriculture, Arboriculture & Landscape Gardening. With 1,000 Woodcuts. 8vo. 21*s.*

De Caisne & Le Maout's

Descriptive and Analytical Botany. Translated by Mrs. HOOKER; edited and arranged by J. D. HOOKER, M.D. With 5,500 Woodcuts. Imperial 8vo. price 31*s.* 6*d.*

Rivers's Orchard-House;

or, the Cultivation of Fruit Trees under Glass. Sixteenth Edition. Crown 8vo. with 25 Woodcuts, 5*s.*

The Rose Amateur's

Guide. By THOMAS RIVERS. Latest Edition. Fcp. 8vo. 4*s.* 6*d.*

Elementary Botany,

Theoretical and Practical; a Text-Book for Students. By H. EDMONDS B.Sc. With 312 Woodcuts. Fcp. 8vo. 2*s.*

CHEMISTRY and PHYSIOLOGY.

Experimental Chemistry for Junior Students. By J. E. REYNOLDS, M.D. F.R.S. Prof. of Chemistry, Univ. of Dublin. Fcp. 8vo. PART I. 1s. 6d. PART II. 2s. 6d.

Practical Chemistry; the Principles of Qualitative Analysis. By W. A. TILDEN, F.C.S. Fcp. 8vo. 1s. 6d.

Miller's Elements of Chemistry, Theoretical and Practical. Re-edited, with Additions, by H. MACLEOD, F.C.S. 3 vols. 8vo.

PART I. CHEMICAL PHYSICS. 16s.
PART II. INORGANIC CHEMISTRY, 24s.
PART III. ORGANIC CHEMISTRY, 31s.6d.

An Introduction to the Study of Inorganic Chemistry. By W. ALLEN MILLER, M.D. LL.D. late Professor of Chemistry, King's College, London. With 71 Woodcuts. Fcp. 8vo. 3s. 6d.

Annals of Chemical Medicine; including the Application of Chemistry to Physiology, Pathology, Therapeutics, Pharmacy, Toxicology & Hygiene. Edited by J. L. W. THUDICHUM, M.D. 2 vols. 8vo. 14s. each.

A Dictionary of Chemistry and the Allied Branches of other Sciences. Edited by HENRY WATTS, F.R.S. 9 vols. medium 8vo. £15.2s. 6d.

Inorganic Chemistry, Theoretical and Practical; an Elementary Text-Book. By W. JAGO, F.C.S. Third Edition, revised, with 37 Woodcuts. Fcp. 8vo. 2s.

Health in the House; Lectures on Elementary Physiology in its Application to the Daily Wants of Man and Animals. By Mrs. BUCKTON. Crown 8vo. Woodcuts, 2s.

The FINE ARTS and ILLUSTRATED EDITIONS.

The New Testament of Our Lord and Saviour Jesus Christ, Illustrated with Engravings on Wood after Paintings by the Early Masters chiefly of the Italian School. New Edition in course of publication in 18 Monthly Parts, 1s. each. 4to.

A Popular Introduction to the History of Greek and Roman Sculpture, designed to Promote the Knowledge and Appreciation of the Remains of Ancient Art. By WALTER C. PERRY. With 268 Illustrations. Square crown 8vo. 31s. 6d.

Japan; its Architecture, Art, and Art-Manufactures. By CHRISTOPHER DRESSER, Ph.D. F.L.S. &c. With 202 Graphic Illustrations engraved on Wood for the most part by Native Artists in Japan, the rest by G. Pearson, after Photographs and Drawings made on the spot. Square crown 8vo. 31s. 6d.

Lord Macaulay's Lays of Ancient Rome. With Ninety Illustrations engraved on Wood from Drawings by G. Scharf. Fcp. 4to. 21s.

Lord Macaulay's Lays of Ancient Rome, with Ivry and the Armada. With 41 Wood Engravings by G. Pearson from Original Drawings by J. R. Weguelin. Crown 8vo. 6s.

The Three Cathedrals dedicated to St. Paul in London. By W. LONGMAN, F.S.A. With Illustrations. Square crown 8vo. 21s.

Moore's Lalla Rookh, TENNIEL'S Edition, with 68 Woodcut Illustrations. Crown 8vo. 10s. 6d.

Moore's Irish Melodies, MACLISE'S Edition, with 161 Steel Plates. Super-royal 8vo. 21s.

Lectures on Harmony,
delivered at the Royal Institution. By G. A. MACFARREN. 8vo. 12*s.*

Jameson's Legends of the
Saints and Martyrs. With 19 Etchings and 187 Woodcuts. 2 vols. 31*s.* 6*d.*

Jameson's Legends of the
Madonna, the Virgin Mary as represented in Sacred and Legendary Art. With 27 Etchings and 165 Woodcuts. 1 vol. 21*s.*

Jameson's Legends of the
Monastic Orders. With 11 Etchings and 88 Woodcuts. 1 vol. 21*s.*

Jameson's History of the
Saviour, His Types and Precursors. Completed by Lady EASTLAKE. With 13 Etchings and 281 Woodcuts. 2 vols. 42*s.*

Art-Instruction in England.
By F. E. HULME, F.L.S. F.S.A. Fcp. 8vo. 3*s.* 6*d.*

The USEFUL ARTS, MANUFACTURES, &c.

The Elements of Mechanism.
By T. M. GOODEVE, M.A. Barrister-at-Law. New Edition, rewritten and enlarged, with 342 Woodcuts. Crown 8vo. 6*s.*

Railways and Locomotives;
a Series of Lectures delivered at the School of Military Engineering, Chatham. *Railways*, by J. W. BARRY, M. Inst. C.E. *Locomotives*, by Sir F. J. BRAMWELL, F.R.S. M. Inst. C.E. With 228 Woodcuts. 8vo. 21*s.*

Gwilt's Encyclopædia of
Architecture, with above 1,600 Woodcuts. Revised and extended by W. PAPWORTH. 8vo. 52*s.* 6*d.*

Lathes and Turning, Simple,
Mechanical, and Ornamental. By W. H. NORTHCOTT. Second Edition, with 338 Illustrations. 8vo. 18*s.*

Industrial Chemistry; a
Manual for Manufacturers and for Colleges or Technical Schools; a Translation of PAYEN'S *Précis de Chimie Industrielle*. Edited by B. H. PAUL. With 698 Woodcuts. Medium 8vo. 42*s.*

The British Navy: its
Strength, Resources, and Administration. By Sir T. BRASSEY, K.C.B. M.P. M.A. In 6 vols. 8vo. with numerous Illustrations. VOL. I. 10*s.* 6*d.* VOLS. II. & III. 3*s.* 6*d.* each.

A Treatise on Mills and
Millwork. By the late Sir W. FAIRBAIRN, Bart. C.E. Fourth Edition, with 18 Plates and 333 Woodcuts. 1 vol. 8vo. 25*s.*

Useful Information for
Engineers. By the late Sir W. FAIRBAIRN, Bart. C.F. With many Plates and Woodcuts. 3 vols. crown 8vo. 31*s.* 6*d.*

Hints on Household
Taste in Furniture, Upholstery, and other Details. By C. L. EASTLAKE. Fourth Edition, with 100 Illustrations. Square crown 8vo. 14*s.*

Handbook of Practical
Telegraphy. By R. S. CULLEY, Memb. Inst. C.E. Seventh Edition. Plates & Woodcuts. 8vo. 16*s.*

The Marine Steam Engine.
A Treatise for the use of Engineering Students and Officers of the Royal Navy. By RICHARD SENNETT, Chief Engineer, Royal Navy. With numerous Illustrations and Diagrams. 8vo. 21*s.*

A Treatise on the Steam
Engine, in its various applications to Mines, Mills, Steam Navigation, Railways and Agriculture. By J. BOURNE, C.E. With Portrait, 37 Plates, and 546 Woodcuts. 4to. 42*s.*

Bourne's Catechism of the Steam Engine, in its various Applications. Fcp. 8vo. Woodcuts, 6s.

Bourne's Recent Improvements in the Steam Engine. Fcp. 8vo. Woodcuts, 6s.

Bourne's Handbook of the Steam Engine, a Key to the Author's Catechism of the Steam Engine. Fcp. 8vo. Woodcuts, 9s.

Bourne's Examples of Steam and Gas Engines of the most recent Approved Types as employed in Mines, Factories, Steam Navigation, Railways and Agriculture. With 54 Plates & 356 Woodcuts. 4to. 70s.

Ure's Dictionary of Arts, Manufactures, and Mines. Seventh Edition, re-written and enlarged by R. Hunt, F.R.S. With 2,604 Woodcuts. 4 vols. medium 8vo. £7. 7s.

Kerl's Practical Treatise on Metallurgy. Adapted from the last German Edition by W. Crookes, F.R.S. &c. and E. Röhrig, Ph.D. 3 vols. 8vo. with 625 Woodcuts, £4. 19s.

Cresy's Encyclopædia of Civil Engineering, Historical, Theoretical, and Practical. With above 3,000 Woodcuts, 8vo. 25s.

Ville on Artificial Manures, their Chemical Selection and Scientific Application to Agriculture. Translated and edited by W. Crookes, F.R.S. With 31 Plates. 8vo. 21s.

Mitchell's Manual of Practical Assaying. Fifth Edition, revised, with the Recent Discoveries incorporated, by W. Crookes, F.R.S. Crown 8vo. Woodcuts, 31s. 6d.

The Art of Perfumery, and the Methods of Obtaining the Odours of Plants; with Instructions for the Manufacture of Perfumes &c. By G. W. S. Piesse, Ph.D. F.C.S. Fourth Edition, with 96 Woodcuts. Square crown 8vo. 21s.

Loudon's Encyclopædia of Gardening; the Theory and Practice of Horticulture, Floriculture, Arboriculture & Landscape Gardening. With 1,000 Woodcuts. 8vo. 21s.

Loudon's Encyclopædia of Agriculture; the Laying-out, Improvement, and Management of Landed Property; the Cultivation and Economy of the Productions of Agriculture. With 1,100 Woodcuts. 8vo. 21s.

RELIGIOUS and MORAL WORKS.

An Introduction to the Study of the New Testament, Critical, Exegetical, and Theological. By the Rev. S. Davidson, D.D. LL.D. Revised Edition. 2 vols. 8vo. 30s.

History of the Papacy During the Reformation. By M. Creighton, M.A. Vol. I. the Great Schism—the Council of Constance, 1378–1418. Vol. II. the Council of Basel—the Papal Restoration, 1418–1464. 2 vols. 8vo. 32s.

A History of the Church of England; Pre-Reformation Period. By the Rev. T. P. Boultbee. LL.D. 8vo. 15s.

Sketch of the History of the Church of England to the Revolution of 1688. By T. V. Short, D.D. Crown 8vo. 7s. 6d.

The English Church in the Eighteenth Century. By the Rev. C. J. Abbey, and the Rev. J. H. Overton. 2 vols. 8vo. 36s.

An Exposition of the 39 Articles, Historical and Doctrinal. By E. H. Browne, D.D. Bishop of Winchester. Twelfth Edition. 8vo. 16s.

A Commentary on the 39 Articles, forming an Introduction to the Theology of the Church of England. By the Rev. T. P. Boultbee, LL.D. New Edition. Crown 8vo. 6s.

Sermons preached most-

ly in the Chapel of Rugby School by the late T. ARNOLD, D.D. 6 vols. crown 8vo. 30*s.* or separately, 5*s.* each.

Historical Lectures on

the Life of Our Lord Jesus Christ. By C. J. ELLICOTT, D.D. 8vo. 12*s.*

The Eclipse of Faith; or

a Visit to a Religious Sceptic. By HENRY ROGERS. Fcp. 8vo. 5*s.*

Defence of the Eclipse of

Faith. By H. ROGERS. Fcp. 8vo. 3*s.* 6*d.*

Nature, the Utility of

Religion, and Theism. Three Essays by JOHN STUART MILL. 8vo. 10*s.* 6*d.*

A Critical and Gram-

matical Commentary on St. Paul's Epistles. By C. J. ELLICOTT, D.D. 8vo. Galatians, 8*s.* 6*d.* Ephesians, 8*s.* 6*d.* Pastoral Epistles, 10*s.* 6*d.* Philippians, Colossians, & Philemon, 10*s.* 6*d.* Thessalonians, 7*s.* 6*d.*

The Life and Letters of

St. Paul. By ALFRED DEWES, M.A. LL.D. D.D. Vicar of St. Augustine's Pendlebury. With 4 Maps. 8vo. 7*s.* 6*d.*

Conybeare & Howson's

Life and Epistles of St. Paul. Three Editions, copiously illustrated.

Library Edition, with all the Original Illustrations, Maps, Landscapes on Steel, Woodcuts, &c. 2 vols. 4to. 42*s.*

Intermediate Edition, with a Selection of Maps, Plates, and Woodcuts. 2 vols. square crown 8vo. 21*s.*

Student's Edition, revised and condensed, with 46 Illustrations and Maps. 1 vol. crown 8vo. 7*s.* 6*d.*

Smith's Voyage & Ship-

wreck of St. Paul; with Dissertations on the Life and Writings of St. Luke, and the Ships and Navigation of the Ancients. Fourth Edition, with numerous Illustrations. Crown 8vo. 7*s.* 6*d.*

A Handbook to the Bible,

or, Guide to the Study of the Holy Scriptures derived from Ancient Monuments and Modern Exploration. By F. R. CONDER, and Lieut. C. R. CONDER, R.E. Third Edition, Maps. Post 8vo. 7*s.* 6*d.*

Bible Studies. By M. M.

KALISCH, Ph.D. PART I. *The Prophecies of Balaam.* 8vo. 10*s.* 6*d.* PART II. *The Book of Jonah.* 8vo. price 10*s.* 6*d.*

Historical and Critical

Commentary on the Old Testament; with a New Translation. By M. M. KALISCH, Ph.D. Vol. I. Genesis, 8vo. 18*s.* or adapted for the General Reader, 12*s.* Vol. II. Exodus, 15*s.* or adapted for the General Reader, 12*s.* Vol. III. Leviticus, Part I. 15*s.* or adapted for the General Reader, 8*s.* Vol. IV. Leviticus, Part II. 15*s.* or adapted for the General Reader, 8*s.*

The Four Gospels in

Greek, with Greek-English Lexicon. By JOHN T. WHITE, D.D. Oxon. Square 32mo. 5*s.*

Ewald's History of Israel.

Translated from the German by J. E. CARPENTER, M.A. with Preface by R. MARTINEAU, M.A. 5 vols. 8vo. 63*s.*

Ewald's History of Christ

and His Time. Translated from the German by J. F. SMITH. 8vo.

[*Nearly ready.*

Ewald's Antiquities of

Israel. Translated from the German by H. S. SOLLY, M.A. 8vo. 12*s.* 6*d.*

The New Man and the

Eternal Life; Notes on the Reiterated Amens of the Son of God. By A. JUKES. Second Edition. Cr. 8vo. 6*s.*

The Types of Genesis,

briefly considered as revealing the Development of Human Nature. By A. JUKES. Crown 8vo. 7*s.* 6*d.*

The Second Death and

the Restitution of all Things; with some Preliminary Remarks on the Nature and Inspiration of Holy Scripture By A. JUKES. Crown 8vo. 3*s.* 6*d.*

Supernatural Religion;

an Inquiry into the Reality of Divine Revelation. Complete Edition, thoroughly revised. 3 vols. 8vo. 36*s.*

Lectures on the Origin

and Growth of Religion, as illustrated by the Religions of India. By F. MAX MÜLLER, M.A. Crown 8vo. price 7s. 6d.

Introduction to the Science of Religion,

Four Lectures delivered at the Royal Institution; with Notes and Illustrations on Vedic Literature, Polynesian Mythology, the Sacred Books of the East, &c. By F. MAX MÜLLER, M.A. Cr. 8vo. 7s. 6d.

The Gospel for the Nineteenth Century.

Fourth Edition. 8vo. price 10s. 6d.

Christ our Ideal,

an Argument from Analogy. By the same Author. 8vo. 8s. 6d.

The Temporal Mission of the Holy Ghost;

or, Reason and Revelation. By H. E. MANNING, D.D. Cardinal-Archbishop. Third Edition. Crown 8vo. 8s. 6d.

Passing Thoughts on Religion.

By Miss SEWELL. Fcp. 8vo. price 3s. 6d.

Preparation for the Holy Communion;

the Devotions chiefly from the works of Jeremy Taylor. By Miss SEWELL. 32mo. 3s.

Private Devotions for Young Persons.

Compiled by Miss SEWELL. 18mo. 2s.

Bishop Jeremy Taylor's Entire Works;

with Life by Bishop Heber. Revised and corrected by the Rev. C. P. EDEN. 10 vols. £5. 5s.

The Psalms of David;

a new Metrical English Translation of the Hebrew Psalter or Book of Praises. By WILLIAM DIGBY SEYMOUR, Q.C. LL.D. Crown 8vo. 7s. 6d.

The Wife's Manual;

or Prayers, Thoughts, and Songs on Several Occasions of a Matron's Life. By the late W. CALVERT, Minor Canon of St. Paul's. Printed and ornamented in the style of *Queen Elizabeth's Prayer Book*. Crown 8vo. 6s.

Hymns of Praise and Prayer.

Corrected and edited by Rev. JOHN MARTINEAU, LL.D. Crown 8vo. 4s. 6d. 32mo. 1s. 6d.

Spiritual Songs for the Sundays and Holidays throughout the Year.

By J. S. B. MONSELL, LL.D. Fcp. 8vo. 5s. 18mo. 2s.

Christ the Consoler;

a Book of Comfort for the Sick. By ELLICE HOPKINS. Second Edition. Fcp. 8vo. 2s. 6d.

Lyra Germanica;

Hymns translated from the German by Miss C. WINKWORTH. Fcp. 8vo. 5s.

Hours of Thought on Sacred Things;

Two Volumes of Sermons. By JAMES MARTINEAU, D.D. LL.D. 2 vols. crown 8vo. 7s. 6d. each.

Endeavours after the Christian Life;

Discourses By JAMES MARTINEAU, D.D. LL.D. Fifth Edition. Crown 8vo. 7s. 6d.

The Pentateuch & Book of Joshua Critically Examined.

By J. W. COLENSO, D.D. Bishop of Natal. Crown 8vo. 6s.

Elements of Morality,

In Easy Lessons for Home and School Teaching. By Mrs. CHARLES BRAY. Crown 8vo. 2s. 6d.

TRAVELS, VOYAGES, &c.

Three in Norway.

By TWO OF THEM. With a Map and 59 Illustrations on Wood from Sketches by the Authors. Crown 8vo. 10s. 6d.

Roumania, Past and Present.

By JAMES SAMUELSON. With 2 Maps, 3 Autotype Plates & 31 Illustrations on Wood. 8vo. 16s.

Sunshine and Storm in the East,

or Cruises to Cyprus and Constantinople. By Lady BRASSEY. Cheaper Edition, with 2 Maps and 114 Illustrations engraved on Wood. Cr. 8vo. 7s. 6d.

A Voyage in the 'Sunbeam,'

our Home on the Ocean for Eleven Months. By Lady BRASSEY. Cheaper Edition, with Map and 65 Wood Engravings. Crown 8vo. 7s. 6d. School Edition, fcp. 2s. Popular Edition, 4to. 6d.

Eight Years in Ceylon.

By Sir SAMUEL W. BAKER, M.A. Crown 8vo. Woodcuts, 7s. 6d.

The Rifle and the Hound in Ceylon.

By Sir SAMUEL W. BAKER, M.A. Crown 8vo. Woodcuts, 7s. 6d.

Sacred Palmlands;

or, the Journal of a Spring Tour in Egypt and the Holy Land. By A. G. WELD. Crown 8vo. 7s. 6d.

Wintering in the Riviera;

with Notes of Travel in Italy and France, and Practical Hints to Travellers. By W. MILLER. With 12 Illustrations. Post 8vo. 7s. 6d.

San Remo and the Western Riviera,

climatically and medically considered. By A. HILL HASSALL, M.D. Map and Woodcuts. Crown 8vo. 10s. 6d.

Himalayan and Sub-Himalayan Districts of British India,

their Climate, Medical Topography, and Disease Distribution. By F. N. MACNAMARA, M.D. With Map and Fever Chart. 8vo. 21s.

The Alpine Club Map of Switzerland,

with parts of the Neighbouring Countries, on the scale of Four Miles to an Inch. Edited by R. C. NICHOLS, F.R.G.S. 4 Sheets in Portfolio, 42s. coloured, or 34s. uncoloured.

Enlarged Alpine Club Map of the Swiss and Italian Alps,

on the Scale of 3 English Statute Miles to 1 Inch, in 8 Sheets, price 1s. 6d. each.

The Alpine Guide.

By JOHN BALL, M.R.I.A. Post 8vo. with Maps and other Illustrations :—

The Eastern Alps, 10s. 6d.

Central Alps,

including all the Oberland District, 7s. 6d.

Western Alps,

including Mont Blanc, Monte Rosa, Zermatt, &c. Price 6s. 6d.

On Alpine Travelling and the Geology of the Alps.

Price 1s. Either of the Three Volumes or Parts of the 'Alpine Guide' may be had with this Introduction prefixed, 1s. extra.

WORKS of FICTION.

In Trust;

the Story of a Lady and her Lover. By Mrs. OLIPHANT. Cabinet Edition. Cr. 8vo. 6s.

The Hughenden Edition

of the Novels and Tales of the Earl of Beaconsfield, K.G. from Vivian Grey to Endymion. With Maclise's Portrait of the Author, a later Portrait on Steel from a recent Photograph, and a Vignette to each volume. Eleven Volumes, cr. 8vo. 42s.

Novels and Tales.

By the Right Hon. the EARL of BEACONSFIELD, K.G. The Cabinet Edition. Eleven Volumes, crown 8vo. 6s. each.

The Novels and Tales of

the Right Hon. the Earl of Beaconsfield, K.G. Modern Novelist's Library Edition, complete in Eleven Volumes, crown 8vo. price 22s. boards, or 27s. 6d. cloth.

Novels and Tales by the
Earl of **Beaconsfield, K.G.** Modern Novelist's Library Edition, complete in Eleven Volumes, crown 8vo. cloth extra, with gilt edges, price 33*s.*

Whispers from Fairyland.
By Lord **Brabourne.** With 9 Illustrations. Crown 8vo. 3*s.* 6*d.*

Higgledy-Piggledy. By
Lord **Brabourne.** With 9 Illustrations. Crown 8vo. 3*s.* 6*d.*

Stories and Tales. By
Elizabeth M. Sewell. Cabinet Edition, in Ten Volumes, crown 8vo. price 3*s.* 6*d.* each, in cloth extra, with gilt edges :—

Amy Herbert.	Gertrude.
The Earl's Daughter.	
The Experience of Life.	
Cleve Hall.	Ivors.
Katharine Ashton.	
Margaret Percival.	
Lancton Parsonage.	Ursula.

The Modern Novelist's
Library. Each work complete in itself, price 2*s.* boards, or 2*s.* 6*d.* cloth :—

By the Earl of **Beaconsfield, K.G.**
Endymion.

Lothair.	Henrietta Temple.
Coningsby.	Contarini Fleming, &c.
Sybil.	Alroy, Ixion, &c.
Tancred.	The Young Duke, &c.
Venetia.	Vivian Grey, &c.

By **Anthony Trollope.**
Barchester Towers.
The Warden.

By Major **Whyte-Melville.**

Digby Grand.	Good for Nothing.
General Bounce.	Holmby House.
Kate Coventry.	The Interpreter.
The Gladiators.	Queen's Maries.

By the Author of 'The Rose Garden.'
Unawares.

By the Author of 'Mlle. Mori.'
The Atelier du Lys.
Mademoiselle Mori.

By Various Writers.
Atherston Priory.
The Burgomaster's Family.
Elsa and her Vulture.
The Six Sisters of the Valleys.

POETRY and THE DRAMA.

Poetical Works of Jean
Ingelow. New Edition, reprinted, with Additional Matter, from the 23rd and 6th Editions of the two volumes respectively; with 2 Vignettes. 2 vols. fcp. 8vo. 12*s.*

Faust. From the German
of **Goethe.** By T. E. Webb, LL.D. Reg. Prof. of Laws & Public Orator in the Univ. of Dublin. 8vo. 12*s.* 6*d.*

Goethe's Faust. A New
Translation, chiefly in Blank Verse; with a complete Introduction and copious Notes. By **James Adey Birds,** B.A. F.G.S. Large crown 8vo. 12*s.* 6*d.*

Goethe's Faust. The Ger-
man Text, with an English Introduction and Notes for Students. By **Albert M. Selss,** M.A. Ph.D. Crown 8vo. 5*s.*

Lays of Ancient Rome;
with Ivry and the Armada. By **Lord Macaulay.**

CABINET EDITION, post 8vo. 3*s.* 6*d.*

CHEAP EDITION, fcp. 8vo. 1*s.* sewed; 1*s.* 6*d.* cloth; 2*s.* 6*d.* cloth extra with gilt edges.

Lord Macaulay's Lays of
Ancient Rome, with Ivry and the Armada. With 41 Wood Engravings by G. Pearson from Original Drawings by J. R. Weguelin. Crown 8vo. 6*s.*

Festus, a Poem. By
Philip James Bailey. 10th Edition, enlarged & revised. Crown 8vo. 12*s.* 6*d.*

The Poems of Virgil trans-
lated into English Prose. By **John Conington,** M.A. Crown 8vo. 9*s.*

The Iliad of Homer, Homometrically translated by C. B. CAYLEY. 8vo. 12s. 6d.

Bowdler's Family Shakspeare. Genuine Edition, in 1 vol. medium 8vo. large type, with 36 Woodcuts, 14s. or in 6 vols. fcp. 8vo. 21s.

The Æneid of Virgil. Translated into English Verse. By J. CONINGTON, M.A. Crown 8vo. 9s.

Southey's Poetical Works, with the Author's last Corrections and Additions. Medium 8vo. with Portrait, 14s.

RURAL SPORTS, HORSE and CATTLE MANAGEMENT, &c.

William Howitt's Visits to Remarkable Places, Old Halls, Battle-Fields, Scenes illustrative of Striking Passages in English History and Poetry. New Edition, with 80 Illustrations engraved on Wood. Crown 8vo. 7s. 6d.

Dixon's Rural Bird Life; Essays on Ornithology, with Instructions for Preserving Objects relating to that Science. With 44 Woodcuts. Crown 8vo. 5s.

A Book on Angling; or, Treatise on the Art of Fishing in every branch; including full Illustrated Lists of Salmon Flies. By FRANCIS FRANCIS. Post 8vo. Portrait and Plates, 15s.

Wilcocks's Sea-Fisherman: comprising the Chief Methods of Hook and Line Fishing, a glance at Nets, and remarks on Boats and Boating. Post 8vo. Woodcuts, 12s. 6d.

The Fly-Fisher's Entomology. By ALFRED RONALDS. With 20 Coloured Plates. 8vo. 14s.

The Dead Shot, or Sportsman's Complete Guide; a Treatise on the Use of the Gun, with Lessons in the Art of Shooting Game of All Kinds, and Wild-Fowl, also Pigeon-Shooting, and Dog-Breaking. By MARKSMAN. Fifth Edition, with 13 Illustrations. Crown 8vo. 10s. 6d.

Horses and Roads; or, How to Keep a Horse Sound on his Legs. By FREE-LANCE. Second Edition. Crown 8vo. 6s.

Horses and Riding. By GEORGE NEVILE, M.A. With 31 Illustrations. Crown 8vo. 6s.

Horses and Stables. By Major-General Sir F. FITZWYGRAM, Bart. Second Edition, revised and enlarged; with 39 pages of Illustrations containing very numerous Figures. 8vo. 10s. 6d.

Youatt on the Horse. Revised and enlarged by W. WATSON, M.R.C.V.S. 8vo. Woodcuts, 7s. 6d.

Youatt's Work on the Dog. Revised and enlarged. 8vo. Woodcuts, 6s.

The Dog in Health and Disease. By STONEHENGE. Third Edition, with 78 Wood Engravings. Square crown 8vo. 7s. 6d.

The Greyhound. By STONEHENGE. Revised Edition, with 25 Portraits of Greyhounds, &c. Square crown 8vo. 15s.

A Treatise on the Diseases of the Ox; being a Manual of Bovine Pathology specially adapted for the use of Veterinary Practitioners and Students. By J. H. STEEL, M.R.C.V.S. F.Z.S. With 2 Plates and 116 Woodcuts. 8vo. 15s.

Stables and Stable Fittings.
By W. MILES. Imp. 8vo. with 13 Plates, 15s.

The Horse's Foot, and
How to keep it Sound. By W. MILES. Imp. 8vo. Woodcuts, 12s. 6d.

A Plain Treatise on
Horse-shoeing. By W. MILES. Post 8vo. Woodcuts, 2s. 6d.

Remarks on Horses'
Teeth, addressed to Purchasers. By W. MILES. Post 8vo. 1s. 6d.

WORKS of UTILITY and GENERAL INFORMATION.

Maunder's Biographical
Treasury. Reconstructed with 1,700 additional Memoirs, by W. L. R. CATES. Fcp. 8vo. 6s.

Maunder's Treasury of
Natural History; or, Popular Dictionary of Zoology. Fcp. 8vo. with 900 Woodcuts, 6s.

Maunder's Treasury of
Geography, Physical, Historical, Descriptive, and Political. With 7 Maps and 16 Plates. Fcp. 8vo. 6s.

Maunder's Historical
Treasury; Outlines of Universal History, Separate Histories of all Nations. Revised by the Rev. Sir G. W. Cox, Bart. M.A. Fcp. 8vo. 6s.

Maunder's Treasury of
Knowledge and Library of Reference; comprising an English Dictionary and Grammar, Universal Gazetteer, Classical Dictionary, Chronology, Law Dictionary, &c. Fcp. 8vo. 6s.

Maunder's Scientific and
Literary Treasury; a Popular Encyclopædia of Science, Literature, and Art. Fcp. 8vo. 6s.

The Treasury of Botany,
or Popular Dictionary of the Vegetable Kingdom. Edited by J. LINDLEY, F.R.S. and T. MOORE, F.L.S. With 274 Woodcuts and 20 Steel Plates. Two Parts, fcp. 8vo. 12s.

The Treasury of Bible
Knowledge; a Dictionary of the Books, Persons, Places, and Events, of which mention is made in Holy Scripture. By the Rev. J. AYRE, M.A. Maps, Plates and Woodcuts. Fcp. 8vo. 6s.

Black's Practical Treatise on Brewing;
with Formulæ for Public Brewers and Instructions for Private Families. 8vo. 10s. 6d.

The Theory of the Modern
Scientific Game of Whist. By W. POLE, F.R.S. Thirteenth Edition. Fcp. 8vo. 2s. 6d.

The Correct Card; or,
How to Play at Whist; a Whist Catechism. By Major A. CAMPBELL-WALKER, F.R.G.S. Fourth Edition. Fcp. 8vo. 2s. 6d.

The Cabinet Lawyer; a
Popular Digest of the Laws of England, Civil, Criminal, and Constitutional. Twenty-Fifth Edition. Fcp. 8vo. 9s.

Chess Openings. By F. W.
LONGMAN, Balliol College, Oxford. New Edition. Fcp. 8vo. 2s. 6d.

Pewtner's Comprehensive Specifier;
a Guide to the Practical Specification of every kind of Building-Artificer's Work. Edited by W. YOUNG. Crown 8vo. 6s.

Cookery and Housekeeping;
a Manual of Domestic Economy for Large and Small Families. By Mrs. HENRY REEVE. Third Edition, with 8 Coloured Plates and 37 Woodcuts. Crown 8vo. 7s. 6d.

Modern Cookery for Private Families,
reduced to a System of Easy Practice in a Series of carefully-tested Receipts. By ELIZA ACTON. With upwards of 150 Woodcuts. Fcp. 8vo. 4s. 6d.

Food and Home Cookery.

A Course of Instruction in Practical Cookery and Cleaning, for Children in Elementary Schools. By Mrs. BUCKTON. Crown 8vo. Woodcuts, 2s.

A Dictionary of Medicine.

Including General Pathology, General Therapeutics, Hygiene, and the Diseases peculiar to Women and Children. By Various Writers. Edited by R. QUAIN, M.D. F.R.S. &c. With 138 Woodcuts. Medium 8vo. 31s. 6d. cloth, or 40s. half-russia.

Bull's Hints to Mothers

on the Management of their Health during the Period of Pregnancy and in the Lying-in Room. Fcp. 8vo. 1s. 6d.

Bull on the Maternal

Management of Children in Health and Disease. Fcp. 8vo. 1s. 6d.

American Farming and

Food. By FINLAY DUN. Crown 8vo. 10s. 6d.

The Farm Valuer. By

JOHN SCOTT. Crown 8vo. 5s.

Rents and Purchases; or,

the Valuation of Landed Property, Woods, Minerals, Buildings, &c. By JOHN SCOTT. Crown 8vo. 6s.

Economic Studies. By

the late WALTER BAGEHOT, M.A. Edited by R. H. HUTTON. 8vo. 10s. 6d.

Health in the House;

Lectures on Elementary Physiology in its Application to the Daily Wants of Man and Animals. By Mrs. BUCKTON. Crown 8vo. Woodcuts, 2s.

Economics for Beginners

By H. D. MACLEOD, M.A. Small crown 8vo. 2s. 6d.

The Elements of Economics.

By H. D. MACLEOD, M.A. In 2 vols. VOL. I. crown 8vo. 7s. 6d.

The Elements of Banking.

By H. D. MACLEOD, M.A. Fourth Edition. Crown 8vo. 5s.

The Theory and Practice

of Banking. By H. D. MACLEOD, M.A. 2 vols. 8vo. 26s.

The Patentee's Manual;

a Treatise on the Law and Practice of Letters Patent, for the use of Patentees and Inventors. By J. JOHNSON and J. H. JOHNSON. Fourth Edition, enlarged. 8vo. price 10s. 6d.

Willich's Popular Tables

Arranged in a New Form, giving Information &c. equally adapted for the Office and the Library. 9th Edition, edited by M. MARRIOTT. Crown 8vo. 10s.

INDEX.